THE *Canary Cage*

ENDORSEMENTS

"*The Canary Cage* will sweep you into a story world filled with romance and intrigue. Beautiful reminders are woven within the story about the danger of wrong assumptions and the healing power of forgiveness. *The Canary Cage* is a must read for lovers of historical fiction!"

—Christy Barritt (award-winning author of *Lantern Beach P.D. series,* Love Inspired Suspense, Squeaky Clean series, Worst Detective Ever series, Fog Lake suspense series)

"A gripping drama that will establish Wagoner as a true master of the craft. I loved this story!"

—Kathleen Kerr, Acquisitions Editor, Harvest House Publishers

"When I sit down with a book I expect to be transported to a different time, a different place, a different life. *The Canary Cage* did exactly that. What a wonderfully crafted character-driven novel that pays strict attention to details of late 19th-century life. The 21st century melted away when I immersed myself in Melissa/Lily's story. She is someone I'd like to call 'friend.' And Tyler? Pass the smelling salts ... this man is swoon-worthy! Kudos to Evelyn Wagoner on this excellent work of historic romance.

—Jayne Ormerod (author of *Blond Faith, The Blond Leading the Blond, To Fetch a Thief*)

"What else can I say? A beautifully crafted tale by Evelyn J. Wagoner, whose awe-inspiring personalities stay true to form to the very last line. Her writing is a breeze to read—refreshing, witty, and full of turnabout wisdom with lyrical detail. I was hooked from the very first line with an unquenchable need to know what was going to happen next. I am in love with Wagoner's ease of weaving the ultimate story of hope through the eyes and lives of her characters. What an amazing storyline with true historical reference! Beautiful story, beautiful characters, beautifully written! Could not ask for more!"—**Joanna Osborne**, CEO, Easter Press, Fort Myers, FL

"*The Canary Cage* reels with powerful emotion. Fast-paced and well-written, Wagoner's debut novel is graced with lyrical descriptions that authenticate the intriguing storyline and leaves the reader wanting more!"—**Ginger Marcinkowski** (author of award-winning *Run, River Currents* and *The Button Legacy: Emily's Inheritance*)

"Reading *The Canary Cage* was like having a movie play in my head. I really enjoyed this engaging story. I couldn't put it down."
—**Erin Brown**, Collections Specialist, Oklahoma Territorial Museum

"*The Canary Cage* captures you from the first page and won't let go. Loved it!"
—**Wendy Griffith**, Co-host, The 700 Club

"In a world of Christian fiction where much is the same, *The Canary Cage* offers us a fresh breath of air. Creative, unique, and just a touch edgy, this redemptive story with its deep characterization will touch your heart and live on in your memory for years to come."
—**Dina Sleiman** (award-winning author of the Valiant Heart series, Bethany House)

THE *Canary Cage*

EVELYN J. WAGONER

For Katherine —
Expect a happy ending!
Blessings
EJWagoner

PUBLISHING THE POSITIVE
ELK LAKE PUBLISHING INC
Plymouth, Massachusetts

Cover and Interior Design: Derinda Babcock

Cover Illustrator: Valerie Fay

Editor(s): Linda Rondeau, Deb Haggerty

Author Represented By: Hartline Literary Agency

PUBLISHED BY: Elk Lake Publishing, Inc., 35 Dogwood Drive, Plymouth, MA 02360, 2019

Library Cataloging Data

Names: Wagoner, Evelyn J. (Evelyn J. Wagoner)

The Canary Cage / Evelyn J. Wagoner

276 p. 23cm × 15cm (9in × 6 in.)

Description: *The Canary Cage* is more than a saloon. It's a place of intrigue, lost love, and regret. As Lily soon discovers, once you enter its doors, you may lose more than your reputation.

Identifiers: ISBN-13: 978-1-951080-08-2 (trade) | 978-1-951080-09-9 (POD) | 978-1-951080-10-5 (e-book)

Key Words: West, Saloon Singers, Romance, Vengeance, 1800s, Prejudice, Cowboys

LCCN: 2019945529 Fiction

DEDICATION

For Pam and Sheila,
who saved my life.

For Joanna,
who never fails to encourage me.

And for Rod.
A girl should always have her very own personal hero.
I'm blessed to have you for mine.

ACKNOWLEDGMENTS

This is the page where I'm blessed to offer a few—albeit it insufficient—words of thanks to those who have been helpful, encouraging, supportive, and, oh, so patient with me during the development and publication of *The Canary Cage*.

I must begin with Deb Haggerty of Elk Lake Publishing. You are the fulfiller of dreams. Thank you for believing in me and allowing me to debut with ELP. Linda Rondeau—editor extraordinaire—thank you for your patience. You taught me so much, and I'm forever grateful.

Diana Flegal of Hartline Literary Agency. Thank you for holding my hand and guiding me through the process. You are a wonder.

My heartfelt thanks to the wonderful folks in Guthrie, Oklahoma—Peggy Cook, retired librarian, for providing the initial historical data; Laurie Fuller with the Convention & Visitors Bureau for guiding me to the right people; and Erin Brown, Collections Specialist for the Oklahoma Territorial Museum, for answering a flood of questions and for reviewing the manuscript for historical accuracy. Believe me, if there are any errors, they're mine alone.

So much love and thanks to my family—Dad, Betty, Matt, Jeremy, and Sue —and, of course, Rod (the best husband in the history of the world)—for their unwavering support and encouragement. I couldn't have done this without you.

Thanks to the KPC Writers Group for sharing the adventure with me. I'm so proud of the writers we're becoming together.

My launch team and prayer warriors—Vera, Pam, Patti, Carol, Karen, Sherrie, Rachel, Eileen (and, again, Betty and Sue)—you held me up, held me together, and served as my brain whenever losing my mind seemed inevitable. How precious you are!

First and foremost—thank You, Lord, for Your unending mercy and gracious favor. You are the reason for everything.

CHAPTER ONE

Guthrie, Oklahoma

April 1899

The whistle wailed as the train, belching black smoke, pulled from the station, deserting her more than a thousand miles from home. She couldn't go back now. Her mouth suddenly dry, Melissa Forrester caught the back of a bench to steady herself, as the determination that had kept her company mile after chugging mile fled. Coming to Guthrie had been a mistake.

Now she could do nothing but move forward. Sucking in a shaky breath, she dredged up the resolve that had brought her this far. She adjusted her hat to just the right tilt, then lifted a gloved hand to catch the attention of a uniformed porter.

"Excuse me, sir. Would you be so kind as to direct me to Harrison Avenue?"

"Yes, ma'am." The porter tipped his hat, then pointed. "You exit the depot over there to West Oklahoma. Take a right, then right again on South Second Street until you come to West Harrison. It's a long street. Are you looking for a particular address?"

She froze. She couldn't tell this man where she was truly heading.

"The Capital City Courier," she said instead.

"Ah," he nodded. "The newspaper building. You'll want to turn right on Harrison. The Courier will be on your left."

"Thank you." She dipped a curtsey.

That doesn't sound far. I can walk there. I can do this.

She left the depot, then stopped short, stunned by her first glimpse of Guthrie. A melee of electric and telephone wires crisscrossed overhead, and traffic choked the street. Buildings of brick, wood, and sandstone—many with intricate architectural moldings—stood two and three stories high.

She hoisted her carpetbags and hatbox and set off toward her destination. Had she ever been so exhausted? Though every joint screamed for mercy, she refused offers of assistance from carriage and wagon drivers. Walking would afford her the opportunity to stretch her legs and assess the town. Picking her way along the crowded sidewalk, she stared agape at the young town teeming with merchants of every kind and marveled at the abundance of businesses, restaurants, and entertainments.

And then she was there.

She stood still on the wooden sidewalk, stunned to hear the strains of Beethoven's *Moonlight Sonata* drifting from the establishment identified by an elaborate wooden sign as *The Canary Cage.* Closing her eyes, she listened for a moment more, and then, trembling, patted Augusta's letter tucked securely in her pocket. After one more deep breath, Melissa gathered her courage and her baggage and, for the first time in her life, stepped through the swinging doors of a saloon.

The music faltered at her entrance, ending on a discordant note. The blonde seated beside the piano player jabbed him in the ribs with her elbow and shot him a sideways glare.

"We're closed," the woman said.

Melissa looked around the darkened saloon, noting the chairs stacked on the tables and the brass spittoons piled in a corner. A mop leaned against the banister near a bucket filled with soapy water.

"Yes, I see that, but I wanted to ask—"

"I said we're closed. Your husband isn't here." The blonde half-rose from the bench, then sat again hastily when an older man joined them.

"I'm Merle Winfield, the proprietor. Is there something I can do for you, ma'am?" he asked, his unreadable face in stark contrast with the polite civility of his voice.

Melissa shifted her gaze from the proprietor to the blonde, as the piano player fingered an innocuous tune on the ivory keys. To her right, a scar-faced bartender wiped the counter with meticulous care. Behind Mr. Winfield, two women peeked through a slightly ajar door in the back of the room.

Tell me about my sister, Augusta, Melissa wanted to say. *Tell me about her life here, who knew her, who called her friend. Tell me why no one noticed her despair—how no one suspected she would take her own life. Tell me about the man she loved, the man who rejected her, who broke her heart and took away her desire to live.*

She wanted to say every bit of that and more, but none of these people seemed eager to talk to her. Gawk, yes. Talk, no. Mr. Winfield appeared courteous—still she doubted he would tell her what she wanted to know any more than the arrogant blonde. Would they answer a few questions about Augusta? Perhaps. Intuition told her the responses would be perfunctory, and she needed more than information. She needed to feel close to her sister again—needed to understand so many things.

In the first dark days after her father died, she'd learned her sister had run away, and all meaning had abandoned her. More than anything, she needed to understand why she was now alone.

Tell me why you let my sister die? she wanted to ask these people. While she had asked God the same question many times, he had refused to answer. Now, apparently, these people would too.

"A drink of water, please," she asked instead.

Merle nodded to the man behind the bar and then, with a jerk of his head, motioned to the blonde. With a scowl, she slid off the bench, seeming totally at ease wearing only a robe that rode high above her knee. Sauntering to the bar, the blonde picked up the glass filled by the bartender. She strolled back and slammed it down on the table nearest Melissa, spilling half its contents.

"Thank you," Melissa murmured, her cheeks heated from the vulgar display and from the woman's rudeness.

"Honey …" Merle muttered, throwing a warning frown at the blonde.

Melissa reached for the glass and took her time drinking the cool water, giving herself time to think. This wasn't going at all as she'd expected. But exactly what *had* she expected? Had she thought she would walk into the saloon and be greeted like long-lost family? That she would be able to say, "Good afternoon, I am Augusta's sister—you knew her as Roxie. I would like to ask you some questions about her and that man."

Even though Merle seemed by far the most genial, Melissa knew neither he, the blonde, the piano player, nor the taciturn bartender would open up to a complete stranger, much less to a woman who had no business walking into a saloon. Especially a woman whose fashionable traveling gown actually touched the floor. The men wore barely polite masks, while the obviously misnamed Honey glowered.

Melissa drained the glass and set it down gently, wiping away a drop of water from her lip with the tip of a gloved finger. "Thank you," she said softly, her gaze encompassing them all. She had no idea how to proceed, and she shifted nervously from one foot to the other. Her uncertainty finally brought a compassionate smile to Merle's taut face.

"What's your name, miss?"

One of Augusta's letters suddenly came to mind.

> I won't say I am ashamed of what I do here, I assure you (you know how I always thumbed my nose at those strait-laced biddies), but I do have a mind for your sacred reputation, dear Melissa. I thought best to use what you might call a stage name. I thought of the names we made up for our childhood plays, using our middle names for fun, and I laughed thinking how you would frown in that way of yours when I wrote I had brought Roxie Mowbray to life …

Augusta Roxanne Forrester had become Roxie Mowbray—Roxie, shortened from her middle name, and Mowbray, the street where they lived with their father. Now Melissa Lillian Forrester would follow her lead, ill-advised though this might be.

"Lily. Lily Woods." Odd how using the play name of her childhood made her feel closer to her sister.

"Are you looking for employment, Miss Woods?" Merle asked.

The newly-named Lily leaped upon the opportunity as a godsend.

"Why, yes—yes, sir, I am. Do you need anyone?" She had no clue what, but there certainly had to be something she could do here, some way she could try to get closer to the people Augusta had lived with. Perhaps Lily could find a way to spend time in the place Roxie had spent her final days, find some way to meet the man who had broken her heart. Lily thought quickly. Perhaps she could cook or clean or keep the books …

"Can you sing?"

"Merle …" Honey's protesting whine earned her another scowl.

Sing? Of course! How silly of her. The women here, including Augusta, had provided entertainment for the customers. Her sister had often written about her popularity and the gratification she received from the applause. Melissa warmed as she recalled how she and Augusta had sung for their father and for his guests—love of music being one of the few things the sisters had in common. She straightened her shoulders and lifted her chin.

"Yes, I can."

Merle took her by the elbow and directed her to where a shaft of sunlight shone through the plate glass window. Gripping her chin, he turned her face from side to side, studying her features in the bright light. Melissa felt her newly-gained assurance fade. Dust and grime covered her from face to boots. Augusta—Roxie, she corrected—had always been the more attractive one. And, despite the blonde's perpetual frown, she couldn't deny Honey's beauty.

"Well, you're certainly pretty enough," Merle said beneath his breath. "Clear skin, and you haven't fried up your hair. You look classier than anything that's been through this town before." He let go of Lily's chin and shot a disapproving glare at Honey's curse. "I don't know how you manage to keep yourself looking so innocent, but we can make that illusion pay off. C'mon, let's hear you sing."

CHAPTER TWO

At Merle's instruction, Melissa relinquished one of her carpet bags to the tall, thin woman and followed her up the stairs and down a darkened corridor.

"I'm Rae Ann," the woman said over her shoulder. "I guess you figured out the blonde is Honey—though I'll never know how she got the name. Toby's the piano player, Malcolm's the bartender." She unlocked a door and swung it wide. "There's two more girls—Sally and Trudy. Trudy's a little shy at first, but Sally will probably be busting your door down before you get a chance to settle."

She stepped aside, allowing Melissa to enter the sun-filled room.

"I'm sorry this is the only room we have. I scrubbed and scrubbed trying to … clean up what I could. I heard Honey telling you about what happened here." Rae Ann lifted a slim shoulder. "Try not to think about it." She offered a sober nod and left.

Melissa sank onto the tarnished brass bed and, with a groan, covered her face with her hands. How could she have been so foolish, so impulsive? Not once in her twenty-two years could she recall ever doing anything not expected of her. And now, within a matter of days, she had committed not one, but two foolish acts. First, she had traveled by train, unaccompanied no less, from her cozy, predictable life in Norfolk, Virginia, to this inhospitable, godforsaken town. That imprudent decision had led directly to a second. A momentary lapse of sanity had landed her in the very room that had once been her sister's.

Her sister's room.

This had been Augusta's room, where she had … Melissa wiped her damp palms on her skirt. She had only wanted to learn what she could about this horrid place where her sister had spent her last days. Just talk to the people Augusta had worked with and lived with—and then confront the rogue her sister had loved, the scoundrel who had driven her vivacious sister to the brink of despair and over the edge.

Melissa stood and steadied herself on the headboard before taking a few steps to the oval rug. Handmade, braided from mismatched, faded scraps, it lay at her feet. Ordinary. Deceitful. She knew what lay beneath— the haughty blonde downstairs had taken obvious satisfaction in the telling of the story. From the moment Melissa had entered the room, the rug had drawn her, relentlessly, inexorably. And so she stood, staring at the bit of floor covering, her heart pounding, her mouth dry as prairie dust. Caught between the need for confirmation and a wild desire to turn tail and run, she clenched and unclenched her fists, her nails digging into her palms. Then, quickly, before she did indeed change her mind and flee, she slipped the tip of her shoe under the edge of the rug and flipped it aside.

And there it was.

Perplexed, she stooped, tucking her long skirts between her legs. What had she expected? Certainly not this. She reached out to stroke the dark stain embedded in the floorboards. Shouldn't there be more than a shadow on the wooden planks, something more than a discoloration, more than a dim reminder of something spilled there? Would she have recognized the stain as blood without having been told? If she had inadvertently kicked aside the rug and found the mark, would she have given the discoloration more than a passing thought? Surely the spot could have been spilled wine, or perhaps bootblack. Someone could have simply laid down a polishing cloth, never giving thought the unvarnished boards thirsted for lemon oil. Had the smear been anything but blood, would anyone have bothered with the rug?

Not taking her eyes from the stain, she tilted her head and listened. Not a sound. No flash of lightning. No clap of thunder. Had she thought she would hear Augusta's voice crying out? Had she expected to experience some mystical connection after confronting what lay beneath the rug? But then she did hear a sound, a ragged cry. She pressed her fist against her lips stifling the sob tearing so unexpectedly from her grief. Squeezing her eyes shut, she gritted her teeth and willed herself to calm down. No one must hear her … no one.

Gaining a semblance of control, Melissa again touched the stain. Rae Ann had indeed spoken truly. She had scrubbed hard, trying to remove the blemish. She had scarred the pine floorboards with her efforts, and yet the distressing proof remained. Augusta's personal belongings were gone. Only the damning brown blotch lingered to declare that her sister had been here.

Augusta's blood.

Melissa jerked away as though the mark had turned to flame. How could she stay in this room when she could only see the horrifying image of Augusta, her beautiful, vibrant sister, lying on the floor—this floor—her life pouring from a self-inflicted gunshot wound?

She slid the rug back into place, and then pushed herself to her feet. Crossing the room to the window, she pulled the frayed gingham curtain aside and pressed her forehead against the pane. She must force herself to look out and think of something—anything—else.

The rear porch roof sloped directly beneath the bedroom. In the bleak backyard, grass grew in parched yellow patches, and rosebushes strangled amidst weeds. How had the roses survived at all? She sighed, longing for the carefully planned symmetry and calming ambience of her small, but diligently tended, garden at home.

A tap sounded at the door and, without invitation, Rae Ann entered with an armload of linens.

"Lily? You settling in okay?"

Lily? Ah, yes, *Lily*. Her new name—best become accustomed to being called *Lily*, or she would be found out, the game quickly over.

Lily—yes—from now on she would think of herself as this character—nodded at her carpetbags on the floor beside the bed and offered a plaintive smile.

"I confess I'm exhausted from the train ride. I haven't done a thing."

Rae Ann shook her head, a frown furrowing her forehead, and uttered a sympathetic "*tsk*." She motioned toward the rocking chair. "Well, of course you're done in. You just sit yourself down and let me fix up the bed for you. Coming all the way from Baltimore—didn't you say you're from Baltimore?"

Lily—yes, this would be her name now—hesitated, then nodded, flushing at the reminder of her lie. Did Rae Ann notice her discomfort? The older woman had already tugged off the worn chenille bedspread and snapped open a sheet with a sharp crack. The fabric settled over the blue-striped mattress like a white sail.

"I've never been to Baltimore." Rae Ann smoothed the crisp cotton over the feather tick.

Neither have I, Lily confessed silently.

"Never been much of anywhere to say the truth. So, what made you want to work here at the Cage? What with your experience in a big city like Baltimore, seems like you'd head for someplace like Boston or Atlanta."

Lily dug her fingernails into her palms, fighting the urge to reveal her true motives. Another lie so soon? She would ask for forgiveness later. Right now, she had to think quickly. She almost laughed aloud. If she'd been thinking at all, she wouldn't be in this predicament.

"I suppose I'm tired of big cities. I've always wanted to go west, and when the train stopped here, I just got off."

Liar.

Rae Ann paused, the edge of a pillow tucked beneath her chin while she fed the other end into a pillowcase. Her hazel eyes widened.

"Just like that? You passed prob'ly five other saloons and the Brooks Opera House to ask for a job at the Canary Cage?"

Lily smiled ruefully. "Well, not exactly."

At least that much is true.

Telling even a little bit of truth felt good. If she included as much fact in her story as she could, perhaps she would keep from tripping in a self-made web. Rae Ann seemed to be a kind-hearted woman, but she stared at Lily with a curious expression. Lily charged ahead, cobbling together the tale as she went along.

"I only intended to take a walk to stretch my legs a little."

Lie.

"I passed other saloons, but I didn't care for the looks of them—"

True.

"—and the Opera House, well, that kind of music isn't my specialty. But I didn't come to the Canary Cage with the intention of asking for employment ..."

I came to ask about my sister, to meet the people she lived with during her last days on earth.

"But when Mr. Winfield offered, I thought—well—why not? There's nowhere else I need to be ... so I found myself saying yes."

Too, too true.

Now, ensconced upstairs in the Canary Cage in the room that had once been her sister's, she watched a stranger handle her most intimate possessions and wondered how she had lost her mind so quickly and completely.

"You sure have some nice clothes," Rae Ann shook out a dress to loosen the wrinkles before hanging the garment in the chifforobe. "You must have made good money where you sang before."

"Yes, I found the pay quite adequate." The misleading admission tasted sour. She had never sung anywhere but in her father's house. He had, however, always given her and Augusta generous allowances. Now alone in the world, both her inheritance and her sister's belonged to her.

Reaching the bottom of the carpetbag, Rae Ann looked puzzled. "Where are your show dresses?"

"My what?"

"You know, the dresses you wear when you work."

Lily's thoughts skittered trying to come up with a plausible explanation. *You'll never pull this off. You're not like Aug—Roxie, you're no good at acting.*

"I reckon you wouldn't have brought them with you, since you probably didn't plan to take a job." Rae Ann voiced her thoughts as a logical answer, and Lily said a silent prayer of thanks.

"I didn't want to travel with more baggage than I could carry myself." She paused for a moment, faced with yet another obstacle her rash behavior had produced. "Um—I can send for the rest of my clothes. I'll need a few things in the meantime. Is there a store nearby?"

Rae Ann gave her another puzzled look and chuckled. "That's a good one, Lily. You have a wit for sure—or the stores where you come from are sure different from ours." Her grin faded, and her voice took on a serious note. "I don't know, you might be bothered, but then—since you didn't know her—you might not. Roxie, the girl whose room this used to be, well …"

The girl whose blood is soaked into the floor beneath the rug …

"We still have her dresses. I think you're a mite skinnier than her, but I can take them in for you if you'd like."

Stunned, Lily forced herself to consider the offer. Wear Augusta's clothes? How could she bear wearing her dresses, knowing the red-haired beauty would never again wear them herself? Lily brightened. On the other hand, the temptation to be close to her sister, to feel the same fabric against her skin, to experience how her sister might have felt when she wore the dresses—perhaps to even prompt a response of some sort when that man—

the man Augusta had written about—hopefully recognized the clothing as Roxie's ... All good reasons. Besides, how could she pull off this exploit without the proper costume?

"How very generous, Rae Ann. As you said, I didn't know—Roxie"—the name stuck in her throat—"so if you think no one will mind ..."

"Oh, pshaw." Rae Ann waved a thin hand in Lily's direction. "They'll mind all right, but believe me, if them dresses coulda been altered to fit anyone else here, they woulda been long gone." She moved the carpetbags next to the chifforobe. "That's everything except the personal things at the bottom. I'll leave those for you to put away." She crossed the room in a few long strides and let herself out. Leaning back into the room, perhaps with an afterthought, her face creased in a friendly smile. "Welcome, Lily. I hope you'll be happy here." Rae Ann's smile faded suddenly, and she shrugged. "Well, as happy as anyone can be in a place like this."

Lily answered with a feeble smile, but Rae Ann had already gone again, the clicking of her quick steps disappearing down the hall. Lily sighed and chided herself. First, remember to respond when called by her new name. Second, figure out how to meet the rogue—Tyler Buchanan—who, for all intents and purposes, had killed her sister.

CHAPTER THREE

Tyler Buchanan pushed away from the stack of papers on the roll-top desk, then rubbed his eyes and yawned. Dang, how could he be this tired? Looking at row after row of numbers had him seeing double. Though the *Capital City Courier*'s bookkeeper had proven reliable, Tyler insisted on going over the accounts himself several times a month. He liked to stay well-informed on every level, ensuring the newspaper retained its rightful place as the most successful periodical in the Oklahoma Territory in terms of influence and affluence.

With an exhausted sigh, he leaned back over the papers for a moment before standing and reaching his arms above him in a long stretch. Truth be told, he didn't care so much about the money. Money never had been the point—the point—the blazes with the point. He'd just as soon forget about that too.

Grabbing his hat, he pulled the black Stetson low over his forehead before turning off the light and locking the door behind him. He could hear the music spilling onto the street. Raucous laughter rolled in waves from the Canary Cage. The girls were no doubt singing one of the more popular bawdy songs.

Tyler often stopped in for an apple cider or ginger beer on his way home. And, perhaps, for a little socializing—one of the best ways to get news in this or any town. Straight from the horses' mouths. Of course, he chuckled, after a few beers, these fellows talked from one end to another. Crossing the street, Tyler stepped aside as two half-drunken ranch hands tried to fit through the saloon's door at the same time.

Tonight, the Canary Cage boasted the arrival of a new singer. Merle Winfield had scurried into the office, grinning like a polecat. He had paid for a quarter-page ad announcing the debut of his *Songbird of the East,* so pleased with himself he hadn't squabbled over the price.

"This one's special, Buchanan." Winfield talked so fast saliva had flown in a fine spray, causing Tyler to take a step backwards. "Real special. About time we had something to shake this town up a little. You just watch and see if I'm not right. This town's been needing a class act, and doggone if I'm not going to give them one." He had flown out the door mumbling something about finally setting the smug so-and-so at the Brooks Opera House back a few paces.

Tyler had grimaced, as he recalled, only half interested. Whatever her talents, he doubted she'd be worth covering in the paper. Still, she couldn't be any worse than the girls who sang there now. Roxie had been the last decent singer they'd had at the Canary Cage or at any of the other saloons in town. She'd had a pretty voice, not well-trained, but appealing, nonetheless. Something about her had always seemed to get under his skin, make him uneasy. He didn't even like thinking about her, and she'd been dead for two months. Shrugging his wide shoulders, he pushed through the swinging double doors and dismissed the deceased singer from his thoughts.

Once inside, he surveyed the room. Cowboys, merchants, businessmen, and farmers stood elbow to elbow at the bar where Malcolm poured drinks as fast as he could. Poker games were in progress—the participants all seemed to have either cigars clamped between their teeth or cheeks distorted with chaws of chewing tobacco. Concentrating on their cards, the gamblers spat indiscriminately and, as often as not, missed the brass spittoons placed generously throughout the saloon.

Tyler threaded his way through the maze of chairs and smoke and sat at a table near the stage. The other occupants at the table didn't acknowledge him at first, their eyes trained on the calves of the three saloon girls dancing to the old Stephen Foster song, *Camptown Races.* Honey, Sally, and Trudy kicked higher and higher as the crowd yelled out "doo-dah" and eagerly anticipated the kicks approaching the same height as the dancers' heads.

Cigar ash fell into the lap of the man beside Tyler and burned through the fabric of the man's trousers. He yelped, leaping to his feet and overturning his chair, as he brushed frantically at his pant leg.

"Evenin', Carson. A little warm tonight, eh?"

The big man righted his chair and sat down again. Tyler nodded toward the stage where the girls took their bows, showing generous amounts of cleavage, then turning around to flip their skirts over their heads to show equally generous amounts of ruffled pantaloons.

"That last kick—what a sight to behold, Carson. I thought they would flip over backwards, they kicked so high. Real pity you were otherwise occupied."

Carson scowled and gulped half his beer in one swallow. "A man has priorities, Buchanan."

"That he does, chief, that he does." Tyler waved to the red-haired woman in an ill-fitting orange dress trimmed in black lace. When she smiled in acknowledgment, he wiggled two fingers in the air. Minutes later, she slapped two mugs onto the table, sloshing ginger beer and ale foam.

"There you go, Mr. Buchanan," she purred, standing with one hand propped on a bony hip in a poor attempt at a provocative stance.

Tyler flipped her a coin and pushed the ale toward Carson.

She stretched her scarlet-colored lips in something resembling a smile, as she simpered hopefully, showing the slight gap between her front teeth. "If there's anything else I can do for you ... any time ... you just say the word, okay?"

Tyler nodded. "Thank you, Trudy. That'll do."

Carson chortled and slapped the table with the flat of one palm while he toasted Tyler with the already half-empty mug. "Pity about Trudy. She's not the sharpest cheese on the platter, don't you know, and that hair"—he shook his head sympathetically—"hair that color don't even look natural on a carrot." He took another swig of the foaming brew and wiped his mouth with the back of his hand. "Don't know how you attract 'em. They just swarm around you like bees around honey."

"Maybe so." Tyler shook his head and sighed. "But my experience tells me that it's just not worth chancing those stingers."

Carson's hazel eyes followed Honey as she sauntered from table to table. "True, my friend, true. Still, if not for the memory of my dear departed Ella being so strong, I might check out the upstairs of this place myself."

Tyler followed Carson's gaze and felt a rush of concern for his friend.

"Ah, Carson, there are plenty of good, God-fearing women in this town. You won't find anything but trouble if you ..."

The piano player rolled an impressive arpeggio, drowning out the rest of Tyler's well-intentioned advice and drawing the crowd's attention to Merle, who had walked onto the stage.

"Gentlemen"—the proprietor boomed in a voice much like a circus ringmaster—"tonight we're going to give you a little taste of our new singing sensation just in from the East."

"A taste?" someone yelled from near the door. "Maybe we'd rather have a free beer!"

The crowd roared its approval, and Merle waved his hands to regain their attention. "Gentlemen, gentlemen," he shouted, "this is not your usual singer—she's the most talented little filly who's ever set foot on this stage—or in this town. She's got a voice that'll knock you dead and a face that's not what you're used to seeing around here. Matter of fact, she's probably too much for even you fellas to handle all at once, so tonight you only get to hear her sing. You don't get to see her until tomorrow night."

He paused as the crowd buzzed with curiosity. When the murmurs finally subsided and the spectators waited expectantly, Merle gestured toward the edge of the stage.

"Gentlemen, welcome the newest addition to the Canary Cage, our very own *Songbird of the East!*"

At that moment, a woman stepped onto the stage, her hands fisted at her sides. She wore a pale pink dress that paid compliments to her slim figure, her bare arms, and camellia-white shoulders. A circlet of pink rosebuds rested on the crown of intricately styled raven hair.

"What the blazes," Tyler muttered. Carson merely stared, mouth agape.

The room hushed as the usually gruff crowd took in the sight of the shapely woman with the gauze veil hanging over her face to just beneath her chin. A heckler broke the silence shouting, "What's the matter, Merle? Your new canary look like a hound dog?"

Holding his belly, Merle bellowed like he knew a private joke. He grasped the woman by the elbow, directing her closer to center stage. She followed with stuttering steps.

"Show 'em what you got, darlin'," Merle whispered but loudly enough to be heard where Tyler sat. Merle's eyes glittered with excitement. And, with a final nod at his *Songbird of the East*, he walked offstage.

CHAPTER FOUR

On stage alone, Lily's breath lodged stubbornly in her throat.

Oh, dear Lord, I can't do this. Why did I ever think I could?

So many men. Their faces swam together in a blur of loutish impatience. The heat seemed to float from their bodies and envelop her in an overly tight caress. She saw the girls—Honey, Sally, and Trudy—staring at her, their makeup garish in the dim light, their stiff faces menacing, hateful, as if willing her to fail.

She swallowed hard and bit her lip. *Is it too late to turn back?* All these strange men staring at her. Unlike Augusta, she didn't crave the attention— she didn't *like* the attention. A bead of perspiration rolled down the back of her neck, and she wiped damp palms on the close-fitting skirt of her dress.

If she didn't open her mouth and sing, this scheme would indeed be over ... and over on the spot. She would lose this job, and she would never find out which of these miserable excuses for men bore the responsibility for Augusta's death. And one of them was indeed responsible, no doubt. She had no family because of him ... and the wretched cur must pay.

The resurgence of anger again strengthened her resolve. She regained her composure and unclasped her hands. Stifling a surge of embarrassment, she forced herself to raise the hem of her skirt, allowing the crowd an enticing glimpse of shapely ankle, and took a step closer to the edge of the stage. She raised one hand, waiting until the room quieted as Merle had instructed her.

"Gentlemen," she said, softly enough so almost every man had to lean forward to catch the words. "My name is Lily."

The room exploded in earsplitting whistles and responses. "I'm Eddie— Hal—Frank" resounded from all corners.

She sighed in relief and waited until the cacophony died down. Still shaking, but determined, she nodded to Toby who waited for her cue. His long fingers moved over the keys, playing the opening bars to a popular song she had learned just that afternoon. She loved "My Wild Irish Rose" with its bright, lilting melody. Lily sang as if her life depended on her performance, as indeed her new life as a saloon singer did. Sultry tones from her throaty voice floated and wound their way around the saloon, beckoning and denying, caressing and rebuffing.

Partway through the second chorus, she relaxed enough to realize every eye in the saloon had fastened on her. No one gambled or dealt cards, and passersby peered through the doors and windows. Even Malcolm the bartender had laid down his dishtowel, his dark eyes narrowed, watching.

An unexpected sense of control she had never known before came over her. How could the same voice that had entertained guests in her father's parlor affect these coarse, crude men so profoundly? Now she understood what Augusta had meant in her letters, what she had experienced. Exhilaration coursed through Lily at the notion that, for the moment, she could mold them like clay in her hands. She reveled in the thought and wielded her voice like a sculptor's tool, pouring every ounce of emotion she had into the words of the passionate song.

As the applause thundered, Lily nodded, her head held high. She took advantage of the moment to scan the faces of the patrons in the smoke-filled tavern. One by one she eliminated each of them—too young, too old, too fat, too bald. One man sitting at a table at the foot of the stage wore a badge of some kind, and though she noted his kindly eyes and his huge hands as he clapped, her gaze immediately traveled on to the man seated beside him. She gasped and her hand reached instinctively to assure herself the veil still covered her face. Yes, but those steel-gray eyes seemed to strip away her protective covering and expose her as an impostor.

He must be the one. She had no doubt. Augusta had described him perfectly from his thick, black hair, slightly tousled and curling at his nape, to his square chin and straight nose. His shoulders, broad beneath the gray jacket, and his hands, one resting negligently on his knee, the other curved around a half-empty mug, proclaimed strength with long fingers and neatly squared-off nails. He had to be Tyler Buchanan. The others still yelled and clapped … but he just sat there, watching her, expressionless, arrogant.

Toby trilled a few tinkling notes, jolting Lily, reminding her of the second song she had practiced for her debut. Now that she had spotted him, the man she had traveled more than a thousand miles to confront, she would begin doing just that. He had not moved. He only nodded at something the lawman said, but he showed no reaction to Lily or to her singing. His apparent indifference annoyed her. She vowed that would change—and quickly.

Toby had taught her a love song, one he swore would enthrall every man within hearing distance, bringing them back the next night, and inviting others along for what Merle touted as her *unveiling*. Tonight, she would beguile them with her voice. Tomorrow night she would woo them with her smile and, with her eyes, promise them things they only dreamed of—or so Merle had predicted. And Tyler Buchanan—Tyler Buchanan would wish he'd never met Augusta.

The opening bars rippled, and Lily closed her eyes.

This really isn't so hard.

Her sister had never wanted to practice, never followed their music tutor's instructions. Augusta sang for fun. Lily also loved to sing, but she wanted to sing as she did everything else—to the best of her ability. Tonight, beneath the veil, she let the music rolling from beneath Toby's able fingers guide her. When she finally began the song, she poured all her young girl's hopes into the words. All of the dreams she had locked away since her father's death surfaced and came to life.

"I have my true love's heart and he has mine. No greater treasure have I ever been given …"

She sang for her father, for her sister, for the young man she hoped to one day meet and marry, and she sang for herself. When the music faded away, the last note hung suspended amidst the stunned silence of the crowd. Lily stood, her arms outstretched, her head thrown back. Her bosom rose and fell quickly with exhaustion and emotion. When the applause began, the thunderous noise roused her, and she dropped to a curtsy deep enough for a throne room.

As if embarrassed by their initial outpouring of true appreciation, the enthusiastic clapping became catcalls and wolf whistles. Ignoring the vulgar shouts as best she could, she lifted her eyes to meet Tyler's gaze. His stare seemed to soften for an instant, and he nodded at her. Lily sensed the respect in his acknowledgment, and her stomach fluttered with elation. Her knees weakened unexpectedly, and she struggled to compose herself. Lifting her hand in a graceful wave, she walked off stage with all the dignity she could muster.

Merle waited for her and offered congratulations with a slap on the back, nearly knocking her over. He grabbed her elbow, his smile huge, his eyes wide with excitement.

"I knew it, Lily, I knew it. Girls with your sweet looks and class act are a rarity on any stage, but here in Guthrie—let me tell you, there's no one like you anywhere in this town. Good going, girl. There won't be room to spit tomorrow night! Now get upstairs before anybody sees you."

Lily saw him as if through a haze. Was she getting ill? Touching her fingertips to her burning forehead, she realized the veil still covered her face and flipped the offending fabric over her head. She disentangled herself from Merle's clinging fingers and forced a smile, her throat too tight to speak.

When Merle returned his attention to the crowd, she made her escape. Pink rosebuds fell from the laurel, and she ground the delicate petals beneath her slippers as she clattered gracelessly up the back stairs. She fled down the dimly lit hallway. Finally reaching her room, she slammed the door behind her and leaned against it, her chest heaving, her skin hot.

She scanned the threadbare room, taking in the still-unfamiliar furnishings and the hated rug that reminded her why she had traveled to this forlorn town. She caught her reflection in the mirror, a thin, shivering body encased in pale pink silk. The veil she had hastily flung over her head and haphazardly tucked behind her ears, now crushed the remaining rosebuds.

Her normally bright blue eyes seemed enormous with the heavy kohl Honey had somehow convinced Lily she should use. Wearing both makeup and a veil had seemed ridiculous to her, especially since Merle had been adamant that none of the barroom customers see her and that she immediately return to her room following her performance. Wearing makeup would have been second nature to a saloon girl, and she could think of no sensible reason to refuse. But she rarely wore makeup, and she felt as though she wore still another veil. She had to get the cloying residue off her face. Now.

Yanking open a drawer in the vanity, she rifled through the sparse contents searching for the face cream she had seen earlier. Not finding the small blue jar, she swept the various containers from the top of the vanity, a frustrated sob tearing from her throat. Her eyes blurred with tears, and her sense of satisfaction at having pulled off her first performance in front of an audience other than the local Daughters of the American Revolution auxiliary faded. Instead, ribald catcalls echoed in her head.

One man, his fleshy face pink from heat and excitement, had banged an empty bottle on the table, spittle clinging to one corner of his mouth. Another man, thin as a flagpole and dressed in black, had leered at her with narrowed dark eyes. He had grinned at her insolently and made a suggestive gesture. Bile rose in the back of her throat at the memory. She resumed her frantic search for the cream. She wrenched open another drawer and, finding it empty, sank to her knees and burst into near-hysterical sobs.

She hadn't heard the door open, but suddenly Rae Ann appeared beside her and murmured in a soothing maternal tone.

"Lily," she said, rubbing the younger woman's arm. "Whatever's the matter? You got a case of nerves? Even the most seasoned can be afflicted. No need to be embarrassed, sugar."

Without knowing how she got there, Lily found herself in Rae Ann's arms, her head cradled against the thin shoulder. "I hate this makeup, and I can't find the cream."

Rae Ann clucked and reached around Lily to where the sought-after jar had rolled. "It's right here, dear—under the rocker. Let me fetch a cloth, and I'll help you."

Before long, Lily found herself perched on the edge of the bed, her eyes closed, as Rae Ann slathered cream on her upturned face.

"I don't know why you put this mess on if you didn't want to. As pretty as you are, you don't need any makeup—especially not tonight since you had that awful veil on. Besides"—she paused long enough to give an expressive shudder—"I don't mind telling you, seeing you in that thing right near gave me the shivers. To my thinkin' you looked more like a body I'd be afraid to come across in the dead of night than like a 'woman of mystery' the way Merle said." She clucked again, shaking her head at the absurdity of the saloon owner's thinking. With a gentle dab, she swiped the last of the makeup and cream from Lily's chin. "There you go, clean as a whistle. Go on now and take a look."

Lily slid off the bed and leaned into the mirror. The harsh electric lamp cast dark shadows beneath her swollen eyes. Her brows and lashes, black as pitch, gleamed with greasy face cream. A paler, starker version of herself stared back, and Lily smiled weakly at her reflection. Behind her, Rae Ann gave a satisfied nod and screwed the lid back on the jar.

"Why did you say you bothered putting this cussed concoction on your pretty skin?"

Lily couldn't stifle a smile. She hadn't had an opportunity to say much of anything since Rae Ann had come into the room.

"Honey convinced me I should wear makeup in case someone saw me or—heaven forbid—in case the veil fell off on stage."

Rae Ann gave a soft harrumph and pursed her lips.

"That Honey. She probably realized you didn't want to wear all that mess on your face and made up her mind right then that you should. She's a sly one. Usually manages to get her way by simper or by claw. Come on now, let's get you out of that dress before you wrinkle it any more than you already have."

Once again Rae Ann took over, unbuttoning the gown and letting it drop at Lily's feet, holding her elbow while she stepped from the pool of shimmering fabric. After hanging the dress in the wardrobe, Rae Ann turned discreetly to one side, allowing Lily a moment of privacy to take off her corset and stockings. At the sound of the bedsprings squeaking, Rae Ann turned back to Lily. If the sight of the young woman wearing a white cotton nightdress with a high lace collar and long ruffled sleeves surprised her, she gave no sign.

"I brought you a sandwich and some coffee—that's what I came in here for," she said, motioning to the tray on top of the bureau. "The coffee's cold by now—I'll bring you another cup—or would you prefer tea?"

Rae Ann smiled at Lily's hesitant nod and crossed the room to motion her off the bed. She pulled back the bedcoverings, then fluffed the pillows before guiding Lily back into bed. She handed Lily the silver-handled brush from the disarray on the vanity.

"Here, child," she said, "take down your hair. A good brushing will help you relax before I get your tea."

After Lily's hair was brushed and braided, Rae Ann encouraged Lily to eat half a sandwich and down a cup of freshly brewed chamomile tea. When Lily's eyes drooped, Rae Ann took the tray and left her charge in peace.

CHAPTER FIVE

Tyler ran his fingers through his dark hair and yawned. If he had been tired before, he was beyond exhausted now, and the seat of the wooden chair grew harder by the minute. The evening had gone nowhere but downhill after Lily left the stage.

He shook his head, then downed the last of his ginger beer, still thinking of the slender, veiled woman with the beguiling voice. He hadn't heard such a voice since leaving his home in Charleston more than ten years earlier.

Her talent—but he forced admiration from his mind. *She chose a strange gimmick.*

Because of that eerie veil the Canary Cage would no doubt be packed tomorrow night. Tyler rubbed the back of his neck. He certainly intended to be here. Pushing his glass away, he stood, his chair scraping loudly across the wooden floor.

"Going already, Tyler?" Carson shouted above the hoots and hollers after Honey's song concluded. Tyler nodded and dug deep into his pants pocket for another coin to flip on the table.

"I'm dead tired, and I have to get some sleep before I tackle the books again tomorrow. The way I left my ledgers, I'm not sure if I'm a millionaire or bankrupt."

Carson chuckled. "I know what you mean. When me and Ella owned that tobacco store back in Philadelphia, she did the bookkeeping. She always managed to keep things straight."

Tyler recalled how Carson had lost his wife to smallpox several years before. The police chief could keep neither the fondness nor the sadness from his eyes when he spoke of her.

"We have to find you a wife," Carson added with a wistful smile.

That statement coming from anyone else would have brought a derisive laugh. But from Carson ... Tyler let the comment slide.

He strolled outside, turning up the collar of his coat against the cool night. His booted steps sounded unnaturally loud as he crossed the sidewalk and headed down West Harrison Avenue. Though he hadn't had anything hard to drink, his head ached, and the noise buzzed behind his ears. He gave up trying to think of anything besides the woman in pink. In his mind, he could still see her slender figure standing alone and vulnerable in the harsh spotlight. His stomach turned in ways he couldn't define. She reminded him of a fragile flower, and he was both grateful for, and yet repulsed by, the veil hiding her face.

Hard to believe a woman with a voice and a shape like hers could be anything but beautiful. Still, a woman of her ilk typically had hardened features. Whatever beauty she may have been blessed with had undoubtedly faded. Too much liquor, late hours, sometimes even drugs and abuse, along with too little nutrition, fresh air, and sunshine—all would have taken their toll. Though she might have attractive features, her face couldn't possibly live up to the promises made by her voice.

Her voice. He shivered, perhaps somewhat because of the chilly evening, but more from the memory of her soothing and provocatively unsettling voice. The rise and fall of her pale, white shoulders made him ache to touch her—just like every other red-blooded male in the place. The thought brought him back to earth like a slap in the face.

"What the devil are you thinking, Buchanan?" he swore aloud to the empty street. He had been so consumed with Lily, he had walked almost the entire distance to his house and had no idea how he had gotten there. He had to make himself stop thinking about her.

Merle had certainly come up with a brilliant strategy. The veil gave the woman an air of mystery any man would find fascinating. The veil and her uncommonly lovely voice—truly he couldn't remember hearing one more passionate. He must rein in his traitorous thoughts before he traveled any further down an ill-advised road.

CHAPTER SIX

Lily rose before the sun. After a restless night, she would have to find time to nap before her official debut—or, unveiling, literally. Hopefully, this would be a big night for Merle and the Canary Cage. He had told her in no uncertain terms not to leave the building during the day. After last night, too many people would try to catch a glimpse of her before the evening show, and Merle was not about to have his plans spoiled.

Lily stood at the window and pulled the sheer, faded curtains aside. The town still slept. In the outlying countryside, the farmers and ranch hands would be rising in the dark to tend to morning chores. In town, streetlights still ablaze, no one walked the streets, and the silent building gave evidence that she alone had risen. The other girls would surely sleep until well into the morning or perhaps even noon. But she had sought her bed much earlier than they, and she habitually awakened early.

For a moment, the events of the night before swept over her ... and she felt incredibly weary. Finally seeing the man who had meant so much to Augusta had been somewhat of a shock. She was not surprised at how easily she had picked him out from the crowd.

Still, even if Augusta hadn't described him so accurately, I would have known him.

The moment she laid eyes on him she knew he was the one Augusta had described so vividly—his strong good looks, his inbred sophistication, and his compelling presence. Her stomach tightened remembering the coolness of his splendid gray eyes. She had earned a little of his respect last night and surely piqued his curiosity. Thanks to Merle and the Canary Cage, a tenuous introduction had been made to the man she now knew as Tyler Buchanan. The first step accomplished—she would take the second step tonight. But that was tonight, and this was still morning.

She sat in the old rocker for a few moments, trying to read her Bible, trying to say her morning prayers. God seemed far away in this place, and she couldn't think of anything but Augusta and that ... that man.

Lily pulled one of her carpetbags out of the oak chifforobe. From the bottom of the valise, she dug out the silver picture frame wrapped in a soft, much-worn scarf. She sat back on her heels, the nightdress bunching behind her knees, and gave a ragged sigh. The photograph had been their father's favorite. She and Augusta sat side by side on the settee in the parlor. Lily held the properly stoic position, her wide eyes somber. Augusta laughed, and her eyes sparkled as she grinned mischievously at the flustered photographer.

Merle or no Merle, this morning—with everyone still abed—she would visit her sister's grave. She refused to accept that Augusta had been buried here in this backside-of-beyond town until she saw the grave herself. By the time Lily had received the box with the few personal items returned to *Melissa Forrester* as Roxie's only surviving relative, Augusta had been dead for almost two months. Dead and probably buried in the cemetery she had seen from the train.

Lily dabbed her dampened cheeks with the sleeve of her nightdress, then stood. She quickly donned her simple black cotton dress, smoothing the wrinkles as best she could, and then washed her face in the tepid water from the pitcher on the washstand. Unbraiding her thick rope of hair, she brushed the curling locks with hurried strokes before pinning it into a severe knot at her nape. She studied her reflection for a moment in the wavy mirror.

Plain. Plain as unsalted porridge.

Even if someone saw her, she would never be connected to the mystery woman at the Canary Cage.

Lily draped a black shawl around her shoulders. Opening the door slowly, she winced when the squeaking hinges seemed to scream her intent down the quiet darkness of the corridor. Seeing no one, she tiptoed down the stairs, through the kitchen, and out the back door. Once outside, she walked briskly across the unkempt yard, down the alleyway and onto the street.

She had spotted the cemetery from the train the morning before. Even at a brisk walk, she would need at least two hours to walk there and back. She had time.

The morning before? She shook her head with wonder. Hadn't a lifetime passed since she stepped off the train less than twenty-four hours earlier? In that lifetime, she had ceased to be Melissa Lillian Forrester, the proper, law-abiding heiress, and became Lily Woods, a common working girl singing in a saloon. She still couldn't believe she had come so far, had come to Guthrie on her own, landed a job at the Canary Cage, and come face to face—well, almost face to face—with her nemesis. Things were falling into place.

Lily turned the corner at a milliner's shop and walked north. She passed the brick building serving as the police station and city jail. She stopped, morbidly fascinated with the outside gallows standing like a sentinel, its long arms casting even longer shadows in the streetlights.

She continued on, walking briskly until she reached the cemetery. A wooden sign hung above the pathway proclaiming the place as *Summit View Cemetery*. She approached, taking in the sparse but closely cropped grass growing between the tombstones. How would she ever find Augusta's grave? The ground, still soggy from a recent rain, sank beneath her boots. She picked her way down a row noting the names on the marble and granite markers on either side. When she neared the back of the cemetery, she saw another, smaller graveyard separated by a low wooden fence with missing slats. Wires held the gate closed, and rough wooden crosses tilted crazily at odd angles. A feeling of dread formed low in Lily's stomach and grew with each step she took toward the desolate cemetery.

Oh God, that's where they bury murderers … and horse thieves … and bank robbers … and debtors.

She added names as she walked, trying to avoid the thought niggling resolutely at the edge of her mind, trying to avoid thinking *prostitutes* and *saloon girls*. But the truth lingered with a numbing certainty … *sweet baby Jesus.* Her darling, her beautiful sister, would not have been buried in the public cemetery among *decent folks*. She would be here with the dredges of humanity in this forgotten, slovenly graveyard.

Moving forward without conscious thought, Lily leaned against the fence, her breath catching in her throat, the splinters snagging her shawl.

Oh, God! This is so unfair. How could you let this happen?

Augusta had died alone in a place where no one loved her, where people called her "Roxie," not even knowing who she was or where she called home. No one knew she had a father and a sister who adored her. No one knew she was an heiress to a small fortune nor that she had been the toast of Norfolk until her adventurous spirit seduced her into running away. She had ended up in Guthrie where she was laid to rest …

No! Lily amended, horrified—Augusta could not be resting, not here, not so far from home, not among the wretches who lay beside her. Not when she had been so miserable, so despondent that she had taken her own life.

Overcome by nausea, Lily clung to the fence, her knees threatening to give way beneath her. A sudden hand on her elbow steadied her and an arm corded with powerful muscles supported her shoulders until her legs righted beneath her. Startled, she turned and looked into the anxious gray eyes of Tyler Buchanan. She stared at the man, fascinated with his classically handsome face. Not until he spoke did she realize her lungs burned from holding her breath.

"Ma'am," he said, his concern evident. "Are you all right? May I help you?"

She had not expected his gentle tone—nor had she imagined the soft Southern accent—a detail Augusta had failed to mention.

"No, thank you," she whispered, her voice shaking. "I'm all right. Really."

He frowned, his arm still around her shoulder. With some difficulty, she managed to pull away.

"You're trembling. Are you ill?"

Lily studied his face for a moment, confused by his seeming concern for a stranger. *No, no,* she reminded herself sternly, mentally churning up the anger she needed to carry out her plan. This man had no compassion. Augusta lay here because of him—a cold-hearted, bloodless creature. If not for his arrogance … his malicious rejection of Augusta's avowal of love … her strong, vibrant sister wouldn't have sunk to the depths of desolation. If he had shown her one-tenth of the concern he displayed for Lily at this moment, Augusta would have been able to deal with their relationship, or the lack of one, and would have gone on until someone or something else caught her fancy.

Lily opened her mouth to give Tyler the scathing set-down he deserved and caught herself at the last moment. She closed her eyes briefly, her thoughts and emotions whirling in too many directions. Yes, he might be the guilty scoundrel she had sought, but she couldn't allow him to see her animosity. At this point, an apology would be the most she might receive. Heartfelt or not, that wouldn't be enough. She must make the most of an untenable situation by pretending to be pleasant and sociable, regardless of how distasteful she found him to be.

"Are you ill?" he asked again, a little louder.

She opened her eyes. "No, I'm fine. I was just a little dizzy. I …" She grappled for an explanation. "I haven't eaten yet this morning, and I walked farther than I'd planned."

Tyler peered over Lily's shoulder toward the cemetery. "This is an unusual place for a morning walk, miss."

What are you doing here, you monster? Are you gloating over another of your conquests?

She so desperately wanted to sling accusations. He would only deny them, and she would tip her hand. At least he was studying her face with poorly disguised interest.

"Can you, ah, make your way home all right or would you like me to walk with you?"

"Good heavens, no!"

At Tyler's startled expression, she followed her emphatic refusal with a sweet smile. "You've been much too kind already, sir—"

"Tyler." He extended his hand in a formal greeting. "Tyler Buchanan. I work for the Capital City Courier."

Surprised by his seeming humility, Lily knew full well that he served as both publisher and editor of the newspaper.

Oh, dear, what in the world do I say now? She had to stall—this was not the time to reveal her identity.

"The newspaper? Oh, how interesting! I'm sure you know absolutely everything about absolutely everybody, don't you?" She fluttered like an awestruck schoolgirl and gave a try at batting her eyelids as she remembered Augusta doing. "It's been so very nice meeting you, Mr. Buchanan. I do appreciate your concern, but I had best be getting back now or everyone will think I have gotten myself lost." And with that she flashed him a dazzling smile and walked briskly towards the entrance of the cemetery, then—in case he still watched her—she turned in the opposite direction of the newspaper office and the Canary Cage.

Lily entered the kitchen through the back door, her cheeks rosy from the chilly morning air and her unexpected encounter with Tyler. In her haste, she nearly collided with Merle.

"Where in tarnation have you been?" he growled, his eyebrows drooped in sharp angles. "I thought I told you to stay put until tonight."

She draped her shawl over her arm, trying to think of an explanation that would placate him. Having had her fill of lying for the morning, she opted for the truth, at least partially.

"Oh, come on, Merle"—she pouted prettily, as she had often seen her sister do—"you and I are probably the only two who are awake at this hour."

"That's not the point, Lil." Merle ran his fingers through his uncombed hair. "Just one person spying you before tonight could ruin everything." He held up his hand to stop her from interrupting. "I don't give a dang what you were doing out there, and if you say no one saw you then I guess there's no harm done *this* time. But"—he wagged his forefinger at Lily's nose—"one thing you'd better learn and learn quick ... what I say around here goes ... or you do." With a grimace probably meant to look stern but far from menacing, he turned to walk away, coffee cup in hand.

"Merle," she called after him, determined to get things back on track. The day was going from bad to worse.

Merle paused mid-step and turned his head to show he heard her. She understood his need to maintain a modicum of discipline. She must abide by the rules like everyone else.

"I am very sorry," Lily said. "I woke up at such an early hour, and the streets were deserted. I felt like I hadn't had a breath of fresh air in days. And, even if someone saw me, I wouldn't be recognized because of that veil. But you told me not to go out and I did—and I apologize. I don't know what else to say."

He didn't answer, though his jaw relaxed. He gave a quick nod, then walked off down the hallway. She'd been forgiven.

The day already seemed interminable as she climbed the stairs to her room, and exhaustion suddenly overtook her. Once inside, she peeled off the black dress with slow, deliberate motions and hung it again in the wardrobe. She hated that dress and every other black dress she owned. This morning, the garment seemed to be the only suitable one she possessed. After tonight, she could wear anything—no matter how outrageous, and no one in town would be shocked. After all, she sang in a saloon and obviously had no self-respect.

Catching sight of her reflection in the cheval mirror, she straightened and studied herself critically, comparing her shape to her sister's. While almost exactly the same height as Augusta, Lily had always seemed to be a little taller because of her slender build. She was not as filled out and could boast a narrower waist, while her hips didn't have quite the same womanly proportions.

"Who would believe that Miss Melissa Lillian Forrester of Norfolk, Virginia—known to everyone who is anyone as a prim and proper bluestocking—would be wondering how to tempt a man like Tyler Buchanan?" she whispered to her reflection, half amazed, half amused. Ludicrous. But true.

Lily thought of the irony of the situation. While both she and Augusta had been properly groomed in all aspects of running a gracious household according to the edicts of an elite society, Lily had felt more at home in the classroom. She excelled in all subjects, including mathematics and history, while only music had held Augusta's interest. As a result, Lily had managed the household accounts and assisted her father in overseeing the shipyard books.

Not using one scrap of her education, she would try to imitate Augusta's sashay of the hips, how she fluttered her lashes, and how she flirted when she smiled. Lily shook her head and sighed. These were things young ladies weren't taught in a classroom.

Perhaps she could relax a little before the rest of the girls began their day. Lily donned the nightdress again and climbed between the sheets. She turned on her side and bunched the pillow beneath her cheek. How ironic that Augusta's need to be freed from the constraints of a rigid and strict society landed her in a place where she still couldn't escape the mundane household chores she abhorred. Everyone pitched in each afternoon to help Rae Ann clean up.

Like counting sheep, Lily reviewed Rae Ann's instructions. Beginning Monday morning, one of her duties would be to wash the windows facing the street. She smiled to herself with the thought. Cleaning the windows would keep her in plain sight of Tyler Buchanan, as the newspaper office was practically across the street. Of course, she would be in plain sight of a lot of other people, too. Unsettling to say the least. Still, she had sworn she would do anything to avenge her sister—to take advantage of any opportunity that brought her closer to her goal—even if she must eschew every moral code society invented.

CHAPTER SEVEN

A loud knock woke Lily from an overlong pleasant sleep. She gave a wide yawn, rubbing her knuckles into her eyes like a child. Sally poked her head into the room and grinned saucily.

"Hey, Songbird of the East, time to get up," Sally giggled. Uninvited, she sauntered into the room, a worn red robe belted loosely around her plump waist. She slapped Lily familiarly on the thigh.

"Up, up! We can't sleep the day away. Merle's already got a long list of things to get done. If we don't get started, he'll have our hides." Her merry voice reflected her doubt Merle would carry out any of his threats.

"All right, all right," Lily grumbled good-naturedly. Throwing back the coverlet, she swung her legs over the side of the bed. She gave a long stretch, then stood, automatically turning to straighten the bedclothes when she heard Sally's giggles.

"You sleep in that thing?" Sally asked, one hand propped carelessly on a fleshy hip. "*Gawlee*, I ain't seen nobody wear nothing like that since my granny."

Lily looked down at her bare toes peeking out from under the lace-trimmed hem of her nightgown, and then glanced back up at Sally.

"This beats the Dutch, sweetie. If we wear anything at all around here, it sure ain't nothin' like that." Sally belted her robe a little more snugly and smoothed her hand down her thigh. "The fellas go for something that feels soft and looks naughty. They don't wanna be reminded of their mamas when they come visiting us."

"Visiting you?" Lily's voice conveyed her confusion, and Sally's eyes widened in disbelief.

"Are you funnin' me or something? 'Course you are. You sang in a saloon back in Baltimore, right?" Sally laughed, her dark brown ringlets bouncing with each cackle. "Girl, you had me goin' for a minute there.

Like you don't know what goes on around here." With another chortle, she left the room.

Lily stared at the closed door, her face hot with embarrassment. How could she be such a ninny. And what was she going to do now?

She donned a navy-blue gabardine skirt and pristine white blouse. Not exactly saloon-girl day attire, but the best she could do in her haste. Then, gathering her nerve on the way, she rushed to Merle's office to set the record straight … even if all her plans went south.

She hesitated for a moment, then knocked timidly. Merle leaned back in his chair and gazed at Lily over the rims of his reading glasses as if studying her, then waved her in.

"Have a seat."

She slipped uneasily into a chair, her glance darting from object to object, avoiding direct eye contact with Merle.

"Lily," he finally prompted, "do you want something or are you here to inspect my office?"

She dropped her gaze and rested her clasped hands on her lap.

"Yes, Merle, I … I …"

Merle couldn't possibly understand her predicament. Did he expect her to perform duties other than singing? How could she refuse without ruining her plans?

"Something bothering you, Lil?" He pulled off his glasses and frowned as he leaned forward. "Just tell me, honey. If you need something, I'll get it. If it's broke, I'll fix it. I don't want you upset, especially not tonight."

"Merle, the problem isn't you—or the girls or anything," Lily began again, whispering her objections. "I just need to clear something up. There's something you need to know."

"What?"

Lily hurried on. "You see, I'm not like the other girls." She paused when he nodded in agreement. "I'm—I'm—"

Again, she hesitated and a flush crept up her neck.

"You're—?" Merle lifted prodded, lifting his eyebrows. Was he growing impatient?

"I'm a singer. That's all." The words said, her shoulders slumped in exhaustion.

Merle's bushy brows rose again as if confused.

"Ah-ha," he said. "You're a singer. That's all you wanted to say? You're a singer?"

"No, no—I mean—yes, I'm a singer—that's all—nothing more than a singer."

Lily pushed herself to her feet, walked to the window, and looked out onto the busy street.

"Get away from that window," Merle groused, "and tell me straight out what the devil you're getting at. I know you're a singer, you know you're a singer, and after tonight everybody in the whole dadblamed town will know you're a singer and a fine-looking one at that. Now what in tarnation is your point, if you indeed have one?" Merle's face was crimson with evident frustration.

Lily whirled away from the window and blurted out the words before she lost her nerve. "I won't be—entertaining gentlemen in my room," she said firmly. "I will sing. I will serve drinks. I will wash dishes, sweep floors, and clean windows. But I will *not*"—again she stumbled, humiliated at having to say the crude words aloud—"I refuse to be intimate with anyone as part of my job."

As understanding dawned, an incredulous grin broke over Merle's craggy features.

"Lily, Lily, Lily," he said, "is that all that's been bothering you? I thought maybe you had the law after you or a husband and a passel of brats waiting in Atlanta."

"No—oh, no! Nothing like that, I assure you."

His grin dissolved, and he leveled his gaze at Lily.

"This isn't a bawdyhouse—that's illegal in this town. But *entertaining*, as you put it, is okay with me if the girls are willing. I hired you to sing, serve drinks, and maybe dance a little. As for the other, well, that's up to you." He stood and stretched, massaging his lower back. "If you want to play the innocent, or if you're just mighty particular, that's okay with me too—actually, even better. That'll make you even more desirable.

"There's just one rule. If the *entertaining* happens on the premises, I get half ... fifty-fifty. If I catch you with a man in your room without my say-so, you're out. No argument."

Lily's shoulders slumped in relief. "Thank you."

"Yeah, well," Merle continued gruffly, "you need anything for tonight, you let me know. As for the rest, like I said, it's up to you. Now get."

Lily was trying to relax in sudsy bathwater when Sally burst through the door, brush in hand and a makeup case tucked under her arm.

"Lord, girl, you still soaking? You're gonna be all shriveled up like a raisin," she clucked and fussed like a good-natured mother hen. "C'mon, up-up—outta there—here, put this robe on—step on this towel so you don't slip. Let's get you upstairs. I'm gonna do your hair and help with your makeup. Merle said to keep Honey out of your room. As I'm sure you've figured, she likes to overdo things a bit. Rae Ann's bringing your dress up in a little while—I think she stayed up all night making the alterations. It's nothing short of a Red-Sea miracle she finished so quick. Of course, Merle hounded her and hounded her—said her life and livelihood depended on that dress—as if any of us could get along without her."

She barely paused to take a breath before continuing. "Heavens-amighty, it's beautiful—almost like a wedding dress. I don't know, seems like I should be jealous of you, getting all this attention. I was at first, but I can't never hold on to a grudge more than a lickity-split. Merle's never treated any of us special, and Lord knows, almost everybody else is fit to be tied—well, anyway, Honey is. Trudy, as usual, don't seem to know what's going on. But I'm not a bit jealous for some reason. I don't know—this is kind of exciting, like being a lady-in-waiting to the queen, you know—" With Lily in tow, Sally continued her stream of endless chatter all the way out the door, up the stairs, down the hall, and into Lily's room.

"Sit here." Sally pointed the brush toward the chair in front of the vanity. She pulled the pins out of the loose bun and began brushing Lily's hair with firm, even strokes. The last defiant rays of the afternoon sun beamed through the window and tinged the dark locks with blue-black sparks.

"Sam Hill and Jesse, but your hair's something else," Sally cooed when the heavy strands curled around her fingers as though alive. "We had another girl here a few months back who had gorgeous hair, too. Thick and full, not all frizzy and frazzled and odd-colored like most of us. But the color was different from yours, kind of gold and red, like yours is kind of black and blue."

Lily smiled at the young woman's words. *Papa used to say Augusta and I were like different parts of the same fire.*

Sally prattled on. "That was Roxie—God rest her soul. You know this used to be her room. She had the best voice any saloon in this town ever heard, until you came along—and I should know because I've been here since the Opening."

"The opening?" Lily met Sally's gaze in the mirror. "You mean the opening of the Canary Cage?"

"Well, since then too, but I mean *the* Opening—of the whole town, the whole territory. Shoot, I was here before the Land Office was even finished, and there weren't nothing but tents as far as you could see, and lawyers set up their desks on crates to file claims. People—the lucky ones—lived in boxcars and tents, because there wasn't any place else to stay. You should have seen how the town just blew up overnight. My mama died when I was little, and my daddy was killed in a fight over a parcel of land, so I set up with Orrin Fletcher over at his place—I was twelve—just serving drinks and helping out."

Sally continued brushing Lily's hair with long, smooth strokes.

"Then Merle bought this place from the Reeves Brothers, and I came to work here. There's been a lot of girls come and go—seems like our kind don't usually stay in one place too long—but I'm … well … I've been here for years and can't call nobody family but Merle and Rae Ann, so I figure this is home."

While Sally chatted, her nimble fingers curled and twisted, pinned and smoothed Lily's hair into a loose chignon woven with strands of imitation pearls and narrow red satin ribbons.

"What do you think?" Sally stepped back, her hands braced on her hips. A satisfied smile plumped her cheeks as she met Lily's gaze.

Lily turned her head from side to side, her eyes wide as she admired Sally's expertise. "You did a beautiful job. I could be going to a gala at the Waldorf-Astoria."

"Well, I don't know anything about the Waldorf-Historical, but I do know you're going to set Guthrie on its ear tonight." She opened the makeup case and began piling bottles, brushes, and sponges on the scarred vanity. "Let's get started on your makeup—we'll just use a touch so you won't look like a ghost. My word, it's a flat-out shame to cover up skin like yours. I've had splotchy skin ever since I was a kid, and I've used every concoction known to man and saloon girl. But nothing's never done me any good. Now, your skin—I'd give my right arm for a complexion like yours."

She applied a touch of rouge to Lily's cheeks, highlighting her natural rosiness, then stepped back and eyed her critically before dusting her face lightly with rice powder.

"My magpie mouth bothering you, Lily? I can shut up, you know. Shoot, once I sat through an entire supper and didn't say word one. 'Course I had an awful toothache, and I was trying to—"

"Sally"—Lily interrupted with a laugh—"Sally … Sally …" Lily finally succeeded in halting the flow of prattle on the third try.

"Yeah, hon, what is it? Too much rouge? I don't think so though, and the powder will help keep the sweat down. Those lights can be real harsh and—whew!—hotter than Hades, pardon my French. I'm sure—"

"Sally!" Lily broke in again, amused but exasperated. "What about this Roxie? Her name's been mentioned in every conversation, but no one ever really says anything much about her besides—"

"Mediocre singer, passable looks, lousy elsewhere according to the real men." The pronouncement came from Honey, who had strolled in without an invitation, a dress wrapped in tissue paper draped carelessly over her arm.

"Heavens-a-mighty, Honey, you're wrinkling it." Sally took the dress from Honey and smoothed out the satin almost reverently. "You're bent on messing something up for Merle tonight, aren't you?"

Honey shrugged, unconcerned, and sat on the edge of the bed, narrowly missing the dress. Gripping a bedpost with both hands, she leaned her cheek against the wood as if skeptically criticizing the Canary Cage's newest entertainment.

"She needs more rouge. In that white shroud, she'll look like a corpse."

"She's fine as she is. She doesn't need to be painted up like a clown like some others around here." Sally stuck out her tongue at the blonde. "Merle said—"

"Merle said … Merle said … Merle said," Honey mimicked. "Let her go out there looking like a scared rabbit, and they'll eat her alive. Then see what Merle says."

"She looks fine, and there's no need for you to get all hoity-toity about Roxie neither, God rest her poor soul. You two scrapped like cats in a water barrel over which one of you Tyler Buchanan was after—you swearin' he couldn't keep his hands off you, and she insistin' he sent her love messages with his eyes." Sally snorted, then continued. "Truth is everybody knows Tyler Buchanan never gives two hoots for any of us, and truth be told every one of us has embarrassed herself trying. All the poor man wants is to come in here, drink a couple of ginger beers—he don't drink hard stuff"—she added in an aside to Lily—"jaw with the police chief, keep half an eye on the show, and then go home. Alone. That's all he wants."

And with flashing eyes, not-so-sweet-at-the-moment Sally Brown stood with her arms folded under her heaving bosom, daring Honey to disagree.

Lily sat, half-turned in the chair, silently watching the drama play out between Honey and Sally, then promptly took advantage of Honey's nonplused silence.

"Tyler Buchanan? Who's Tyler Buchanan?"

Honey stood, flicked a disgusted look at Sally, and strode towards the door with a toss of her golden hair. "Miss Know-It-All will be more than happy to fill you in, I'm sure—with her version at least. Me, I've got better things to do than sit around and discuss Roxie's delusions about a future with Tyler. Good riddance to her, I say." She slammed the door behind her with a sharp crack.

"Good riddance to *you*, *I* say!" Sally yelled fiercely at the closed door. She clenched her fists and drummed her heels in a rapid staccato. "*Oooohh,* she makes me so mad!"

"Obviously," Lily said dryly, barely able to restrain her own anger at Honey's callousness. "If I understand correctly, she and Augus—Roxie both loved this Tyler fellow while hating each other."

"That about sums it up." Sally returned her attention to Lily's makeup. "Honey and Roxie became enemies the second they laid eyes on each other. They were equally pretty, but Roxie was nicer to me and Trudy and Rae Ann. As you can tell, Honey thinks the rest of us are here for her to walk on. But I wouldn't say love is the right word to describe the battle for Tyler Buchanan. Not that every woman and girl-child in Guthrie isn't half in love with that gorgeous man, but Honey and Roxie ... they were obsessed."

Lily's smooth forehead creased in bewilderment. This was a different twist.

"Obsessed?"

Sally dipped a thinly tipped brush in a delicate pink mixture and bent to apply the pigment to Lily's lips.

"Everything was a contest between the two of them. Now I'm not saying Roxie didn't really think she cared about the man. And Honey—well—Honey thinks she needs to have every man in the territory wrapped around her finger—"

"You said Roxie *thought* she cared for Tyler. You think she didn't?"

Sally shrugged and picked up a kohl pencil, then lightly outlined Lily's eyes.

"Well, you'd have to know Roxie. She was like a butterfly, you know?"

"No. I don't know."

"Guess you wouldn't. Roxie was beautiful and wanted to be in the middle of everything. She sort of flitted from one thing to another, one person to another, like a butterfly going from flower to flower."

Lily nodded, caught up in her own memories—how Augusta made the rounds of Norfolk society, never able to turn down an invitation to a soiree, a ball, or even an afternoon tea. While her best friends changed from week to week, her infatuations rarely lasted even that long.

Sally hardly took a breath before continuing. "Not like I didn't believe her when she said he smiled at her in a special way, or he had winked at her." Sally's expression oozed sympathy. "I think she saw things the way she wanted them to be and not exactly the way they really was. And honest to goodness, Tyler has never been anything more than polite to any of us—which is unusual enough in itself. It's almost unnatural … he's such a man, and yet, he's not ever been seen on a regular basis with any woman. We've joked that maybe something's, you know, *wrong* with him. But we know that's not true. Everybody knows Theo Peebles has her eye on him, and he escorts her around sometimes."

"Theo Peebles?" Lily's attention snapped to full throttle with this new information.

"Theo's short for Theodora—she's named after her father Theodore. He owns one of the biggest banks in town. She's spoiled rotten. You'll run into her sooner or later. As for Tyler, he's a man who knows what he wants and he waits until it—or in this case—*she* comes along. And Roxie wasn't the one no more than Honey or any of the rest of us are."

Lily digested this for a moment, sitting still while Sally stepped back and studied her workmanship. Perhaps now was a good time to ask a few questions and take advantage of Sally's lull.

"I know this used to be her room and that she—died here. What happened?" Lily braced herself for the answer. She knew what Sally would say, and Lily's heart was already breaking at having to hear the words. Still, she had to keep up the pretense of ignorance. She had to know everything, gather all the missing bits and pieces.

Sally's brown eyes filled with tears, and she shook her head sadly. "Yeah, she's dead. Shot by her own hand."

Lily swallowed hard, the words no easier to hear now than when she first learned of her sister's suicide. "Killed herself? How terrible. And sad. What caused her to be so unhappy? Did something happen to her?"

"I don't know, I really don't. Late one night, I heard low voices through the wall—you know my room is right next door. There was this gunshot, and then we all crowded in the hallway trying to get in her room. There she lay—on the floor—the front of her robe all covered in blood, the gun by her hand—and I just stood there. I kept thinking how hot the room was even though her back window was wide open. Then Merle came running in with Chief Ward and made us all leave."

Tears dripped off Sally's chin and splashed onto the back of Lily's hand, burning into her skin. Grief and thankfulness surged, almost choking Lily. At least one person had cared about Roxie.

"When we buried her, only Tyler and Chief Ward came. I mean all of us were there, the girls, Toby, Malcolm, Merle, and Rae Ann—but from the town, only Tyler and the chief. The most awful thing was we couldn't get a minister to speak over her. Reverend Scott was out of town, or I'm sure he would have been willing to do a service. Merle even asked Sexton LaMotte, but that hateful man refused because, given the way she lived and the way she died, for him to speak would be a slap in the face of decent folks. I was surprised, because I thought they had sort of become friends. I mean, he always came around trying to convert her, and she would tease him about converting him. Then he'd get all flustered. So, Merle did—speak over her that is. He did a fine job, too. Then Tyler spoke the Shepherd's Psalm and said a real nice prayer."

Stunned, Lily stared at her, mouth agape. "Tyler? Tyler Buchanan? He prayed over her? Why was he even there?"

Sally shrugged. "I admit I was a little surprised to see Tyler there considering the gossip that had been going around about him and Roxie. I knew Honey started most of it, trying to cause trouble for Roxie. Then

I heard the chief tell Tyler there was a letter on Roxie's vanity addressed to him—to Tyler, not the chief. Honey said she'd make sure Tyler got it. Everybody figured she'd written him a love letter, because there was all the talk about Roxie killing herself after Tyler broke her heart."

Lily sprang to her feet and paced the room, avoiding the rug covering the blood stain. "Well, that makes sense. In her despair over being rejected by the man she loved, she took her own life."

"No, well … yes, I mean, maybe—I don't know. It's just that we've all been turned down by Tyler—but real nice-like. I mean, he's never been mean to any of us or anything. He always manages to sound like he's not interested right now. But if he changed his mind, you'd be the one he'd call on. Shoot fire, he's the best this town has to offer, and we're all flesh and blood. But none of us has killed herself over a man before. It seems like such a waste. After all, there are so many of them. Just because you can't get one don't mean you can't comfort yourself with lots of others."

Out of her element in that regard, Lily rarely flirted. On the other hand, her sister managed to attract suitors by the dozens. With her teasing smiles and alluring looks, Augusta couldn't be happier than when holding court, her dance card filled, and the house overwhelmed by the scent of flowers delivered daily by her smitten admirers.

Content to remain in her sister's shadow, Lily ran the household—accepting only enough invitations to be considered sociable—and staying up late only to hear Augusta's enthusiastic recounts of her latest conquests. Augusta always teased, calling Lily's belief in one true love a "Sir Lancelot dream."

A loud knock made both girls jump.

"What the blazes are you doing in there, Sally? You should be on the floor already—the show starts in thirty minutes." Merle could most likely be heard half-way down the street. "You hear me? The place is packed, and they're standing on the sidewalks. Get moving!"

"Oh my-my-my," Sally sniffed and wiped her face. "Look at us. Biggest night we've had around here since I can remember, and we're sittin' here blubberin'. I've gotta run and get myself ready, but there's only so much I can do. No matter what, I won't be lookin' like you. That's for sure. Put on your dress and touch up your face a bit. You sure are a soft-hearted thing to be sheddin' tears over someone you never knew—though I suppose anyone with half a heart would feel a little sadness for such a situation. You practice breathing deep to help calm your nerves ..." Sally finally left the room, her words trailing behind her in an unbroken stream.

Lily opened the window facing the backyard, letting in the cool evening breeze. Through the open downstairs windows, she heard loud banter underscored by Toby's energetic piano playing. The floor vibrated beneath her thin slippers, and her stomach fluttered.

"You're crazy, you know," she told herself, turning away from the window to don the dress. "You've never even *seen* a crowd like that downstairs much less tried to sing in front of one, except for last night." She almost laughed at her reasoning. Last night hardly counted, considering the safety afforded by the veil. Tonight, she was on her own. The thought echoed—*on her own—on her own*. Because of Tyler Buchanan. If not for him, she would still have her sister. No doubt Augusta would have come home at some point. If she didn't want to come back to Norfolk, then perhaps the two of them would have moved somewhere and started a new life together.

A blast of laughter shattered her reverie, and she anxiously examined her attire. Her gown, a sheath fashioned of spotless white satin, bared her shoulders and fit tightly through the waist and hips, flaring slightly above the knee. White silk stockings hugged her exposed calves and ankles. Merle decided she would portray a paragon of virtue, a woman of quality and breeding. "Lily white," he had said, and then laughed. Lily choked on her own laugh. As if anyone would believe a woman singing in a saloon to be any of those things. To Merle and to the men downstairs, she wore a costume, the pretense of a chaste innocent, untouched, and unsullied. The apparel would be a joke, belying the woman they believed her to be, a wanton, painted creature with no morals, no decency, no rightful place in society, and who sold her favors for a coin or two. In their eyes, only the red ribbons in her hair would herald the truth.

Indeed, the whole charade was laughable. For the most part, she would be dressing up as herself tonight. While not quite up to Norfolk's—or Guthrie's—social standards, she was the only woman on the premises entitled to wear white. Her thoughts went back to the earlier conversation with Sally. Lily sighed. Had she made a mistake? Augusta's letters had given no hint as to the possibility Tyler refused favors the girls at the Canary Cage offered. If he truly did—for whatever reason—avoid entanglements of that nature, perhaps Lily could have found another way to stay in Guthrie, one that would have given her more access to Tyler under different—

and certainly more comfortable—circumstances. Perhaps as a telephone operator or a schoolteacher or bookkeeper. But no—only by this way could Lily learn the truth about Augusta's life. No other path would have enabled her to get to know—or even meet—Sally or Rae Ann or any other denizen of the saloon life.

Too late now. She must remain committed to her adopted identity. Learning that the typical wiles of a common saloon girl had no effect on Tyler had been the only useful information gleaned from today's revelations.

Perhaps this information could be put to good use. Acting out her part realistically already proved to be difficult, as the lifestyle was so foreign to her upbringing. Still, if she could somehow intertwine her own thoroughly proper personality with her recollection of Augusta's flirtatious mannerisms and her careful observations of Honey, Sally, and Trudy ...

That just might be a winning combination.

CHAPTER EIGHT

Tyler turned the knob on his front door and, finding it locked, knew Libby had gone home. Usually, he hoped she would still be there. He'd never become accustomed to entering a cold, empty house bereft of an army of servants and the laughter and warmth of his family. He sighed at the memory. He'd always thought Libby was good for him—compassionate, dependable, and filled to the brim with plain common sense. He could count on her to lend an ear or a shoulder. Next to Carson, she might be the only true friend he had in Guthrie.

He'd been in town only a month, already printing four issues a week, when Libby came to the newly-constructed newspaper office.

"My name is Olivia Preston, Mr. Buchanan—Libby will do." She had studied him with somber brown eyes. "I'm a widow, got two boys to feed. You're a single man, and as far as I know, don't have anyone looking after you. I've come to offer my services as a housekeeper. I do laundry for a few of the folks here in town, but I'm done with that by noon each day. I'll do your laundry, clean up around your quarters—and your office, too, if you want—do the floors, the windows when necessary, whatever you need, and I'll cook dinner for you once a day. I can come five days a week … six if it makes a difference. I'm honest, hardworking, and healthy." Her speech finished, she had swallowed hard and waited for his response, rubbing her red knuckles nervously with her thumb.

Ten years had gone by. Tyler had long since moved from a back room at the newspaper office to his own home at the edge of town, and Libby was still with him. They had grown close, and she sometimes seemed to provide the only stability in his life. The town constantly changed, and the newspaper business proved to be nothing short of chaotic. Then there had been that muddle with Roxie. But Libby kept one part of his life neat, simple, uncluttered. Walking through his front door felt like stepping into the eye of a hurricane, a peaceful harbor, an oasis.

Tyler couldn't remember the first time he had asked Libby to stay a while to talk after he'd come home. He only remembered that the day had been long, and he had been particularly homesick. For the first time, he told another human being the truth about Allegra and his brother Rogan. He had wept his first tears over the events that had forced him to leave Charleston to begin a new life in Guthrie. Libby had comforted him with the warmth of a hug. There was no passion but love of a sort between them, along with true friendship and the kind of healing found in simple understanding and trust.

Tonight, as Tyler fished the key out of his pocket and unlocked the door, relief washed over him. Libby had gone home. He didn't want to talk, nor did he want to think. He only wanted to block Lily's image from his mind. He hung his hat and jacket on the rack behind the door, then kicked off his boots and left them on the floor. He walked in his socks to the kitchen. A plate covered with a linen napkin sat on the still-warm stove. As he lifted the corner of the napkin, the aroma of baked chicken and fried potatoes filled Tyler's nostrils at the same time his stomach growled. Had he eaten today? He frowned when he couldn't remember. No matter. He didn't want to eat—he wanted a drink. Tyler dropped the cloth and rummaged in the pantry until he found a bottle of whiskey. Dusting it off, he poured a liberal amount in a coffee cup, then carried the cup and the bottle to the living room.

He built a fire against the unseasonably cool night before collapsing in a chair, his long legs stretched out in front of him. One arm hung over the side, his fingers draped around the neck of the bottle as it dragged the floor.

Lifting the cup to his lips, he took a sip of the hazel liquid and held it in his mouth a moment before swallowing. He hadn't had a drink in over ten years. Not since he had changed his life. But tonight, he deserved one drink. Or more. He closed his eyes and leaned his head against the back of the chair, the whiskey forging a burning path from his throat to his stomach. A couple of sips more and the cup was empty. A feeling of resigned lethargy spread through his limbs.

"Blast it all," he said aloud, disgusted with himself. All day, he had tried to keep his mind on his work, to think about the upcoming Novelty Parade and about the party the Peebles planned to celebrate their daughter's twentieth birthday. Despite his efforts, his recalcitrant mind refused to stray far from two women … one he had heard sing the night before, and the other he had met at the cemetery. And tonight, no matter how hard he tried, he again had no control over his thoughts. Finally, with a groan of defeat, Tyler surrendered. Staring blankly into the flames now burning low, he let his mind stray to where it had wandered all day—to Lily.

The Canary Cage had been packed to the rafters. Though curious about the unveiling of Merle's new singer, Tyler—already tired to the bone—almost went home rather than try to elbow his way through the crowd. Merle had hired several cowboys to help handle the additional crowd, and one of them had been watching for Tyler.

"Mr. Buchanan," the stocky young man called, "this way. Merle saved you a seat up front with the chief."

Tyler followed him through the crowd and sat down next to Carson at the same table they had occupied the night before. He accepted a mug of ginger beer from Honey, flashed her a vacant smile, and turned his attention to Carson. A few minutes later, he settled back as the house lights dimmed, and the spotlight directed everyone's gaze to, of all places, the top of the drawn red velvet curtain. Toby's nimble fingers flitted across the keys as the curtain rose to reveal a bare stage. The crowd's puzzled murmurs gave way to guffaws when an immense, golden birdcage slowly descended from the ceiling on a pulley. The lights hit the cage and enveloped a woman dressed in white swinging on the perch.

She had needed no introduction. The men came to their feet with a tremendous roar and chanted her name. The cage landed on the stage with a gentle thump, and Merle strode across the platform, his face split ear to ear with a grin. He unlatched the door and held out his hand for Lily. She stepped through the opening and swept into an elaborate curtsy—her head bowed low. With every eye trained on her, she lifted her face to the audience, a move Tyler had been certain was practiced. Smiling sweetly, her gaze roamed leisurely around the room, so that each man would later swear she had looked directly at him with promise in her incredible blue eyes. Then her smile widened as her rose-tinted lips parted, revealing pearl-white teeth. When she began to sing, Tyler had no doubt each man in the room silently swore his eternal devotion to the vision in white.

The woman at the graveyard. Tyler's jaw dropped at the realization. Tonight, though her complexion was slightly heightened by artifice, he immediately recognized her translucent beauty. If he had leaned close enough to catch her scent, he knew she would have smelled like delicate gardenias. The same face, the same lips, the same eyes had haunted him all day, until he had finally determined he would find the mysterious woman through all available means.

And he had found her—in the last place he would ever have expected. The last place he *wanted* to find her.

He couldn't keep his eyes from devouring her. The white dress clung to her curves, and her pulse fluttered at her throat, a sure but surprising sign of her nervousness. He found her bravery as alluring as her face and her anxiety as seductive as her voice. This was no showgirl. More like a misplaced fairy princess. Though his flesh tried relentlessly to convince him otherwise, he had no doubt in his mind—he couldn't have her.

Now, slouched in his favorite overstuffed chair, after several drinks, he admitted he hadn't been in such a state in a very long time. He regretted his lack of willpower. Though quite drunk, he could still swear at himself.

"Blast you, Buchanan," he said to his blurred reflection in the now-empty bottle. "Is there some defect in your brain? Some fatal flaw in your character that provokes you to become bewitched by the most unsuitable of women? Didn't you learn your lesson the hardest way possible? You will not become involved."

Even as he spoke the words, Lily's smiling visage floated in the glow of the fire. With another curse, Tyler hurled the whiskey bottle at the grate.

CHAPTER NINE

Melissa had always been grateful God created the world in six days, and then saw fit to declare the seventh day one of rest. After a busy week of household duties and social engagements, events she had also regarded as duties, she had looked forward to the hour she could spend in church in quiet reverence. The remainder of the day she would relax peacefully, sometimes reading, catching up on her correspondence, or maybe even taking a much-needed nap. Augusta, on the other hand, had always chafed under the inactivity of the Sabbath household devoid of servants. A dozen half-done embroidery projects filled her sewing basket, and she would toss book after book of sonnets aside in frustration, wandering from the bookcase to the window to the wing-backed chair and back again.

Every Sunday morning since they were little girls, their father had bundled them off to church. Providing the weather wasn't prohibitive, John Patrick Forrester took great pride in walking the four blocks to the church on St. Paul's Boulevard, holding his lovely daughters' hands. As they grew older, and their skirts grew wider, he walked with one daughter on his arm while the other followed behind, alternating each successive Sunday so neither daughter would feel slighted.

While Augusta's startling beauty drew the initial attention, Mr. Forrester found conversation with Melissa to be far more interesting. Augusta perpetually grumbled about walking to church and exclaimed she preferred truly foul weather, which dictated they use the carriage. Melissa had always been amused by Augusta's courteous nod and beguiling smile at a passerby while complaining bitterly under her breath. Though always eager to accept a ride from one of her many friends, Augusta obviously enjoyed the attention she received on those Sunday morning walks. Melissa, however, always took advantage of a few stolen moments alone with her father.

His memory made her smile. As a child, she had adored him, staring up at his seemingly great height, loving the smell of pipe tobacco that pervaded his clothing. As the sisters matured, and his black hair grayed, Melissa took his plea to take care of her little sister more and more seriously. As Augusta grew more headstrong, keeping her reined-in became increasingly difficult. Gratefully, even after their father's sudden death from heart failure, the Sunday walks to church remained a ritual until Augusta left on her fateful journey.

Lily sighed. She was no longer Melissa. But, on this first Sunday morning in Guthrie, Lily would do as Melissa had done nearly every Sunday morning of her life. Lily performed her morning ablutions and unbraided her waist-length hair. After a thorough brushing, she styled the heavy tresses in a simple chignon. Thinking the effect a little severe, she pulled a few curling strands around her forehead. She donned one of her favorite dresses, a lovely garment in a pale blue muslin with a deep blue sash. Embroidered irises in pink, green, and yellow adorned the skirt. Lace framed the high neck in a white froth and decorated the shoulders and sleeves. Digging out her small Bible from the bottom of the carpetbag, she cast one final appraisal in the mirror and left her room.

Making her way through the silent halls and down the stairs, she followed the aroma of freshly brewed coffee to the kitchen. Surprised to see anyone else up and about, she found Toby sitting at the table, a newspaper spread out and anchored by his elbows. He held a steaming cup in one hand, while the other supported his head, palm on forehead, fingers buried in his tousled hair. Honey stood at the stove, pouring herself a cup of coffee. She turned at Lily's friendly greeting. Honey's eyes widened when she noticed Lily's attire—dressed for an outing.

Honey swung her gaze to Toby, then made her way to the table, hips swaying provocatively, her robe gaping. Lily's cheeks burned with embarrassment at Honey's titillating behavior.

"You look like you've got plans," Honey drawled.

Lily took a cup from the cabinet. "Yes, I thought I might—is there any tea?"

Honey glanced toward Toby, then rolled her eyes. "Nope. Around here we drink plain old coffee. Chase & Sanborn and sometimes Maxwell House. If what we drink's not good enough for you, you'll just have to get your own special supply of whatever."

Lily sighed, remembering the tea Rae Ann had brewed for her, perhaps from the good-hearted woman's *special supply*. She poured a cup, adding sugar and a liberal amount of cream to the black brew. Coffee and Honey's vituperation—not exactly conducive to starting the day as she'd hoped.

"Where are you going in that get-up anyway?" Honey asked, smoothing her hair while critically eyeing Lily's fashionable outfit.

Lily checked the gold filigree watch pinned to her bodice and took another tentative sip before answering. "I thought I'd go to church."

Honey, caught mid-swallow, choked, sputtering coffee between pursed lips, and Toby's jaw dropped. He recovered first and slapped her heartily on the back. "But Lily, you can't—*oooww!*" Honey elbowed him soundly, and he turned his red-rimmed eyes to her glaring stare.

Lily frowned. "Can't what, Toby?"

Toby looked back to Honey as if asking direction.

"You can't possibly get there on time unless you leave right now." Honey stroked Toby's injured arm. Toby, pink-faced, only nodded.

Lily drained her cup, then set it in the sink. Smoothing her skirt one last time, she picked up her Bible and smiled. "I'd better hurry, then." She waved and rushed out the back door.

For a town that had been founded only a few years earlier, Guthrie had its share of churches. Among the smaller Catholic and Jewish communities, a United Methodist Church, the Trinity Church, the First Baptist Church, a Method Episcopal Church, and the Presbyterian Church each boasted impressive edifices. Lily paused in front of the First Presbyterian Church, staring at the placard in the churchyard. The Right Reverend Nathan Scott, and beneath the pastor's name in smaller letters, Sexton, Eldon LaMotte. LaMotte. The sexton who had refused to eulogize Augusta and denied her the right of a decent burial. Lily seethed with righteous anger, wanting to march up to the monster and give him a piece of her mind. How dare he refuse to allow Augusta rest among the so-called decent citizens of Guthrie, those who had embraced the same beliefs by which she and her sister had been raised? As a so-called man of God, how dare he refuse to preside over her burial regardless of his opinion of her?

But Lily couldn't denounce him, not yet anyway. Besides, at this point, she only had Sally's version of events. Though Sally had been convincing, Sexton LaMotte, supposedly a man of God, at least deserved the benefit of the doubt. Moreover, Reverend Scott, from what Lily had heard, had a fine reputation. He would certainly know the heart of the sexton who took care of the church.

What about Tyler Buchanan?

The thought came, unbidden, unwelcomed. She thrust the notion away with a sneer and a ready reply. Tyler Buchanan was a different story. She had learned from Augusta's own hand that he had hurt her, scoffed at her feelings, and spurned her like dirt beneath his heel—as though a man who frequented a saloon could think himself somehow better than a woman who worked there.

What if Tyler is in church?

The possibility seemed remote, especially with the number of churches in town. Still, she considered the prospect. Lily looked forward to an hour of serenity, but now anxiety washed over her. If she found Tyler inside, she would need to set aside her need for vengeance for a few moments, at least long enough to enjoy a short respite to replenish her spirit. Tyler had taken too much from her already. She wouldn't allow him to steal this hour.

When Lily opened the carved oak door, the congregation was standing, already singing the first hymn. She spied a vacant spot on the center aisle in a pew about halfway down. Closing the door quietly, she made her way toward the front of the church. A few women looked up at her with curiosity as she passed, most of them eyeing the newcomer's lovely dress. More than a handful of the men had witnessed her debut the evening before. Lily did her best to avoid their hungry stares and kept her gaze on her destination. Lily stepped to the place she had spotted and, intent on the singing, didn't notice the hubbub behind her.

"Onward, Christian Soldiers." She knew the hymn by heart. Lily added her voice to those of the congregation, singing full-throated, confident in the words and melody. As she sang, she noticed the man in front of her hunch his shoulders. His dark blue suit jacket rippled across bunched muscles until he relaxed again, and the material smoothed across his broad back.

Lily's voice cramped in her throat. She recognized the man's crisp black curls curving over the collar of his white shirt. *Tyler.* He shared a hymn book with a young blonde woman who sang loudly and off key. When Lily heard his fine baritone again pick up the words in the middle of the chorus, she fought back a wave of pique.

She had planned to become a fixture in his life. Now, she seemed to encounter him everywhere. She had hoped … prayed, for a reprieve, for a few moments where she could set aside her animosity and, for that short while, be herself—be Melissa once more. She yearned to be the kind, generous woman who practiced the Golden Rule, treating others as she hoped to be treated. The woman who took time to point out the good qualities of those her sister had mercilessly criticized. Now she was filled with hatred, thirsty for vengeance, and overwhelmed by the desire to do unto Tyler as he had done to her sister and, subsequently, to her. Would her adopted persona change her inner being? Could she already be losing herself in this malevolence—a maliciousness that had no place in a house of worship?

Standing here, staring at Tyler's broad back, knowing what he had done, she found the feelings impossible to set aside. Her breath came faster, and her heart seemed lodged in her throat.

When the blonde tugged on Tyler's sleeve, he bent his tall frame toward her. She whispered in his ear, and Lily felt her stomach muscles tighten. What was the woman saying to Tyler? Something about Lily? An endearment to Tyler? At that moment, Lily didn't know which she thought was worse.

The hymn ended with the small choir singing a seven-fold amen. Once the congregation took their seats, the din grew louder. Some of the men, presumably those who had been at the Canary Cage the night before, stared ahead red-faced. Other men gawked with inappropriate appreciation. The women, on the other hand, were not so divided. Their faces hard, their eyes blazing, they glared at Lily and whispered furiously to each other behind gloved hands.

Lily refused to fidget and betray her discomfort. Straightening her shoulders and lifting her chin, she clasped her Bible securely in her lap. A man who had been seated in the front pew walked to the pulpit and caught the Reverend's attention for a private moment. As the man spoke, the Reverend scanned the congregation until his gaze met Lily's. His eyebrows raised just a fraction. Lily colored unexpectedly, feeling suddenly naked as his eyes, glinting behind his spectacles, appraised her.

The buzzing whispers grew louder. Realizing she was the cause of the commotion, she stiffened. She shouldn't be here. No, she thought again, she really *should* be here. She had as much right to be in church as anyone. No one else could understand that. She could imagine what they thought—*the nerve, the bald-faced, unmitigated gall of the woman that she would dare strut so boldly into a house of worship. She surely would be struck dead. How could she live as she does during the week and then come to church with God-fearing folks and have her sins absolved?*

Lily chewed her lower lip. She hadn't thought this through. She remembered the exchange between Toby and Honey. They could have stopped her from walking into this snake pit, and they hadn't. What had she done to cause offense?

The Reverend flipped through the pages of his Bible and cleared his throat to draw the attention of the congregation. Of medium height, his thin, narrow shoulders were barely discernible beneath the black robe. Though a young man, his straight, sandy brown hair showed signs of thinning. Gold wire-rimmed spectacles reflected the sunlight and intermittently hid his pale green eyes.

The Reverend waited until the commotion subsided. Lily fought the urge to hike up her skirts and run down the aisle, down the stairs, down the streets, and all the way back to Norfolk.

"Reading from the Book of Ezekiel, chapter 16, beginning with verse 35 … 'Wherefore, o harlot, hear the word of the Lord!'"

The minister's voice rang out in the sanctuary, and Lily's horrified exclamation was lost amid the collective gasp of the congregation. The Reverend continued reading, ignoring the shocked surprise of the townspeople, his reedy voice gaining momentum.

"'Thus saith the Lord God: Because thy filthiness was poured out, and thy nakedness discovered through thy whoredoms with thy loves, and with all the idols of thy abominations, and by the blood of thy children, which thou didst give unto them. Behold, there I will gather all thy lovers with whom thou hast taken pleasure, and all them that thou has loved, with all them that thou has hated. I will even gather them round about against thee, and will discover thy nakedness unto them, that they may see all thy nakedness.'"

Lily, numb and cold all over, wondered if this was how death felt. Her urge to flee remained just that—an urge. She couldn't stand, much less run. She could do nothing but sit and endure the shame.

The Reverend swiped at his perspiring forehead with a handkerchief he had pulled from the pockets of his robe before continuing with the reading.

"'And I will judge thee, as women that break wedlock and shed blood are judged, and I will give thee blood in fury and jealousy. They shall strip thee also of thy clothes, and shall take thy fair jewels, and leave thee naked and bare. They shall also bring up a company against thee, and they shall stone thee with stones, and thrust thee through with their swords. And they shall burn thine houses with fire, and execute judgments upon thee in the sight of many women: and I will cause thee to cease from playing the harlot, and thou shalt give no hire any more.'"

The Reverend fixed a stern, steady gaze toward the congregation, his probable intent contradicted by the nervous sweat beading on his upper lip. When he broke the silence, half the church jumped.

"There is a disease, a deadly, cancerous disease that has infected this town," he bellowed. "This town to so many people represented the Promised Land, represented a new opportunity to so many people leaving a hundred different Egypts to begin again in a land that was fresh and new. A land flowing with milk and honey. We came to live and work and raise our families in a new land, a good land, a land of brooks of water, of fountains and springs, that flow out of valley and hills—a land of wheat and barley, of vines and fig trees and pomegranates, a land of olive oil and honey—a land where we could eat bread without scarcity, where we would lack nothing—a land whose stones are iron and out of whose hills we could dig copper."

He dabbed at his upper lip with the handkerchief, ignoring the congregation's indignant murmurs.

"What have we done with this new Jerusalem? What have we done with this clean slate God has given us? What have we done with our Promised Land? We have mutilated it! We have perverted it into a Sodom, into a Gomorrah, into a land riddled with drunkenness and debauchery. Into a metropolis ravaged by gambling, insobriety, with fornication and prostitution. We have compromised our principles. We have compromised our salvation."

The more the congregation stirred, the more feeling Lily regained in her limbs. Initial murmurs of approval had agreed with what had seemed to be a direct assault on her and her apparent lifestyle. But she was not the only one to be castigated this morning, and the church members didn't refrain from expressing their displeasure.

"We have accepted the blessings of the Almighty and, in return, have shown him contempt. We have, in spirit, slapped the face of God! And who is at fault? Who do we blame? At whom should we point the finger of accusation? Ah, all of us have the answers, don't we? We sit here, in the house of God, and we know. We all know who is to blame. There's no doubt in our minds. Let us blame the breweries and the men who work in the breweries. Let us blame the tavern owners and the bartenders. Let us point our fingers at the musicians and the poor, unfortunate women who, for whatever misguided reasons, find themselves in the unenviable position of being in the employ of unscrupulous and unprincipled reprobates. Let us say to them all, 'You—you—and you, it is your fault. You are the reason our town is in such straits. If not for you—you—and you, things would be different.'"

He pointed a long, bony finger at no one in particular, and members turned to look at one another in suspicion.

"Let us not for one moment look inward. Let us not for one moment remember the men who buy the liquor. Let us not accuse the men, the husbands, the fathers who listen to the devil's music, drink the devil's drink, and watch the devil's dances. Let us not point our fingers at those who avail themselves of the favors of wayward women who have fallen upon hard times. Nor let us for one moment remember the proverb … 'It is better to dwell in the wilderness than with a contentious and angry woman.' "

"Let us not consider that the Holy Bible reminds us … 'It is better to dwell in a corner of the housetop than with a brawling woman in a wide house.'"

Taking a deep breath, he swiped at the sweat on his forehead with the back of his hand.

"Let us not remember that the Scriptures urge us men to rejoice with the wives of our youth, to be enraptured with her love, not to be captivated by an immoral woman, or allow ourselves to be embraced in the arms of a seductress.

"Scripture says, 'He who has found a wife has found a good thing and obtains favor from the Lord.' And again, 'A virtuous wife does her husband good and not evil all the days of her life.' Let us consider that a virtuous woman opens her mouth with wisdom, and in her tongue is the law of kindness. Her husband shall praise her, and her children shall call her blessed."

Despite her relief that the Reverend had taken the sermon in another direction, Lily prickled beneath the murderous glances still swirling around her. Not only was she viewed as a *wayward woman*, she was the reason the Reverend called down the wrath of God upon their heads.

"There is no excuse for drunkenness ... no defense for debauchery ... no justification for fornication or adultery. Let us think again about who is deserving of blame. We are. We are all to blame because we have accepted the state of our town. We have closed our eyes and refused to accept responsibility for our role in the corruption. We are to blame because we have condoned the goings-on. We have done this by our silence, by our inactivity and our refusal to do as God would have us do in gratitude for all he has given us.

"And what does God ask of us in exchange for all these many blessings? He asks that we remember from whence comes our blessings. He asks us to give him the honor due him through righteous lives."

The Reverend stared directly at several members, impaling them with his fervor.

"I urge each of you, when you leave this place, to go home to your prayer closets and search your hearts and your lives. Look inward, citizens of Guthrie, and remember, 'He that covereth his sins shall not prosper: but whoso confesseth and forsaketh them shall have mercy.'

"Let us all do our part, for God's sake, for our sake, for the sakes of our children and those who have yet to join us in building a new life here in Guthrie. And what is our part? The prophet Micah tells us, 'He hath shewed thee, O man, what is good, and what doth the Lord require of thee, but to do justly, and to love mercy, and to walk humbly with thy God.'"

The Reverend turned from the pulpit and ran a shaking hand through his hair, now matted with perspiration. He seemed to be surprised he had the passion, the righteous anger, the nerve to actually step on the toes of the good people of Guthrie.

While the congregation sang the "Doxology" with noticeably less enthusiasm than "Onward, Christian Solders," the Reverend strode down the aisle to the door where he waited to shake hands with the exiting congregants.

Trapped by the murmuring crowd, Lily kept her gaze on the Reverend. The young man wiped his palms on his robe between handshakes. She inched closer, impatience mounting as he accepted two supper invitations—one for that evening, one for Wednesday—promised to pray for three ailing relatives and agreed to speak at the next meeting of the Chautauqua Circle.

When she finally reached the exit, Lily held her breath. What would he say to the saloon girl? Not waiting to find out, Lily skittered out the door while he congratulated a woman on the birth of her first grandchild.

Tyler's head pounded mercilessly, thanks to the previous night's dalliance with Jack Daniels No. 7. He nodded perfunctorily, mumbled a hasty "Good morning, Sexton," and pumped the stand-in pastor's hand twice as Lily shouldered her way through the crowd in the churchyard. The women gave her wide berth, but the few men without female companionship impeded her progress. A cowboy, garbed in his worn Sunday-best, grasped her arm as she passed. Tyler clenched his jaw in irritation as he hurried toward her. Theodora called his name. He half-turned impatiently to acknowledge her, and then observed Lily glance first at the cowboy's face, then at the hand clutching her forearm, and then once more to her captor's leering grin.

Tyler stopped mid-step as Lily raised her chin and stared coldly at the bully. Her lips moved. Though he stood too far away to hear her words, he noted their immediate effect. The cowboy dropped her arm as if burned and backed up a step, raising his hands in mock surrender. Tyler relaxed, admiration bunching in his chest. Lily no longer ran but strode deliberately and with dignity across the churchyard. She had held her own. He finally turned his attention to the young woman tugging petulantly at his sleeve.

CHAPTER TEN

"How about a glass of fresh lemonade?" Rae Ann called to Lily through the screen door.

"That sounds wonderful. I'd love a glass if you're sure it's no trouble." Lily lowered the Saturday edition of the *Capital City Courier* and toyed with an errant strand of hair. Sitting on the back-porch swing, she brooded in the warm afternoon sun looking out over her favorite spot, the small backyard. She seemed to be the only one needing fresh air, and so the time spent on the porch swing was her own. The morning had been disastrous, and she still reeled from the mix of anger, indignation, humiliation. Then, when she had recognized Tyler, a faint, annoying tremor of something she couldn't quite identify unnerved her.

"Here you are," Rae Ann said. She handed Lily a glass of lemonade with ice shavings, then collapsed on the swing. "I've got a couple of pies cooling and a pot roast in the oven for supper." Rae Ann slapped her apron, raising a cloud of flour.

Lily took a sip of the icy lemonade and sighed in appreciation. "Since you're obviously on a different calendar than the rest of us, when exactly is *your* day of rest?"

Rae Ann's laugh sounded surprisingly youthful and lighthearted. She stood and arched her back, specks of flour floating around her.

"This is my family," Rae Ann said. "The only family I have. And I'm doing what every mother or wife does twenty-four hours a day, seven days a week. She takes care of her family. They need me, whether they'll admit they do or not. I love my work. I don't have anything else."

She looked out across the backyard to the narrow alley that ran behind the Canary Cage and the neighboring buildings. Her smile faded.

"He'll be wanting a glass of lemonade, I reckon," she said and disappeared into the kitchen, the door slamming behind her.

Puzzled, Lily watched Rae Ann's sudden retreat until the rattling of the gate drew Lily's attention. She gasped as the thin figure strode up the path formed by beaten-down grass. Reverend Scott. One hand half-raised in greeting, he approached, sweeping his hat from his head in a surprising show of respect when he mounted the uneven wood steps. Lily remained seated, indolently swaying, the creaking chains and Rae Ann's movements in the kitchen the only sounds punctuating the lazy afternoon. Lily hoped she remained outwardly calm and poised, every bit the well-bred young woman. Inwardly, she seethed. What did this man want? Why had he come?

The black-garbed man stood for a moment under her frosty perusal, licking his parched lips with an air of uncertainty.

"Good …," he began, his voice unnaturally high. He coughed into a clenched fist and tried again. "Good afternoon."

Lily nodded, hoping she kept her discomfort hidden. "Reverend Scott," she acknowledged coolly.

"I … I …"

Lily waited patiently, the man's uncertainty growing more and more apparent.

"Please sit down, Reverend." She gestured to one of the rocking chairs lining the porch.

"First of all, let me properly introduce myself," he said. "I'm not Reverend Scott—he's officiating at his niece's wedding in Atlanta. I am filling the pulpit in his absence. I'm the sexton—Eldon LaMotte." He held out his hand but dropped it to his side when she did not respond.

Not the reverend? She hesitated a moment to absorb this new information. She would have to adjust her impressions of Reverend Scott until—*if*—she met him. Of course, knowing that he employed LaMotte as sexton and allowed him to occasionally preach formed another first impression of Reverend Scott.

"Do sit down, Sexton LaMotte," she again offered.

Just then, Rae Ann pushed the door open with her shoulder, a glass of lemonade in one hand and a plate laden with a huge slice of steaming apple pie in the other.

"Why, thank you," the sexton exclaimed when Rae Ann held out the refreshments, her hospitable actions a contrast to her scowl. "That smells delicious." Rae Ann merely nodded. Turning toward Lily, she said "I've got some for you, too." True to her word, she returned a few seconds later with another serving of pie.

Lily picked at the flaky crust, exposing warm browned apples and plumped raisins in a sweet, syrupy juice.

Sexton LaMotte took a huge bite and yelped just as Rae Ann called through the screen door. "Watch your tongue. It's still real hot in the middle."

Lily bit her lip to hide her smile at Rae Ann's timing. "This is delicious, isn't it?" she ventured a few moments later, her ingrained breeding forcing her to break the strained silence. She despised parlor small talk, but her expertise came to her rescue.

"Yes," the thin-faced man gulped, blinking rapidly. "It's been a long time since I've had a treat this tasty."

Silence fell between them again until Lily broke the awkwardness.

"Tell me, Reverend—Sexton LaMotte—what brings you out this way? I would have thought that after such an *exhausting* morning, you might have preferred to rest."

He pushed his spectacles with a forefinger and sat the empty plate on the floor beside the rocking chair. He fastidiously wiped his lips with a handkerchief and, folding it neatly, tucked it back inside his pocket before answering. "Frankly, I've come to apologize."

Not what she had expected, but she said nothing. She too placed her empty plate and glass on the floor and, clasping her hands in her lap, waited for him to continue. His words didn't erase the disparagement she had experienced.

"The people in Guthrie are basically good people," he continued after a moment. "But I'm sure you understand how everyone categorizes everyone else. You simply surprised our good townsfolk by stepping out of your class."

Stunned, she stared at him for a moment before she could respond. Good townsfolk? "And what class would that be?"

His eyes widened. Had it not occurred to him that she might demand clarification? She would not let him off the hook so easily. Let him pronounce those in her profession to be less than first-class citizens. Let him say to her face that any woman who flaunted her limbs suggestively in public, jested with men in a clearly coarse manner in a bar room, and then sold her favors had no place in church. She took a small measure of pleasure in his apparent uncertainty.

Sexton LaMotte pulled uneasily at his collar and cleared his throat, his cheeks turning to pinkened splotches. "Why did you come to church this morning, Miss Lily?"

"Why does anyone go to church?"

When he didn't respond immediately, she continued. "Do you question everyone who attends a church service? Is there an examination one must pass to determine worthiness? Am I to understand that the man who attends church sporting a hangover, or the man who is only there because his wife nagged him into attendance, or the society simpleton who merely wishes to parade her Sunday best in the hopes of impressing her friends or—more importantly—snare a husband, or the woman who attends for the pleasure of criticizing and gossiping about others—am I to understand that these are more acceptable candidates for membership than someone who is, shall we say, of *my* class?" She ended her angry outburst abruptly, then, out of breath, waited for a response.

Sexton LaMotte sat motionless in the rocker, staring at her.

"Miss Lily," he ventured finally. "I know what you are saying, and you know I have to agree with you. I am simply interested in why you came. I was touched by your visit this morning. And, I, too, was angered by the congregation's response to your appearance. I'm not judging. I'm asking. Tell me *your* motives for coming to the Lord's house."

Lily stood, the swing slamming into the wooden siding. She strode to the edge of the porch and stared out across the ramshackle yard.

"Because I've always gone to church," she said.

"Alone?"

"No, with my father. And my sister."

"What of your mother?"

"She died when my sister was born."

"And your family—your father and your sister—where are they now?"

Lily hesitated before answering. How much did she want him to know?

"They're gone. I'm the only one left." From the corner of her eye, she saw the sexton stand and reach out to her before he instead wiped his palm on his trousers.

She suspected what he was thinking. Even though he may have felt something akin to compassion, he refused to touch her. Though somewhat isolated, they were still in public. No doubt he didn't want anyone seeing him acting familiarly with a saloon girl … like Jesus at the well with the harlot.

"I'm sorry, Miss Lily. I myself have no family, and I understand how bereft one can sometimes feel. Especially when ostracization is added. And that is, after all, why I am here."

Lily half-turned. "And that is?"

"As I said earlier, to apologize. Not only for the behavior of the townspeople, but for my insensitivity. I'm sure you realize that the intent of my sermon was not to humiliate you further or to make your presence more marked. Rather, I hoped to equalize the situation. However, I have no doubt that more than a few people completely missed both the point and the correlation between Israel playing the harlot compared to the goings-on here in our city. I'm afraid, though, the only thing most of them heard was the word *harlot*. And that, quite frankly, was what I was trying to avoid."

Sexton LaMotte finished his discourse and stood to leave, wiping his upper lip which was again perspiring.

The sexton was probably right. Those hypocrites had only heard *harlot*. Synonymous with Lily, the Songbird of the East. How she hated that silly name. Unbidden, the faces of the church congregation appeared before her, stern and disapproving and, among them, Tyler's troubled visage. Lily turned full around and leaned against the porch railing.

"Yes, I'm sure you're right," she said. "Needless to say, I won't be attending again. Not because they've chased me away or because I'm ashamed. I won't be attending because I don't care to associate with the likes of those I saw this morning. Thank you for coming by. Your concern is … unexpected."

If Sexton LaMotte didn't know how to respond, she didn't care. He hesitated, apparently not quite ready to leave, but she had quite skillfully ended both the conversation and his visit.

"Thank you for your hospitality, Miss Lily. While I understand your reluctance to again submit yourself to the censure of the congregation, I would appreciate the opportunity to stop by and visit with you occasionally."

Caught off-guard, Lily stared at him. He wanted to visit her? What did that mean? He refused to officiate at Augusta's funeral, refused to allow her to be buried in the church graveyard. Yet, he would be willing to associate with someone like her? In the few moments Lily had faced the narrow alley running behind the building, no less than three of Guthrie's *good townsfolk* had walked past and recognized her visitor with no apparent signs of surprise other than smug smiles. Perhaps they accepted a sexton's role in saving the souls of the town's soiled doves, yet her attendance at church—in the company of those whose souls were supposedly already saved—was deemed disrespectful.

Lily swallowed a sigh and forced a smile to her curving lips. Regardless of her inclination to refuse him, her upbringing demanded she not be intentionally rude under any circumstances. Perhaps, if she pursued a friendship of some sort, she might be able to discover a little more about Augusta and Tyler. After all, according to Sally, the sexton had visited Augusta on several occasions and had developed a friendly relationship with her. Which once again gave rise to the question … why did he refuse to speak at her funeral service? Had Reverend Scott forbidden him? Lily rebuked the nagging thought.

"That would be delightful," she said with as much grace as she could muster. "Quite obviously you understand how difficult it is for women … like me … to make friends."

Sexton LaMotte offered a rigid half-bow. "It would be a pleasure to be considered one of yours, Miss Lily. Good day." He turned abruptly but not quickly enough to hide his reddened face. Was he embarrassed at making such a forward statement? Almost running down the path, he paused at the gate, answered her wave with one of his own, and then hurried down the alley.

Lily again sat on the swing and picked up the *Capital City Courier*. She shook her head in amazement. This certainly had been a strange day—one she didn't care to repeat in any way. *Except for Rae Ann's apple pie.*

Tyler's image loomed before her. Lily sobered instantly, wondering how she could ever progress with her scheme. Her only opportunities to see him thus far had been while performing or in passing him on the street where he would do no more than acknowledge her presence.

If he would even do that. After all, he had been in church that morning … had witnessed her humiliation … had sat on the jury, judging her, condemning her effrontery in daring to attempt associating with Guthrie's citizenry. But then, she'd expected that of him.

She already knew he considered himself part of the upper echelon. Like the other men who had hidden their faces from her in church, to associate with her type behind closed doors or in places like the Canary Cage was one matter. However, pursuing any type of relationship that could be witnessed by the general public was quite another. Augusta had been explicit about Tyler's interest in her until their friendship endangered his social standing. Of course, Lily recalled with some confusion, Sally's story read somewhat differently from Augusta's and from Honey's. She had seen the spark in Tyler's eye both nights only to be snubbed by him along with the rest of the congregation.

Lily leaned back on the swing and studied the porch ceiling, the newspaper laying crumpled in her lap. Things might take a little longer than she'd planned, what little planning she had done. She felt foolish, actually. How naïve to think she could orchestrate her plan in only a few days.

She must be more patient. She had no reason to go back to Norfolk. She was alone in the world … because of Tyler Buchanan. A sudden sense of desolation came over her. She pushed the emotion aside and turned her attention to the newspaper. After reading several local stories, she scanned the advertisements. The editorial surprised her, and she reluctantly admired Tyler's talent for succinct, impassioned writing. For lighter reading, she found Chapter Three of a serial entitled "Mr. Severenson's Bride," which seemed to be about a young woman from Baltimore who had answered an advertisement from a rancher in Texas who wanted a bride. The story was fairly well written, but Lily only read the first few paragraphs before deciding against trying to pick up the threads of the story without reading the first two chapters. Chances were slim she would find the previous two Saturday editions at the Canary Cage, as Rae Ann used the newspaper for kindling.

Lily perked with sudden inspiration. Who was the obvious person to ask about back issues? The newspaper offices would likely be dark on Sunday. No harm in verifying her assumption. Unable to contain her excitement, she folded the paper, then stood to smooth the wrinkles from her skirt. Pinching her cheeks for a little color, she almost skipped down the back path.

CHAPTER ELEVEN

Lights dotted a few of the windows along West Harrison Avenue, and the streetlamps glowed. Lily found the newspaper office dark except for a light on the first floor. Could she be so fortunate? Tyler or perhaps the cleaning lady? Lily crossed the street and rubbed her suddenly cold hands together. Stepping onto the wooden sidewalk, she peeked through the glass. Tyler stood in front of an open cabinet rifling through supplies. Though afforded only a view of his back, she jumped as though stung, suddenly unsure of what to say to him. What if he snubbed her as he had that morning? She would never grow accustomed to the type of treatment she had been subjected to since donning the first dress that officially pronounced her a saloon girl.

Calm yourself. Just a few moments ago you bemoaned the fact that opportunities to get near Tyler will be scarce and that you need to seize any chance that arises. This might be providential.

After sucking in a deep breath and smoothing her hair, Lily opened the door, smothering a pleased smile at Tyler's surprise as he glanced over his shoulder. He shut the cabinet and waved her in, his coal-black hair falling across his forehead.

"Good evening," he said, the resonance in his deep voice stirring a reluctant response within her.

"Good evening, Mr. Buchanan." Her reply sounded breathless and strange to her ears. "I apologize for not introducing myself properly yesterday morning when we met, but I'm sure you understand," she continued, fluttering a hand. "I had broken a promise and escaped for a bit of fresh air. I was supposed to be under lock and key until last night."

He laughed, the sound thick and rich, triggering an answering tremor along Lily's spine. "I understand completely, Miss Woods." His eyes swept over her. "I admit I was floored when I saw you last night. I would never have made the connection between the attractive young woman I saw yesterday morning and the beautiful singer on stage."

Lily raised her eyebrows. "And just what is that supposed to mean, Mr. Buchanan?"

"Tyler, please. I only meant that the woman standing by the fence at the cemetery seemed very real, very earthbound. On the other hand, the celebrated *Songbird of the East* seemed untouchable, ethereal."

"You're as eloquent as your editorial, but I must admit I despise that ridiculous sobriquet—Songbird of the East. Ugh."

Tyler ran his fingers through his hair and scowled. He scraped two chairs across the floor. At his unspoken invitation, Lily perched on the edge of the wooden seat, noticing the sudden change in his demeanor.

Anxiety mounted, skittering her thoughts in too many directions. She had a valid reason for coming to see him, not to mention taking advantage of an opportunity to spend a few moments with Tyler. Why had his cordiality vanished with a sudden scowl? What had she said to prompt such a glower? Uncertain how to proceed, she tried to suppress a surge of panic. How would she ever be able to attract him if she couldn't put together an intelligent, or at least coherent, sentence? Lily urged another smile and plunged ahead.

"I just finished reading yesterday's *Capital City Courier*, and I must say, I was most impressed. The editorial was especially noteworthy."

Tyler's answering smile seemed genuine. "Thank you. How nice to know someone actually reads the editorial. It's not often I get favorable remarks. Usually only the grousers bother to comment."

"Actually, I read almost the entire paper, including the advertisements. There was only one section I was unable to muddle through."

He drew his heavy brows together. "What article was that?"

"I started reading, 'Mr. Severenson's Bride.' Unfortunately, the first two chapters had long since disappeared, most likely into the stove. And I was unable to make heads or tails of the story." Her mind scrambled for words to further her purpose. "Of course, I knew exactly where to go to find what I need." Lily fluttered her eyelashes. Was she coming across as an experienced coquette? She awaited his response and, as she waited, she felt her smile growing stiff and uncertain. Somewhat relieved when Tyler ignored the double-entendre, she tried to hold his gaze. He stood and shook his pantlegs down over his boots.

"I certainly wouldn't want to be the one to discourage your literary pursuits." His quip held a decidedly sarcastic edge she couldn't miss. "I'll have those back issues for you in a minute." He turned and made his way up a darkened staircase to the second floor, his steps loud and measured.

Lily sat, still on the edge of the chair, her heart beating uncomfortably fast. She had tried to keep her tone playful and her words clever and enticing. Instead of tantalizing Tyler, he sounded annoyed. Too much? Had she laid the artifice on too thickly? Perhaps her inexperience proved so apparent that Tyler was laughing at her attempt at enticement. Even though alone in the office, she felt another blush creep up her neck.

Flight filled her thoughts for the second time that day. Though brought up to handle almost any type of social situation with grace and aplomb, her inability to deal with the myriad emotions terrified her.

Tyler's booted steps on the stairs sounded a warning, and Lily took a shaky breath.

Smile. Accept the papers with a sweet thank you. Promise to return them soon. Exit with dignity.

She must reconsider her strategy, perhaps study Sally and Honey a bit more. She would never be able to snare Tyler the way things were progressing, or actually *not* progressing. She needed more time.

"Here you are." Tyler held out the newspapers. "I've been pleased with the response we've received running the serials. I was doubtful at first. I was brought up to believe a newspaper should be a pure news publication, so including fiction seemed ill advised." He shrugged his broad shoulders. "But folks can't always afford books or won't take the time to visit Miss Cook at the library, so …"

The rest of Tyler's sentence was lost on Lily so intent was she on the word *library*. How could she be so foolish? Of course, she could have found the newspapers at the library.

"I … I didn't think … where is the library?"

"Not a library as in big cities. F.B. Lillie—he's president of the literary association and Oklahoma's first pharmacist—set aside the second floor of his drugstore for use as the library. We'll start construction on a library building as soon as we have the funds."

Lily's intent had been to find an opportunity to spend a few minutes alone with Tyler, but he couldn't know that, and quite obviously, he didn't care. She had disturbed him for something she could have found just as easily through logical channels.

Tyler still held the papers out to her, and Lily reached for them at the same time she stood. Her heel caught in the hem of her skirt, her thoughts scattering in blind panic as she felt herself falling. Tyler dropped the newspapers and caught her by her shoulders. She clutched frantically at his shirt.

Something akin to lightning streaked through her. She stared into eyes the color of molten steel—eyes that made her feel like too many things were melting ... her knees, her heart, her resolve. His breath, warm on her face, smelled of spearmint. His heart pounded beneath her palm, as if beating in riotous tandem with her own. The heat from his body flowed into her, and she felt in danger of never regaining her equilibrium.

"Lily?" His warm, gruff voice flowed through her like lava.

Mesmerized by his nearness, she nodded instinctively though unsure of the question.

He bent his head, his kiss imminent—and, she was quite sure, the only thing she had ever truly wanted. Before his lips could capture hers, the sound of heavy steps on the boardwalk penetrated. They broke apart and both fumbled to retrieve the scattered papers.

"Tyler, I know you're in there, you ornery work mule," Carson Ward bellowed before swinging open the door. He stopped in his tracks.

Lily stood first, smoothing her skirt, careful not to catch her heel again in the torn hem. Judging from the smug smile on Carson's face, Lily was certain the lawman had a pretty good idea what he had interrupted.

"It's nice to see you again." Lily hoped Carson hadn't noticed the tremor in her voice. "I hope you'll catch another show at the Canary Cage soon."

Carson pulled his hat from his head in a hasty swipe and shook her extended hand, engulfing her fingers in his beefy paw. "It'll be my pleasure, ma'am."

"Once again, Tyler, thank you." Lily's heart fluttered like hummingbird wings when Tyler's ardent gray gaze met hers. "I mean, for the back issues. I'll return them in a couple of days."

"At your convenience," Tyler pushed his hands deep into his pockets. "Enjoy the story."

"I'm sure I will." She nodded, first at Tyler and then at Carson, and closed the door quietly behind her, grateful for the mercifully cool evening air. She took a step, then paused to catch her breath, surprised she could hear their voices through the door.

"So much for keeping the Sabbath day holy, eh, Tyler?"

"Not that I need to explain myself to you, but I was looking for an eraser when she came in. She wanted to borrow back issues."

"For sure? She's a mystery that one."

"You got that right."

Lily lifted her skirts and ran.

Sleep eluded Lily as she tossed and turned. She bunched her pillow beneath her cheek and stared at a slash of moonlight on the wall. What exactly had transpired that afternoon? Everything happened so quickly, the day's events strewn like puzzle pieces. She had managed to get a little closer to Tyler, but she hadn't been prepared to get quite so close. One moment, her attempts at flirtation fell short of the desired effect. Then, caught up in his arms, the expectation of being kissed stole her breath. Remembering his lips so close to hers caused her heart to beat uncomfortably fast. An unfamiliar feeling tingled through her limbs.

She rolled onto her back and squeezed her eyes closed, trying to erase the image of Tyler's consuming gaze. She had underestimated him. For a moment, she had forgotten all she knew about him. Obviously a predator by nature, he had somehow turned the tables on her. No wonder she couldn't figure out how she had encouraged him to kiss her. She had done nothing. He simply took command and became the aggressor.

Had he done that to Augusta? Had she started out flirting harmlessly with him as was her nature? Had she then been captivated by his gray eyes, his finely chiseled features, and his muscular build? He had a certain power over most women. Sally had admitted as much. His inherent charm made him a dangerous man. He allowed a woman to pursue him, thinking she had no effect, then—once her confidence was shaken—he took advantage of her vulnerability. One of Augusta's letters came to mind, and Lily was convinced her theory was on target.

> I can only say that I am nearing my wits end, Melissa, darling. I have told you often of how I am enamored by a certain gentleman in this town. Truly, I cannot think of what more I

might do to encourage him to declare himself. You know my persistence when I desire someone's attention, dear heart, and I am not ashamed to admit that I have flirted outrageously with him. Of course, you cannot imagine exactly how outrageous that could be, as the mores for a saloon singer are altogether different from those to which you and I were raised. Still, I have pursued him for so long with such tenacity and boldness (and with no apparent success) that I am now uncertain as to how I might behave were he to respond favorably ...

Lily knew exactly what her sister would have done—anything the fiend demanded. In her elation over finally having gained his attention, Augusta would simply hand over the reins and let him ride roughshod over her emotions. As strong-willed as her sister had been, her nature was passionate, and she could be easily hurt. Clearly, Tyler Buchanan hadn't considered the consequences of dealing harshly with a woman's tender heart.

Lily determined not to make that mistake. She would not fall victim to Tyler's charisma. The situation had gotten a bit out of control today, but she vowed to keep the upper hand in the future. With her resolve firmly in place, Lily finally slept.

CHAPTER TWELVE

Tyler congratulated himself on his restraint. By working to the point of exhaustion every night for the past week, he hadn't left the newspaper office until well after the entertainment at the Canary Cage had concluded. He kept his gaze straight ahead and ignored the laughter and tinkling piano music as he walked past the saloon. He wasn't a fool. He knew he wouldn't have been nearly as successful if Lily's voice had drifted through the swinging doors.

A whole week had passed since his slip with the liquor bottle. He knew the good Lord had forgiven him for falling back into old ways for one night. He had done what the Good Book said he should do—confessed his sin and received forgiveness. He had set aside strong drink when he had knelt at the altar with Reverend Scott almost ten years earlier. He had set aside other behavior at the same time, and he would not backslide further. Though he had succumbed to the temptation to drink for the first time in a decade, he would not yield to those other temptations.

Tyler had told Lily she seemed untouchable, ethereal. He grimaced at the memory. As he had spoken the words, he recalled overhearing the exorbitant offer Theodore Peebles had made to Merle for Lily's company. Ethereal. Untouchable.

You're a fool, Tyler Buchanan.

Even so, he couldn't forget the creaminess of Lily's shoulders hidden beneath her high-necked blouse. Her smile may have been vaguely flirtatious … but Tyler had seen nothing more than her pink, curving lips. His throat seemed to close on him, and he coughed.

Confused, he had gone upstairs to fetch the papers. She was an enigma. Flirtatiousness should have flowed from her as naturally as a spring from a mountainside. Instead, he found himself drawn to her when she wasn't being coy. True, an almost irresistible physical attraction overcame him even when she was silent. Her saucy tone seemed incongruous with her natural manner, as though uneasy with the words coming from her own mouth. And yet, she didn't sound the least pretentious using such phrases as *ridiculous sobriquet*—another side of an already multi-faceted paradox.

True, he had managed to go a whole week without seeing Lily—a whole week without hearing her voice—a whole week recovering from the memory of her body pressed against his. After a little more time to callous himself against her sweetness and charm, he would again meet Carson after work and enjoy the show. The performances were mediocre at best, except when Lily took the stage. Ah, Lily. Whenever he allowed himself to think of her, she seemed the exception to everything.

CHAPTER THIRTEEN

Lily settled on the swing and nudged it into motion while sipping her morning tea. Rae Ann had purchased a fresh can for them to share, and Lily had hugged the older woman in delight. Lily's gaze wandered over the yard, taking in the sole rose bush strangling in a patch of black-eyed Susans. The yard's mix of weeds, struggling flowers, and dwarfed bushes again brought to mind her own small courtyard in Norfolk. Meticulously tended boxwood hedges, prize-winning roses, and borders of pansies, peonies, and violets had been her pride and joy. Her garden, carefully landscaped so something bloomed all year, served as a haven, a respite from Augusta's haphazard efforts at hosting socials.

Behind the Canary Cage, a sturdy, barren trellis clung to the clapboard beneath her bedroom window. Lily wondered what, if anything, had grown there. From the moment she had set eyes on the overgrown tangle behind the saloon, Lily's fingers itched to pluck out the weeds and set the yard in some semblance of order. This morning, however, she felt tolerant of its primitive beauty. At home, she dared weeds to intrude into her garden. Here, some of the weeds bore tiny flowers, and she wondered at her reluctance to tear them loose. Had she changed so much?

Though she lived among immoral women, sang, served drinks, and showed her ankles more than she should, she had managed to remain untouched and was determined to stay pure until she married. The townspeople's opinions didn't really matter—she knew the truth. When she returned to Norfolk, she would fall back into her former lifestyle. No one need know of her foray into society's seamy side. She had been wise to follow Augusta's example and use another name. That provision, added to the slim chance of running into anyone who would recognize her from the Canary Cage, made the odds too extreme to be of concern.

A still, small voice insisted she was no longer the timid woman who came to Guthrie to solve the riddle of her sister's death. Lily couldn't deny the truth, try as she might. Recalling how she had felt the first night behind the veil—the fear, the panic—she now looked forward to performing each evening and yearned for the euphoria accompanying the applause. Though Tyler had hurried away, she knew she had touched him too. The surprise in his eyes—she could see the exact moment he recognized her as the woman at the cemetery—had given her inordinate satisfaction. An almost sinful excitement bloomed with the sensation of power, along with the certainty that she could actually accomplish her purpose. No doubt the feeling was wicked. She meant to destroy the man.

Lily battled uncertainty by rereading Augusta's letters, embracing the surge of bitterness at every mention of Tyler. She must strengthen her resolve and forget how she had weakened in his arms.

Still, wasn't this desire to destroy Tyler Buchanan sinful, almost evil? Doubt plagued her. When had she ever welcomed anything so vile into her life? How could she urge these emotions to remain, to grow, to outshout her sense of decency and her tendency for forgiveness? Who had she so quickly, so easily, become? Someone uncomfortably similar to the woman everyone thought she might be?

Frustrated by the nagging questions, Lily rolled up her sleeves and refastened a pin in her loosening chignon. The day threatened to be a scorcher. She would suffocate if she didn't get away from this place.

Hurrying down the path to the back gate, she gripped the picket fence with its cracked paint and looked both ways down the narrow alley the Canary Cage shared with a number of businesses and several private residences. A woman dressed in a faded cotton dress, her hair bound in a kerchief, came out a back door and shook a rug over the porch railing. The smells of frying sausage and baking bread drifted in the morning heat, the combination making Lily slightly nauseated. From the side streets, she could hear the clip-clopping of horses' hooves. The sound brought a delighted smile to her face. That was the ticket! She could ride for a couple of hours and still be back before the other girls rolled out of bed. Running back up the walk, she burst into the kitchen, startling Rae Ann as she poured herself a cup of coffee.

Rae Ann smiled. "Lily, you're up early, dear."

"So are you. Pardon me for not stopping to chat, but can you tell me where I might find a livery?"

Rae Ann stopped, the cup inches from her lips and raised her eyebrows. "A livery? Whatever for?"

"I'd like to go riding for a couple of hours. It's been ages, and I really need to get out for a while."

Setting the cup carefully on the counter, Rae Ann struggled to hide her bewilderment. "Riding," she repeated. "On a horse?"

"Yes, on a horse, silly. What did you think?"

Obviously, Rae Ann didn't know what to think. Had Sally, Honey, Trudy, or any of the other girls who had passed through the saloon ever gone riding for pleasure? Not likely.

Another incongruity.

At the moment, Lily didn't care.

"There's a livery on North Division. You head left, go two blocks to South Division. Hang a left, and Tallman's Livery and Transport is three blocks down. But, Lil—"

"Thanks, Rae Ann," Lily called over her shoulder and ran to her room to change into something suitable for riding.

She reappeared twenty minutes later wearing a navy-blue split skirt with a matching jacket, a white blouse with tiny pearl buttons down the front, and a straw bonnet with navy blue ribbons tied beneath her chin. Rae Ann stared at her as if she had strolled in stark naked and painted purple. Lily could read the woman's mind. Why in the world would a saloon girl have a riding outfit? And how had that hat managed the journey without being crushed?

"Here," Rae Ann said, thrusting a bag at Lily. "Take this with you in case you get hungry. You didn't eat."

With a quick kiss on Rae Ann's cheek, Lily skipped out the door, leaving Rae Ann to ponder the remaining wonders of her small world.

Lily found the livery without difficulty. After a few moments of haggling with the dour-faced owner, she started on her way. She scoffed, thinking Traveller, the aging horse's name, certainly bore no resemblance to the same-named noble stallion once owned by General Robert E. Lee. Still, Lily reveled in the feel of warm horseflesh between her thighs and the control she wielded with the reins. In Norfolk, she primarily rode sidesaddle, but her father had occasionally taken her on cross-country treks and insisted she learn to ride astride. As the livery had no sidesaddles to offer, she blew a little kiss skyward.

Lily turned the horse north and crossed Cottonwood River at the Noble Avenue bridge, trying to ignore the curious glances thrown her way. She rode alongside the train tracks until the town disappeared behind her. Lily dug in her heels and urged Traveller into as much of a gallop as the gelding could manage. She followed the meandering Cottonwood to where it joined the Cimarron, and Traveller's breath grew labored. Dismounting in a small grove, she pulled off her hat and, with a flick of her wrist, sent it sailing under a tree. A breeze teased her hair, and she pulled out the hairpins, tucking them in her pocket before tossing her jacket beside her hat. She unbuttoned the top three buttons and then rolled up her sleeves, as she watched the horse drinking long draughts. Realizing that she too thirsted, she unpacked the small jar of apple cider and the egg biscuit Rae Ann insisted she bring along.

She lay back in the tall green grass, satisfied for the moment, and stared at the cloudless sky through the branches of a cottonwood tree. Growing drowsy in the morning sun, the chirping of the katydids and the buzzing of the bees combined with the rustling leaves composed a melody too lulling to resist. Her eyes drifted closed, and her lips parted in true rest for the first time in days.

Warmth, peace, and her father's voice. He hadn't gone away after all, and she felt safe again. Papa stroked her hair with calloused fingers, then touched her cheek. His deep, gentle voice called her his "pretty little girl." She turned her face into his hand and smiled. She had missed him so much. Alone. She had been so alone ...

"What's your name, little girl?"

Suddenly confused, she floundered in the thick, sun-induced sleep. Papa knew her name—Melissa—his little honeybee. He reminded her often that he had named her after her mother. No, wait, she was Lily, a flower, not a bee.

"What's your name, little girl?"

Lily stirred restlessly, her forehead creasing in dismay. How could Papa not remember her name? The reedy voice didn't sound right. And the hands. Papa's hands were hard, not rough and callous like ...

She opened her eyes and tried to focus. A man's face, but not that of her handsome father. A narrow face with small black eyes too close together and a scraggly growth of whiskers—not enough to call a beard—loomed over her. His twisted teeth lent him a feral look, like a weasel or a rat. His fetid breath blew hot on her face, and fear knotted in Lily's belly.

A dirty finger traced along her jaw to her chin and then down her neck. Stung out of her fear by outrage, Lily slapped his hand away. She dug her heels into the ground and heaved herself up with the palms of her hands, intent on reaching Traveller who still munched grass peacefully at the river's edge. She tried to run. But, before she could take more than a step, the man seized her ankle. Falling face first into the grass, the jolt knocked the wind out of her. She gasped. The wretch scooped up a couple of rocks and threw them in the direction of the horses. His nag moved out of the way, still drinking, when a pebble hit Traveller on the flank. Whinnying, the gelding skittered sideways until a second stone hit him in his soft underbelly. He ran off, reins flying behind him. Regaining her breath, Lily struggled to her feet and warily eyed the stranger, his smile more frightening than anything she had ever seen.

"Now, now, little girl," he cooed, "I ain't gonna hurt ya none. I just wanna have a look at ya. It's been a long spell since I seen anybody pretty as you. After we have a little … talk, you can walk on back to wherever you come from."

Terrified, Lily scanned the countryside. No one. Without warning, he grabbed her, driving her back against a tree.

"I said I ain't gonna hurt ya. I just wanna talk to ya," he said. "Don't be fightin' me, darlin', or I'll have to make ya stop."

Despite his warning, Lily tried to escape him, pressing back into the tree, not caring that the bark dug into her skin. She twisted her head back and forth doing all she could to avoid his foul breath and cracked lips. His hands tore at her clothing and squeezed her shoulders painfully. She pushed against his chest, but he held her captive with a sinewy strength that belied his height and build.

Tears rolled from Lily's eyes—she gasped, the only breath she could manage to take. She must have been whimpering, because he shook her, knocking her head against the tree, and—from somewhere far off—she heard him warning her to be quiet. Her head smacked against the tree again, and she didn't mind the pain—something to think about besides his groping hands and his rough beard against her neck. Terror turned into hysteria, and she kicked and screamed as though deranged. Caught by surprise, he lost his grip. Her hands freed, she managed to scratch his face, leaving four bleeding lines down his cheek. She had no time to savor her small victory before he hit her across the jaw, knocking her to the ground.

Rolling to her hands and knees, Lily tried to crawl away, her hands clawing at the ground. He grabbed her by the waistband and hauled her backwards. He flipped her over and slapped her again. Dazed, she stared numbly as he stood over her, his face twisted into an ugly leer, ripping his shirttails from his faded corduroy trousers.

"Are you gonna scream any more, little girl?"

When she didn't answer, his eyes narrowed. He leaned over her, holding the gun within a few inches of her nose.

"It don't matter to me if you're dead or alive, just so long as you're quiet. You gonna be quiet?"

Lily managed to nod, his close-set eyes watching her as he reached for the neckline of her blouse. He rubbed the lace trim between his rough fingertips.

"*Oooh*, fancy, aren't ya? I guess you must be quality. I'm only used to harlots … you're prob'ly only used to fine gents, so I guess this'll be a treat for both of us."

He lowered himself to kiss her neck, and Lily squeezed her eyes closed. She screamed and thrashed despite her earlier promise. He grunted when she brought her heel down hard on his calf and tried to brace herself for the punishment she knew must follow. The man yelped again. Suddenly, miraculously, his weight lifted. She opened her eyes. Jerked backward as though by an invisible string, his eyes widened with surprise and confusion, a string of saliva hanging from his mouth. He landed beside Lily in an ignominious heap, his gun knocked away and disappearing in the grass.

Lily clawed her way toward the weapon, her breath escaping in ragged sobs. She reached the gun and grasped it frantically, then pushed herself to her feet. Holding the gun in both hands, she turned to face her attacker just as Tyler picked the man up off the ground. Tyler here? How? Blood poured from her attacker's nose, but he fought as though insane, swinging wildly at Tyler. The man caught Tyler with a surprisingly strong punch in the stomach that sent her rescuer stumbling backwards. Regaining his balance, Tyler lunged, catching her attacker around the waist and slamming him into a tree. His head smacked against the trunk, and he slid down the length of the tree, collapsing on the ground.

Tyler turned toward Lily. She stood, clothing torn and covered with dirt and grass, legs akimbo. She held the gun in front of her with both hands, her hair tumbling in a tangled mess over a swelling cheek.

Tyler edged toward her—palms outward. "It's okay, Lily," he said in a low voice.

Soothing. Harmless.

"He can't hurt you now. Give me the gun. You're safe."

Shifting her disoriented gaze, she looked somewhere over his shoulder, her eyes widening. She shifted the direction of the gun, the barrel wavering in her shaking hands. He whirled to follow her line of vision as the horrible man leaped onto his horse and galloped away. Instead of giving chase, Tyler turned back to Lily. Meeting her gaze, he again held out his hand. "Lily, give me the gun."

She stared into his steady gray eyes. Finally, her shoulders slumped, and with a sob, she let him take the gun from her shaking fingers.

"There's a good girl. It's all right now. He's gone. He won't hurt you anymore."

She stared at him again, her face throbbing, her chest shuddering with dry sobs. Confusion overtook her. This man had saved her life, she was certain of that—but hadn't he killed her sister? She was certain of that, too. Did one good deed cancel out the sin? She took a step backwards, a wave of nausea sweeping over her. Tyler's countenance swam before her. When her knees buckled beneath her, Tyler caught her and lowered her to the ground. He kissed the top of her head, his whispers lullaby-soft, murmuring comforting words she couldn't comprehend.

Nausea again erupted, and he supported her shoulders while she emptied the meager contents of her stomach. He left her for a moment and returned with the remainder of the apple cider and a handkerchief dampened in cool river water. She wiped her face with the cloth and gratefully gulped down the last of the drink. Lowering the jar, she turned to find Tyler's face only inches away, his gray eyes worried, lines bracketing his mouth with deep concern.

"Thank you," she said.

"You're welcome." Reaching out, he gently touched her swollen cheek.

Disconcerted by his kindness, Lily fought the urge to throw herself into his arms and feel safe again. She let caution fly and leaned toward him. He didn't hesitate but pulled her close, rubbing her back, shushing her sobs with sweet words. She felt sheltered in his arms. How long since she had felt so secure? She realized with discomfiting clarity that the feeling had been missing since her father died, leaving her and Augusta alone. Then, even before the grief had become bearable, Augusta, too, had left her, claiming she craved adventure. But to find safety and sanctuary with Tyler? Alarm and confusion swept over Lily, filling her with doubt.

Her shoulder tucked beneath the comforting curve of his arm, fire from the heat of his body penetrated to her very bones. If she leaned forward just a little more, might he kiss her? Sudden and intense longing—but unsure for exactly what—assailed her.

Tyler's horse whinnied, interrupting Lily's thoughts. She scrambled to her feet, bewildered by her reaction to being so close to him. Beside her in an instant, his strong hand steadied her again when she swayed.

"Lily? Are you sure you're okay?"

She tried to smile, only to find the left side of her face refusing to cooperate. Her head throbbed. A sudden breeze blew up from the river—and, for the first time, Lily noticed the warmth on her skin. Looking down, she gasped at her torn clothes and clutched her ruined blouse together in a fist.

Tyler cleared his throat and averted his gaze. Yanking off his soiled jacket, he held the garment out to Lily. She seized it with relief, sliding her arms into the sleeves and folding the lapels high across her chest.

"I'll get my horse." Tyler whistled between his teeth and started off toward the river. "Darlin'!" The mare lifted her head and whinnied.

Tyler strode down the hill, his thigh muscles flexing against finely tailored trousers now dusty and torn at one knee. His dark hair fell across his forehead, giving him an almost-boyish look that contrasted with the somber gray of his eyes and the stern line of his lips.

He is almost beautiful. She gripped the jacket even higher at her throat. What was she saying? What was she thinking? How could she so easily forget Augusta and what Tyler had done to her?

Oh, Father God, what is happening to me?

Tyler made his way back to her, leading Darlin' by the reins. Lily tried to squelch her unwelcomed feelings.

A moment of weakness. He has an unfair advantage.

With a great sense of relief, she grasped onto that rationale. Yes, he sensed her vulnerability and felt no compunction in taking advantage of her. How perfectly understandable for her to feel grateful to anyone who would rescue her from such a nightmare. She, in truth—under normal circumstances— felt nothing more than loathing for this man. Her plight had simply confused her.

Her plan proved more difficult to execute by the minute. How could she capture his heart while keeping a firm grip on her emotions? How could she flirt and play the coquette when she spent every bit of her resolve being civil to the man? Lily closed her eyes and let the memory of her sister's face surface. Roxie's long, dark lashes fluttering coyly, her lips curving in an entrancing half-smile, the practiced tilt of her head, the toss of her beautiful red hair. Augusta had flirted so easily. She had wrapped them all—from the butcher to the gardener to the mayor—around her little finger.

Opening her eyes, Lily tried to smile. Pain shot from her cheek to her ear. She leaned back against a tree, gripping the lapels of Tyler's jacket impossibly tighter.

"Your mouth is bleeding," he said.

"Is it?" She raised the still-damp handkerchief and dabbed gingerly. "I fear my teeth have been jarred loose."

"I'm familiar with the feeling." He rubbed the horse's muzzle, then reached out a hand to Lily. "Here, let me help you up."

Tyler settled Lily onto Darlin's back, then swung up behind her. She stiffened when his legs cradled hers, and he reached around her to control the reins.

"I'm taking you to my house, so you can get cleaned up." She started to protest until he added, "Libby, my housekeeper, should be there, if that makes you feel any better. Then I'll take you home."

She wanted to argue but admitted she would like to repair as much damage as she could before riding through town in the middle of the afternoon. Her body already ached all over, and her head pounded with a pain that grew worse with each passing moment. She gave up trying to hold herself away from Tyler and leaned back, relaxing against his chest, resting her head on his shoulder. It seemed that his arms folded protectively around her, and she gave herself up once more to the cocoon of safety she found there. She roused a few moments later.

"Tyler?"

"Hmm?"

"How did you find me?"

Tyler shifted in the saddle and clicked his tongue, urging Darlin' into a faster pace.

"I was on my way back from the Lazy M Ranch. I rode out early to interview MacGranahan about …"

Lily half-turned to peer up at his stern face.

"About?"

He hesitated. "Later, Lily. Let's not talk about that now."

She gave a mental shrug and relaxed again into the warmth of his strong arms.

Later.

Later she would move her scheme forward. Right now, she only wanted to pull herself together … and sleep.

CHAPTER FOURTEEN

Tyler had managed to reach his house without meeting anyone along the way. Once inside, he ushered Lily to a small, modern bathroom where she removed his jacket and surveyed the damage.

She looked dreadful. Tears welled at the evidence verifying that the assault had truly happened. A nasty bruise already colored one cheek. She inspected a scrape beside her distended lower lip. She groaned at the sight of her lovely blouse torn beyond repair and the realization of what Tyler must have witnessed. As if to confirm her thoughts, Tyler tapped on the door.

"Lily? I'm hanging one of my shirts on the doorknob for you—and a brush. I'll get a compress for your cheek."

Waiting until his footsteps retreated down the hall, she grabbed the garment from the doorknob and the brush from the floor. She rubbed the soft garment between her fingers for an appreciative moment before slipping her arms into the sleeves and buttoning the shirt to the collar. Feeling a bit more presentable after knotting the shirttails at her waist, she rolled the too-long sleeves over her wrists.

After washing her face, she brushed the grass from her tangled hair and braided the tresses into a thick plait. Tearing a thin strip of lace from the remains of her blouse, she secured the end of the braid.

Ten minutes later, Lily stood awkwardly in the kitchen doorway, watching Tyler turn on a new electric stove to boil a kettle of water. He froze when he turned.

"Is something wrong?" She instinctively cupped her palm around her throat. When she swayed, Tyler snapped to life. Taking her by the elbow, he guided her to the living room.

"Here, lie down and rest. I'll bring you that compress—I'm sure your cheek hurts like the blazes. I'll just be a minute."

As good as his word, he returned in no time to lay a cold cloth against her cheek.

"Thank you," she murmured. "For everything."

"No need for that. I'm only sorry I didn't get to you sooner and that I let him get away from me. But I'll get Carson on the—"

"No!" She couldn't bear the thought of anyone else learning of her humiliation.

"He needs to be caught and held accountable," he said. "I know this is hard for you, but he's a criminal and—"

"And he tried to molest a saloon girl. Oh, yes, I'm sure the police will go after him immediately."

"A crime has been committed," he said firmly, "and something needs to be done before he attacks somebody else, somebody who—"

"Who doesn't deserve such treatment?"

"Somebody who might not be fortunate enough to get away as you did," he continued. "And I'd appreciate it if you would stop finishing my sentences, especially since you're not very good at reading my mind."

Lily closed her eyes and sighed. "I'm sorry. I guess this morning added on to Sunday morning, and it's been a little more trying than I'm accustomed to."

"No … I'm sorry. I'll check on that tea."

Lily lay back on the divan, her thoughts scattering. She needed to get back to her room where she could rest. She knew, after seeing herself in the mirror, she couldn't appear in public, much less sing. Merle would probably fire her for disappearing for almost an entire day. At least Rae Ann knew she'd gone for a ride. And the horse. Hopefully the horse had found his way back to the livery. That would be something else she had to explain. So, she couldn't sing tonight. She could barely talk, and more than a little makeup would be necessary to cover the bruise on her cheek. Her swollen lip couldn't be disguised by any means. Exhaustion overcame her. She doubted she would ever move again.

Tyler came out of the kitchen and glanced around the living room, carrying two cups of steaming tea. Late afternoon bathed the cool room in shadows. He set the cups down and scanned the room. Where had Lily gone? Then he saw her hands, pale and slender, hanging over the side of the divan. Stepping closer, he peered down at her. She was asleep, her thick black braid across one shoulder, tendrils of hair escaping and curling around her oval face. From that angle, he could only see a classic, fragile beauty at odds with everything else he knew about her. Her personality, her speech, her mannerisms all marked her as a woman of class, of gentle upbringing and education.

He couldn't deny how drawn he felt toward her. Her lips slightly parted in sleep, he recalled how she had felt in his arms Sunday, at how close he had come to kissing her. If Carson hadn't come in when he did ... Tyler hadn't planned to kiss her, but he knew that he would have if he'd had one more second alone with her. Planned? The desire to kiss her was instinctive and spontaneous. Desire came close to sabotaging the self-discipline he'd managed for the past ten years. Kissing her would have been a stupid thing to do.

Tightness gripped his chest when he thought of how close Lily had come to being ravaged. If he hadn't ridden out to see how Blue MacGranahan fared after his accident ... if Blue hadn't told Tyler the details of the assault on his ranch ... Lord God ... if he hadn't seen the riderless horse galloping toward town ...

He'd rounded the crest of the hill and found that no-account hoodlum beating Lily. He could still see the whiteness of her skin beneath those filthy hands, her hair in wild disarray. Only once in his life had he ever felt such rage, and he had thought himself incapable of experiencing that depth of anger again. He was wrong. What if he'd followed his impulses and killed Lily's attacker? Once before he'd been responsible for another human being's death—something he never wanted to experience again.

Lily turned her head restlessly, a little moan escaping. He winced at the sight of her injured face—swollen, bruises blooming purple and ugly, anathema to her perfect complexion. A crime had been committed not only against humanity but against beauty. And the perpetrator should be punished, not just for attacking a woman, but for marring a marvelous beauty, even if only temporarily.

His fists clenched at his sides, and he again fought his warring emotions. He didn't want to feel anything for Lily—or for any woman of her type. Tyler had spent years analyzing what he considered to be his dark nature. He had been so grateful to have found a Savior, and he never forgot he had been made a new creature. Old things had passed away. Still, he reminded himself daily not to trust his own strength, his own will. Today's rage proved he hadn't changed as much as he had hoped. Sure, fury against the crime was to be expected, even merited. But this anger was personal—personal because the crime had been committed against Lily.

Tyler set the cups on a side table and settled in his favorite chair, one of the few pieces he had brought with him from his study in Charleston. His small house bore no resemblance to his family's three-story home on the Battery, filled with elegant cherry furniture, Oriental carpets, wallpaper and tile imported from Italy, and curtains and bedspreads from France. He had left everything behind, fleeing the city in disgrace, unable to bear his father's disappointment and his mother's silent grief.

He had planned to build a new life here in Oklahoma—a new life in a new town in what would soon be a new state. But he had brought too much baggage along. Even here, after all these years of subjugation, his baser instincts emerged. Wasn't his attraction to Lily proof? Attraction? He laughed in self-derision. If he didn't rein himself in, that attraction would snowball into obsession ending in nothing but trouble. This he knew from experience.

Lord, help me.

What did the Apostle Paul say? *For the good that I would I do not, but the evil which I would not, that I do …* He understood the passage from Romans too well. Especially today.

He had thought to have a wife and family by now. But the years had sped by, and he had felt no more than a mild interest in any available female. Theo Peebles's interest in him held no subtlety, but—while attractive physically—self-centeredness spoiled her. As she was prone to pout and whine when not getting her way, Tyler found her both cloying and annoying.

And he was well aware of the Scripture regarding being equally yoked.

Tyler took a sip of the now tepid tea and let his gaze wander around his quarters.

The scantily furnished room boasted only the chair he sat in, an oak roll-top desk with a chair against one wall, two small tables with brass electrical lamps, a rug nearly the size of the entire room, and the divan Lily lay on. He hadn't taken time to make the place homier, though Libby had made curtains and fabric squares for the arms of the chair and divan and crocheted doilies for underneath the lamps. A dish filled with struggling

African violets sat on the kitchen table. While he appreciated Libby's efforts, he really didn't care. He only needed a place to sleep.

He turned back to Lily and smiled despite himself. Today, he liked having her here, he admitted, safe and relatively sound, under his roof and watchful eye. She looked peaceful, almost as though nothing had happened. As he gazed at her, she tossed her head, her face twisting in fear. She cried, a pitiful little wail that drew Tyler to his knees beside her in an instant.

"No, no, please—please don't hurt me—don't touch me—please stop—please ..."

Taking her by the shoulders, Tyler shook her gently. "Lily, wake up. You're dreaming. Wake up, you're okay. I've got you."

Lily opened her eyes and uttered a gurgling scream.

"No—no," she cried, beating at Tyler's chest with her fists.

"There, there, Lily, it's me—Tyler. You're dreaming, you're just dreaming."

Tyler could see in her eyes when awareness finally dawned and her fear turned to renewed horror of her ordeal. Capturing her flailing hands against his chest, Tyler pulled her to him, tucking her head beneath his chin. His arms enveloped her, and she sobbed, her slender body shuddering.

"You're safe, Lily. You're safe."

He stroked the back of her head, admiring the silkiness of her dark hair. She smelled like sunshine, and the faint scent of gardenias drifted around her. Tyler closed his eyes and leaned his cheek against her head, one hand now stroking her back while he gathered her closer with his other arm. His heart ached hearing her pitiful cries, and he murmured soft whispers intended to soothe. He held a warm, soft, beautiful woman in his arms, but he couldn't allow her into his heart.

Finally, her tears subsided, and she pushed herself away, struggling to stifle the little hiccoughs.

"I'm sorry," she gulped, raising wide eyes to his. "I can't seem to stop crying. That man's face ... and breath and teeth ... his grimy hands..." She shuddered and looked away. "Thank you for helping me ... for not looking the other way."

Tyler frowned. "Look the other way? I told you I was coming back from the Lazy M—Blue MacGranahan's place. One of his ranch hands had nearly ravaged his daughter. He stole two hundred dollars from a strongbox and beat Blue with a rifle stock to within inches of his life. Blue heard a description of a man who robbed a bank in Oklahoma City a few days ago and thought it might be the same guy. I saw a horse with an empty saddle tearing toward town, and then I heard a woman's scream. I suspected Blue's miserable ranch hand was up to no good, though he should have been miles away by now."

Lily gasped. "Surely it can't be the same man."

Tyler shook his head. "I wouldn't think so. It would be pure idiocy for him to double back this way. Still," Tyler shrugged, "he—"

"He doesn't sound very intelligent to start with, does he?" Lily's eyes widened, and she put her fingertips over her mouth. "I'm sorry. I finished your sentence again, didn't I?"

Tyler smiled. "But this time, you said exactly what I was thinking." He paused for a moment. "Lily, we have to tell Carson what happened."

She swung to her feet, shaking her head wildly, her face pink. "No, no—really, there's no reason. You frightened him off. He won't be back. I'm fine, just a little bruised, so there's no need for anyone to know, all right?" Her eyes shimmered bright with tears and her swollen lip trembled.

A wave of compassion washed over Tyler as he also stood, reaching out to gather her pale, fine-boned hands in his fingers.

"I have—*we* have to tell Carson," he repeated, his eyes roaming over her cheek, noting the blue tinge and the swelling around her eye. "A serious crime has been committed and—"

"A crime? Do you think he'll care? Do you think anybody will care?" She jerked her hands free of his grasp and whirled around, turning her back and speaking over her shoulder, as if unable to look him in the eye any longer. "They'll just laugh. Everyone will laugh." Her voice took on a harsh, angry edge, but a slight tremble betrayed her hurt.

"Laugh? Why would anyone laugh? What happened to you was a terrible thing, and he should be hunted down and treated like the animal he is," Tyler said, trying to reassure her but not exactly understanding her thinking.

She shook her head, her long braid swinging across her narrow back. Tyler stepped forward and put his hands on her shoulders. She shrugged him off and moved farther away, wrapping her arms around herself.

"You tell the police chief or anyone else that a girl from the Canary Cage was nearly ... molested, and they *will* laugh. A saloon girl? They *live* for that, don't they? The news will be all over town in a matter of hours. Everyone will know, but nothing will be done."

Behind her, Tyler felt his own face flush, glad she still had her back turned, as she voiced his earlier concern.

"That's not going to happen," he said, tamping his own doubts to reassure her. "Carson Ward is a fine man, and he will see justice done regardless of the crime, regardless of the victim. You have my word."

CHAPTER FIFTEEN

She had his word?

Her sister sprang to mind, and Lily's discomfiture changed to angry disdain in an instant. She whirled, one eyebrow raised haughtily, her arms crossed in a defiant pose.

"Your word? Is that so?" she said. "I believe I heard something about a death at the Canary Cage a few months ago. What did the good chief of police do about that?"

Lily searched Tyler's face for a telltale sign of guilt, both relieved and disappointed to see only a confused frown.

"A death at the Cage?" His expression cleared, and Lily knew he had made the connection. "That was a totally different situation. There was no crime—an unfortunate situation but no crime."

Lily's temper flared again at his casual dismissal of Augusta's senseless death.

"An unfortunate situation? *An unfortunate situation*? A beautiful, vibrant young woman is dead, and there was no crime? What kind of ridiculous gibberish is that?"

She knew she had said too much. Tyler's eyes narrowed, his gray eyes penetrating hers in the darkening room.

"You seem to know a lot, but not a lot that's right," he said. His gaze held hers, waiting for her to reply.

"Yes, well, I—Sally and Honey—"

One dark brow rose when she mentioned Honey, and Lily mentally congratulated herself for at least startling him.

"Sally and Honey had plenty to say about Au—Roxie—wasn't that her name?"

Tyler nodded, not seeming to notice her near slip.

"I know she was beautiful and vivacious and popular and that she was found in her room in a pool"—Lily faltered with emotion but kept talking, grief and righteous indignation spurring her on—"in a pool of blood. And no one did anything. Her death was declared a suicide, and she was dumped in a box and buried in a derelict cemetery, her meager possessions shipped off to a sister whose name no one can remember—"

"Melissa," Tyler said.

Lily's eyes widened in surprise, her heart skipping a beat at the sound of her own name, her *real* name coming from Tyler's lips.

"What?" she whispered.

"Melissa," he repeated, "her sister's name was Melissa."

"How do you know?"

He shrugged, raking his fingers through his dark hair. "I'm the one who mailed the package to her."

Lily's thoughts flew to the box she had received, wrapped neatly in plain brown paper and secured with rough twine.

She had stared at the square, black printing in trepidation, recognizing the return address from Augusta's correspondence, the handwriting neat and strong, totally unlike Augusta's spidery scrawl. The letters inside had been written by Chief Ward and Merle, but Tyler had shipped the box himself.

Why?

"Why?" she asked. "What did the girl's death have to do with you?"

Tyler shrugged—one-shouldered this time—and Lily swore she saw discomfort cross his face.

"I was in Carson's office when Merle came in with the box. He'd written a personal letter. Carson was writing an official one. He hadn't finished, so Merle left the box with Carson along with an envelope Roxie had addressed to someone in Norfolk. He had no idea who the woman was, but hers was the only name or address he found in her belongings. I remembered Roxie once said she had a sister in Virginia she hadn't seen in a while. I figured Melissa Forrester must be her sister. I recall thinking Forrester must have been Roxie's real surname, and I wondered if all women like her—you know, saloon girls, actresses, dancers—take other names ..."

Lily stared, curious, until he shook himself free of whatever memories had caught him.

"Anyway, Carson finished the letter and got called away for something or other. He asked me to take care of mailing the box, so I did."

Lily digested his simple story with difficulty.

"You still haven't explained why nothing was ever done about her death. The misfortune happened ... too bad. Bury her, ship off whatever things would fit in a little box, and forget about her. That's all?"

"Look, Lily, the girl ..." he began, his voice low and measured.

Did he think her a wild horse to be calmed? His audacity only served to anger her further.

"She had a name."

He frowned at her tone but nodded and began again. "*Roxie* was found in her room—*alone* in her room—a gun only inches from her hand. She'd had no arguments with anyone and no one she called enemy. There was no evidence and no reason to think her death was anything more than a suicide. What else could be done?"

"No arguments, no enemies ... so murder is ruled out. But—if she killed herself—why did she do such a heinous thing? Did no one ask the question? Did anyone even care?"

Tyler wiped his hand across his face and stood up. Hooking his thumbs in his back pockets, he walked to the front window and looked out over the yard. "I didn't know her that well. I only saw her at the Canary Cage. On a couple of slow nights, we had something that barely passed for conversation. I don't know what she was thinking or what she was feeling. I don't know why she apparently felt she had no reason to go on living. I'm not the one who has to tell you that the path you and Roxie and the others have chosen is a rough one. I guess she just didn't see any other way out."

He seemed sincere, and for a moment, his response left Lily perplexed. Did he believe what he said or was he a practiced liar? How could he not have known how her sister felt about him? Augusta—Roxie—she had to think of her as Roxie—Roxie had never been shy about letting people, men or women, know how she felt or what she thought. Did he honestly have no memory of rejecting Roxie's overtures? Roxie's letters had been filled with compliments he paid her and descriptions of gifts he gave her, reports of kisses stolen in the moonlight, and promises of a future together. Tyler said what passed between them could barely be described as conversation, that he hardly knew her. Lily sighed. How could she discern truth from lie?

Guilt rose, leaving an acid taste in her mouth and a feeling of disgust at her own treason. Augusta was dead, and somehow Lily found herself close to taking the word of a man whose story called her sister a liar.

"Had she seemed depressed? Did anyone notice? How can someone be so distraught, feel so helpless as to want to end her life and no one notice?"

Again, Tyler shook his head. He turned and held out his hands in supplication. "How can I know the answers? I agree with you. You would think her despondency would be obvious if someone were that desperately unhappy. But aren't you all actresses of a sort? Perhaps she put a brave face on and kept her tears private. Maybe she received some bad news and didn't tell anyone. But people did care. Merle, Rae Ann, and Sally were devastated. Toby wrote a beautiful song in her honor, and Malcolm couldn't seem to keep his mind on anything for days."

"And the sexton wouldn't speak at her funeral or allow her to be buried in the *acceptable* section of Summit View."

"Yes, well, that was unfortunate. I believe LaMotte may regret that decision."

"A lot of good that does now."

Tyler cocked his head. "None of us can undo anything we've done, but regret should count for something, I think. I've seen LaMotte at the cemetery several times, and I'm sure he's praying for their souls."

Lily gave a short laugh. "Oh my, then, that makes up for everything, doesn't it?"

"Well, I think your question is answered—at least somewhat. Yes … people cared." Silent for a moment, he peered at her, his brow furrowed. "My question is, Lily, why do *you* seem to care so much?"

Lily felt as though she'd been slapped. Her chin quivered, and she fluttered her eyelids trying to blink away sudden, unwanted tears. *Because she was my sister. She loved you and you broke her heart. Now she's gone, and I'm all alone.* But she couldn't say anything—not to this man who could be both callous and kind, brilliant in his work but somehow an imbecile when trying to discern a woman's feelings.

"Because her blood has stained the floorboards in my room. Even though the spot is covered by a rug, I can't forget her blood is there. It haunts me night and day."

Tyler closed the physical distance between them in one long step and pulled Lily into his arms. He held her head against his chest, his cheek resting on her hair. Resisting him at first, she relented and let him hold her, let him caress her back in gentle, soothing motions.

How could she allow her destroyer to also be her rescuer? How could she seek healing in the arms of the man who had wounded her so deeply? How could she seek restoration from the man who had stolen from her the person she loved most? Yet she still stood there, safe in his embrace, until her tears subsided.

Again, her loss overwhelmed her. Totally alone in the world, the last of her family, she had no friends to speak of in Norfolk. Childhood friends had married and moved away. And here? She couldn't even imagine making true friends in Guthrie. Perhaps she could gain a certain closeness with Rae Ann and maybe Sally. But, under ordinary circumstances, she never would have met Rae Ann or Sally, much less befriend them. Under *these* circumstances, her whole life was an invention—no honest relationship could blossom when regularly watered with lies.

Even Tyler who held her so gently in his arms, unaware he offered comfort to a woman sworn to have her revenge, even he was attracted not to her true self, not to prim and proper Melissa but to Lily, the saloon singer who bared her limbs and dared to be alone with a man in his home.

She pulled away slowly, and he let her go until his hands rested on her shoulders. He held her there, his gaze searching her face, staring first into her eyes, then dropping to her parted lips and then back to her eyes. Her breath came faster and, with one hand splayed across his chest, she felt the thundering of his heart beneath her palm. He closed his eyes for a second—could he not bear the sight of her so close? When he opened his eyes again, she stared at him still, and he leaned toward her. She inhaled sharply, knowing he would kiss her. She didn't pull away—she didn't want to pull away or quiet the warning voices as he bent his head, drawing her close again.

Providence interrupted just as his lips touched hers. The kitchen door slammed, and they sprang apart, startled and guilty.

"Tyler?" a female voice called out.

"In here, Libby," he answered, releasing Lily and stepping away from her.

Lily smoothed her skirt and cinched the knot at her waist. Libby?

A woman came in from the kitchen, her hands already at work tying apron strings at the small of her back. She stopped when she noticed Tyler and Lily standing so close to each other.

"Lily, this is Libby, my—um—housekeeper—" He searched for the right word, tossing an apologetic smile to Libby. Her returning smile wary, he hastened to add, "—and my friend. Libby, this is Lily. She—"

"I know who she is." Libby closed her eyes for just a second. When she reopened them, she added a smile. Stiff and uncomfortable, but a smile all the same. "You're the new singer at the Canary Cage. You have a beautiful voice," she said.

How would Libby know? "Thank you, but how—"

"You sat behind me at church Sunday morning."

"Oh, yes. Well ..." Lily's face heated with renewed humiliation. Her gaze darted to Tyler who watched the exchange with a worried frown. He caught Lily's stare and, smoothing the lines from his forehead, smiled encouragingly.

"I ran into Carson—um, Chief Ward—in front of Prescott's. Turns out Merle reported you as missing," Libby said.

"Lily was attacked this morning near the river. I came along in time to run the scalawag off."

"Attacked?" Libby gasped, and she gawked at the bruises on Lily's cheek. "My heavens, child. Are you all right?" At Lily's nod, Libby turned back to Tyler. "And you? Are you okay? You could have gotten yourself killed!"

"I'm fine, Libby," he said.

Lily suddenly felt like an interloper. She noted the genuine affection between Libby and Tyler, something more than cordial relationship between homeowner and housekeeper. An unfamiliar feeling spasmed in Lily, and she fought the urge to interrupt their interchange.

Libby's rough, work-reddened hands and mousy brown hair streaked with gray pulled into a neat bun at the nape of her neck indicated she had a few years on Tyler. Though sturdy and solid with a thick waist and flat derriere, her bosom still rode full and high. Tiny wrinkles spread along the corners of her amber eyes, and tanned forearms peeked from the turned-up sleeves of her plain beige dress. Strong. Capable. Libby knew her way around work ... and Tyler's house.

Beside her, Lily felt thin, pale, and useless. Here was a woman used to labor, who had probably borne a tribe of children and went home to a husband who loved her. Lily's gaze darted to Libby's left hand and her heart sank. No wedding ring, no tan line to testify that she had merely taken one off to do the laundry. Whether unmarried or a widow, she had free rein under Tyler's roof on an almost-daily basis.

"You'll be wanting dinner after taking her home, won't you?" Libby asked Tyler as she headed toward the kitchen.

"No, don't bother yourself. I need to check in at the paper and talk to Carson, so I won't be back for a while."

"At least let me fix you a sandwich to take along. I dare say you haven't had a bite to eat since breakfast."

His sheepish smile admitted as much.

"Lily, would you like a sandwich before I take you home?"

Lily's stomach turned over at the thought of eating. But the pinched line of Libby's lips almost convinced Lily to accept, if only to spite the woman and her obvious reluctance to prepare anything for her. Lily shook her head. "No—but thank you. My appetite is quite gone. Please, you go ahead—in fact, why don't I just head on" —she couldn't bring herself to say *home*, so she glossed over her distaste and continued—"I'll find my way back to …"

Tyler shook his head. "It's too far, Lily."

"But Libby just walked here all the way from Prescott's."

"Yes, she did, and normally you could as well. Not today. You're exhausted and tomorrow you're going to be sore—if you're not already. Humor me on this. Give me a minute to telephone the Canary Cage to let Merle know where you are. Then I'll help Libby wrap up some supper, and I'll give you a ride." When Lily nodded, he turned to follow Libby into the kitchen.

Lily wandered around the living room, trying to ignore the voices murmuring in the kitchen, the sounds of domesticity and two people totally at ease with each other. Realigning Tyler's already smooth doilies and absently noting his few decorations, she paused at the open lid of the oak roll-top desk. She shouldn't … she couldn't … rummaging through someone's private papers was ill bred … and rude. She could imagine Papa's disapproving frown.

I could learn something helpful … something to use …

She tilted her head, listening to the couple in the kitchen to be certain of their continued preoccupation. Then, succumbing to curiosity, she pulled old envelopes and slips of paper out of the pigeonholes. A photograph captured her attention. A handsome couple perched on a settee, flanked by a younger-looking Tyler and an even younger man, a blond version of Tyler. A brother? She frowned thoughtfully and tucked the photograph away. Something scrunched, and the photograph jammed.

Oh, wonderful. I'm poking around in Tyler's desk, and I have to destroy something.

She retrieved a piece of crumpled newspaper. Laying it on the cluttered desktop, she smoothed the article out with the heel of one hand. Her breath caught in her throat at the headline. *Brother's Death Ruled Accidental—Elder Buchanan Acquitted.* In disbelief, she scanned the supporting article.

After more than sixteen hours of deliberation, Rogan Buchanan's death was ruled to be accidental. Buchanan was shot through the heart during a struggle in the dressing room of actress Allegra D'arcy ...

"Thank you, Libby. I'll see you tomorrow."

Tyler's voice penetrated Lily's stunned sensibilities, and she crammed the article back into the desk. Whirling around, she smoothed her hair and did her best to paste an innocent expression on her face.

"Ready?"

She answered with a weak smile and walked onto the front porch and into what little remained of the afternoon sunshine.

Though Tyler seemed to take as many backstreets as he could, they were still met with wide-mouthed stares and shocked whispers of recognition. When they dismounted at the back gate to the Canary Cage, Lily thanked Tyler and left him standing in the alley. She scurried through the kitchen, covering her injured cheek with her hand, ducking past a worried Rae Ann and Merle, his face ominous as a thundercloud, and took the stairs two at a time to the haven of her room.

Behind her, she heard Tyler's deep voice followed by exclamations and horrified questions. She leaned against her closed door, her heart thumping. She should feel at least a little bit grateful for Tyler's intercession, but one thought drowned out every other.

Tyler Buchanan is a murderer. He killed his own brother over an actress.

Lily leapt from this thought to the next ... *If he could cold-heartedly murder his brother, maybe he killed Augusta, too.*

She had thought she had no tears left. Her knees gave way beneath her, and she sank to the floor, her ruined skirt billowing around her like a dark cloud.

CHAPTER SIXTEEN

Lily stood before the cheval mirror, her nightgown bunched around her waist, examining evidence of the assault. After a soft tap, Rae Ann pushed the door open before Lily could respond. At Rae Ann's gasp, Lily instinctively covered herself.

"My sakes, Lily, let me see."

Rae Ann bustled into the room and gently pushed Lily's hands away. The gown slipped down again, and Rae Ann's eyes filled with tears.

"Oh, child," she whispered plaintively.

Lily turned her eyes to the mirror, uncomfortable under Rae Ann's perusal. Honey, Sally, and Trudy often roamed the upstairs halls in their undergarments or sometimes even bare skinned, but Lily still hadn't grown accustomed to such immodesty. Except for late night whispered conversations when Augusta would tiptoe into Lily's room in her nightgown, even she and her sister had respected one another's privacy. Had Augusta become so relaxed with her body that she too had no qualms about nakedness? Lily sighed. Of course she had. If she had been that different from the other women, Honey most certainly wouldn't have hesitated to share that bit of gossip.

Lily calmed herself with the reminder that Rae Ann filled the role of housemother. Kind and sympathetic, she studied Lily with concern, not out of curiosity or a desire to be critical. At that moment, Rae Ann murmured a few vile things that ought to be done to the lunatic who had dared hurt Lily.

Lily might have laughed under different circumstances. Instead, she shuddered at the memory of his hands on her. She had hoped to feel somewhat better after the full evening's rest she had been allowed. After soaking in the tub, a protective Rae Ann had escorted Lily up the back stairs. Merle, too, had put aside his questions and had only frowned angrily at her battered appearance.

Today her cheek turned a different shade of purple, and the swelling had receded from her lip. Fresh bruises spread across her throat, though she couldn't remember his hands having been around her neck. More black and blue discolorations spotted her chest and ribs, and reddened abrasions covered her back and knees where he had dragged her across the grass.

Lily pulled the hem of her gown over her head in one swift motion, then tossed the garment on the bed, no longer mindful of the woman beside her. Marks on her legs, rounded and spaced like fingerprints, exposed the gruesome reminder of her attacker's intent.

"Lily, did he—did he ..." Rae Ann finished her question with a sideways glance.

"No, Tyler got there in time," Lily whispered, her eyes still fixed on her reflection. She had suspected there might be more to her injuries when aching limbs and stiff muscles hampered her attempt to climb out of bed.

"This is simply outrageous. It's a violation and a crime. Carson Ward better find that man and make sure he pays," Rae Ann said.

"Oh, they'll catch him, but not because of me. He'll be made to pay for that man he beat, the other woman he almost ravaged, and the bank he tried to rob. But for me?" Lily shook her head. "No, there'll be little sympathy and no retribution. They'll all just say I deserved it."

Tears slipped down Rae Ann's lined cheeks. She turned away from the mirror and helped Lily slip her arms into the robe she held out for her.

"I know you'd rather not, but Merle wants you to meet him in his office as soon as you can."

Lily nodded and poured water from a pitcher into a washing bowl. She splashed the cold water on her face and shivered.

"A little rice powder will help cover the bruising on your cheek, and a little touch of color on your lips will draw attention there. Your eyes usually work like a magnet, but you—I mean ..."

"Thank you, and you're right. I didn't sleep very well. I look bad enough without these dark circles."

"I'm sorry, honey. I'll leave you alone to get dressed, unless you need my help?" Lily shook her head, and Rae Ann continued. "Well, I'll be in the kitchen starting breakfast. I'll have some tea ready for you and toast. Wouldn't you like eggs or something else this morning?"

"Thanks, but no. Tea and toast will be fine. I'll be down in a few minutes."

Lily dressed, then dragged herself reluctantly into Merle's office, trying her best to explain what had happened the previous day.

Merle studied her from behind his desk, cursing under his breath. "The first we realized something was up was when Honey burst in here complaining that you had skipped out on your share of the work," he said. "We figured you'd gone on one of your walks and lost track of the time. Then a couple of hours later, Tallman himself came over from the livery yelling that you'd taken one of his horses and the gelding had wandered back into town with an empty saddle. He said you hadn't paid his stable hand, and he expected to see you as soon as you showed up, if you showed up at all. I went on and gave him his money—"

"That's a lie," Lily said angrily. "I had to pay him before he would let me take the horse. In fact, he made me pay for a whole day, saying he would refund the unused portion when I returned. Now he not only owes me money, he owes you, too."

Merle shook his head. "That miserable cuss." He gave a heavy sigh and raised his hands as if in defeat. "We might as well kiss that money goodbye. With your word against his—"

"And nobody would take the word of a saloon girl over that of a good gentleman of Guthrie?"

Merle shrugged. "Well, Sam Hill, Lil, aren't you used to that sort of treatment by now? It's always been like that."

"That doesn't make it right."

"No. But, right or wrong, folks aren't likely to change."

Lily had no response and stared miserably out the window, waiting for Merle to fire her or send her back to work.

"Rae Ann says you're beat up pretty bad."

His eyes swept over her. Lily shifted uncomfortably knowing the powder she had patted on her face didn't totally disguise the discoloration on her cheek, and the stand-up lace collar couldn't cover the ugly bruises around her throat.

"Take today and rest up. We had some unhappy customers last night when *you* didn't come down, and they'll get even more riled up tonight. Truth be told, this little hiccup'll keep 'em interested. Just watch how big a crowd we get tomorrow night when you're back on stage."

"Thank you, Merle," Lily said. "Every move I make feels like I'm being torn apart. I'm certain I can't sing anyway given how sore my throat feels."

Merle slapped his hand on the desk and stood. "Go on over and talk to Ward. Rae Ann and Buchanan convinced him not to question you last night, but he's not likely to wait long."

"I'll go over straightaway." Afterwards, she would seek out Tyler, make a stop at the post office, and then at least try to help out in the kitchen.

The Capital City Courier made its home in a building three stories high and made of native red sandstone with several plate glass windows spaced symmetrically on each floor. A wooden sign hung across the doorway and identified the newspaper, the date established, and Tyler Buchanan as its publisher.

Lily pushed through the front door and stepped inside. The floors thrummed beneath her boots, and the entire space seemed to vibrate. The presses must be in the basement.

A teenaged boy sat at a table deftly folding stacks of finished papers. He looked up at her with obvious interest and sprang to his feet.

"Help you?" He swept off his hat with ink-stained fingers.

"I'm here to see Tyler Buchanan."

"Sure, this way." He hitched up his britches and motioned for her to follow.

Lily's abused muscles screamed as she climbed the stairs behind the boy. She lagged a few steps behind him, catching glimpses of a conference room on her left and offices on her right. In one, a gray-haired man sat at a drawing desk, surrounded by brushes and bottles of ink. Another room housed telegraph equipment. Several doors were closed.

The boy paused in front of an open doorway and leaned in. Lily waited at his side, noting with interest the two women pounding methodically on typewriters.

"Miss Leatherwood?" the boy said loudly. "There's a lady here to see Mr. Buchanan."

A thin, elderly woman with gray hair pulled into a severe bun continued typing. The second, a younger woman, whose rather long nose supported thick-lensed spectacles, glanced at Lily and rose, pushing her chair back with a scrape.

"Thank you, Gus," she said to the boy who smiled cheekily at Lily and headed back down the hallway. Miss Leatherwood returned her attention to Lily.

"Yes?"

"I'm here to see Tyler Buchanan."

The woman pointedly let her gaze sweep Lily from her hair to her shoes and back again.

"Is he expecting you?"

Lily hesitated only a second. "Yes." She lied.

Miss Leatherwood considered Lily. "His office is the last door on the left." Without another word, she sat down and continued with her work.

Lily turned away, her face burning from the curt dismissal. She found Tyler's office with no trouble. The door was open, and he sat behind an oak partner's desk, his elbow propped on its surface, his cheek resting in his palm. He bent over a sheet of paper, deep thought creasing between his eyebrows, a fountain pen in his other hand.

No doubt he would ask questions about her interview with Carson Ward. Though uncomfortable at the prospect of once again discussing what she was doing her best not to think about, she reminded herself of her purpose—trying to fashion a relationship with Tyler. If she wanted him to care for her, for his heart to become emotionally entangled, she had to take advantage of every opportunity to share confidences, feelings, and experiences. If that failed in the end, she could always resort to what she instinctively knew he must fear—scandal. He surely had fled Charleston under a cloak of shame.

According to Sally, Honey, and her own observations, he never frequented the company of any of the girls at the Canary Cage—including Roxie. Did that mean he intentionally avoided relationships with women of a certain ilk? After the disaster involving an actress and the rumors surrounding Roxie, one would assume he'd have sworn off public entanglements with women in the so-called entertainment field. If that proved to be true, Lily had chosen a difficult path to try getting close to Tyler. If he tried to maintain what he considered an appropriate distance from her, what would she do if he managed to succeed?

Watching him, Lily fought off the odd feeling once again tightening her chest.

I'm just nervous. I found out yesterday that this man is a murderer. A voice in her head taunted her. She might be nervous, but not from what she had learned.

Doesn't his past prove he really is responsible for Augusta's death?

Why did you feel so safe in his arms if you're truly convinced he's a killer?

With no answer forthcoming, she pasted on a bright smile and tapped lightly on the door.

CHAPTER SEVENTEEN

"Good morning, Tyler."

At the interruption, he glanced up with a frown. Then he smiled. "Lily! Come in." As he pushed back his chair, he rolled down the sleeves of his white shirt, fastening the cuffs and gestured for her to take a seat.

She lowered herself into the wing-backed chair, a spasm of pain flashing across her face.

"Are you all right?"

"Just a bit sore. I'm a little more bruised than I thought."

Tyler narrowed his eyes.

"That miserable cuss," he said beneath his breath, taking in the bruises visible above her lace collar and the purple shadow still evident beneath the light powder on her cheek. "Please excuse my language. I'm sure you hear enough foul words at the Cage."

Lily nodded. "Thank you." A thoughtful expression flitted across her face. "I fear I'll never grow accustomed to the casual use of vulgarity. For the life of me, I can't remember my father, his friends, or any of the servants ever swearing in my presence. Here, men speak in whatever manner they please, despite the presence of a woman."

Lily's eyes widened as though shocked by the absurdity of her words.

"I meant despite the presence of a *saloon girl*. Of course, I was talking about when I was a girl ..."

Tyler marveled again at the myriad expressions that raced pell-mell across her lovely features. He wouldn't get involved with her. He *couldn't* get involved with her. He'd learned his lesson with Allegra. After losing his brother, devastating his parents, and ruining his reputation, he wasn't about to take a chance like that again. Lily might have the speech, style, and manners of a woman who had been raised in polite society, but the fact that she sang at the Canary Cage told the true story. He'd be a fool to get involved. He had acted irresponsibly and made too many mistakes in his youth. A lot of names could still be attached to him today, but fool wasn't one of them.

"Have you seen Carson?" he asked, determined to guide his thoughts in another direction.

"Yes, I have. I came here after speaking with him. Thank you for persuading him to give me time to pull myself together first. Merle said you and Rae Ann kept everyone away last night."

"I figured you'd had enough questions for one day."

"The chief was actually quite solicitous. He did his best to keep from embarrassing me, I think. He apparently already knew the details from the point when you happened upon the scene. I really only needed to fill in what passed before."

Tyler couldn't help but compare the differences between Lily and other actresses, singers, dancers, and saloon girls he had known. She had none of the harshness, the rough edges, or the crudeness. If Honey—or Allegra— had been seated before him, her bodice would reveal cleavage, her skirt would not quite cover her ankles, and her eyelashes would flutter at him flirtatiously. The look she would shoot him would have a beckoning glint, and she would do what she could to draw his attention to her mouth. A few exaggerated sighs would ensure he gave her bosom due consideration.

But Lily … whenever he had seen her away from the saloon … dressed conservatively, though quite stylishly. Perched on the edge of the chair, her hands folded demurely in her lap. She held her knees together and her feet flat on the floor. She had swept her hair into a French twist, and his fingers remembered its silkiness. With her eyes bluer than the clear morning sky, he could hardly believe this poised young woman was the same frantic girl who had cried in his arms just the day before.

"We never did talk about how you found yourself in that situation. Would you mind telling me what you told Carson?"

Lily shifted in the chair and grimaced delicately. Her gaze drifted to the window over Tyler's shoulder, and he waited patiently for her to respond.

"Penny?"

Tyler's question roused Lily from wherever her thoughts had taken her. "Pardon me?"

"Penny. For your thoughts."

Lily shook her head. "I'm afraid they're not worth that much."

"It's my penny to spend however I like. What about Carson?"

She leaned back in the chair and took a deep breath.

"I was up early—I still somehow manage to wake up before almost everyone else—and just had to get away from—from the Cage. I walked to the livery, paid for a horse, and rode toward the river. I ate a little of the snack Rae Ann had insisted I take along, and then rested in the grass. With the warm breeze, the lullaby of the river, and the birdsong, I dozed off and started to dream. I hadn't been sleeping well with the constant hubbub at the Cage."

"What did you dream about?"

Lily responded without hesitating, though she had yet to meet his gaze.

"About my father. I dreamt he was there, comforting me like he did when I was a child. He was stroking my cheek and calling me his pretty little girl. But when he asked my name, the dream became a nightmare. I opened my eyes and couldn't believe that horrid man was real. He smelled as though he hadn't bathed in a decade. You saw him—unkempt beard and hair, filthy clothes, rotting teeth. He breathed on me, and I thought I would be ill. He touched my face …"

She shuddered and stood up suddenly, wrapping her arms around her stomach, as though sick or cold. She paced in front of the desk. Her eyes took on a wild look, and Tyler pushed back his chair and rose in concern, though she didn't seem to notice.

"When I tried to get up, he scared off my horse and forced me against a tree. I tried to fight him off, I swear I did. No man—no one—had ever touched me the way he did. I was so frightened. I struggled and struggled, but all I accomplished was to make him angry enough to hit me.

"I thought he had broken my jaw. My whole face went numb, but I couldn't make myself acquiesce. I don't remember screaming, but he kept telling me to be quiet. He must have put his hands around my throat, because I have horrific bruises—I don't remember that either."

As she spoke, Lily clearly became more and more distraught, nearly quivering with agitation. Tyler moved around his desk and took her by the shoulders. Staring intently into her wide blue eyes, he shook her just a little until he could see her return from her hellish memories and refocus her gaze on him.

"Lily, it's okay. It's over. You don't have to talk about—or think about—the incident anymore. They're going to catch this no-count scoundrel unless he's long gone. Either way, we won't be seeing him again. You're safe, Lily … safe."

Bending his knees to put himself at eye level, he grasped her shoulders firmly but not tightly enough to frighten her. He spoke in an urgent whisper, hoping his intensity would convince her that his words rang true.

He remembered every time he had seen this woman. The first night when she sang from beneath the veil, her voice, so pure, wound its way around his frozen heart. Even then, he reminded himself he could not have her, even if she turned out to have a face that matched her lovely voice and shapely figure. She had haunted his dreams that night. When he met her by the derelict graveyard the next morning, not knowing she was the Songbird of the East, he had been filled with concern and admiration for the young woman. He *could* be interested in this woman, he remembered thinking with relief. If nothing else, she could prove to be a distraction at least long enough for the voice of the new singer at the Canary Cage to become familiar and less dangerous.

That night, his heart fell to his boots when he realized the two women were one and the same. He had listened to Lily sing that night, determined to simply enjoy the music, the beer, and remind himself of Allegra and the ruination of life.

But Lily had been his companion, though only in thought, as he went home. Thoughts of her had followed him there just as those thoughts had followed him the night before and all day. Determined to harden his heart and harness his thoughts, he only managed to get himself drunk. As if real, her image ignored his desire for privacy and invaded his dreams once again.

When she had attended church Sunday morning, he had known she stood behind him from the first note she sang. Then her gardenia scent flowed over him until his chest tightened, and he could hardly breathe. He thought her a brave woman. Or perhaps she lacked intelligence, showing up where she should have expected to be ostracized. Tyler hadn't stopped to reconsider before deciding to make sure Lily made it out of the churchyard with no trouble. But he had been held up by the crowd, and when he was close enough to help her, there was no need. She had taken care of herself quite capably.

That afternoon when she stopped in at the newspaper for the back issues, he wondered about her again. Hard to believe she made her living singing in a saloon and serving drinks. Only on stage did she dress the part of one of Merle's fallen birds. Otherwise her clothing, her manners and mannerisms, everything about her screamed she was not who or what she claimed to be.

Perhaps that explained why he could hold her so easily when she had toppled into his arms that first afternoon. And why he had been about to kiss her. He knew she, too, would have been willing. He had been surprised, though he couldn't explain why. After all, he could, no doubt, do much more than kiss her for a dollar or two. He had never been intimate with anyone from the Canary Cage or any of the dozens of saloons and brothels in town. Not after Allegra. Never again.

Still, thoughts of that near-kiss also followed him home that evening, and he refused Libby's offer for conversation. It wouldn't be fair to Libby if his mind strayed to another woman. He had awakened the next day filled with confidence. He could do this. He could stay away from Lily, and he would eventually stop thinking about her. Besides, she might not stay in town long. Her type often became restless and moved on without notice.

He thought perhaps the good Lord was testing him when he heard a woman's scream. He had, of course, no idea he would play rescuer to Lily until he saw her pale face twisted in terror. His anger grew disproportionately, and he remembered the rage that had made him want to kill the beast for daring to put his hands on her.

Spending the afternoon taking care of her and getting to know her a little better had only put him in dire straits. He had wanted to hold her and keep her safe. And more. But he ached to somehow chase away the fear in her eyes. Protectiveness overwhelmed him and thrust aside all fleshly thoughts and urges.

Now, here in his office, he wanted to unlock his elbows and pull her into his arms. She stared up at him, and his mind again warred with his instincts, his well-intentioned vows battling with his emotions. After one moment of looking into her ocean-blue eyes, he recognized the danger of being lost forever. He only had to bend his elbows a little ... she would be closer, pull her toward him and she would come ... willingly, he was certain. As usual, he had doubts about his judgment concerning women. Must he always be inevitably drawn to the wrong kind? Surely, the devil must be to blame. Involvement with Allegra had ruined his life, a fact he reminded himself of more and more often. He had met the Lord in the pit of desperation, and his sins had been forgiven, his life finally taking an upward turn.

But danger lurked. This attraction, different, more compelling—more confusing than any other he had experienced, threatened his undoing.

Dragging his stare from her hypnotic eyes to her lips, his resolve crumbled. With a groan he lowered his head, claiming her lips with unerring accuracy. He sampled the sweetness of her mouth purposely, gently. Urging her closer, his hand flat against her lower back, he pressed her against him.

Tyler finally lifted his head. Lily's eyelashes fluttered open, her gaze startled and impassioned. Unable to stop himself, he kissed her again, tenderly, questing, testing. Lily's arms crept around his neck, and she seemed suddenly frantic to be closer. Surprised by her response, he deepened the kiss, seeking to somehow satisfy the desperation thundering through his body.

CHAPTER EIGHTEEN

Lily's thoughts spun wildly, a strange heat radiating from some unknown, untapped well deep within her. The strength in her legs melted, and she swayed. Unprepared for the passionate assault on her innocent senses, she felt the world outside of Tyler's lips and hands fade into nothingness. She had never been kissed like this before, her previous experience only a brief encounter consisting solely of a chaste kiss from a young man as inexperienced as she. Though bewildered by the wild flood of heat that enveloped her, she was unable to pull away and found herself seeking more.

They finally broke apart, each panting, Lily confused and exhilarated by her thrumming emotions.

What is happening to me? Lily touched her swollen lips in wonder.

"What are you doing to me?" Tyler breathed in a voice so low she barely heard him.

I can't be feeling this way, I can't, I can't.

"Why does it have to be you? Why don't I feel this way about someone else, anyone else ... Libby ... or Theo ..." Was Tyler aware he'd whispered his plea aloud? As though Tyler's speaking her name conjured her out of thin air, the door burst open and a young woman, her pale blonde hair piled high in intricate ringlets and curls, strode in, a napkin embroidered with cornflowers covered the basket carried in the crook of her elbow. She turned to close the door behind her, her voice high with effusive cheerfulness.

"I wanted to surprise you, so I managed to slip by while that woman downstairs was preoccupied. I brought you ..." The full-figured blonde skidded to a halt when Tyler turned. Lily realized she must have been hidden from the girl's view by Tyler's broad shoulders.

The blonde scowled.

"Tyler? I trust I'm not interrupting anything terribly important." Her sugary tone made Lily feel as though she'd been dismissed. "I awakened to the aroma of Belle's lemon poppy-seed muffins, and you immediately came to mind." She gave Tyler a flirtatious smile and raised the basket a little. "I know how you love Belle's muffins, so I brought some right over. They're still warm."

"Thank you, Theo," Tyler said, his voice like a gruff bark. He cleared his throat. "Thank you. That was thoughtful."

Theo's too-bright smile faded, and she directed a supercilious look at Lily but refused to acknowledge her directly.

"Who is this, Tyler?"

She said his name with such an air of proprietary Lily felt a rush of annoyance. She recognized—what had Tyler called her? Theo?—yes, that was her name. She recognized Theo from the church.

She sings off key. And she's rude.

Theo continued to address Tyler and, except by her question, ignore Lily.

Perhaps Tyler had found himself in a quandary. No doubt Theo's jealousy was constantly on simmer. How could he introduce two women who would not speak or even acknowledge each other if they passed on the sidewalk? Assuredly, Theo would cross the street rather than let the hem of her skirt skim the same dirt as Lily's.

That thought angered her unreasonably. Before Tyler could speak, Lily stepped forward, squaring her shoulders and lifting her chin a notch. "I'm Lily Woods. I sing at the Canary Cage."

If only Theo would be as civilized. Instead, she dashed that hope the second she opened her pursed mouth. "The church! That's where I saw you. And you work at the Canary Cage?" She said the name of the saloon with such repugnance that Lily took a step backwards.

"Theo," Tyler interjected, his face flushed with something Lily couldn't quite define—Anger? Embarrassment on her behalf?

"Tyler," Theo whimpered, her full lower lip thrust out in a childish pout. "Tyler, how could you be seen with this—this *strumpet* in broad daylight? Have you no thought for your reputation or mine? And to have her here in your office, behind closed doors … why, Tyler, I don't know what to think!"

How could Tyler bear the company of such a simpering noodlehead? Lily, her stomach roiling with disgust, directed a small, tight smile at Tyler. "Thank you again, Tyler," she said. She should stop there. But some minute bit of impudence flared, and she seized it with relish. Society's rules apparently did not apply to saloon girls, so she might as well make use of the fact and steer Theo in the direction she so clearly wished to travel.

"I'm deeply appreciative of your intervention on my behalf," Lily continued. "I look forward to the opportunity of repaying the favor sometime soon." She gazed up at Tyler and smiled. "Very soon," she added with an inviting smile for Theo's benefit rather than Tyler's. Lily gave his forearm a brief squeeze before curtsying and heading for the door. Head held high, she barely skimmed a glance over Theo.

Lily suppressed a smile at Theo's seeming indignation at a saloon girl's abrupt dismissal. Theo hurriedly pulled her skirts aside as Lily passed, missing Tyler's resulting glower. Theo followed Lily and pointedly slammed the door behind her.

CHAPTER NINETEEN

"Tyler," Theo wheedled, her tone akin to that of an infant. "You're not consorting with that saloon girl, are you? I would be so terribly humiliated if my friends found out. I would be a laughingstock. I couldn't possibly hold my head up in this small town. And Papa … why, Papa would be so disappointed."

Tyler sighed and rubbed his brow, his head already beginning to ache from Theo's dramatics. He hated when she lapsed into the childlike voice she no doubt used with great success on her doting father. He, on the other hand, found her ploy to be anything but endearing.

"Tyler," she went on, peevishness seeping into her cajoling tone, "what reason could that soiled dove possibly have for thinking she owes you a favor?" Oblivious to the muscle spasm in Tyler's clenched jaw, she set the basket down and rearranged the stacks of paper, cups of pens and pencils, paperweights, and inkpots on his desk. "Honestly, I don't understand why you simply did not put her in her place. I cannot imagine she could think it appropriate for her to be seen in broad daylight with such a distinguished citizen as yourself and in such a place as reputable and important as a newspaper office. She quite obviously has ideas above her station and *someone*"—she directed a pointed glare at Tyler—"someone should have already done that. Honestly, Tyler, what were you thinking, allowing her in your office in plain sight? Being alone with her could be social suicide. Honestly, Tyler." She ended her monologue with a disapproving cluck and stood, arms folded.

The contradiction in her argument was not lost on Tyler. He could either be with Lily in plain sight or alone with her, not both at the same time. But he had no interest in pointing out the gaps in Theo's logic. His patience ended long before her irritating prattle reached a conclusion. And if she said *honestly* one more time, he would throttle her. He willed the biting reply on the tip of his tongue back into his throat. Rounding the desk, he sat down, automatically replacing his desktop accessories where they had been before Theo brassily rearranged them.

Offending Theo would only ruin his friendship with her father. Though Tyler found her shallow, he didn't want to hurt her feelings.

"Thank you for the muffins. I'm sure they're as delicious as always. I'll see that the basket is returned."

"What about that woman?" she insisted, again ignoring the warning tic in Tyler's jaw. "Did you notice the cosmetics she was wearing? And in daytime! Still, they didn't help one bit. Her lifestyle cannot be hidden by any amount of makeup. The sallowness of her complexion was plain to see along with the blue shadows under her eyes. Someone should tell her—no, telling a woman like that anything would obviously be a waste of time and breath."

Tyler stared at Theo in disbelief, noting her unnaturally pinkened cheeks and lips. Once again, he bit back the words that rose so readily. There could be no gain in defending Lily. Telling Theo he had never seen Lily wear cosmetics of any kind except while on stage would only cause more discussion. Explaining the reason for the rice powder Lily had applied that morning would be an even greater mistake. Word of Lily's attack would undoubtedly be spread all over town by nightfall and greatly distorted by Theo's vindictiveness.

"That *woman* is not a matter I care—or intend—to discuss with you. There is no need for us to dwell any longer in thought or conversation on this subject. Thank you for the muffins."

He hadn't meant to speak so sternly, but relief washed over him when Theo took a step backward. Had he not been so angry, he might have been amused at the expressions parading across her face. She finally settled on a measure of dignity.

"Tyler, you are so right. There's absolutely no need for *either* of us to consider that woman any longer. She couldn't possibly be of any consequence and—oh, dear!" she cried, darting a look at the clock on the table behind Tyler's desk. "The time has completely escaped me. I still have to run errands for Mother, and I must tear myself from your company." She smiled prettily at him and crossed the room to the door. "Don't concern yourself with the basket. I'll be happy to stop by later."

Before Tyler could protest or agree, she waved gloved fingers at him and swept out the door as abruptly as she had swept in.

CHAPTER TWENTY

Having left Tyler's office in a hurry, Lily came upon the post office in good time, though the building was a few blocks away on South 2nd Street. She left there quite pleased with her ingenuity. She had written to her solicitor asking that he make inquiries into a certain Tyler Buchanan, formerly of Charleston, South Carolina, specifically regarding a scandal that had erupted roughly eleven years earlier. She had signed the letter *Melissa Forrester* but requested that he direct his reply to Miss Lily Woods in care of the post office. She explained she had arranged to transact business through Augusta's friend rather than set up accounts throughout town for a visit of such short duration. Mr. Barlow had a reputation for dependability, and Lily had no doubt he would fulfill her requests as efficiently as possible.

Her earlier anger dissipated only slightly when she allowed her thoughts to return to the events of the morning. Theo's entrance had been both timely and ill-timed. On one hand, Lily had been irritated by the interruption when Tyler was obviously softening toward her once again. He had held her at arm's length at first, and she had been both relieved and disappointed. It was evident by his uncertain gazes that he warred with himself. She both welcomed and feared his battle. More contradictions. Always contradictions with Tyler.

Theo's appearance had left them with unfinished business, and perhaps that was just as well. The kiss left Lily—and surely, him as well—with rampaging emotions and no resolutions. She would find time and opportunity to complete that business at another time, after she had a few moments to sort out her thoughts.

Lily gave a little huff of disgust, then continued down the wooden sidewalk. What about Theo? Lily felt no contradictory feelings toward the young lady, having grown up with women like Theo. She considered the majority of them silly, only thinking of the next party, the next social event, their only ambition to find a man wealthy and handsome enough to marry.

In that, they could be as tenacious as hungry lionesses stalking prey. Overly concerned with their social standing, they had little interest in intellectual pursuits. No need trying to discuss literature, history, philosophy, or even current events. Lily dismissed them as featherbrained ninnies. Even Augusta would laugh at their friends' lack of substance.

But today, Lily had been embarrassed by Theo's superior attitude. Lily's father claimed intelligence was a valuable commodity with pretty faces being a dime a dozen. Smart people could be had for the same price. But a beautiful, *intelligent* woman? Now there was a priceless gem.

Oh, Papa, you just didn't realize that vapid socialites are somehow more valuable than intelligent showgirls.

She could almost hear her father telling her, "People can only make you feel as bad as you allow them to."

She had allowed an impudent socialite to make her feel tawdry. And simply because she worked at the Canary Cage. She was not cheap, and she could still proclaim herself unsullied. Just because Theo, or anyone else, couldn't possibly know the showgirl role was a ruse didn't make this any less true. Lily sighed. Her not-so-brilliant plot had been hatched on the spur of the moment as a means to an end. Playing a saloon singer shouldn't change her. Yet, she could feel herself changing, though not all of the changes were unwelcomed.

Until that moment, Lily hadn't realized what pride she had taken in her social position in Norfolk. Several thriving shipyards had earned her father great wealth, affording his daughters with many opportunities—the best tutors, the finest instruments, and richly-tailored wardrobes. They had filled their home, one of the largest and most elegantly furnished houses on elite Mowbray Arch, with valuable collections both contemporary and historical. The library included a selection of books envied by scholars and libraries up and down the east coast, several manuscripts dating back to the Middle Ages, complete works of Shakespeare, and first editions of Byron, Shelley, the Brownings, Austin, Elliott, Thoreau, Emerson, and Longfellow. Papa collected ancient Mayan and Aztec pottery, blown glass from Ireland, and even owned a small Renoir that hung in the parlor.

Lily had been proud of her life, of her father, her home, her possessions, and even her intelligence. A sense of guilt overwhelmed her. She had looked down her nose at the young women she considered scatterbrained in much the same way as the women in Guthrie who turned away as she approached. While these women were social snobs, Lily admitted she was an intellectual one.

Had she come into town in all her finery and social status and taken rooms at the best hotel, she would have been inundated with invitations to every luncheon, soiree, and party in town. Every woman of any social consequence would have been sitting on her doorstep eager to make her acquaintance. These same women who pulled their skirts aside as Theo had would never dream of treating her in such a manner had she introduced herself as Miss Melissa Forrester.

Why should she be treated with such disdain here in Guthrie? She had more money hidden in her carpetbag than most of these people would make in a year. If necessary, she'd simply instruct Mr. Barlow to wire whatever amount she required directly to any local bank. Lily had observed the townspeople's reactions to her, how they seemed envious of her appearance.

Neither was she deficient in intelligence, though perhaps she wasn't making the best choices these days. Pretending she actually had experience singing on stage as a showgirl, serving drinks to men who were everything from refined to rowdy … didn't that prove she had at least partially lost her good sense?

No, she reminded herself, *this is for Augusta.*

She need only be here for a short time, another month or two, and she would be close enough to Tyler to be able to walk out on him, and let him experience the humiliation he had forced on Augusta. If that failed, she would ruin his reputation. Such damage could be done by innuendo, gossip, and double entendre. Either way, her mission would be accomplished and both she and Augusta could rest in peace.

In the meantime, she would have to endure being ostracized by the so-called good people of Guthrie. Perhaps she would reveal her identity before leaving town and have the last laugh.

Lily chewed her bottom lip thoughtfully, stopping with a wince when she bit into the injury from the day before. She could divulge the truth about herself only if she managed to engage Tyler's heart. If she had to resort to the scandal angle, announcing she wasn't who everyone thought might be counterproductive. Indeed, if she let the entire town know they had been duped, their anger and resentment might be redirected at her, and Tyler might become a martyr of her deception. That simply wouldn't do.

Another scenario occurred to her for the first time. What impact would this plan of hers have on her life in Norfolk if someone found evidence of her actions in Guthrie? She shivered at the thought. No, she had best leave town as ignominiously as she had arrived. The old Sir Walter Scott adage came to mind … *O, what a tangled web we weave, when first we practise to deceive!*

Lily's thoughts flew by in such rapid succession that she had already arrived at Gibson's Sundries. On East Oklahoma Avenue, sandwiched between the First National Bank of Guthrie and Daniel's Drugs, the narrow, two-storied wood building seemed dwarfed by the architectural stylings of the neighboring buildings. Lily pushed open the glass-plated door and stepped into the cool, quiet interior.

A thin woman with auburn hair pulled into a severe bun stood on a stepstool arranging tins on a shelf behind the counter. The bell over the door jingled when Lily entered, and the woman turned toward her customer. When she saw Lily, the woman's freckled face turned brighter than her hair. She hastily climbed down from the stool, wiping her hands nervously on her blue-and-white checked apron.

"Can I … may I …" the woman stared at Lily with wide brown eyes and gulped. "Are you looking for anything special?"

The storekeeper's obvious distress bothered Lily more than Theo's earlier insulting behavior. While polite society would expect the clerk to avoid small talk with Lily on the street, here a proprietor must wait on customers and sell stock. The clerk might be embarrassed to encounter a woman from the Canary Cage, but she should do a passable job hiding her true feelings behind a polite demeanor.

Lily smiled at the flustered redhead. "I only need a tin of rice powder, and I'd like to see some hair ribbons. I won't be long," she said.

The woman, Miss Gibson, according to the pin on the bib of her apron, smiled back a little tentatively and nodded toward the back of the store.

"The powders are in the cabinet in that corner, and you'll find the hair ribbons on the table at the end of the counter. If you have any questions, let me know."

Lily nodded and smiled again. Walking toward the cabinet as directed, she could feel the clerk's stares. At least the woman was professional enough to be courteous to a customer. Did such a necessary thing as shopping have to be this difficult? Did Honey, Sally, and Trudy bear this same response every time they patronized a shop? Then again, groceries were delivered directly to the Canary Cage, and Rae Ann picked up cosmetic supplies for the girls.

Lily found the cabinet and looked over the attractive display of powder puffs, silver-plated brushes, combs, mirrors, and tins of powders and rouges. She found the shade Rae Ann had requested. Bottles of cologne crowded the shelf beside the cabinet, and Lily almost squealed when she found her favorite scent. She browsed for a few more moments before setting both items on the end of the counter, drawing Miss Gibson's attention once again.

"Find everything you need?" the clerk asked, her thin fingers fluttering nervously at her throat.

"Yes, thank you, Miss Gibson," Lily answered. "I'll just take another minute to look at these ribbons."

From the wooden spools in varying widths and colors of satin, silk, and other fabrics, she chose a vivid red to match a dress Rae Ann promised to alter for her. On impulse, she decided on another length of baby blue for Rae Ann, yellow for Honey, bright green for Trudy, and a rose color that would look lovely in Sally's brown hair. Behind her, the bell tinkled again, and she cringed at the sound of a voice already gratingly familiar.

"Good morning, Amy. Are my hairpins in yet?" Theo's voice rang through the store.

The clerk gave an audible sigh before answering.

"Miss Peebles, when you placed the order, I explained shipment could take anywhere from six to eight weeks. Scarcely three weeks have gone by."

"But Amy, my dear girl, you *simply* don't understand. I ordered those pins to match the gown that's being custom made for my birthday party next week," Theo said, her petulance obvious. "My outfit will *simply* not be *complete* without the pins. I'm counting on having them. Nothing else will do. I looked in every store in Guthrie before I realized the only way I could possibly find what I had in mind was *simply* to special order them. And you, my dear Amy, I chose you because you had managed to get the fabric for me so quickly."

Throughout Theo's harangue, Lily kept her back turned, hoping to remain hidden by the bolts of cloth stacked behind her on the counter. One encounter with Theo had been more than enough.

"Miss Peebles," Amy began, speaking slowly and clearly as if to a dull-witted child. "I realize how important your birthday party is to you, but I'm afraid you are the one who *simply* does not understand. The fabric you ordered was in Oklahoma City, and I picked it up myself. The amber hairpins are another matter. They are being shipped from New York City and *simply* cannot be delivered in less than six weeks. I explained this to you before you placed the order, and you said you understood. I *simply* have no control over the situation."

Lily took a peek in time to see Theo's eyes narrow and any pretense of civility disappear.

"Well, you'd better get control over the situation," the self-important woman said. "If those pins do not arrive in time, and the effect of my gown is ruined, then I will be sure to let my friends know that Gibson's Sundries cannot be trusted to handle such a thing as a simple order of hairpins. I've no doubt you'll find the quality of your clientele will suffer sadly. After all, the fact that my mother and I choose to frequent your establishment is a feather in your hat—even if the sole reason is because the location is near my father's bank …"

By Theo's sudden silence, Lily suspected she'd been found out. She painted a blank expression on her face before turning around. Perhaps she could avoid another ugly scene if Theo thought Lily hadn't overhead the argument with Amy.

"It appears you're already skimming the gutter for customers, Amy."

"What?" Amy followed Theo's glare to Lily, who now approached carrying her selections.

"Hello again, Theo," Lily said, setting the spools of ribbon on the counter. "Imagine, meeting twice in one morning. What do you suppose are the odds of that happening?" Without waiting for an answer, she turned her attention to the red-headed woman. Miss Gibson's face, again washed in vivid color, tore at Lily's heartstrings.

"I would like one yard each of these ribbons and five yards of the red. They are of a lovely quality, by the way."

The bell tinkled again, but none of the women turned.

"That would be Miss Peebles to you—since you have the nerve to speak to me at all. And what would you know of quality?" Theo said with a sneer.

Amy Gibson gasped, and Lily tamped her anger, determined not to waste her temper on the likes of Theo Peebles.

"Well, I do know that quality is fine and inferiority is coarse. Much like the difference between courtesy and rudeness." Lily turned toward the counter to peruse the varieties of tea. In her peripheral vision, she saw Theo blanch, her face turning a pasty white before immediately flaring to a mottled red.

"How dare you address me in that manner—or even at all, you guttersnipe. Look at me when I speak to you!" She took a step forward and grabbed Lily's arm to pull her around. Lily instinctively jerked away, and Theo's hand knocked against the cologne, sending the bottle crashing to the floor.

"Oh, no!" Lily cried in genuine dismay when the glass shattered, the fragrant liquid splashing onto both her and Theo's skirts and shoes. "Now see what you've done."

"What *I've* done?" Theo screeched. "You're the one to blame. You purposely knocked my hand against the bottle. I refuse to pay for your clumsiness."

The flowered scent of the cologne filled the air. Theo stepped back, her features pulled into an ugly frown, her nostrils flaring as though the room stank of manure instead of gardenias.

"What a stench. I'll have to go straight home and burn this dress and my shoes, too. I simply cannot go about Guthrie smelling like a harlot—"

"That's enough, Theo." Tyler Buchanan's voice startled all three women.

"Tyler!" Theo quickly found the perfect balance between pleasant surprise and injured feelings. "How long have you been standing there? I can't believe you didn't come to my rescue sooner." Theo pointed at Lily. "Did you see what *she* did? Did you hear how she spoke to me?"

"I've been here long enough to realize the situation wasn't going to improve any time soon," he answered, his deep, resonant voice edged with disapproval.

Theo's pale eyebrows drew together in irritation. "Surely you don't think any of this is my fault? I simply came in to check on some hairpins Amy *promised* to have here by my birthday," she simpered, ignoring Amy's affronted gasp. "You can't possibly disagree that I have every right to be upset."

"That's what this is about?" Tyler asked. "Hairpins? I could hear you shrieking from the sidewalk."

"Shrieking? I don't shriek," Theo denied in a voice that did just that. "This woman"—she pointed to Amy Gibson—"convinced me to purchase hairpins when she knew they wouldn't arrive in time to wear with my birthday gown. And *that* woman"—Theo now pointed at Lily—"has no business speaking to me at all. She's rude, coarse, and not fit to wipe the dust from my shoes—or from any decent woman in Guthrie. And look at me, just look at me! She's ruined my dress and my shoes, and I smell like a … a …" Theo hesitated for a second or two. "A saloon girl," she said, her animosity as overpowering as the cologne.

Tyler sighed and wiped his broad hand across his face.

"Theo," he said, "go home."

"What?" Color drained from her face. "Surely you can't be taking the side of this … this …"

"Go home, Theo," he said, this time louder and more firmly. With effort, he softened his tone. "I'll take care of everything. Just go home. Please."

She must have thought Tyler would champion her, as she smiled smugly at Lily and the clerk, both who had remained silent the entire time. Before leaving, she gave Lily one more scornful glare.

"Don't believe anything she says, Tyler," Theo said, almost hissing. "And Amy, if those pins aren't here in time for my birthday party, I refuse to pay for them."

Dismay clouded Amy's face. "But Miss Peebles, the pins are amber tipped. They cost almost twenty-five dollars. I ordered them in good faith. You can't refuse to pay for them."

Theo raised her eyebrows haughtily and thrust her nose a little higher in the air. "I wanted them especially for my party. If they're not here in time, they are of no use to me. Explain good business practices to her, would you, Tyler? Ta-ta!" She slammed the door behind her, the bell jangling wildly. Three sighs of relief followed her.

Lily immediately stooped to pick up the shattered glass. "I'm so sorry, Miss Gibson," she said, carefully placing shards of splintered glass in the palm of one hand. "I suppose I should have gone to the back of the store when she came in, but I was already looking at the ribbons. I hoped she wouldn't notice me."

"Please don't apologize, Miss Woods," Amy replied earnestly, "and please don't worry yourselves with that. I'll get the broom and sweep up in no time."

Tyler had gone down on one knee to help clean up the debris. "I've always liked the smell of gardenias," he said under his breath.

Lily looked up in surprise. Inches from Tyler and his warm gray eyes, her heartbeat quickened in response. "They're my favorite," she said, her breath coming quickly between barely parted lips.

"Here we go, let me get that." Amy reappeared, broom in hand. Lily and Tyler stepped aside while she swept the remaining glass into a pile against the counter.

Tyler pulled a handkerchief from his pocket and wiped first his forehead and then bent to wipe up a small pool of cologne that had not yet seeped into the floorboards.

"Oh, my," Lily said with a sheepish smile. "This place smells like a fully bloomed gardenia bush."

Amy laughed and nodded. "I'll just open a back window and in less than an hour the smell won't be quite so strong. With such a lovely scent in the air, I'll sell every bottle in stock in no time at all."

"I will pay for this bottle plus buy another."

Amy came back around the counter and hurried toward the perfume shelf. "Don't you give it a second thought, Miss Woods. Things get broken in here all the time. And, like I said, I was standing right there. You're not the one who was nasty, nor did you knock the perfume over." She returned with another bottle and began measuring out the lengths of ribbon. "Thank you for stepping in, Mr. Buchanan," she said. "Truth is, that's the first time such a thing has ever happened in my store, and I didn't quite know how to handle the situation."

"You shouldn't have had to handle it," Lily said. "I apologize. I never imagined she would be quite so …" The word wouldn't come.

"Ridiculous?" Miss Gibson snickered.

Lily and Tyler laughed in sync.

"That wasn't quite the word I was searching for, but it will do," Lily said.

"Well, I see you ladies have no need of me. I apologize for barging in. I've known Theo for quite a while, and I could see neither of you wished to use the degree of firmness she requires at times. I thought I could help."

"You certainly did, Mr. Buchanan. Thank you again."

Tyler bowed his head toward the redhead and then to Lily, his gaze settling on her a little longer than necessary before leaving.

"Here you go, Miss Woods." Amy wrapped the items in tissue paper and rang up the total on the cash register.

Lily counted out the proper amount and tried once again to apologize. "Are you sure I can't pay for the broken bottle? I feel responsible."

"Theo had worked herself up into a temper even before she spotted you." Amy blew out a heavy breath and shook her head. "Truth is, I should be apologizing to you for one of my customers treating you so rudely. I didn't quite know what to do."

Lily gave Amy a friendly smile. "I appreciate that, especially since I could see your discomfort with my being here in the first place."

"I beg your pardon?"

"I'm sorry. I don't mean to embarrass you further. I saw your reaction when I came in the door. I understand I'm not the first person you'd like for a customer."

"Oh, no, no …" Amy shook her head vigorously. "That's not it at all! Yes, I recognized you. I saw you at church, and I overheard someone say your name and that you … uh … work at the Canary Cage. But that had nothing to do with my …" Amy blushed again, and Lily's heart went out to the sensitive young woman.

"Your reaction was typical," Lily assured her. "I'm growing accustomed to it, believe me." The last was a bit of a stretch, but she felt the white lie justified given Amy's obvious discomfort.

"No, what I mean is that you misread my reaction."

"Misread?"

"You're just so pretty. I saw you come in the door, and you're perfect. Your hair, your face, your clothes and, it turns out, even your manners are perfect. I felt so—plain. I didn't want you to notice me." Amy ducked her head, then looked up in surprise at Lily's comforting touch.

"Thank you so much for your kind compliments, but you shouldn't call yourself plain. You have lovely eyes, a sweet smile, and marvelous hair."

Amy reached up as if self-conscious and touched the bun twisted at the back of her head. "Hair? Oh, no, ma'am, my hair is a nightmare with a mind of its own and curls that spring in every direction. The only control I have is to tame it into this hideous bun."

"Miss Gibson," Lily began thoughtfully, a slender index finger laid against her chin.

"Amy, please, just Amy."

"And I'm Lily. Amy, did you know the latest style is perfect for you? You would have to find the courage to cut your hair short, though, with a little fluffy fringe. You can catch it back on the sides with combs and take advantage of your natural curls. It would look lovely."

Amy offered a small smile. "I think I saw that style in last month's *Ladies Home Journal,* but I never thought …" Her face crumpled into dejection. "Oh, Lily, even if I tried—and I know Nora Beauvais can copy any picture I show her—everyone would laugh at me."

"Then you just put your cute nose in the air and remind them being stylish is in your best interest as a merchant. After all, your hats and fabrics are all the rage."

"I do try to keep on top of things as best I can," Amy's face brightened and her smile broadened. "I'll do it. I'm so tired of wearing my hair like this." She sighed and her smile faded once again. "But my hair is only one thing. I can't change my face."

"Amy," Lily said, "there's nothing wrong with your face."

"That's nice of you, but so untrue. I have all these horrible freckles."

"Your propensity to freckle is not your fault. Make sure you wear one of your lovely hats when you're out of doors—remember, you can be a walking advertisement for the store. Have you considered wearing a little of this rice powder you sell? Just a touch will tone down the freckles, and no one will even notice."

"You think so?"

"I'm certain. As I said, your eyes and your smile are two of your best features. But even more so, you're sweet and you're smart. My father always said that's a hard combination to beat."

"My pa used to say that too, but I always thought he said things like that because he was my pa and was supposed to," she said, a wistful note in her voice. "Thank you so much, Lily." The young woman's gratitude touched Lily, and she resisted the urge to embrace her.

"You're more than welcome. Now I'd better go before someone sends a posse after me." Lily picked up the tissue-wrapped items and opened the door. "Remember to smile."

Amy did and called out, "Come again! Please!"

A lump rose in Lily's throat. She had just spent half an hour with a woman who had actually treated her like a human being.

"I will," she promised.

CHAPTER TWENTY-ONE

The next week passed with Lily doing a little more each day until she recovered enough to sing again. As she and Merle had agreed, her activities remained confined to the main hall downstairs. During the evening, one or two of the others would occasionally disappear upstairs for up to half-an-hour at a time.

At least two girls had to be in the hall at all times. But when Lily climbed into bed, she couldn't ignore what went on upstairs in the other rooms. Every so often she could hear a groan or a muffled curse or laugh penetrating the walls. She covered her head with her pillow and tried not to think of her sister.

She hadn't seen Tyler in days. He hadn't come by the Canary Cage nor had she caught a glimpse of him walking to or from his office, even though she took an exceptionally long time cleaning the two large plate-glass windows at the front of the saloon every other morning.

Two nights earlier, she stepped off the stage just when Merle slapped a mug of beer down in front of Carson Ward.

"You seen Buchanan lately?" Merle asked the police chief.

Carson took a long drink of the cold brew and shook his head slowly. He wiped the foam off his mustache with the sleeve of his jacket.

"Sure haven't. He was going to Oklahoma City for a couple of days, but he should have been back by now." Carson reached into his pocket for a cigar. Sally appeared in an instant with a match. He leaned over, puffing on the cigar until the tip caught. "He's probably got himself all worked up over some political meeting he went to and is writing one of his infernal editorials."

"Well, that's fine then. Just wanted to make sure none of my girls done chased him off again," Merle chuckled.

Lily turned away, tugging at her lower lip with her teeth. Was Tyler avoiding her? What Carson said sounded legitimate, but an uneasy feeling in the pit of her stomach made her wonder if she hadn't provided a bit too much dissension for the taciturn newspaperman.

His career, his livelihood, centered around searching out and reporting the news. Seemingly, he clearly intended to keep his private life confidential. He had gone to great lengths in the past to do so, even moving almost halfway across the country to escape notoriety. Was he already escaping from her?

Another two days passed without any sign of Tyler, and Lily quickly grew tired of life without him. She didn't miss him—no, that thought she plucked just as quickly as it blossomed. Without him, she had no reason to remain in Guthrie, no motivation for staying at the Canary Cage. Without being able to move forward with Tyler, her days fell into a routine she neither enjoyed nor desired. Though she gained a small measure of satisfaction when she sang and the floorboards vibrated beneath her feet from the stomps of the crowd, she rarely sang a song she liked. One of the most requested favorites was a tune from the War Between the States called, "The Luck of the Wife of a Sailor." Though she despised the song, she belted the words just as Toby had taught her. The fact that she couldn't keep from blushing from the beginning of the song until the last note faded seemed to make the men enjoy the bawdy song all the more.

She hated the unwanted advances from men who grabbed at her as she passed and who offered her anything from eternal devotion to a month's salary if she would only spend a few minutes fulfilling their varied fantasies. This she found worse than the embarrassing lyrics she sang and the less-than-modest clothing she wore. Lily didn't even want to think about what those fantasies might be.

CHAPTER TWENTY-TWO

After helping Rae Ann with the breakfast dishes, Lily swept the kitchen floor and then picked up a dusty scatter rug. Humming to herself, she pushed the screen door open with her shoulder and stepped onto the back porch. She gave the rug two healthy shakes before a loud sneeze caught her attention.

"Oh, my, Sexton LaMotte." She gasped at the sight of the clergyman, his glasses and black coat speckled with dust. Lily pursed her lips to keep from smiling at his comical expression. "I'm sorry. I didn't see you there."

"Obviously," he said with a scowl. He pulled off his glasses and allowed Lily to take them from him to wipe on her apron. He slapped at his jacket to brush off the dirt and then, retrieving his glasses, settled them firmly on his nose.

"I'm sorry," Lily said again. "I wasn't expecting anyone to be out here."

"That's all right, Lily. No harm done," he nodded magnanimously. "I wanted to see you for a moment, and I thought it more prudent to come in the back way. After all, I shouldn't make a spectacle of myself walking into the front door of a saloon."

Lily stifled another grin and the urge to tell him he had wasted his time. Instead she ushered him onto the porch and gestured for him to sit down in the rocker.

"Would you like a cup of tea?"

"I'd prefer coffee. With sugar and cream."

"Certainly." She disappeared into the kitchen, returning a moment later with a steaming cup. "It's a little cool out here. Would you rather go into the kitchen?"

"Oh, no, no," he answered, rising from the rocker to take the cup from her. He stood courteously until she sat down on the porch swing.

"I hoped to see you in church again, Lily."

Caught off guard, Lily laughed and then quieted when LaMotte's face turned red with indignation.

"Oh—sorry—for a moment I thought you were jesting. I appreciate your concern, but I confess I'm not willing to suffer that ordeal again."

He nodded in understanding and took a sip of his coffee. "Are you happy with your life here?"

Touched by the gentleness of his tone, Lily looked out across the yard and sighed. "Well, singing in a saloon certainly wasn't my dream as a little girl. For now, it's my life. And I'm dealing with my circumstances the best I can."

"What *was* your dream as a little girl?"

"Just that of almost every other little girl—to marry, have children, make a valuable contribution to society in some manner."

LaMotte nodded. "You should have that, Lily."

She laughed again, this time at the irony in the man's words. Marriage. Children. A life of service. She might have had all that had she not come to Guthrie. Would she have the chance ever again? "At this point, it doesn't look likely."

"You could leave this town, go someplace where no one knows you, and start over. I could help you. Let me help you." He reached over and put his hand over hers.

Startled, she looked up at him but couldn't see his eyes behind the reflection of his glasses. She pulled away and, refusing to oblige the desire to wipe off her hand, smoothed her hair instead. "You're very kind, but I couldn't possibly take advantage of your good heart."

LaMotte leaned back and, shaking his head, sighed. He dabbed at his forehead with a handkerchief. "I heard you had a little trouble recently."

Lily stared at him. The spat with Theo had happened two weeks ago. How absurd that the altercation had even been brought to his attention.

"It was simply a misunderstanding."

"A misunderstanding. I assure you it was much more than that."

She fought against a feeling of annoyance. "I suppose you think I should just stay within the confines of the Canary Cage and never venture onto the streets with good folks—unless, of course, I'm on my way to church to repent."

He looked startled and sweat again broke out on his forehead. "I only meant to suggest that perhaps you shouldn't venture so far from town alone. While they have, from what I understand, caught the scalawag who attacked you and Blue MacGranahan's daughter, this is still somewhat uncivilized territory."

With embarrassment, Lily realized her mistake. "Ah, yes. You are right, of course. I was referring to something else."

"Something else?"

"Of no consequence." Lily waved her hand as though to brush away an insect. "I simply have a great deal to learn."

"I'll pray for you, my dear."

She smiled uncomfortably. How horrified would the minister be if he knew her purpose for staying in Guthrie? Anxious to change the subject, she asked, "Do you know Tyler Buchanan?"

"Buchanan?" LaMotte's face stiffened, and one corner of his mouth pulled down sharply. "He's an upstanding citizen and a member of my congregation. Other than that ... why do you ask?"

"He chased off that horrid man and was quite kind to me. I hear the girls talk about him, but I don't know much about him. I thought you could give an objective ... masculine opinion."

LaMotte frowned. "I, of course, cannot dabble in gossip. But I feel I can say this much—while he's technically an eligible bachelor, I don't think the ... uh ... ladies here should think there's any future for them where he's concerned. Talk is, there may be an engagement to Miss Theodora Peebles soon. They'll make a fine match. Since they are both members of the church, I hope to officiate at the wedding ... that is if Reverend Scott is indisposed for any reason."

Lily's heart sank, surprising her with a sudden sense of devastation. A somewhat smug smile flitted across LaMotte's thin face, and she was somehow certain he enjoyed her discomfiture.

"Best that you not harbor any hopes where Buchanan is concerned. Far better that you be disappointed now than heartbroken later. I could tell you a few things about Buchanan." He hesitated. "Again, that would be gossip, and I cannot indulge."

"Well, thank you for coming by. I hope your reputation won't be injured if you're seen."

LaMotte stood and gave a slight bow. "If they know the Scriptures, they'll be familiar with the parable of the shepherd who leaves his flock of ninety-nine to search for the one sheep that is lost." He paused for a moment. "And I vow you are one lamb I will not lose."

CHAPTER TWENTY-THREE

Lily slid onto the bench beside Sally who was spearing green beans with her fork.

"I heard Edwina Peebles isn't organizing the Flower Parade this year," Sally said between bites.

Honey gave an unladylike snort and rolled her eyes heavenward. "As usual, Sally, you know just enough to know nothing that matters. She's not organizing the parade, but she might as well be. Miss Theodora herself is in charge this year." She plopped a large mound of creamed potatoes on her plate and passed the bowl to Toby. "Why should we care?"

"Parade? What parade?" Lily asked. She took the nearly empty bowl from Toby.

"The Flower Parade," Sally mumbled, her mouth full.

"Which is?"

Still chewing, Sally motioned to Rae Ann with her fork to answer the question.

"It's just a silly parade, Lily. The town has held one every year since the Opening. Most of the businesses, social clubs, and townsfolk decorate floats, their wagons, horses, carriages, whatever, with flowers. Then they parade up and down the streets. There are ribbons for first, second, and third places. After, there's a Flower Ball at night, usually at the Ione Hotel."

"And Theodora Peebles is chairing the organizing committee?" Lily probed, her irritation at that particular young woman's self-righteous attitude still not totally dissipated.

"I don't think anybody put it quite that way, but yes," Rae Ann again answered. "Edwina nominated her daughter with the excuse she wasn't well enough to head the committee herself this year. With Edwina's nomination, nobody dared suggest anybody else, so the vote was unanimous."

"All hail the mighty Peebles." Honey ripped a piece of chicken off the bone.

"Who decides the winners? Are there judges or does everybody vote?" This time, Toby answered.

"Judges. Three of them—the mayor, the editor of the *Capital City Courier*, and the manager of the Royal Opera House."

Tyler will be one of the judges. As always, he's in the thick of things. And Miss Priss is in charge of the parade. How convenient. No doubt Theo will expect—no, demand—that Tyler cast his vote for whichever float she's riding.

Considering they were among the ostracized segment of the community, Lily was amazed that her companions knew the goings-on in Guthrie in surprising detail. Whatever the event, someone at the Canary Cage knew something and somebody else knew a little more. Soon, assembling all the pieces—usually around the supper table—they came surprisingly close to the entire truth of a matter.

"The ladies of the Excelsior Club are dressing up as flowers this year. Theo's outfit is gonna be white—Queen Anne's Lace, I think," Trudy said.

All eyes turned to her in surprise. Trudy could click her heels in complex syncopation and bellow out a bawdy song with the rest of them, but she rarely had anything to add to a conversation.

"Where did you hear that?" Honey asked, lowering her fork and narrowing her eyes to golden-fringed slits.

Trudy chewed her bottom lip between uneven teeth. Her gaze darted around the room, above the heads of her supper companions. "Her daddy told me," she finally choked out.

"When?" Honey snapped.

"Last night."

"Last night?" Honey almost hissed the words. "You were with him last night?" At Trudy's skittish nod, Honey redirected her snarl to Merle. "What's going on here? He's *my* regular. I've been with him for months. What are you doing letting Trudy have him? She barely knows how to find her way upstairs much less what to do when she gets there." She let loose a string of expletives that would have surprised even hardened sensibilities.

Everyone froze as though caught under a sudden avalanche. Each face slowly turned to Merle, who calmly laid down his knife and fork and raised a somber gaze to Honey. He held her eye steadily, until she dropped her own angry stare and shifted uncomfortably on the bench.

"Number one—I thought you knew better than to use that kind of language or tone when you're talking to me. If you don't want to live by my rules, you know you're free to find some place else to hang your corset. Somebody else'll come along to fill your shoes and whatever else just fine. Number two—I don't have to explain myself to you or to nobody else. You best add that to your list of things to remember. Number three …"

Merle paused and took a drink, his eyes never leaving Honey's pale face. She managed to look at him every few seconds, so he couldn't reprimand her for not paying attention, but she primarily kept her gaze directed at her plate. Merle gently set the glass on the table and dabbed his lips with the cotton napkin. His controlled tone and the precision of his motions provided further proof of the extent of his anger.

A fly buzzed lazily above a plate still piled high with Rae Ann's fluffy biscuits, and no one bothered to shoo the insect away.

"Number three," Merle repeated, "you don't have to tell me who the regulars are—but, as always, the customer decides who he wants to spend time with. I don't have to tell you, but maybe—if you'll listen—you'll figure something out before you lose all your regulars.

"Peebles pointed out Trudy when he came in last night. Said he didn't want to listen to any whining females. Seemed he'd already had his fill at home."

That comment elicited choked giggles, and Merle gave them all a wry smile, relaxing the tension. "I don't want you hassling Trudy," Merle warned, picking up his fork and pointing the tines at Honey. "You hear?"

Honey looked up and gave him a nervous little nod.

"He didn't want me first anyways, Honey," Trudy said, her eyes wide and pleading. "He's been after Lily ever since she come here, but she won't have him. So, he settled for me. You know nobody never wants me over you."

Only Rae Ann smiled at Trudy for her genuine effort to comfort Honey. Unfortunately, everyone but Trudy knew her explanation would only escalate Honey's animosity toward Lily. Indeed, all eyes followed Honey's smoldering stare as it shifted from Trudy to Lily.

"I think we should finish our dinners before everything is totally ruined," Rae Ann said quickly, as Merle pierced a piece of baked chicken and resumed his meal.

"Trudy, did you say Theo is supposed to be Queen Anne's Lace?" Lily asked, picking up the threads of conversation and trying to retie them.

"Seems to me she'd be better suited as a snapdragon," Sally quipped.

"Or a prickly pear," Toby suggested.

"How about a plain old stinkweed?" Merle grinned—his good mood restored. Everyone appeared to be following Lily's lead in restoring camaraderie. Confirmation of this effort came, surprisingly, from Honey, now appropriately subdued.

"What about the others, Trudy?"

Toby reached over and gave Honey's hand a squeeze.

"I think he said something about a rose, a violet maybe? And, oh … now I don't remember. I'm so stupid." Trudy's lower lip trembled.

"It's okay, sweetie," Sally comforted, reaching across the table to pat the back of Trudy's hand. "You knew more than the rest of us, didn't you?"

Trudy smiled, a shy, pleased smile, and nodded hesitantly.

"So, how do we decorate our float?"

Stunned, the group turned in unison toward Lily.

"*Our* float?" they repeated in one voice.

"Yes, *our* float. Or wagon. What's our theme? What did you do last year?"

They stared at her, as though she'd lost her mind and then laughed.

"We don't have a float, Lil," Toby finally managed. "You honestly think they'd let us be in the Flower Parade?"

"Why not? You said the whole town gets involved. We're a legitimate business concern, and we're part of this town whether the *ladies* of the Excelsior Club like it or not. So why shouldn't we be in the parade?"

The women looked from one to another, knowing the answer, no one wanting to say the words aloud. The saloon girls were the less-than-desirable citizens of Guthrie. The business community respected Merle as a legitimate business owner. Malcolm had tended bar from New Orleans to San Francisco, and Toby had been offered a position at the Royal Opera House so many times he finally began hiding whenever he saw Max Benard.

What if the Canary Cage had been a restaurant instead of a saloon with the women serving steak and chicken instead of beer and hard liquor? Perhaps if men came to the Cage merely to drink, smoke, and gamble, the women who worked there would have been as acceptable as those who worked in Slocum's Cafe or Bailey's Dinner House.

"Lily's right, Merle." This time they all turned to Honey whose eyes had again narrowed, this time deep in thought. "Why shouldn't we be in the parade? It would be like advertising, right?"

Merle laid his fork down again. "Sure would be. The women would hate our participation, but then they don't like anything about us anyway, do they?" He shook his head regretfully. "They won't let us just line up with everybody and be part of the parade. I don't really see how we could manage such a thing."

"I do."

The group's attention swung to Rae Ann. "We could at least be in it for a block or two. The parade always starts at Capitol Hill. It goes west down Oklahoma around to First Street, then down Harrison back to Division. It ends at Island Park for a big picnic."

"Okay. Where does that get us?" Merle asked.

"The livery!" Toby exclaimed.

Rae Ann leaned back in her chair and nodded with satisfaction.

Sally sighed. "I still don't get it."

"I do!" Lily said, excitement creeping into her voice. "They may not let us participate in the whole parade like everyone else, but—like Rae Ann says—we can tag onto the end for at least a block or two. If we set up our wagon in the livery, we can wait in the alley near Division and Oklahoma and pull out after the last wagon goes by."

The room almost buzzed with enthusiasm. They had never considered doing something as a group, especially something that would solidify them as a unit and most likely bring down even more censure. Later, after the initial fervor wore off, they probably would decide against participating in the parade. At least, for the moment, they reveled in the idea that they could actually defy the segment of the township that snubbed them.

"A theme. We need a theme," Honey interrupted the hubbub.

"Why not just *the Canary Cage*?" All eyes turned to Toby. "We could make a wire cage, like the one we have on stage, and cover the entire structure with flowers."

"The committee's dressing as flowers. Why don't we dress you girls as birds? It's a fitting theme," Rae Ann added.

"Birds?" Trudy wrinkled her nose. "How can we be birds?"

"Like canaries," Lily responded, "blue jays, cardinals. There are so many colorful birds."

"I'll make simple gowns in different colors, and you can wear feathers in your hair." Rae Ann rummaged through a drawer for paper and pencil.

"I can make the cage," Toby said.

"What kind of bird would I be?" Trudy's plaintive voice broke in.

"Maybe you could be a bluebird. You look lovely in blue," Rae Ann looked at the others for confirmation.

"And Sally looks fabulous in red—she could be a cardinal," Lily added, wondering how long the group effort would continue without one of the birds flying south.

"I like red," Sally said with a smile. "I was afraid you'd make me the brown sparrow."

"That's an idea," Toby chuckled. "You could be a robin dressed all in brown except for the red chest."

Everyone turned to stare at him, and Toby's face turned as red as the robin's breast in question but laughed with everyone else.

"The canary." Merle leaned back in his chair.

"That's the most important," Sally said.

Everyone's eyes skittered from Honey to Lily and back again.

"There's no question as far as I'm concerned," Lily finally said. They watched as one of Honey's eyebrows rose in silent challenge.

"It has to be Honey. The canary has to be yellow, and I can't wear yellow even on my best day. Honey looks beautiful in yellow."

The canary would be the focal point, the figurehead. When all eyes turned toward Honey, she nodded. Then she looked to Merle. "That okay with you?"

Merle held her gaze steadily before he spoke. "I think it's fitting. You've been here the longest next to Sally. You suggested the two of you try putting on a little show." He nodded again, and Honey smiled at him.

"That leaves Lily," Sally said.

"She looks real nice in white," Trudy said.

"A dove," Merle said without hesitation. "She seems to spend a lot of her time peacemaking. And Trudy's right. Lily looks great in white with that dark hair and fair skin." He grinned. "She'll sure look better than Miss Queen Anne's Lace."

"Theo's gonna look like a washed-out weed next to our dove," Rae Ann said, laughing.

"*Ooooh,* she's gonna be so mad." Sally giggled, and the rest of the table agreed with equal amounts of joviality.

"Merle, what about you, Rae Ann, Toby, and Malcolm? Shouldn't we all be on the float?" Lily asked.

Rae Ann slapped her hand on the table in protest. "Dear heavens, no, child. You don't need a scarecrow like me up there."

All four women objected to her choice of words, but she waved them down. "I've got enough to do—we all do—without spending time being worried out of my wits. I'm definitely an in-the-back person."

"And I'm not comfortable in front of people unless I have a piano to protect me," Toby said.

"I think you birds are enough," Merle pushed back his chair and stood, putting an end to the question.

"Are we just gonna stand there and ride down the street?" Trudy asked, her voice trembling. "I don't know if I like that."

"We could sing," Honey said.

"Of course!" Lily seconded. "Maybe something that would surprise people."

Merle frowned, his lips pulled down in a mock disapproving scowl. "Something like 'Amazing Grace?' Forget it. The parade would turn into a lynching."

"Lily's not stupid," Honey spoke up, obviously not appreciating his attempt at humor. "She means something people wouldn't expect from us. They'd expect something like 'Garden of Delights' or 'Bed of Roses,' but what if we sing something—oh, I don't know—pretty, something that shows we actually have a little talent." Honey paused and gestured at Lily though her attention remained focused on Merle. "Maybe something like the song Lily sang for you that first day."

Lily felt a little catch in her chest at yet another attempt by Honey to seemingly repair their strained relationship. How could Honey have changed so radically over the course of one meal? She'd ponder that later. Right now, she would meet Honey at least halfway.

"That's brilliant, Honey." Lily smiled, pleasantly surprised to see Honey blush. "She's right, you know." Lily directed her statement to the rest of the table. "The committee's going to be furious enough at us for disrupting their perfectly planned parade. We might as well really heap coals of fire on their heads by singing something to turn the church choir or the manager of the Opera House green with envy."

Sally lifted her chin, her brown eyes soft and sad. "They talk about us like we're trash, like we're not fit to walk on the same street with them. Like the only thing we're good for is takin' care of their husbands on occasion to save them from their wifely duties. They say we sing like croakin' bullfrogs … that it doesn't matter because the fellas go deaf when we show our legs and don't hear how we sound anyway. So I agree. Let's show 'em all. Maybe we could—"

"Show them we're as talented downstairs as we are upstairs," Honey finished.

"Or vice versa," Toby mumbled, smothering a grin and holding up his hands to fend off Honey's playful slap.

"Then the decision's made," Rae Ann stood and stacked the empty dishes. "I'll get started on the outfits … Toby, why don't you draw up a pattern for the cage. Girls, you pick out your music, and Merle …" She stopped and turned to their boss who stood at the stove pouring himself another cup of coffee. "Merle? Do you want to be in on this or would you rather plead ignorant?"

Merle ran his tongue over the edges of his front teeth and took a tentative sip of the steaming coffee. "Both," he decided, grinning over the rim of the mug. "I'll set things up at the livery. Tallman owes me." His gaze flickered to the instigator of the escapade. "And he owes Lily, and he knows it. He'll lend us a spare stall and keep his mouth shut. I'll arrange to have the flowers sent over—"

"That won't work," Rae Ann said. "His wife is a gossip, and it'll be all over town that we're up to something."

The group gave a collective moan, and their high spirits settled like a sudden fog.

"Now wait a minute," Lily said, not willing to give up so easily. "Let me talk to Amy Gibson. Maybe she can place the order for us."

Rae Ann nodded. "You know, that might work. Gibson's used to have a float every year. Poor Amy hasn't had the time or enough help to decorate a float or even a wheelbarrow for the parade since her pa passed. She wouldn't raise any suspicions if she got flowers."

"But why would she help?" Honey cut in. "I've been in her store too many times to count, and she won't even look me in the face. She'll probably have Theo on our tails faster than a blink."

Lily smiled. "She's nothing like the other so-called ladies in this town. She wouldn't look at you because she thinks you're pretty."

Honey eyed her skeptically but held her tongue.

"Truly. I thought the same thing when she avoided me a couple of weeks ago. Theo came in and started giving her a hard time over a special order. Then Theo spotted me, and she lit into both of us—Amy for allowing *our kind* in the store and fouling it for decent women—and then she took me to task for having the audacity to breathe the same air as she. Tyler Buchanan came in and—well, anyway, I apologized to Amy for causing such a to-do. But she would have none of it. She admitted she's self-conscious about her appearance. That's why she looks away when someone pretty comes through the door. It's actually a compliment, Honey."

Sally chimed in excitedly. "I was in there yesterday, and I thought she seemed friendlier than usual. She had a new haircut that made her look like a different girl. I told her she looked real uptown, and she turned so red her freckles disappeared. She said a friend had suggested she try the new style."

They all turned to Lily, who merely shrugged.

Toby scratched the end of his nose with his index finger. "You might have a friend there, Lily, but she still has a business to run. She might not want to publicly take sides with us."

At the unison murmur of disappointed agreement, Lily stood and put her hands on her hips in exasperation. "Let me talk to her before we agree the plan's not going to work. Since she used to be in the parade, she may at the very least have a few helpful suggestions as to how we might pull this off."

Trudy brought up the one point the rest of them had overlooked.

"I've spent all my money on a new corset and real silk stockings. I don't have anything left to pay for my costume," she fretted.

Money. Lily—no, *Melissa*—could have financed the whole thing with money she usually kept in a cookie jar. But *Lily* shouldn't have any more money than Sally, Trudy or Honey. Less, in fact, since she refused the opportunities to earn anything extra. How could she offer to pay?

Merle barked a short laugh and handed his empty coffee cup to Rae Ann.

"Oh, don't go dragging your tailfeathers in the dust. If you pull this off, I'll foot the bill." He smiled craftily as he opened the door leading to the hallway. "Truth be told, I'd pay a lot more just to see the look on Edwina Peebles's face. Enough of this for now, kids. Get moving. We open in an hour."

CHAPTER TWENTY-FOUR

Lily entered Gibson's Sundries just as Amy hurried out of the storeroom carrying a bolt of cloth. A smile brightened her face when she spotted Lily.

"I did it!" Amy set the cloth on the counter and patted her stylish new hairdo. "What do you think?"

"Let me see." Lily crossed her arms, laid one finger against her lips, and circled Amy as if purchasing a mare.

"Well … what *do* you think?"

Lily drew her brows together as she faced Amy. "I think it's"—pausing as though searching for the proper description— "perfect!" She clapped her hands and grinned.

Amy's anxious look faded at Lily's enthusiastic pronouncement, and the young redhead threw her arms around Lily and hugged her tightly.

"Thank you, thank you, thank you. I've had so many compliments, and I don't even recognize myself in the mirror. In fact," she dropped her voice to a whisper and looked around conspiratorially even though no one else had come into the shop. "I've even been asked to join a certain police chief for dinner at the Royal."

Lily, warmed by Amy's excitement and her spontaneous show of affection, could only congratulate her with sincerity. Lily watched with dismay as Amy's confidence faded quickly.

"I've only changed my hairstyle. I'm sure the novelty will wear off. Underneath, I'm the same old boring Amy."

Lily gave Amy a little shake. "Now you just stop that. The haircut only made someone stop and take a second look. Now that he has, he can't help but see what a wonderful woman you are. If you really like him, then let him see the real you. Look him straight in the eye and smile, Amy … for goodness sake, smile."

Relieved when Amy's good humor returned, Lily changed the topic of conversation.

"By the way, did Theo's hairpins come in yet?"

Amy grimaced. "In a word, no. Her party is tonight, and she has come by twice a day for the past two weeks. She doesn't care one bit that the mail comes once a day or that I promised her I would shut down the shop and deliver them myself immediately. Of course, I've braved her wrath and reminded her each time that we can't expect them this soon. I knew they couldn't possibly be delivered on time."

"She will pay you for them when they finally come in, won't she?"

Amy shrugged. "Oh, she'll want them all right. Even if she doesn't, she never pays me directly. I send her father a bill, and he pays without question."

"What about her threats? Has she—or will she follow through? I would hate for our friendship to harm your business."

Amy smiled warmly as she dusted the already-clean counter with her apron. "Even if she does, and even if they actually listened to her, I doubt any harm would last long. They'd have to go clear across town to buy most of the items they can get here. And most of them have accounts with me. Besides, anyone who would listen to Theo isn't someone I care much about losing as a customer. I tell you, I wish somebody would do something—anything—to knock that young woman down a few pegs."

At that, Lily smiled. "If you're serious about that, Amy, there just might be a little something we can do."

Amy raised her eyebrows and leaned toward Lily. "Exactly what do you have in mind?

CHAPTER TWENTY-FIVE

Dinner dragged on interminably. Between Theo's simpering and Winifred Mandeval's viperish antagonism toward Oklahoma gaining statehood, Tyler thought he would go mad. On the one hand, the idea of an apathetic featherbrain like Theo having equal rights in a political arena almost made Tyler feel the fight unworthy of the effort. Winifred's combative fervor also had him reconsidering his supportive stance.

While the cuisine at the Peebles's usually rivaled that in Charleston's best restaurants, tonight the food tasted as bland and dry as Mojave sand. With almost genuine eagerness, Tyler agreed to Theo's suggestion of a moonlight walk in the garden. He inhaled deeply, pulling the cool evening air into his lungs, clearing his head. Though he clasped his hands behind his back, Theo still managed to loop her arm through his. Sashaying down the stairs, she led him down the torch-lit path. Her skirts brushed his legs, and she took every opportunity to rub against his elbow. She remained silent for a moment. They could hear nature's night songs, as well as horses, carriages, noisy ranch hands, and other evidence of the world beyond the ten-foot-high hedge that bordered the yard.

He had been in another garden eerily similar to this one, years ago in Charleston. Invited to an anniversary party after Rogan's death had been ruled accidental, he mistakenly thought the humiliation of the trial had ended.

Wrong.

No sooner had he stepped down from his carriage than a horde of reporters surrounded him. His host fought through the badgering swarm and dragged Tyler into the house. Trying to shut the front door against the intruders, Henry gave a reporter who tried to shoulder his way into the house a mighty shove and slammed the bolt.

"I didn't know you planned to bring your friends along, Tyler," Henry had said good-naturedly, slapping Tyler on the back.

"Neither did I," Tyler said, embarrassed. His shame sprang not only from the scene he had caused. Before the trial, the reporters out front had been his friends and peers. At the first word of Rogan Buchanan's death, they had turned on him. Tyler had learned how much many of them actually despised him. He was heir to the largest shipping empire in the South. In addition, his father owned *The Charleston Courier*, where Tyler and Rogan had cut their teeth. They had worked every job from custodian to delivery boy, typesetter to pressman, reporter to copy editor. Just before the accident, Tyler had been named executive editor and was astounded to find himself the object of much resentment.

Though reluctant to attend Henry and Ellen Cadwell's anniversary party, yet loath to turn aside any offers of friendship, he accepted at their insistence. The gala had scarcely begun before the police arrived and an officer pounded on the door.

"I'll handle this, Tyler," Henry had assured him. "Why don't you get some fresh air? Go out to the garden."

Awash in shame, Tyler had done as he was told. He had hidden, yes, *hidden*, he would later admit to himself, until Henry had diffused the situation. The reporter Henry pushed had fallen down the stairs and twisted his ankle. Henry agreed not to press trespassing and harassment charges against the reporters still amassed on the front lawn, trampling his wife's prize-winning rose bushes, if the reporter would drop assault charges against Henry. The police officer directed the reporters back onto public property and then stood guard to protect the property and privacy of the highly-respected businessman.

Tyler waited in the garden until Henry came with the news that the situation had been handled. Tyler stayed only a short while longer, smiling stiffly, offering his congratulations and his most sincere apologies to his host and hostess. He left in humiliation, taking the back door and managing to elude the crowd still lurking at the front gate.

He couldn't believe his life had come to this. Because of him, a policeman had come to the door of the Cadwell mansion to investigate another incident. Tyler berated himself—he was a coward. He had been strong for so long. Strong for his parents, strong for Allegra, strong for himself. He had shouldered the scandal with all the dignity and pride he could muster.

He hadn't even been allowed time to grieve for Rogan, his beloved brother, who had been caught in an emotional crossfire between Tyler and his latest paramour Allegra. He had held all his grief, his despair, at bay until after the trial. Then he would have time, whether that be time in prison or while putting his life back together. But the ordeal went on, and the constant publicity continued to hurt not only those few who had remained his friends but his parents as well.

Tyler vowed never again to put himself, his family, or his friends in the position of being ridiculed because of his mistakes. He had fled and settled in Guthrie where he found himself once more in the garden of a friend.

Most people in Guthrie knew nothing of the scandal in Charleston. Even if they had read the reports, they never made the connection between the hard-working, somber, and well-respected newspaper publisher and the rash hell-raiser he had once been. He had worked tenaciously to become a man his parents could at long last be proud to call their son, the man his brother should have emulated, a man whose reflection he could finally see without feeling shame.

The guilt would always be there. Though he had not pulled the trigger, he had protected Allegra and had taken full responsibility for Rogan's death, carrying the tragedy with him every moment, every day. He couldn't undo the past, but he could live his life so as to never again bring shame to his parents, his family name, or his heavenly Father. Here in Guthrie he would marry, have children, and be a good husband, a good father, a good citizen.

Theo tugged on his arm, her petulant tone pulling him back to the present. Tyler stared down at her.

She's actually a pretty girl. His gaze roamed over her apricot-hued skin.

Theo's smile faded uncertainly as he studied her, but she held his gaze, her blue eyes seemingly filled with affection.

She expects me to marry her.

The thought, for once not unpleasant, arose abruptly. Saddened by his thoughts of the past and somewhat benumbed by the moonlight, the torchlight, and the beautiful garden, he reminded himself of his resolution.

Theo's pale blond hair wisped softly around her face in the breeze, and he reached out to smooth a drifting lock. She closed her eyes and turned her face into his hand, pressing her lips against his palm. Though surprised at another display of her forwardness, he bent down and brushed a gentle, fleeting kiss on her lips.

"Happy birthday, Theo," he whispered.

She opened her eyes and smiled up at him, her eyes bright with ecstasy. "Oh, it is, Tyler! It truly is, and you have made it so."

Her obvious pleasure gave Tyler sudden pause. What the blazes was he thinking? He couldn't marry her. Regardless of her apparent suitability, marriage to Theo was out of the question. He had always known the truth. *I don't love her ... even if I tried, I never could.*

He quickly tallied his impressions of her much as he would a balance sheet, comparing assets and liabilities and arriving at a net worth or, in his thinking, a responsible decision.

On the plus side, she had a pretty face and a fine figure. Good family with good standing in the community. And she obviously cared for him. On the other hand, if he put stock in such things as physical attributes, her looks and figure would soon go the way of her mother's. Vapid and self-centered, petty, pretentious, and—recalling Theo's vitriolic quarrel with Lily and Amy Gibson—he could add cruel and spiteful to the list. And, of the utmost importance, he had never once had a conversation with her that revealed any devotion to God, regardless of her weekly attendance in church.

As much as he admired her father, Tyler could not picture himself with Theo by his side. She would demand to be pampered and petted. She would expect him to accompany her on Guthrie's social circuit which, while not nearly as extensive as that in Charleston, could still take up an inordinate amount of time. Would Theo enjoy sitting by the fireside, content to talk or perhaps spend the evening reading? He almost laughed aloud. He had never enjoyed a conversation with Theo, his thoughts often wandering, as they did now, whenever in her company.

She could never be his partner, working at his side toward a common, worthwhile goal. Living in a beautiful house with modern furnishings, wearing the latest fashions, and holding a prominent place in society— only these things mattered to her. Yes, she would give him children or at least a child. Tyler almost shuddered at the thought.

She would not, however, be much of a mother. And he had no doubt she would demand a nanny. Thinking back to his own happy and nurturing childhood, he knew his heart would break to see his own children suffer from the lack of a loving, committed mother.

"Tyler," Theo said in a whine that made Tyler cringe, "what's wrong? You've been staring for ever so long. What are you thinking? You gave me such a divine kiss—simply divine—but you haven't said a word since." Her eyelids fluttered, and she pouted coquettishly. "Didn't you like kissing me?"

Tyler raked his fingers through his hair and loosened her hold on his arm, then took a step backward. He sat on a low, stone wall that encircled a goldfish pond and looked up at her. For a man who wrote for a living, he was having a remarkably difficult time finding the right words.

Theo stood above him expectantly, her yellow gown drenched in moonlight, her eyes sparkling. He sighed and bit the bullet.

"No, Theo, of course it's not you. It's me," he said and glanced away, not wanting to see the hurt in her eyes. "I haven't been playing fair." He laughed inwardly at his choice of words and the childish pout she once again employed. "Your friendship and that of your parents mean a great deal to me, but"—he paused at the ominous look on her face—"I am concerned that my affection …"

Theo's expression again brightened at the word *affection*. She bent over him, her hands framing his rugged jawbones, her face inches away from his.

"Tyler, don't say any more. I know we've been out here a long time, and you're concerned about compromising me. But don't worry, please don't worry. No one's even missed us. Besides, Mama and Papa know how I feel about you and have felt about you since I was a little girl." She placed a finger against his lips when he started to interrupt. "They'll understand. Believe me, they'll understand."

Before he could respond or even blink, she turned his face upwards and desperately pressed her lips to his. He grasped her wrists, but she held him fast. Since she stood and he was seated, she had the advantage. He could not shake free without using more force than was appropriate. When she finally released him and stepped back, laughing and blushing, his hair was mussed and his mouth hung open from her thorough kiss. He couldn't think of anything remotely suitable to say.

Theo tugged at him, urging him to stand.

"Tyler, this is the most wonderful night of my life. All I want to do now is dance, dance, dance!" She started toward the house with Tyler in tow but jerked to a stop when Tyler refused to take another step.

"Wait, Theo," he began, an unpleasant taste filling his mouth. "I'm afraid I've expressed myself badly, and I have to set things straight between us. Now."

Theo turned, her smile fading. His somber tone finally seemed to have gotten through to her. He held her gaze and shook his head.

"No, Tyler. There's no need to say anything. I believe I understand perfectly. But I want you to understand two things—that strumpet Lily will ruin you, and I won't wait for you forever."

Her face contorted with fury and humiliation, she turned and made her way back to the house, her head held high, her shoulders well back.

CHAPTER TWENTY-SIX

Lily added the final touches to the harnesses and straw hats that would be worn by the two horses pulling the flatbed.

"Done," Toby announced, fastening one last flower to the top of the wire cage before jumping down from the wagon.

Sally and Honey had already finished lining the outside of the wagon in alternating rows of lavender and violet flowers.

Trudy clasped her hands. "It's so beautiful," she said with a sigh.

Rae Ann urged them to hurry. "I've got your dresses and makeup in the stall next door. Merle paid the boy to clean it up nice and then he hung up a mirror for you."

The young women started for the makeshift dressing room, and Rae Ann hurried after them. "Maybe you could go a little lighter on the makeup than usual?"

"Sounds like a good idea," Toby agreed. "It's broad daylight and you're pretty enough without greasepaint."

"I can't believe I'm so nervous," Sally said, stepping into her scarlet dress. "You'd think I'd never sung in public before."

"It sure feels different than singing at the saloon," Trudy echoed. She trembled all over, and Lily touched her shoulder reassuringly.

Honey sniffed and vigorously brushed her lush blond hair until it crackled.

"The only difference is that we're showing off our voices instead of our legs. Besides, the men will probably be as drunk as usual."

Rae Ann shushed them. "You girls are going to do just fine. You all look beautiful, and you've worked hard on your song. You're gonna do Merle and yourselves proud—even if Miss Theo comes after us like a she-devil."

Everyone laughed but Lily. She suddenly felt as if the weight of the world, at least her little corner, rested on her shoulders. This whole escapade had been her idea, and now she wondered if they should see their plan through. While the men of Guthrie enjoyed spending an evening drinking, gambling, and gawking at the entertainment at the Cage, what would be their reactions when in the company of their wives and daughters? Would this be a triumph or a debacle?

If all went according to plan, they would share in the small victory. If they failed, the responsibility would be Lily's alone. And then there was Tyler. What would Tyler think? Would he applaud their bravado or shun them to maintain his own status?

Lily blew out a sigh and smoothed the skirt of the white sheath Rae Ann had fashioned for her. She settled the white feather boa around her neck and fastened white feathers in her hair.

"Here comes the first float," the livery boy called from his position in the hayloft.

"Easy, girls. There's plenty of time," Rae Ann soothed. "Don't go gettin' your tailfeathers ruffled."

Tyler pulled off his hat and wiped the sweat from his forehead with his sleeve. Whoever would have expected such a heat wave this late in the year? The seemingly endless stream of flower-bedecked floats, wagons, carriages, and horses kicked up clouds of dust that settled in a fine powder on everything and everyone.

Tyler squinted and shielded his eyes with his hat to see if the end was in sight. Not yet. He looked over the mayor's shoulder and scanned the list of registrants. Fifty-six carriages and single riders. Amy Gibson, float number forty-seven, had failed to check in. Tyler frowned. He'd stop in at the store later to make sure she was all right. Turning his attention back to the parade, he nodded in response to the coy smiles and waves from the young ladies of the Shakespeare Club in their gaily decorated wagon representing their interpretation of *A Midsummer Night's Dream.*

"That's an interesting attempt," said Max Benard, the manager of the Opera House.

Mayor Berkey concurred. "Perhaps we could consider the Shakespeare Club for second place. After all, first place should go to the ladies of the Excelsior Club considering they've done a fine job organizing the parade. I hear they've put in quite an effort this year."

"That's true." Max loosened his tie with a gnarled forefinger.

"Oh, for heaven's sake," Tyler said. "Their float hasn't even gone by, and you've already decided? I thought everyone got a fair shake in this country."

Berkey turned, his eyebrows raised. "What the blazes got in your ear, Buchanan? We're just trying to get this thing done with as quick as we can, so we can get out of this blasted heat." He stopped for a breath and leveled a curious eye at Tyler. "What's your objection?"

Tyler shrugged and shook his head wearily.

"None, Lucas. I guess I'm just tired and sweltering like everybody else. Awful hot for this time of year. I was up too late last night, and I've got dirt in my mouth. Actually, I don't care who we pin the blue ribbon on." Pulling his hat lower, he peered down the street again, vainly seeking the end of the line. "Just as long as we get it over with soon."

His eyes wandered idly over the entries from the Capitol National Bank, Beadles Shoe House, and Miller's Kitchen. He had turned his gaze toward the Canary Cage too many times that morning. Out on the sidewalk, Merle, Rae Ann, and Malcolm leaned elbow to elbow against the railing. Toby and the girls must be somewhere inside. Tyler frowned. Unusual. In all the years since the first Novelty Parade, the staff of the Canary Cage had lined the front of the saloon, purposely wearing their most ostentatious garments, whistling and yelling at the passing floats, and making nuisances of themselves. Changing the route had been considered at one point, but the route was as much a tradition as the parade itself. Besides, a course that avoided every saloon in town would be as meandering as a goat path. So, the townswomen tolerated the saloon girls as necessary evils, much like the dust clinging to their heated complexions and the flies hovering around the horses. Meanwhile, the men managed to nod their heads in seeming accord with their wives' distaste, as they surreptitiously ogled the girls more than they watched the parade.

Gritting his teeth in aggravation, Tyler simultaneously clenched his fists. He'd been looking for Lily again, a thought he hadn't admitted until this moment. His gaze continuously wandered up the street, along the boardwalk to the Canary Cage, and even to the open upstairs windows … up and down the avenue where people leaned out to get a better vantage point.

Disgusted anew with his apparent lack of self-control regarding Lily, Tyler purposely leveled his concentration on the parade, determined to keep his mind off her. More club floats passed … the Guthrie Club, the Benevolent Society, the Cambridge Club, the Sorosis Club, and the Acorn Club. He took off his hat and wiped his perspiring forehead with a handkerchief. He hadn't lied about staying up too late the night before. In fact, he had been working late almost every night for weeks—not so much because of a heavy workload, but because he hadn't accomplished all he needed to during the day.

He considered himself to be level-headed … most of the time … and berated himself almost hourly for the number of times his attention wandered to search the pedestrians or the windows of the Canary Cage for a glimpse of Lily. He had seen her there on Tuesday, standing on a chair washing the plate glass window, her cotton dress stretching with her movements. A glimpse of her slim ankles had replayed in his memory all afternoon and far into the night. Even more often his mind returned to the afternoon in his office when he had thrown all his resolution to the wind and kissed her. Just remembering her ardent response to his impetuous show of desire caused his blood to stir. Tyler smoothed his tie.

She's a confusing little bit. When he unexpectedly succumbed to her enticing invitation, her response seemed somehow inexperienced. She had none of the practiced technique of the women with whom he had been involved. Instead she had responded with a passion that seemed innocent and surprisingly genuine.

He had felt the fluttering of her heart, and his pulse raced again as he remembered her body pressing against him. He wondered then what her response would have been had he urged her further. Would she have stayed in character, playing her role as an uncertain novice or would she, with the rising of desire, betray herself and show her true level of expertise? Then again, he acknowledged, the professional women he had known preferred to playact at passion—rarely feeling the authentic article.

On the other hand, Tyler grinned cynically to himself, they'd all claimed him to be the exception, that he could arouse feelings that had long lain dormant. He hadn't cared one way or the other. After all, these hadn't been affairs of the heart, just conveniences of a physical nature. He'd kept himself from those physical entanglements ever since he'd come to know the Lord. Nor had he allowed his heart to become involved with anyone since Allegra. At the sudden intrusion of that unwelcome image, Tyler shook recollection from his mind and refocused on the parade.

And just in time. He gave Theo a half-hearted nod, and she seemed more than a little piqued. Had she been trying to attract his attention before now? Her miffed expression lifted as she curtsied regally to Tyler and the other judges, favoring Tyler with a smile that to a besotted suitor would have been dazzling. To Tyler, Theo simply became more and more tiresome.

The members of the Excelsior Club had outfitted themselves to represent flowers, although Tyler was at a loss as to what some of those flowers might be. Theo wore a tiara on her pale blond hair to further symbolize her blossom of choice—Queen Anne's Lace. Though her cheeks flushed from the heat, the white lace gown made her pallid skin look even more colorless. Still, Tyler reluctantly admitted, the blue ribbon should be awarded to the imaginative and colorful Excelsior hostess float.

As the applause began to wane, melodic female voices wafted up toward the judges' stand. Conversation stalled as people turned, craning their necks and standing on tiptoe, to see the origin of the lovely strains. Suddenly, the air came alive with exclamations of surprise and dismay as the Canary Cage float turned the corner and continued up the street.

Toby drove the buckboard, clicking his tongue and slapping the reins gently against the horses' rumps. A cage, fabricated of wire with yellow chrysanthemums entwined on the bars, sat in the center of the wagon bed. Honey, dressed in buttercup yellow, stood in the door of the cage. Their gowns fashioned in a simple Grecian style with Trudy in cornflower blue, Sally in ruby red, and Lily in snow white. They had smoothed their hair straight back with curls cascading down the back. Matching feathers fastened in bands surrounded their heads, and feathers sewn on gauzy shawls draped around their shoulders. No one could deny the elegance of the unusual costumes, or what they represented.

Chatter dwindled in amazement as the float neared and the voices grew clearer and stronger. The girls were singing a love song, their voices blending in perfect four-part harmony.

> I'll follow you, however far
> Or hard the fate to which you're going
> I'll follow you, my shining star
> Where gentle breeze or gales are blowing
> Across land and sea, I'll follow you.

As usual, Lily carried the melody line, and the sound of her lovely, clear voice went straight through Tyler as if he heard the popular song for the first time. His stunned reaction quickly gave way to reluctant admiration, and he struggled to hide his grin.

> I've said my last goodbyes to all
> And cried to think I'll see them never
> But when I heard your dear voice call
> I knew I'd follow you forever
> Across land and sea, I'll follow you.

"They are good, aren't they?" Max Benard murmured. "I could use them at the Opera House. Who in tarnation are they?"

The mayor frowned, scanning the long list of participants he held in his hand. "The Excelsior Club was supposed to be last. Amy Gibson registered and is the only one who didn't sign in—but that obviously isn't Miss Gibson. Whoever they are, they're not registered, but they sure sound familiar. Maybe they're in the church choir?"

Tyler snorted, hardly able to contain his laughter. "Not likely. Those talented young ladies work at the Canary Cage. That's why you recognize them, Mayor."

Max's eyes widened in surprise, and he stared at the mayor's suddenly flushed face. "The Canary Cage? Why, of course, Merle has been crowing about his Songbird of the East. But I paid him no mind. What's her name?"

The mayor and Tyler answered in unison. "Lily."

"Lily," Max nodded, his eyes narrowing as he stared at her. "I wonder if Brooks has heard her sing ..."

Toby drove the wagon past the judges and continued down the block. Tyler scanned the mixed reactions of the onlookers. Women expressed their offended sensibilities with clenched jaws and eyes spitting fire. The single men whooped and hollered, applauding the saloon girls' audacity, while the married men took their cues from their wives and either frowned in condemnation or looked away red-faced.

"A real looker with actual talent," Max mused. "What the Sam Hill is she doing at the Canary Cage?"

Tyler shook his head, his gaze following the wagon … and Lily … down the street. "I don't have the faintest idea, Max."

"Well, more to the point," Berkey cut in, "what are we going to do about this?"

Tyler and Max turned their attention to the mayor.

"Do about what?" Max asked.

"This mess. It's an affront to the decent folks of this community. Should we have them arrested?"

"Arrested?" Tyler barked. "For what?"

"For having imagination and talent?" Max moved to stand shoulder to shoulder with Tyler.

"Look here, I'm the mayor. I've got to do something." Berkey gestured toward the crowd who had turned as a group to watch as Toby turned the wagon off the main road and the voices faded. "The townspeople are not happy."

"Blast it, Berkey, who cares?" Tyler scoffed, fully irritated. "They haven't broken any laws. If anything, they're guilty of either a little poor judgment or maybe a lot of guts. Let's just decide the winners and get out of this heat."

"He's right," Max said. "If you've got to do something, just go have a talk with Merle and advise him to keep his birds in their cage where they belong—even though they were by far the most entertaining thing I've seen in a while. And though I admit I wouldn't mind stealing his Songbird, the girls don't need to be riling up the citizens."

The mayor thought a moment and then nodded. "Okay, then. Let's choose the winners. Tyler, are you going to be at the dance at the Opera House when I award the ribbons?"

"Depends," Tyler said warily, watching as a wilted but irate young woman dressed as Queen Anne's Lace stalked in long, unladylike strides toward her father.

CHAPTER TWENTY-SEVEN

Lily could barely hear herself think above the hubbub. The parade may have ended, but excitement over their escapade filled the saloon.

"Do something, Daddy! You've simply got to *doooooo* something!" Toby wailed in mocking falsetto. Malcolm swiped a damp cloth across the bar and tried not to grin, but the others in the saloon had no such compulsion.

Laughing, Honey joined Toby on the piano bench. She thrust her shoulders back and ducked her chin, barking out in a gruff tone, "Now, now, Theodora, settle down, darlin'. You're causin' a scene."

"But they've ruined everything!" Sally whined in a shrill voice. "It's not fair! It's just not fair!"

The laughter dwindled when the entrance doors swung open. Merle suddenly stood, his grin fading. "Good evening, mayor. Good evening, Theodore," he said.

Mayor Berkey and Theodore Peebles, dressed in their evening finery, nodded formally in return.

"I'd like a word, Merle."

"Sure, Mayor. My office?"

"Out front will be fine," Theodore said. "Ladies," he added, his gaze sweeping across the occupants of the saloon, finally settling on Honey and spearing her with cold disapproval. She looked away and scooted a little closer to Toby.

Merle coughed, drawing Theodore's attention, and moved to follow the mayor through the swinging doors. "Toby, play something. Girls, probably won't be much business tonight, so we'll take it easy. Enjoy yourselves."

Lily took advantage of Merle's directive and slipped out the back door to settle on the swing. She spent more and more of her free moments on the porch, unable to bear her room for much more than changing her clothes and sleeping. The memory of Augusta was too heavy there.

A mournful melody threaded its way out the open door, as Toby played a few chords and then began an old Civil War ballad. The song had at one time been banned by several commanding officers as its plaintive melody and haunting lyrics caused homesick soldiers to abandon their posts and head for home. After a few bars, Toby began to sing, his voice a lilting tenor.

> The years creep slowly by, Lorena
> The snow is on the grass again
> The sun's low down the sky, Lorena
> The frost gleams where the flowers have been
> But the heart throbs on as warmly now
> As when the summer days were nigh
> Oh, the sun can never dip so low
> A-down affection's cloudless sky …

Lily had heard Toby sing once before, and she again marveled at his talent. Why had he chosen to play in a saloon? And Honey, with her obvious intelligence, could have been a schoolteacher or worked in a shop. With the exception of Trudy, who truly seemed to need someone to look after her, she could picture them all with reputable occupations. These people, still a mystery to her, called the Canary Cage home by choice. What had prompted those choices? Why did they seem to believe they now had no choice but to stay?

The temperature dropped when the sun set, and Lily pulled her shawl tighter around her shoulders. For a moment, she fingered the finely woven wool, noting the contrast between its rich texture and the cheap satin of her dress. The gown had been Roxie's, and while the emerald green flattered Lily's complexion, the stiffness of the second-rate fabric chafed her skin. Had Roxie grown accustomed to wearing a tawdry wardrobe? Had she totally forgotten the comforts of her youth? Had she too felt imprisoned by the regrettable choices that had brought her to the Canary Cage? Did she remember how being loved, safe, and pampered had felt?

Lily sighed and laughed disdainfully at herself. How could she judge— or even question—the others? She too had made choices, and she now lived the consequences of those choices. Had her initial motivation been a desire to know the truth, instead of an obsession with vengeance, she may have found her answers long ago without becoming ensnared in her own lies.

The truth had been evident, but nowadays confusion overwhelmed her. Tyler *had* to be responsible for Roxie's death—Augusta's death. Lily groaned and covered her face with her hands. Augusta. Roxie. Augusta the little sister. Roxie the saloon girl. How could they be the same person? How could Roxie now seem more real to her than Augusta? Lily sighed. And Tyler—how could he be the cause of her sister's death and yet cause her heart to flutter with an emotion she hesitated to admit? She had become a traitor—not only to Augusta, but to herself, and to her father and all he had taught her.

"Good evening, Lily. Why are you here?"

Startled, Lily peered into the darkened backyard. Whose voice was this? Not Tyler's. She knew both his voice and his form. This gruffer, yet gentle voice, belonged to an older man, someone with rounded shoulders and a fuller middle.

"Who's there?" she called, hoping her voice carried more confidence than she felt.

The man leaned over to unlock the gate and walked up the path toward Lily. Reverend Scott. She had met him briefly in Gibson's weeks earlier and hadn't spoken to him since. Something about him reminded her of her father, perhaps his unwavering gaze that seemed to discern her motives. Regardless, she had decided early on to give him a wide berth.

Now he stood at the bottom step, his hat in his hands, looking at her expectantly. She gave him a tentative smile.

"Good evening, Reverend."

He nodded. "I asked you a question."

"Yes, but I thought it was rhetorical."

"It wasn't. Why are you here?"

She waved a hand airily and gave him her most gracious smile. "Why, enjoying the lovely evening. Such a refreshingly cool breeze after a hot day, don't you think?"

He leaned forward a little, his expression serious, holding her with his gaze until her smile wavered.

"Why are you here, Miss Lily? What is your purpose?"

"My purpose?" She stared at him blankly, her heart beginning to pound. "To entertain, to sing … um … to bring a little happiness—"

"*Pshaw.*"

Pshaw? Had he actually said *pshaw*? He had, and Lily didn't quite know how to respond.

"I don't understand, Reverend."

"There you go, that's it right there." He waved a finger at her. "You say 'Reverend' with a respect I don't typically get from women who work in your so-called profession. And it's not a surface respect but a profound respect. You're an educated woman, Lily. It shows in your speech, in the way you carry yourself, and in the way you deal with people. You don't belong here. And so you must have a reason. I'm asking you that reason, Lily. Why are you here?"

A strange numbness crept over her as he spoke. He knew, didn't he? Of course not—how could he possibly know? How ridiculous. Even so, guilt threatened to engulf her. If he knew why she had come to Guthrie, if he could truly see through her, he would be appalled. As a true man of God, he would attempt to talk her out of her plan. But perhaps she was ready to be talked out of her plan. Maybe he could help her. Maybe he would tell her what to do.

"You aren't alone," he said.

Not alone? She had been alone since her father died and her sister ran away. She straightened her shoulders and raised her chin.

"Yes, I am alone." She flung the words at him. "And that is the problem. I have been deserted. My father is dead and my sister is dead. Now I am left alone to face an uncertain future. I had dreams. I had a future—I knew where I was going … what was expected of me … and now I have no future, because I no longer fit in the life that was supposed to be mine."

Reverend Scott wagged his gray head slowly. "I can't even begin to understand what you mean, but I'm willing to try. Would you like to talk?"

Lily's eyes filled with tears, but she refused to let them fall. Afraid to speak, she simply closed her eyes and shook her head. She heard him sigh wearily and turn to leave.

"I'm not convinced. You're welcome anytime, Lily. In fact, I'll expect to see you sometime soon. I have a feeling about you. You'll straighten things out … if you listen to God and to your heart. Good evening."

She didn't answer but watched as he retreated down the path, through the gate, and down the alleyway toward the church. She leaned her head back against the swing, curled one leg beneath her, and pushed off with her other foot. The chain creaked fretfully as she closed her eyes, listening to Toby …

> It matters little now, Lorena
> The past is in the eternal past
> Our hearts will soon lie low, Lorena
> Life's tide is ebbing out so fast
> There is a future, oh, thank God!
> Of life this is so small a part
> 'tis dust to dust beneath the sod
> But there, up there, 'tis heart to heart.

Lily could not recall when she last heard God's voice. He seemed further away each time she ignored the gentle rebukes reminding her—these lies—this sought-after vengeance could only lead to disaster. Perhaps she should talk to the Reverend. But what if he told her to go home? Maybe she *should* go home. Maybe she should give up this foolishness since her brilliant plan seemed destined for failure. Tyler was no closer to falling in love with her than she was to falling in love with him. That thought caused her to squirm. Truth be told, falling in love with him proved almost inevitable, while he seemed fully capable of remaining at arm's length. That was all wrong. All wrong. She wanted to break his heart. An eye for an eye, a tooth for a tooth, a heart for a heart—Augusta's heart, not her own.

Tyler walked down the back path toward the Opera House, his hands in his pockets, wondering for at least the hundredth time why he couldn't keep Lily out of his thoughts.

Lord, I promised you I'd stay away from women like her. I thought that side of me died when I came to know you. Why, after all these years, is this a problem again? Why am I so drawn to her when I don't want to be—when I know I shouldn't be?

I know you have a plan for my life, Lord—You've told me so often enough—and I believe you. And yes, I know that in the Bible you told the prophet Hosea to marry a prostitute as an example—but I'm not Hosea, and I almost totally ruined my life once before—not to mention losing my brother. Tell me what to do, Father. Lead me.

The tinkling sound of a piano drew Tyler's attention. He looked up, surprised to find himself at the back gate of the Canary Cage. Lily sat alone on the porch, swaying idly, her head resting against the swing, eyes closed. She reached up and wiped her cheek with the edge of her shawl. He frowned when he heard her weeping. She couldn't attend the gala at the Opera House, but shouldn't she be inside with the girls? He could hear them singing from where he stood.

"Lily, why are you out here?"

Obviously startled, she sat up suddenly and clutched her shawl. She said nothing, and he swung open the gate and strode up the path. "Is everything all right?"

She eyed him warily, heaved a long, hard sigh, and then relaxed.

"Everything is fine," she said, irritation edging her tone. "I just don't know why a woman can't sit on a porch in the moonlight without everyone questioning her."

Tyler took a step back and raised his eyebrows. "Everyone? I just wanted to make sure you were all right, Lily. Sorry to have bothered you." He turned to leave.

"Wait!"

He stopped and looked over his shoulder at her.

"I'm sorry," she said. "I didn't mean to be rude. I'm just a little—"

"Tired?" he offered. He turned and walked toward her again.

"Yes, that ... it's been a long day."

"It has." He placed one foot on a porch step and leaned forward, resting his forearm on his thigh. "The Flower Parade was definitely more interesting this year than last."

Lily nodded somewhat regally.

"Yes. I understand there was a bit of excitement today."

"You could say that."

"I believe some of the townsfolk expressed a bit of outrage for some reason."

"I recall hearing something similar."

"Well," she said, smoothing her skirt and looking up at him mischievously, "a little feather-ruffling would be a service to some people, don't you think, Mr. Buchanan."

"I heartily agree, Miss Lily. And feather-ruffling seems to be your specialty, I might add. As a compliment of course."

Again, she nodded. "You might say the Flower Parade was a success then?"

"Most … successful."

They chuckled companionably, and Lily motioned toward the rocking chair.

"Sit for a moment?"

He stared at the chair, debating the wisdom of allowing himself to spend any more time in Lily's company. But what harm could a few moments do?

"You're already here. What harm could a few moments do?" Lily asked softly.

"What?" Had she really echoed his thoughts?

"I said what harm could a few moments do? I know you have a reputation to protect. It's one thing to be in the Cage with the chief, drinking a few ginger beers, and trying to pick up some news stories—and it's a totally different thing to be sitting here after dark keeping company with a saloon girl. How about if I promise to stay over here, and you can stay over there—to help protect your stellar reputation?"

Did she realize her sultry voice assured a warm response in his belly? She evoked the strongest reaction when she didn't even seem to be trying.

"What if I don't want to stay over there?" The words came out unbidden, his voice low and gruff.

After a moment, instead of saying anything in response, Lily simply slid over on the swing, moving her skirts aside to make room for him. He settled beside her, the swing groaning under his weight, his shoulder and thigh warm against hers. Tyler stretched one leg out, bending the other long leg beneath the bench, and again set the swing to swaying gently, the chain creaking through the ceiling hook from the added burden.

They swung back and forth, listening peacefully to the piano, until Toby played a familiar English ballad. Lily hummed along, a strange nostalgic smile playing at her lips.

Sleep, my love, and peace attend thee … all through the night …

If Tyler's baritone startled her, she gave no sign and joined him on the second line.

Guardian angels God will lend thee … all through the night …

"Lily, where do you hail from?"

"Back east. What about you?"

"Where in the east?"

"Virginia. What about you?"

"Charleston."

"Ah. South Carolina."

"There's a Charleston in West Virginia, too."

"A West Virginia accent is totally different."

"Accent? I don't have an accent!" Tyler pretended affront.

"Oh, but it's a very genteel accent, I assure you."

"Well, as long as it's genteel."

Inside the saloon, murmured conversation followed the final flourish of the ballad before a jaunty tune, "Hot Time in the Old Town Tonight," filled the air.

Lily groaned.

"You don't care for ragtime?"

Lily shook her head. "I know Scott Joplin is all the rage, but my father …"

"Your father?" Tyler prompted gently. "What about him? He didn't like ragtime either?" When she didn't answer, he continued the one-sided conversation, hoping to put her at ease once again. "I actually have no idea if my parents like ragtime or not. I've been here in Guthrie since the Opening, and I haven't been home. Our letters haven't touched on the subject of modern music." Toby's playing filled the night for a moment before he spoke again. "What about your parents?"

He kept his gaze on the starry night so she wouldn't feel studied, but he knew when she again raised her shawl to wipe her eyes.

"I have no parents," she finally answered.

"You mentioned your father …"

"He died two years ago."

"Your mother?"

"She died giving birth to my sister."

"Ah, so you have a sister."

"I *had* a sister … she's gone too."

Tyler took a moment to digest this. The lonesomeness in her voice tore at his very soul. He ached to turn toward her, to take her in his arms.

"Well, then. That's something we have in common."

Immediately, Lily's tear-streaked face turned toward his. Even in the pale moonlight with just the scant light from the kitchen behind them, he could see astonishment on her lovely face.

"In common? What do you mean?"

"I mean …" Suddenly, Tyler realized he yearned to lay bare his soul to this woman, and the compulsion had sprung out of nowhere. He reined himself in. *Be careful. You don't know if she can be trusted.* Still, there he felt pressed to follow one compulsion at least to a point. "I had a brother. A younger brother. He's gone too."

"But you're not alone … you still have your parents."

Tyler considered this.

"That's true. But there's a distance between us that wasn't there before. Not just a distance in miles, but a distance … of the heart."

He felt her hand then, fine-boned and soft, touch his where it lay fisted on his knee. He uncurled his fingers and intertwined his with hers, finding an unusual comfort in her unassuming touch.

"But surely they love you." The tone in her voice held such longing that Tyler again felt his heart ache for her.

"Love me, yes—they will always love me—and stand by me, as all good parents do. But I disappointed them in a way they never could have imagined, and the loss of my brother is one they will never recover from."

"And you came here?"

"I thought a fresh start would be the best thing for us all. So I came west—a new town, a new business, a new life. What about you? Your father …"

She pulled her hand free and busied herself arranging her shawl around her shoulders. "Yes, well, with my father and my sister gone, I … I … want to talk about something else. Can we do that, Tyler?" Her voice took on an air of hysteria or perhaps panic, and he wanted desperately to lighten the mood. He reached out and found her hand again. He splayed open his fingers and spread hers over his, palm to palm.

"I was wondering who had the idea to infiltrate the Flower Parade."

"Well, the cage was Toby's idea."

"Mm-hm. The Canary Cage. Makes sense."

"And Rae Ann thought of dressing us as birds."

"Birds inside the Canary Cage. Got it."

"There you have it."

"Still I find it quite interesting that I've been here ten years."

"Yes?"

"And the Canary Cage has been here that long."

"Yes?"

"And the Flower Parade has been an annual event for almost that long ..."

"And your point is?"

"My point is that the Canary Cage never showed the slightest interest in being a part of the Flower Parade until the Songbird of the East flew into town. I find that mighty interesting."

Lily gazed at their hands, gently tracing patterns on his palm with the tip of a nail, a smile playing at her lips.

"Am I to infer that you think, kind sir, I am personally responsible for insinuating ourselves wrongfully in the highly virtuous and morally upstanding Flower Parade?"

"I just find it interesting that the one most likely to stir up trouble is the one dressed as a bird of peace."

Before she could ask what trouble he meant, the strains of a popular waltz filtered onto the porch. Tyler stood and swung one arm wide as he bowed deeply.

"Would you care to dance, Miss Songbird?"

Lily's delicately arched brows rose slightly in surprise, and she studied him for a moment before she stood and straightened her skirts.

"My pleasure." She held her hand before her like a duchess and allowed Tyler to lead her down the steps and into the yard. He gave her an elaborate twirl, swept her into his arms, his hand on her trim waist, her small hand in his, and whirled her around on the sparse grass. Lily gracefully matched him step for step. He doubted any of the other girls at the Canary Cage could dance with her grace and precision. Questions began to assail him once again.

"Aren't you on your way to the Opera House for the gala?" she asked, stroking the fabric of his fine woolen coat.

"I had planned not to go. I'm not much for parties, and I'm already committed to the New Year's Eve ball at the Ione Hotel. Then I decided to go tonight ... and I ended up here."

"A lot of people seem to end up here," she said beneath her breath. Again, the edge of sadness in her voice touched him. He held her a little closer, and she leaned her head back to look up at him. The moonlight shone on her face, and he found himself startled by her beauty. She seemed to study his face, and he wondered what she searched for, what she hoped to find. He realized they no longer danced, and instead he felt himself bending toward her. Her eyes closed expectantly. He pulled her against him, marveling at how naturally she wound her arms around him.

"Lily," he whispered, his lips very near hers.

"Yes?"

He could feel her breath, warm and sweet, on his lips. He dipped his head lower still, capturing her lower lip gently between his, tugging gently, beckoning her closer. And she came, rising up on her toes, pressing against him.

Desire sang through his veins as he crowded all opposing voices from his mind, giving himself permission to kiss her. He moved his lips against hers in a hungry, yearning kiss that felt as though he was both exploring a new paradise and finally coming home. His heart hammered wildly, and he could feel hers fluttering riotously like a frightened bird caught between them. As Lily responded, her mouth softening, Tyler groaned and pulled her even more tightly against himself. It had been so long since he had felt true tenderness for anyone, since he had ...

Enough.

A warning roared in his head.

Let your heart keep my commands ...

He took her by the shoulders and pushed her away abruptly, reminding himself that, not only were they still in an essentially public place, but that he shouldn't be there at all. He had stayed much too long. Lily stumbled against him, and he felt a pang of guilt at her bewildered look. Still, he dropped his hands and took a step backward, giving her a gallant bow and the coolest smile he could muster.

"Pardon me, Lily. I should be leaving. Enjoy your evening," he said formally and strode toward the gate. Closing it behind him, he looked back to see Lily still standing in the middle of the yard, her arms hanging limply at her sides, her face a mixture of hurt and confusion. His heart softened, and he stopped, his hand still resting on the gate.

"You should have won. I was outvoted." Before she could respond, he set off resolutely down the path toward home.

"Shh! Here she comes!" Toby played another tune.

"Don't shush me!" Honey hissed, turning to glare at Lily as she entered the saloon from the kitchen. She raised her eyebrows knowingly and sneered, looking Lily up and down with repugnance.

Suddenly, Lily felt dirty and ashamed. A hot blush crept up her neck, burning her ears, and turning her face as pink as her favorite petunias. Had Honey seen her with Tyler? Of course she had. That could be the only explanation for her behavior. The plan to trespass on the Flower Parade had forged a truce of sorts between them. But the treaty was broken … and before day's end. Lily turned away from Honey's glare to survey the rest of the room.

Merle sat alone at a table with papers spread before him. Sally and Trudy sat at another table in the far corner playing a card game and manicuring their nails. Rae Ann sat with them sewing lace on the neckline of a dress. She looked up at Lily and smiled a silent invitation. Lily nodded back. Though not in the mood for superficial chatter, she didn't want to be alone either. A few exhausted fellows wandered in periodically, threw back shots of whiskey, and then left. She could go to her room as she typically did but found the idea of solitude unappealing. She spent enough time alone.

Malcolm sat at the table nearest the bar rolling dice, a whiskey bottle and an empty shot glass on the table, an unlit cigar clamped in his back teeth. He also seemed to be always alone, even in a crowded room. Maybe they could be lonely together tonight. She wandered toward him and pulled out a chair, scraping it loudly against the floorboards.

"Mind if I join you?"

He barely gave her a glance but shrugged and continued rolling the dice.

"Suit yourself."

They sat in silence, Malcolm playing a game Lily had yet to understand while the bartender concentrated on throwing the white cubes.

As she watched him play, she realized how little she knew about Malcolm. The only employee who didn't have a room at the Cage, he rarely ate his meals there. His black-eyed glare could stop a punch in mid-swing, and he only had to move one hand toward the sawed-off shotgun he kept behind the bar for a troublemaker to have second thoughts.

A scar nearly the size of his little finger stretched from the corner of his mouth to his ear, added to his mystery. No one knew how he came by the ferocious-looking wound though plenty of customers speculated over drinks and cards. Some said a bullet while others swore an Apache's flaming arrow had taken half his earlobe. Someone swore he'd heard that Malcolm had worked on a railroad out west and the scar resulted from a spike wielded during a fight.

Malcolm rarely smiled. When he did, his pencil-thin mustache didn't move, held in place by the offending scar. Only one side of his mouth curved, lending him an even more sinister air. Despite his small stature and his compact, wiry physique, both men and women cut a wide swathe around Malcolm.

Lily finally spoke, breaking the silence.

"What are you playing? I haven't been able to figure out anything, except that you're trying to roll fives and sixes."

He looked up at her finally, his almost-black eyes piercing hers. He had never been unpleasant to Lily or to anyone in her hearing.

"Fours, fives, and sixes. The game's called Ship, Captain, Crew," he said finally, his gravelly voice low.

"Will you teach me?"

He studied her for a moment. She let him, meeting his steely gaze evenly, until he gave a short nod, and rolled the dice.

"You get three chances to roll a six—that's the ship—a five, the captain—and a four—that's the crew. Once you have those three—ship, captain, and crew—you can roll again, if you have any rolls left, and count the total on the remaining dice. That's your score."

"What happens if I don't roll a four, five, and six?"

"Then you get a zero score."

"And how far do you play?"

Malcolm sat back in his chair and rolled the cigar to the other side of his mouth.

"You can play to a certain number or roll a determined number of turns. Whichever."

"Shall we?" Lily gave him a bright smile, and she could swear a smile threatened to crack Malcolm's grim façade.

Without answering, he retrieved pencil and paper from behind the bar. At her questioning look, he explained, "For markers. Merle lets certain customers drink on credit. I keep track."

After several turns, Lily motioned to the whiskey bottle.

"You haven't opened that."

"I don't drink."

Startled, Lily stared at him. "You have a whiskey bottle and a shot glass on the table, but you don't drink?"

"Gave it up."

"But you work in a bar."

"Yep."

"So why do you put the bottle on the table? Aren't you tempted to drink?"

"Sometimes."

"And the cigar? Don't you light it?"

"Don't smoke."

"I don't understand."

"Who says you need to?"

Lily laughed softly and shook her head.

"You're right, Malcolm. Who says I need to? You're quite an enigma, aren't you?"

"That's what they say." After a moment he added, "They say it about you, too."

CHAPTER TWENTY-EIGHT

Swathes of pink and peach tinted the early morning horizon, nudging away the deep purple of pre-dawn. Lily had been on her knees an hour before sunup, yanking at the weeds crawling across Roxie's grave. The walk was long and tiring, but she was determined to frequent the cemetery as often as possible. Leaving the saloon while still dark, she brought a lantern to light her efforts graveside. As far as she knew, no one had ever seen her, except for Tyler that first morning. Hopefully, if someone did notice her, she would pass for a mourner. No one would give her a second thought, except perhaps to wonder who would grieve over anyone in this wretched little cemetery. But this morning, she found herself with unexpected company. Squatting back on her heels, she wiped the dust off her hands with a handkerchief and gasped when a man knelt beside her.

"Good morning, Lily," he said. "Sorry. I didn't mean to startle you."

"Reverend Scott," she nodded, wondering how to explain her presence. Perhaps go on the offense. "You're up and about early this morning."

"As are you. Yes, well, walking is my daily habit … and to begin the day with prayer for the town—and so I walk."

"Here? Do you walk past here and pray for these poor, neglected souls?" Too late. She had spoken too quickly, the bitterness in her voice almost palpable. Lily stiffened, indignant, when he chuckled.

"No, my dear, these souls are wherever their eternal homes are. No amount of praying will change that. But I do pray for their families."

Had she heard him correctly? Lily watched him tug at a hawkweed near his knee and toss it onto the small pile she had amassed, as though he waited for her to prompt him before he would say more.

"You pray for their families?"

"Yes. I pray first of all that they know where their loved ones are—that they know at least that they have passed on. I hate to think of a mother or father waiting somewhere for a letter or a visit that never comes. Always wondering where that son or daughter … or brother or sister … or even mother or father is." He sighed heavily. He waved a hand expansively over the slatternly gravesites. "Have you noticed that some of these markers don't even have names?" He shook his head. "Sad. So sad. At least this one here"—he pointed to Roxie's wooden marker painted with her name and the date of her death—"at least people knew her and mourned her."

Lily stared at the marker. Not even a complete name. No birthdate. No loving sentiment—*Beloved daughter and sister…* Just *Roxie* and the date she had died … alone. Senselessly.

"For what? A week?" Again, the resentment, the anger. Where in the world had her restraint flown? She had always been quite capable of controlling her tongue like the genteel young woman she had been brought up to be. One couldn't go about speaking one's mind at every opportunity. Even the Bible was quite clear on the subject in Proverbs and also in … Jude? … no, Colossians … perhaps James?

"So, you knew Roxie." Both question and statement. Perhaps Reverend Scott thought he had figured out a great deal about Lily.

Startled, Lily first thought to deny the fact and then, quite strangely, she wondered if she did, if he would pursue the accusation. Would he force her to deny her sister twice more before a cock crowed somewhere?

"I knew her," Lily stated as a matter of fact.

"How? She died before you came to town."

"Died? *Died?* You mean murdered—and buried here in this ramshackle, derelict excuse for a cemetery."

Reverend Scott rose and held out his hand to help Lily stand. She accepted, yet refused to meet his eyes, choosing instead to make a show of shaking the dust from her black dress.

"I believe," the cleric began softly, "the general consensus was that she had killed herself, yet you say murdered. Do you believe someone murdered her?"

Lily shook her head, scrambling for words and an excuse. "No—no—of course not. I meant killed—not murdered—how would I know? But what a shame anyone has to be buried here."

"You're right," Reverend Scott agreed. "One should be buried in a family plot near loved ones who have gone on before and near loved ones who may come to grieve. How sad that Roxie died with no one. Unfortunately, I had gone out of town. I never would have allowed her to be buried here. With no family in Guthrie, she could at least have been in the town cemetery."

"Would the town have allowed that?" she asked, hearing the bitterness in her own voice.

"Well, there was a two-fold problem—or case—against her, you might say."

"Something more than the townsfolk not wanting a saloon singer to be buried beside their arrogant remains?"

"To be quite correct, the remains you speak of could no longer be arrogant themselves, as they were all quite dead and suddenly quite equal to all other remains regardless of class. But I take your point. So, Lily, yes, there is that—but she also was a suicide, considered by many to be an unforgivable sin. Several churches have petitioned to not allow suicides to be buried in the common graveyard. A few of the graves you see here are actually of other suicides also not granted burial in the Christian churchyard for that reason."

A wave of sorrow broke over Lily. Not only sorrow. Hatred—had she ever felt such hate? Hate actually felt good. The fierce emotion made her feel strong, alive, and purposeful, as though she could vanquish a vicious enemy on her own. Perhaps she would hold on to this loathing. Perhaps this is what she truly needed in order to do what needed to be done and then leave this place.

"And just what would you have done about that, Reverend?"

He put his hands in his pockets and looked up at the brightening sky.

"This is the first suicide that has taken place since I've been pastor here, and I've thought about how it was handled. Prayed about it. And I hope that I would have the courage to do what Martin Luther, the great reformer, did."

She was in no mood to hear parables, to have her anger assuaged. But he continued without any prompting from her.

"There was a teenaged boy who had committed suicide. His parents not only grieved his loss, they grieved the judgment passed on him by the church. You see, he was not to be buried in their Christian cemetery but in a pagan graveyard. Luther took the boy in his arms and carried him to the churchyard. Once there, Luther began to dig the grave with his own hands. Of course, the church authorities challenged him on the appropriateness of his actions."

The story, not only the events but the cleric's passionate telling of the tale, drew Lily in despite her resistance.

"What did he say?"

"He was angry—and rightfully so. He said to them, 'Do we blame the victims if a robber assaults them in the forest and takes their money? Of course not! Scripture tells us that Satan is a thief and a murderer. He came upon this boy and overwhelmed him with despair, stealing from him his sensibilities and then his life. He will be buried in the church cemetery, because he was a child of God. And while Satan stole his life, he cannot steal his salvation.' The church authorities retreated. The boy was buried properly, and the visible demonstration of God's grace for their son greatly comforted his parents."

The reverend remained quiet for a moment before adding, "And that's what I hope I would have been courageous enough to do for Roxie had I been here for her. Because, assuredly, that can only be what happened to her. Her sensibilities and her life were stolen from her. She would not have given them up of her own accord."

Reverend Scott's kind voice stabbed Lily's heart. He truly sounded as if he cared. He had not made the decision where to bury Roxie—that had been made by the odious little rector. She felt an urging to confess—no, she meant *confide*—in Reverend Scott.

"She had family, you know," she began.

The reverend nodded. "A sister—whom she loved very much. Roxie grieved that she had hurt her by running away. She never quite forgave herself for that."

Lily's eyes widened. "You knew her?"

He smiled. "Oh, yes. Roxie and I grew to be friends of a sort during her last month. She came to me to talk several afternoons. Quite an amazing young woman. I grew quite fond of her."

"What did she want?"

"To change her life. To make amends. She was planning to go home for a while. She said she didn't think she could live there anymore—she was too different—she had changed too much. But she hoped to perhaps persuade her sister to make a fresh start and move somewhere with her, perhaps farther west."

Lily's throat tightened and her eyes burned. Augusta planned to come home? The possibility filled her heart with a cruel joy.

"She said she had made many mistakes, but she couldn't forget how she was raised. She wanted to know God and have him change her if it was still possible."

"What did you tell her?" Lily leaned forward so as not to miss even one word.

"I told her that with God all things are possible. She could indeed be forgiven for anything she had done wrong. That the Lord would forgive her sins, throw them into the sea of forgetfulness, and remember them no more. I told her to make a fresh start ... and to go home to her sister."

Lily froze, and she could barely breathe. Augusta was truly planning to come home? That same thought kept rattling around in her mind, too wonderful, too horrible to contemplate.

"She was coming home?"

Reverend Scott nodded. "I believe so. She was to leave the next week."

A week? That made no sense. If Augusta had truly been determined to get her life back on track and come home—even if only for a while—why in the world would she have killed herself?

"I don't understand," Lily whispered, her voice breaking.

Reverend Scott nodded. "I don't either. She was very excited. She was going to go back to the Canary Cage, tell everyone about her decision, and then make plans to leave for home. I left to attend my niece's wedding. When I returned, I found out that she had ... died—and by her own hand."

"What did you think?"

"Truthfully, I didn't know what to think. She had been so determined—she seemed to be an exceptionally strong-willed young lady—I couldn't possibly understand how she could have gone from such elation to such desperation so quickly. Believe me, I've spent many hours wondering about her."

"So have I."

"And you're the sister." Again, the words composed both question and statement.

Lily nodded. "How did you know?"

"I'm not exactly sure," he said, shrugging, "You said *coming* home, instead of *going* home. Other things. It just made sense to me quite suddenly."

"I suppose I'm glad something makes sense."

"Why are you here?" He smiled. "I seem to recall asking you that same question the evening after the parade."

"Yes, and I was not very forthcoming as *I* recall."

"To everything there is a season, my child."

My child. Suddenly those simple words, coupled with his genuine concern, broke open the floodgate.

"I came to avenge Augusta."

"Augusta?"

"Roxie—her name was Augusta Roxanne."

"Ah—avenge her death?"

Lily nodded.

"Hm." The elderly man stroked his chin, his eyebrows furrowed. "It seems to me that Roxie—Augusta—mentioned that you both had been very well educated and that you attended church weekly, held devotionals daily, and study groups regularly. Is that correct?"

Lily murmured an assent.

"So then, young lady, I would think you are at least somewhat familiar with Scripture."

At Lily's nod, he continued. "Then, my dear, first of all, you should recall what the Good Book says about vengeance. To whom does vengeance belong?"

"I know, but—" Lily began.

"Tut-tut—no hedging. Just answer the question. Allow me to simplify. Complete the verse ... *Vengeance is mine, sayeth the—?*" He snapped his fingers in front of her nose. "Come now, quickly. You should know this. I'll give you a hint—the passage is in Romans."

At first, Lily just stared at him. Where had the kindly old cleric gone? Before her eyes, he had transformed into a scowling, scolding, long-lost uncle. Lily drew herself up and managed to keep from slapping his hand away. What was wrong with her? From what errant root did these rebellious feelings sprout?

"If you're talking about the verse in Romans, then the correct wording is, *Vengeance is mine, I will repay, sayeth the Lord,*" she said.

Reverend Scott smiled. "Ah, yes!" He clapped his hands once and sent dust flying into the air. Sneezing, he reached into his pocket for a handkerchief, wiping first his nose, then his hands. He lifted her chin, forcing her to meet his gaze. "And do you recall the rest of the passage?"

Lily pushed his hand away. She could look at him no longer. Shaking her head no, she wished he would leave her alone, let her finish her task in peace. Peace? She had forgotten how that felt.

"The Apostle Paul reminds us of another passage in Proverbs, telling us to feed our enemy if he is hungry. Give our enemy something to drink if he is thirsty and that, by doing so, we will be heaping coals of fire on his head. He tells us to overcome evil with good. Is that what you're doing in Guthrie, Lily? Overcoming evil with good?"

She didn't answer but smoothed her crumpled skirt.

"Excuse me, Reverend, I must be going. Seeing me here would raise questions. I would imagine being seeing with me probably wouldn't do much for your reputation either—"

"What are you doing in the Canary Cage? You of all people should know better. The others, they have their reasons—and I am not excusing them—but you—you are there of your own accord. You have no excuse." At her silence, he insisted, louder this time, "Well, speak up, girl! What have you to say for yourself?"

She reached to find her earlier indignation, but instead happened upon a bit of ingrained respect for her elders. She knew, after all, not only was he trying to help but that he was right. Even so, he didn't know as much as he thought he did.

"I came to find out about Augusta. I—I wanted to know the people she knew, live life the way she lived ..." At his appalled expression, she hastened to add, "to a point, Reverend—I only sing and work downstairs. I promise you, I have never, ever—you know—upstairs." She blushed furiously, her hands straying to her hair, busily tucking stray strands under the bonnet.

"I believe you, child. But you've continually lied about who you are. Why is that?"

Several reasons sprang to mind, but Lily clutched at the one she comforted herself with most often.

"So that after I leave here, I can go home, and no one need ever know that I—for a brief time—was Lily Woods. She will simply cease to exist."

"Will she?"

The simple question struck Lily with the force of a tornado. She braved a smile.

"Absolutely. I've simply been acting. Lily isn't real."

Reverend Scott considered her thoughtfully.

"You are a professional actress."

"Of course not."

"But you've said you've been acting."

"Well, I've been pretending to be someone I'm not."

"Then you've just been lying. Day in and day out. Lying about who you are, lying about where you've been, why you're here, lying about—"

"Yes, yes! I understand what you're saying. But I have my reasons!"

"And those reasons are based on anger, vengeance, bitterness …"

Frustration overwhelmed her, and she struggled to keep her thoughts straight. "I didn't decide to feel a certain way. Feeling however one feels is not a sin. One has no control over feelings."

"Perhaps not. The sin would be in how someone deals with those feelings."

"I'm doing the best I can."

"Are you?"

Instead of answering, she latched onto something he had said a moment earlier, something that had piqued her interest.

"You said that the others have their reasons for being at the Canary Cage. I've often wondered about those reasons, hoping to understand Augusta better. Please tell me about them—Honey, Rae Ann—"

"No, Lily, I will not—cannot. I am a man of the cloth, not a gossip. But as Roxie—Augusta—has passed and you are her sister, I will tell you that she found herself here in Guthrie without a penny to her name."

Stunned, Lily's thoughts skittered. How could that be?

"She had no money? But she took a good amount with her when she ran away—and she had jewelry … Mama's ring, the pearls Papa gave her for her sixteenth birthday, an emerald brooch. And still, all she had to do was write or telegraph, I would have sent her anything she needed. What happened? I don't understand."

"Like too many other naïve young women before her, she believed promises she shouldn't have believed and found herself duped. Her jewelry, possessions, and whatever money she possessed had been stolen from her. She was abandoned here in Guthrie, left with only the belongings she carried in one carpetbag."

Lily digested that information, her mind cataloging Augusta's letters.

"She never mentioned any such thing."

"She never told you that she tried reputable business after business only to find that no one would hire her? No one trusted a woman who so obviously carried her worldly possessions around in a dusty carpetbag. She was never even given the opportunity to introduce herself, so she never gave her name. She simply walked in the door and asked for work. She was given the once-over and thrown out. After several humiliating attempts, she reached the Canary Cage. And they took her in, no questions asked. Of course, she lied about who she was—just as you're doing."

"It's only for a season."

"But you seem to think that you can take off the Lily costume, pull off the Lily mask—and, oh, never sing again?—and voilà!—as the French say—there you have it!—the return of the sedate, demure sister—the proper opposite of the flamboyant, free-spirited Augusta Roxanne ... the much-loved but audacious sibling who was too ashamed to ask her good sister for money so she could come home ... and instead took a position in a saloon to earn her way home."

"What?" The implied question stuck in Lily's throat. The reverend's words whirled around and around in her mind. "What?" she said again, louder this time. "She was too ashamed to tell me the truth? To ask me for money? That's ridiculous! She knew I would do anything for her. I would have given her anything—everything!"

"Along with a lecture—along with your disapproval—your criticism," he said.

Lily lifted her gaze to his, hoping to find understanding.

"But I loved her—I was simply concerned about the repercussions of her actions. The dowagers could be so cruel. The gossip mill in Norfolk is prolific and inexhaustible. One must behave according to certain dictates of society in order to fit in, to conform, and if we were to have any kind of decent life after Papa died, Augusta had to stop ..." She trailed off—her eyes wide.

"Ah, need I express the obvious? Oh, why not? Norfolk sounds a great deal like Guthrie ... a great deal, in fact, like every other town in our fair country."

"Yes," Lily whispered, "and I sound, I'm sure, no different than Theo Peebles."

CHAPTER TWENTY-NINE

Lily strode up the alley behind the Canary Cage, her feet aching from the long walk back from the cemetery. Opening the back gate, she finally looked up and groaned to see the kitchen light on. There would be more questions. After a deep, sustaining breath, she squared her shoulders and opened the screen door. Its hinges announced her entrance with a screech before she opened the inside door. Rae Ann stood at the counter kneading bread dough. Trudy and Honey sat at the table each nursing toast, tea, and head colds.

Shutting the door behind her, Lily pulled off her bonnet and cape, hanging them on the coat tree. She smiled innocently at all three inquiring looks.

"Mornin', Lily." Rae Ann said and then yawned into her shoulder.

"I'm not the only one up early this morning," Lily said pleasantly. "And drinking tea for those colds? I believe I'll join you." She retrieved a cup and tea tin from the cabinet and filled the cup with boiling water from the kettle simmering on the stove. Noting the honey pot on the table, she added, "Are your throats feeling any better?"

Trudy gave a pitiful moan and shook her head.

"No," she croaked, "and I can hardly breathe a lick. I don't think I've ever been so sick. I can't sleep, and I ache all the way to my bones. This toast's the first thing that's managed to stay down in two days."

"Well, that's a start. You'll just have to rest until you're better. And you, Honey, any better?" Lily turned to Honey to find her glaring at her with a look so venomous that if looks could indeed kill, Lily would have found herself slaughtered, stuffed, and mounted conveniently on a wall where Honey could use her for target practice.

"Guess you weren't asleep either. You been out all night? Even if you weren't upstairs, if you got money, you still owe Merle half."

"Excuse me?" The question so startled Lily she couldn't believe she had heard Honey correctly.

"You heard me. You have some explaining to do, sister."

Ire rose—indeed, the emotion perched so near the surface today, it hadn't far to climb. "I'm not your sister, and I don't need to explain myself to you."

"Uh-oh," Trudy murmured warily.

"Now, girls." Rae Ann turned her attention from her task.

"Don't '*now, girls*' me, Rae Ann," Honey flung out. "She gets enough special treatment—Miss Songbird of the East. She sings when she wants, works when she wants, wears the best of what we've got, waltzes through town like she's better than we are …"

"I've defended you—" Lily began.

"Defended me? Defended us?" Honey's hoarse voice could still manage an irate snarl. "Who asked you? Who appointed you our lawyer—our superior? You're no better than the blue-blooded biddies who draw their skirts aside on the streets so they don't touch us. You're as uppity as the worst of them, and you don't even see yourself."

"That ain't true, Honey. She's sweet—" Trudy objected.

"Don't be an idiot, Trudy. She wants something. What do you want, Lily?" Honey skewered Lily with another flaming glower and waited.

Rae Ann frowned as she glanced from Honey to Lily, her hands resting on the dough.

"I'm not an idiot." Trudy's lower lip trembled.

Lily sheltered Trudy in an embrace. She sniffled against Lily's neck.

"Of course you aren't, dear. Honey didn't mean what she said. She's angry with me, not you. I'm sure she's sorry."

Honey slammed her open palm on the table causing the teacups to rattle and the other women to jump.

"Would you stuff something in your mouth, woman? Stop making excuses for me! I can speak for myself!"

Trudy whimpered, and Lily tightened her grip around the girl's thin shoulders. "Well, then speak! You've been cruel to Trudy for absolutely no reason. She was miserable to begin with, and now, you've added insult to injury and made her cry. If you have something to say for yourself, then say it!"

The two women stared at each other, daring one another to be the first to look away. Only the sound of Trudy's snuffling broke the silence.

"So, Lil, where did you go? Honey, just apologize to Trudy and get it over with? Rae Ann, is that coffee I smell?"

Four heads turned in unison toward the voice. Toby lounged in the doorway, a lazy smile playing at his lips, his legs crossed at the knee, shirttail still untucked, and his chocolate-brown hair boyishly rumpled.

"This isn't your argument, Toby." Honey turned her attention back to Lily.

Toby sighed, uncrossed his legs, and took the few steps to the table. He sat beside Honey and gave Rae Ann a grateful smile for the steaming cup of coffee she put before him.

"You made it my argument when your caterwauling woke me up. You forget my room is right next to the kitchen." He leaned back and knocked on the wall behind him. "The wall isn't very thick, and I—unfortunately— am a light sleeper. I hear every time that door opens and closes, every time somebody slams a cabinet, drags a chair across the floor ... and every time somebody calls somebody else an idiot. Sorry, Trudy."

"It's not your fault Honey's so mean," Trudy said.

"Hey!" Honey punctuated her protest with another slap on the table.

"Well, you are!" Trudy suddenly found a remnant of pluck from somewhere.

"And *you* don't have a smidgen of sense!"

"Enough, ladies!" Rae Ann slammed the oven door and whirled around, her floured hands in the air as though she had just surrendered to General Grant. "My word and all I own, what has gotten into everyone? Can't you get along for ten minutes? Trudy, Honey—take your blankets and back to bed with you—no! Not a word more from either one! Go! Right now! I'll bring your tea."

Trudy scampered out of the room, dragging her blanket behind her. Honey followed but at her own more leisurely, regal pace, her blanket wrapped around her like a mantle. Rae Ann refilled their teacups and added a dollop more honey before trailing behind them, shaking her head, and muttering beneath her breath.

Toby chuckled, taking a slice of toast off the plate in the middle of the table. He spread an ample helping of apple butter, then folded the bread in half before taking a generous bite. He munched for a moment while Lily sipped on her tea.

"So, where *did* you go so early this morning?"

Lily looked up, startled, but Toby continued examining his toast as though determining where to take the next bite.

"I couldn't sleep. I just went for a walk."

He looked up at her, his face expressionless. "Most people who can't sleep just toss and turn. Or maybe read something until they get sleepy. But get up, dress, and go for a walk around town in the dark? A woman? That seems a bit strange. Not to mention dangerous."

Lily's thoughts flew. How could she explain herself? What should she say? What would her sister have said? She took her teacup to the sink.

"Toby, thank you for your concern. I don't have to answer to Honey, and I don't have to answer to you. I think I'll go upstairs and see if I can catch an hour or so of sleep now. Enjoy your coffee." And with that she left the kitchen, passing Rae Ann on her way back in.

"She tell you anything?" Rae Ann asked, still within Lily's hearing.

"Not a thing," Toby answered, his mouth full. "But I have a few ideas."

CHAPTER THIRTY

Christmas at the Canary Cage came and went with barely more than a nod of recognition. Trudy had bemoaned that no one ever bought presents for anyone. Lily asked Sally and confirmed that no one exchanged gifts. Honey overheard the conversation and added, "No one has the money or the inclination." According to her, on Christmas Day, Rae Ann had always baked an enormous breakfast, including her specialty—cinnamon rolls with raisins and icing—and Merle gave everyone a silver dollar.

The saloon opened for business and did a fairly brisk business off and on during the day. Solitary ranch hands, cowboys, and those with no family and nowhere else to go stopped in for a hand or two of poker, but mostly for company and to listen to Toby play the piano. He played special requests almost exclusively, and the girls encouraged the lonely customers to sing along.

By the end of the day, Lily could barely drag herself up the stairs. She lay awake staring at the ceiling. Tyler continued to avoid her. She had taken on the chore of checking daily for mail at the post office. In addition, she had made several trips to visit Amy. She enjoyed the young woman's company, and the visits gave her another excuse to walk past the newspaper offices. The one time she had passed Tyler, he had only nodded, kept a straight face, and touched the brim of his hat. She might as well have been a complete stranger. Her heart had pounded loudly in her ears, and her smile froze on her face. Unfortunately, she could think of nothing witty or charming to say to him. He stayed away from the Canary Cage. Merle had asked at supper one evening if anyone knew of any reason Buchanan no longer regularly shared the table with Chief Ward. Lily hadn't said a word even though Honey had stared pointedly at her.

The morning after Christmas brought little reason to rise and shine. Lily did so out of habit and, also out of habit, stopped into the post office.

At long last, she had received a packet as requested from her family attorney in Norfolk.

Lily hid the oversized envelope under her cloak. After delivering the rest of the mail to Merle's office, she ran upstairs and ripped the packet open. The contents spilled onto her bed. Soon after, her tears, both distraught and angry, spilled into her pillow.

She couldn't stay secluded in her room to indulge studying the material. Another busy evening approached, with even Merle and Rae Ann helping out while Honey and Trudy remained confined to their beds.

Lily needed a new plan—a simple plan. She could carry out the plot on New Year's Eve, and then she would go home. Home. The thought brought her no joy. Surely joy would return to her life once she finished with this place ... this town ... with Tyler.

Getting dressed took longer than usual. Cool water helped ease the swelling and extra rice powder covered the dark shadows under her eyes. She dressed in another of Roxie's garments, as though pulling on a fresh layer of resolve.

On New Year's Eve, Lily studied her reflection with her typical critical eye. Rae Ann had followed Lily's instructions to the letter. The blouse, hanging precariously on the tips of her shoulders, was fashioned of fine, white lawn and featured a wide neckline trimmed in lace. She tucked the blouse into the waistband of a black skirt cinched narrowly at the waist. Flaring to her ankles, the hem revealed a glimpse of red crinoline. On the bed lay a black lace mantilla to be held in place by a black-and-red lacquered hair comb. She practiced flourishing a black lace fan to cover the part of her face not disguised by the black silk demi-masque.

For what seemed the hundredth time, Lily re-read the well-worn newspaper advertisement for the Charleston production of *The Matador* starring Allegra D'arcy as the love interest. Something akin to jealousy stirred as Lily studied the accompanying photograph of a stunning redhead in costume. Indeed, according to the *Charleston Tribune*, Allegra had still been wearing the outfit when the police, followed closely by the press, had burst into the actress's dressing room and found Rogan Buchanan lying dead on the floor. He had been slain by a bullet through the heart, and the actress had crumpled to the floor. The report indicated the victim's brother, Tyler, had stood over the two bodies, the smoking gun, literally, held limply in his hand, his face twisted in anguish.

From the articles her lawyer had sent, Lily pieced together much information. Allegra D'arcy and *The Matador* had taken Charleston by storm and boasted standing-room-only attendance for the first month of the production. She and Rogan Buchanan, eight years younger than Tyler, engaged in a widely publicized affair, culminating in Rogan's death and Tyler's indictment for murder.

The courts ruled the younger Buchanan's demise an accident, and Tyler had been absolved of his brother's death. Reporters circulated the story that the brothers had been quarreling over the beautiful actress and the gun had fired during the struggle.

The publicity boosted attendance at *The Matador,* and the producer took full advantage of the public's morbid fascination with the woman who had come between two brothers, bringing about the death of one and the ruination of the other. The theater extended the performance an additional two months before the production continued the tour. Tyler left Charleston less than one week after his acquittal, leaving behind a mother and father grieving over the loss of still another son.

Mr. Barlow recounted additional information Lily found disheartening and conclusive. Tyler Buchanan had a penchant for women involved in the theater—ballet dancers, opera singers, and, of course, actresses. Considered to be one of Charleston's most eligible bachelors, heir to a shipping fortune and a successful newspaper, he had managed to avoid involvement with myriad marriage-minded debutantes. He attended soirees and balls only when prompted by his mother or when his absence might be construed as an insult. Always well behaved, he danced with a different young lady at every turn and deftly side-stepped all attempts at flirtation. Evidently, Tyler Buchanan proved to be a major frustration to the mothers and daughters of Charleston society.

Lily had crumpled the paper in her fist before throwing it across the room, anger clenching in her chest, her breath coming in uneven jerks. Roxie was not the first woman whose relationship with Tyler had ended in violence.

Now, she paced the room in hurried strides, the petticoats rustling around her legs with faint *shushing* sounds. At Rae Ann's urging, she stopped and turned slowly, while the older woman smoothed the skirt and fluffed the petticoat at the hemline. After pronouncing the costume as perfect, the seamstress shook her head in frustration.

"What's wrong?" Lily asked, twisting around and inspecting herself from all angles in the cheval mirror.

"It's your hair, Lily," Rae Ann declared, pursing her lips. "You look beautiful in that get-up. The mask and fan will disguise your face with no problem, but your hair …" She shook her head again and propped her hands on her hips. "Sweetie, you wear your hair like that and the fellas will figure you out right quick."

Lily looked in the mirror again. She had pulled her hair back in a loose chignon, doing her best to imitate a painting her father had owned of a Spanish *señorita*. But Rae Ann was right. The style was too similar to the one Lily usually wore. She could plait her hair into a long, heavy braid, but Tyler had seen this style several times, and she wanted to dupe him above all others. She met Rae Ann's gaze—her brows raised in question.

Rae Ann clicked her tongue as if solving a puzzle. "You never wear your hair down." Stepping closer, she pulled out the comb fastening the lace mantilla. Together she and Lily hurriedly plucked out the pins holding the chignon in place. The tresses tumbled down Lily's back, the ends curling naturally. In Rae Ann's hand, the tortoiseshell brush became that of an artist, each stroke bringing the strands to life, blue-black lights flashing in silken sparks.

"Are you sure you want to do this?"

Lily nodded without hesitation—thoughts of Augusta, Rogan, and even Allegra, the poor actress, spinning through her mind. Victims. All victims of Tyler's ego, his selfishness, his *savoir-faire*. Tonight, he would be the victim—*her* victim. Her chin lifted a little, and she smiled at the thought of Tyler's expression when he saw her tonight. He would remember his secret, his sordid history, and he would wonder how Lily knew and whether she had told anyone. He only needed one glimpse of her costume.

Tonight, she would shock him, intrigue and entice him, and then spurn him. Yes, spurn him privately—all else she would do in front of everyone. Rae Ann's concern interrupted Lily's thoughts.

"I know how you feel, wanting to be part of things and hating the way we're treated like lepers. If you want to go and dance and have a good time like everyone else in town, well, that's fine by me. I just don't want you to get hurt. And you can't let anyone find out who you are. If Merle finds out, there'll be the blazes to pay … that's why I'm asking if you're sure."

"Oh, yes," Lily answered firmly, staring into the future. "I'm very sure." At Rae Ann's expression in the mirror, she entertained a moment of concern. She turned and caught Rae Ann's hand. "I haven't been fair to you, coercing you into being my cohort in crime."

"You did what?"

Lily smiled. "I mean, I'm sorry I've asked you to lie for me just so I can go to a costume ball. And you've spent your time secretly sewing this beautiful costume for me …"

Rae Ann shrugged. "Well, sewing is a pleasure. And you were so sweet to give me the extra pocket money. I'll be able to buy a few things I've been wanting. Besides, the rest is just a little white lie. With Honey and Trudy just getting over their colds a day or so ago, no one was surprised when I said you felt bad this morning. So, when I told Merle you couldn't work tonight and needed to stay in bed, he only grumbled a mite."

Lily wrapped a charcoal-gray woolen cape around her shoulders and tiptoed down the backstairs to the kitchen. She could hear Honey—most likely sitting beside Toby—singing old Stephen Foster songs. Rae Ann stood guard at the door to the main hall, ready to intercept anyone who might unexpectedly decide to come into the kitchen. The concerned look in her eye served as an unspoken reminder to be careful.

"Thank you. You're a miracle worker." Lily drew Rae Ann into a fierce hug, then stepped onto the back porch and pulled the cloak tightly around her, her breath fogging in the frigid night air. Shuddering from cold and anticipation, she hurried across the backyard, casting furtive glances over her shoulder to be sure no one witnessed her escape.

Shops and businesses lurked in darkness along the empty streets. Only the lights from the saloons glowed. Even these, like the Canary Cage, had few customers. Many of the devout citizens would be gathering at the churches at eleven o'clock to await the new century, but most of the townsfolk would celebrate privately or gather at the Ione Hotel for the largest public party in the history of the town … Lily's destination as well. Light spilled from the windows and the buzz of music and conversation vibrated in the air.

Stopping in a darkened doorway to adjust her mask and flip open the fan, she steadied herself with a deep breath before walking up the stairs. Two men in traditional doorman uniforms tipped their top hats and winked at her from behind emerald green masks while opening the carved oak doors. Inside, a young woman dressed as a French maid took Lily's cloak and directed her toward the ballroom. There another doorman, this one dressed in the flowing robes of an Arab, opened the door with a flourish. A blast of noise assaulted her and threatened her with a wave of dizziness. She stepped quickly behind a stand of potted trees to catch her breath and gain her bearings.

A small orchestra played a lively waltz, and an ocean of couples somehow managed to whirl around the dance floor without colliding. Amazed at the variety of costumes, Lily's gaze darted from kings to court jesters, train conductors to medieval damsels, Indian maidens to chiefs, and at least half a dozen Abraham Lincolns. One young woman, whom Lily immediately recognized as Theo, created quite a stir in her cowboy costume. Her fleshy curves filled out a pair of popular Levi Strauss denim trousers. A white shirt, string tie, Stetson, and leather vest completed the outfit. As all weapons had been confiscated at the door, the holster at her hip hung empty.

A burly lumberjack blocked Lily's view, and she ventured out of her hiding place, fluttering her fan nervously, covering the lower half of her face. Her eyes scanned the throng for a glimpse of Tyler, finding him in short order. She inhaled sharply, her pulse quickening. Leaning negligently against a wall and holding a glass of fruit punch, he seemed to be in deep conversation with a Lincoln and a clown. Tyler was dressed in a black shirt and a black bandanna hung around his neck in a loose triangle. Black trousers, tucked into shiny black knee-high boots, hugged his lean legs. A black cloak hung from his shoulders, its hem swirling around his calves as he gestured with his glass and laughed at something Lincoln said.

A highwayman. A thief of hearts for sure … and dressed in black to hide in the darkness like the devil he is.

She took a step toward him, willing him to look up and see her. Before he did, she felt a tap on her shoulder. She turned to face a swarthy pirate.

"Dance, m'lady?" he asked gallantly, bowing low. He grinned at her saucily and flashed a mouthful of soot-blackened teeth.

Lily curtsied. "*Sí, señor.*" She allowed him to sweep her onto the dance floor.

"Ye've only been here a couple o' minutes and already ye have everybody a-tryin' to figure out who ye be," her dance partner remarked, his eyes scrutinizing her with undisguised admiration.

"*Ees this so, señor?*" Lily answered with what she hoped was a sultry smile, keeping her voice soft and low, further camouflaged by the best Spanish accent she could muster. She was unconcerned her voice might give her away. Few people had ever spoken with her at any length, and she, of course, would not be singing.

"Aye, lass," the pirate confirmed, also doing his best imitation of how he thought a pirate might speak. "Ye dance like an angel, and ye have looks a man would die for. Give me a hint, will ye? I'll make it worth your while," he cajoled, obviously enjoying the freedom afforded by his mask.

Lily tapped him playfully on the shoulder with her fan. "For shame, señor," she exclaimed with mock dismay. "*Eef* I tell you who I am, then where *ees* the mystery?"

The pirate pulled her closer and whispered, his breath tickling her ear. "Expect to see me nearby at midnight, little señorita. Wherever there be treasure unveiled, ye'll be sure to find a pirate."

Lily laughed and allowed herself to be swept away to finish the dance with an Indian chief who managed to step painfully on her toes despite his soft moccasins.

Midnight. Fireworks would announce the arrival of the new century with masks lowered during the ensuing melee. To keep her identity hidden, she would simply leave before midnight like Cinderella in the children's story, "The Little Glass Slipper." And, if all went according to plan, she would take Tyler with her.

She tried to keep an eye on him. But being passed from one partner to the next with such frequency, along with the heat from the crush of people and the exertion of the dancing, soon had her head spinning.

Tyler continued to engage in conversation and avoid the dance floor. In his element, he and a short, round Abe Lincoln debated the inevitability of Oklahoma statehood when a shapely woman whirled past him in the arms of a jovial Robin Hood, her skirts flying and her smile flashing. He balked, a glass raised halfway to his lips, his heart lurching when he saw her costume.

Allegra? His thoughts whirled. Downing the remainder of the punch in one huge gulp, he swiped at his mouth with the back of his hand, his eyes following the dancing señorita. Tyler grabbed another glass from a passing waiter and guzzled half its contents in a series of suddenly thirsty swallows. He leaned against a doorframe and declined a waiter's offer to refill his again-empty glass.

No, *not* Allegra. Too tall, with a smaller waist and a fuller bosom, to be the actress. This woman's glorious hair cascaded down her back with a life of its own and shimmered several shades darker than that of his ex-mistress. And, although Allegra had been an extremely talented actress, his much-trod-upon toes almost ached with the memory of her clumsy dancing.

No, Tyler mused. Definitely not Allegra. This woman's gracefulness and the shape of her chin tugged at the corners of his memory. But the costume? Could its similarity to Allegra's be a coincidence? Or could this unknown woman, thinking she had uncovered his scandalous secret, be hatching some sort of plot to blackmail him? Tyler laughed silently. She wouldn't get very far with that plan. Anybody who meant anything to him knew the whole story … well, most of it anyway. The reputation he had built would speak for itself—and, if some turned on him, then they could buy someone else's newspaper.

"Evenin', Tyler," a voice cooed. Tyler drew his gaze away from the slim back of the dancing señorita and refocused reluctantly on Theo's smiling face.

"Hello, Theo," he said. She pouted a little and batted her eyes flirtatiously from behind a sky-blue mask.

"Now how did you recognize me so easily? I never would have worn so outrageous a costume if I thought anyone would recognize me. Why, now I'm positively mortified." Her stance displayed her trouser-clad curves and provocatively belied her words.

Tyler allowed his gaze to travel up and down her figure. His reporter's mind once again affirmed that in the too-near future Theo's figure would most likely turn to fat, and she would be an exact replica of her mother. In temperament too, remembering the whiny twang Theo's voice so often took on, even while she was trying her utmost to sound seductive.

That's unkind. He vowed to be more gracious. "Must have been your voice," Tyler answered finally, the corners of his mouth twitching a little when the vapid blonde simpered and took the comment as a compliment.

"Anyone would recognize you, too, Tyler," she said breathlessly. Tyler was certain her courage had been bolstered by champagne punch. "Compared to the other men in this town, you're so—"

"Yes, well, a lot of people are easy to figure out, aren't they?" No one had to tell him the girl was still infatuated with him, but he wasn't about to let her say something well-brought up young ladies shouldn't say. Especially since her gushing made him somewhat queasy. "That's definitely Jack Marsdale over there dressed as Nero," he said, pointing at a portly figure draped in a toga and wearing a garland of greenery around his head. A violin tucked beneath one beefy arm, he asked anyone and everyone if they had a match and then laughed uproariously. His bushy black beard declared his silver mask a waste of fabric and revealed his identity as the grocer.

A young sultan approached and timidly asked Theo to dance. She accepted his invitation with a blinding smile, perhaps grasping the opportunity to make Tyler jealous. As she danced away, he searched for the slender woman in the Spanish costume. She was standing by a partially open window, sipping a goblet of punch, alone for what had to be the first time that evening. Tyler set his glass on a nearby table, reflexively straightened the kerchief around his neck, and headed toward her.

Lily took another swallow of the cool punch, then fanned herself. Behind the fan, she studied the pressing crowd for the imposing figure in black. She had been whirling past him when he seemed to notice her. Unprepared for the paroxysm of pain that flashed across Tyler's handsome face, Lily had felt a twinge of guilt. The emotion gave way to a certain measure of satisfaction when his eyes quickly narrowed, his jaw clenched, and he downed a full glass of punch in one long draught.

Let him be angry … let him be annoyed … let his poise be shaken … let him realize he can't wreak havoc in the lives of innocent people and go his way unscathed.

A bead of perspiration rolled down Lily's spine. She accepted yet another glass of fruity refreshment before spotting Tyler crossing the room in long, purposeful strides, the crowd automatically clearing the way for his broad-shouldered frame. Their gazes locked, and Lily sipped on the punch, outwardly calm, her heart pounding overtime. A slow, lazy smile formed on Tyler's lips while his overt scrutiny raked across her costume. A blush crept up her neckline and, staring for a moment at Tyler's highly polished black boots, she almost missed the creasing of his forehead as he witnessed her sudden confusion.

"Quite an outfit you have on, señorita," he said, his eyes admiring her slender figure. In self-defense, she purposely swept her gaze across him from hat to boots and back again.

"Yours too is quite impressive," she answered in a voice a few tones lower than natural, forgetting to use her contrived accent.

The orchestra began playing a slow, sweeping waltz, and Tyler offered his hand.

"Shall we?"

Had she heard both longing and challenge in those two words?

She stared at his outstretched hand for a long moment before extending her own. His long, cool fingers closed over her soft, warm ones, and he pulled her to him, settling his other hand possessively on her waist. He drew her into the festive throng, skillfully guiding her across the floor.

"I recognize your costume," he finally said.

"Is that so? From where?" Lily replied, struggling to hide her satisfaction.

"It's a long story—perhaps I'll tell you later if you so desire."

"I desire," she said, amazing herself at how easily she spoke the double entendre.

Tyler didn't respond and only continued guiding her gracefully around the crowded dance floor. The music had scarcely stopped before another partner tugged Lily back onto the dance floor. She watched helplessly over the man's shoulder as Tyler saluted her with two fingers and disappeared into the crowd.

Lily glanced at the clock … eleven … time to leave. She scanned the ballroom one last time. Where was Tyler? Her head spun from too much heat and too much twirling. How disappointing. After that one dance, Tyler had vanished, leaving her with no opportunity to further her plan. She shook her head in frustration and managed to make herself even dizzier. She could wait no longer. She had to be back at the Cage by midnight. The revelry in the streets would undoubtedly be dangerous for a woman alone, and she might be unable to conceal her identity. Just one person recognizing her would be disastrous. Word would soon spread all over town that one of the saloon girls had again endeavored to socialize above her station. The Flower Parade escapade had brought in more business for Merle but had made the female citizens even more hostile.

No doubt due to the histrionics of Miss Theodora Peebles.

That young lady had been making quite a spectacle of herself all evening in her tight breeches. Even Tyler had danced with her three times. Lily remembered the rebuke Merle had received from the Mayor and Theo's father.

And they criticize the women at the Canary Cage for being brazen. Miss Theo could teach Jezebel herself a thing or two.

Lily dared wait no longer. She retrieved her cape from the coat room and slung it across her shoulders before stepping onto the street. Within seconds, the freezing night penetrated the cocoon of warmth that had followed her from the ballroom. She gathered the cape more tightly. Dense clouds covered the moon, and the streetlights threw only dim circles around their poles. Tucking her chin and hunching her shoulders, Lily started off at a brisk pace, thinking she might try to find a shorter way back to the Canary Cage. Perhaps if she took the alley behind the barber shop.

Where had Tyler gone? He said he recognized the costume. Had he recognized her? He hadn't said so, and he seemed to enjoy their dance. When she had said that she *desired* … wasn't that clever of her? Had she not said so with the right amount of flirtatiousness? She had watched Honey and had even practiced before the mirror.

Ambling past the Baptist church, Lily heard the muted sounds of voices singing a familiar hymn.

'tis grace that brought me safe thus far
And grace will lead me home …

Home. Her throat threatened to close. As children, she and Augusta, accompanied by their father and grandmother, attended the Watch Night services at St. Paul's. Then Grandmother had died, and the sisters grew into young ladies and attended New Year's Eve soirees instead. Augusta could dance until two, her eyes wide and bright with excitement. Conversely,

Lily would readily have traded the hubbub for the warmth and serenity of a church pew, tucked securely between her father and grandmother.

Her eyes misted. Homesickness threatened to choke her. She had no one, nothing. The only thing that had kept her going for months had been her desire for revenge. Everything she had done, every word she had spoken, and every song she had sung had been motivated by this obsession. But now, suddenly, she didn't care.

She had deluded herself, thinking tonight would end her pain. Tonight, she would stir up old feelings in Tyler—maybe panic, maybe memories of a shameful romance, maybe guilt—no matter. She had been certain he would be caught up in the excitement of the evening and in the aura of sensuality she surely could project. She had been so sure she could convince him to give in, to loose his feelings. He would want her so desperately that at the last moment, after he had declared himself and she pulled away, when she denied him all that he thought she promised, she would laugh in his face. And then he would feel what Roxie had felt when he had rebuffed her.

Lily had pictured Tyler's hurt over and over in her mind. Tyler, his male pride shredding as he felt the agony of unreturned yearning—one moment of being unwanted or being less in someone's eyes. Then she could rejoice in having caused that pain … for Augusta's sake.

But, at this moment, her quest for revenge seemed futile. Nothing changed the emptiness inside her. She had failed to avenge Augusta's death and, for some reason, she no longer cared. A new age dawned, the twentieth century, and as she heard the congregation singing, she wanted nothing more than to feel like she belonged somewhere.

Lily paused and leaned against a building, staring wearily at the brightness of the stained-glass windows.

Dear Lord, what should I do? I have made such a mess of everything. I should have listened to you all along and let you take vengeance for Roxie. Please forgive me for my foolishness.

She pushed away from the rough siding with a surge of determination and continued walking. She would go home. She would forget everything. She would shed the past few months like a dying snakeskin and begin the new century fresh and clean. She could carry the burden no longer.

How well she remembered her father's lectures on the dangers of lying. Deception becomes part of a person, a habit. Continue to tell lies, and you became a liar in your bones. When you don't tell the truth, you begin to mistrust everyone, wondering if they believe they have reasons to lie to you just as you lie to them. And then, when you finally tell the truth, how is anyone to know?

Lily had wanted to finally bring her foolish plan to fruition. But her crafted opportunity had slipped away when Tyler had not taken the bait. He had danced with her once and then had not spoken to her for the rest of the evening. She had lost, and she must give up the chase or lose herself, too. She couldn't pursue revenge any longer, she just couldn't. She said that now, but what would she say in the morning? How many times had she threatened to cave only to find new resolve? Had she become totally spineless? She could neither convince herself to give up nor maintain resolve long enough to follow through. What did that say about her?

What did the Bible say in the book of James about being double-minded? Something about attaining nothing? That certainly told her story. She had spent months in Guthrie and her confusion only grew. She hated Tyler one moment, then the next she ... no, she wouldn't allow herself to put a name to how she felt and betray not only Roxie, but every other woman Tyler had ruined.

Her steps again faltered, and she sagged against the smooth clapboard of a house, overwhelmed with despair. She wrenched off the mask, trying to smother her sobs with her hand. The sound of booted steps caught her attention a split second before a hand touched her shoulder and turned her around, pulling her into the warmth of strong arms beneath a woolen cloak. Security enveloped her, and she knew without question that Tyler had found her.

CHAPTER THIRTY-ONE

"Hey, hey," Tyler soothed, "what can be so bad?" He laid his cheek against the top of her head and felt his pulse quicken at the sweet scent of gardenias. He shouldn't be touching her, he told himself. Every time he touched her, he wanted her. Every time he touched her, his brain ceased functioning. Being this near to her, his blood churned so that he could hardly comprehend her words. He pushed away the memory of what he thought he'd heard the Lord tell him, certain his flesh had been speaking.

"I'm so tired," she said, the words muffled against his shirtfront.

"So many tears because you're tired?" he said. "Surely that can't be all."

"I want to go home."

"To the Canary Cage?" How sad that she, that anyone, would consider such a place home. "I'll walk you over," he said, feeling both relief and dismay. He thought she would pull away. Instead she moved closer, wrapping her arms around his waist, shaking her head miserably.

"No. Not there. That's not home."

Almost overwhelmed by her nearness, her warmth, and her scent, he struggled to make sense of her words. He nodded, understanding finally.

"Ah, I see. You mean back east then." Though not a question, the top of her head nudged his chin in affirmation. "Why is that, Lily? Don't you like Guthrie?" His insides shifted as he realized with wonder how much her answer mattered.

Lily shook her head almost violently, the motion causing her to clutch at him again. He sensed her unsteadiness and, in one swift movement, disentangled his arm, placed it beneath her knees, and lifted her.

"Let's go inside. You're freezing."

"Inside where?" She wiped her face with the lapel of his cloak.

He chuckled and bent his head a little, touching his forehead to hers. "My house. Don't you know how far you've walked?"

"Oh." Her face crinkled, and she blinked. "I must have turned the wrong way. I tried finding a shorter way back to the Cage, but I guess I didn't."

"No, you didn't. You passed by the saloon behind buildings on the other side of the street and all the way here. You've walked a long way."

"I'm very cold. I could have had some of that champagne punch to warm up, but Papa taught us not to drink."

Tyler's mouth twitched. He pondered the confession of a saloon girl who didn't believe in drinking. "Then I guess we'd better go inside."

Settling her head on his shoulder, her arms looped around his neck, she sighed wearily.

"I'm so cold. And the world won't stop moving."

He managed to open the door and, once inside, set her down gently. When her feet touched the floor, she wilted like a dying flower. Tyler tightened his grip on the narrow curve of her waist.

"Here ... this way, Lily. Sit down." He guided her to the divan and eased her down. He turned on a lamp and then coaxed a blaze from a pile of kindling.

"You should be warmer soon." He rose and brushed off his hands.

"Yes." The huskiness of her voice affirmed that she was indeed forgetting her earlier chill.

"When did you last eat, Lily?"

"I had something this morning, but the day was so busy ..."

No wonder she was lightheaded.

Without a word Tyler disappeared into the kitchen, returning a moment later with a plate, a cloth napkin, and a glass of water.

"Here, eat this. It's just a piece of apple cake, but it's good. It'll put something in your stomach. You can't forget to eat and then dance like a whirling dervish. It's no wonder you're finding the world atilt."

As if a sentry, he guarded her while she took dainty bites.

"Delicious. My compliments to Libby." She picked a stray crumb from her lap, then set the plate on the side table. "Thank you. You've come to my rescue once again."

Feeling like anything but a champion, Tyler struggled to shake the memory of her softness. His restraint finally disintegrated when she lifted searching eyes to his. Her head thrown back, the long column of her throat, pale and gleaming in the firelight, demanded his caress. With one commanding tug, he drew her to her feet. He bent and kissed the hollow of her throat. He felt her shiver in response, and she tilted her head to one side, encouraging the burning course of his lips. Tyler touched her face tenderly, the tips of his fingers barely tracing the outline of her heated cheek, her sweeping brows, the tip-tilted ridge of her nose. He paused and her eyes drifted open, meeting his molten gaze, and he froze there, mesmerized.

For one brief moment, reason reared its ugly head, and the nightmare of Allegra laughing and taunting rose before him. But then Lily swallowed, and his eyes followed the delicate movement of her throat. He crushed her to him in a frantic embrace, and her lips parted expectantly in invitation. Lowering his head, he kissed her gently, belying the ferocity of the feeling flaring through his veins. He angled his head and, fitting his lips more perfectly to hers, drank in the sweet moistness of her mouth. At that moment, the world exploded.

Thunder crashed and rolled in overlapping ribbons and streams. Lightning flared and burst in multi-colored rainbows and a myriad of designs and shapes. Whistles and pops, bangs and shouts, hoots, hollers, and cheers filled the air.

And the earth moved beneath their feet.

Tyler lifted his head to see reflections of reds, yellows, and oranges playing across her porcelain skin, her half-closed eyelids.

"Oh, my," Lily breathed.

"Fireworks."

"Yes, it's like fireworks."

Tyler smiled. "Happy New Year, Lily."

Her eyes widened then, and she looked as though she had awakened from a dream.

"Oh—fireworks!" She gave him a sheepish smile. "Happy New Year, Tyler." She raised her face for another kiss when another a series of loud cracks sounded from somewhere nearby, and she jumped. He laughed and moved his hands soothingly over her shoulders.

"Firecrackers."

She gave him a little frown. "I hate firecrackers! Fireworks are lovely. Papa used to take us every year to the waterfront to watch them, but firecrackers are just bothersome noise."

Us. Again, he was reminded that she had been a girl with a father and a sister and a life like any normal young woman—a life that had nothing to do with saloons and bawdy songs.

Lily raised her head and gave Tyler an encouraging smile. She moved her hands restlessly over his muscled forearms and shoulders, then looped her arms around his neck urging him closer. Rubbing her soft cheek against his stubbled chin, she kissed the corner of his mouth, then tugged at his lower lip.

Tyler sucked in a ragged breath and pulled her to him, years of loneliness melting away in her touch …

No … no … no … What was he doing to her? To himself?

He jerked away, taking a step back, and she fell against him, grasping his shirt with both hands. He automatically reached out to steady her, but then set her down firmly on the divan. He moved across the room and stared into the fire.

"Tyler? What's wrong?" Her voice sounded small and weak, embarrassed and uncertain, filling him with pain. "Please, Tyler …"

"Tell her, son."

Tell her? But why?

"Do you trust me?"

Yes, I trust you.

"Tell her. Everything."

He would. In his own way. He sat in the overstuffed chair, close enough to see the firelight reflected in her eyes but far enough away so he couldn't quite touch her.

"Lily, this has to stop. I *have* to make this stop. We can't keep doing this." He held up his hand when she started to interrupt. "It's not your fault. You've done nothing wrong. I have my reasons, I assure you. You're a lovely, desirable woman, and there's something about you …"

Color drained from Lily's face. Was she about to faint? Perhaps the room was too warm.

Lily stood. "Yes, I know what you find objectionable about me. I sing in a saloon, and—oh, my—you can't have that, can you, Tyler Buchanan? You presume to sit on your tall horse and judge me? Well, maybe I shall judge you! I know a thing or two about you, mister. I know you like to have your fun with girls of a certain station, and then you toss them—us—aside, brokenhearted and inconsolable. I know all about your big secret too—I know you shot your brother in a rivalry over an actress. Oh, yes, it was ruled an accident, but the fact of the matter remains. Your brother is dead, another woman is abandoned, and you are here with your reputation and your heart intact, about to—about to …"

Her expression contorted, and she crumpled to the sofa, her face in her hands.

Tyler froze in stunned disbelief. He crossed the room in three long strides. He looked down at her. Illogically, compassion threatened war with his white-hot fury.

"I don't know where you got your story, but …"

He reached down to pull her to her feet. She jerked away, gesturing for him to back away.

"No! Don't touch me! Ever again! I've allowed you to touch me too many times." She scrambled to her feet and busily straightened her cloak.

"You're not interested in the truth?" He stepped in her way, blocking her path.

"I'm not interested in anything you have to offer. I neither want, nor need, your explanations. I just want to leave. Now. Move out of my way."

When he stood his ground, she shoved him, a pitiful little push, but powerful enough to stagger him backwards so she could slide around him.

"Fine then. You stay out of my business, and I'll stay out of yours. I'll take you back to the Canary Cage. I'm sure your customers are wondering where you are."

She spun toward him, pointing a finger at his chest, her blue eyes narrowed and spitting fire.

"Stay away from me! I know the way—and I don't want your company or your"—one short, hysterical sound escaped—"protection." Her sarcasm both infuriated him and split his heart.

Lily redonned her demi-masque and left without a backwards glance. She fairly flew the entire way to the Canary Cage. Tyler followed her, not caring if she saw him or not. He was relieved she kept to the darkened alleys and back streets, as the main roads teemed with a boisterous crowd celebrating the birth of the new century.

He had handled the entire situation badly. Lily had found out something about Allegra. The coincidence with *The Matador* costume was too great to be explained otherwise, and she knew only the common misconceptions.

He hadn't followed God's leading. He had gone his own way, with this the result.

He watched as Lily scurried up the back path to the Cage, glancing at the darkened windows on the second floor before entering through the kitchen door. The main hall was ablaze with light, and the main streets still teemed with merrymakers. Solemnly, Tyler waited in the shadows until a light in the second-story corner room flickered on. Turning on his heel, he shivered violently and started for home. Only then did he realize he'd forgotten his coat.

CHAPTER THIRTY-TWO

The new century seemed no different to Lily except for the decision to go home. On New Year's Eve, she had given up on her mission only to be handed the opportunity she had so hoped to have. But when the moment came, she—not Tyler—had been swept away by passion. She had neither the capability nor the wherewithal to hurt Tyler. Instead, she had thrown herself at him, and he had humiliated her—not the other way around.

How foolish she had been. At least no one but Tyler knew what a laughingstock she had made of herself. Hopefully, she would never have to face him again. He wanted no more to do with her, and she felt the same. If they passed unintentionally on the street, she would look away—he would be a gentleman and comply with her wishes. In the unlikely event he had the gall to enter the saloon, she would simply turn her attentions elsewhere. Honey, Sally, or Trudy would be more than happy to serve his needs.

Two thumps on the door and Sally's voice rang out.

"Shake a leg, Lily! It's getting crowded downstairs. We need you."

Lily sighed. She should refuse. She *could* refuse. She could go downstairs and announce her resignation. She could pack her bags tonight, buy a train ticket tomorrow, and take the next train east. Hopefully, there would be one within a day or two. She couldn't stay here any longer. But she would go downstairs tonight. She would hold her head high, sing a song or two, serve drinks, dodge wayward hands, pretend appreciation at cheeky compliments, refuse coarse invitations, and then—in the morning—she would tell Merle and the girls her plan to leave.

Donning a red dress with blue ribbons, she righted the stool, checked her makeup and hair and then shut the door behind her. From the top of the staircase, she surveyed the saloon. As usual, smoke, music, and laughter filled the room. Trudy and Sally smiled and sang while serving drinks to tables, and Malcolm worked the bar. Toby played a lively tune—the old popular sing-along, "Little Brown Jug." But the moment he spotted Lily, he brought the tune to a close and segued into the newest song, "On the Banks of the Wabash."

Lily took the cue and slowly descended the stairs, singing the melody and smiling sweetly. As had become her habit, she made eye contact with no one but instead looked just over their heads. Trudy and Sally made their way toward Lily, and Honey appeared from wherever she had been, all three harmonizing with Lily above the clamor of the exuberant crowd, who, for the most part, sang along.

> Oh, the moonlight's fair tonight along the Wabash,
> From the fields there comes the smell of new mown hay.
> Through the sycamores, the candle lights are gleaming,
> On the banks of the Wabash far away.

The girls joined Lily at the bottom of the staircase, and all four bowed as though they had just performed at Carnegie Hall. Hoots, hollers, whistles, and catcalls accompanied the applause and stomping. Lily grabbed Honey's hand and pulled her along toward the stage.

"What are you doing?" Honey hissed.

"Come along … just follow me for once, will you?" Lily climbed the steps and, after a second's hesitation, Honey trailed behind her.

"What'll it be, boys?" Lily called out.

Someone from the back of the hall bellowed, "Beautiful Dreamer."

"Ah," Lily smiled, "Honey and I love singing Stephen Foster, don't we? Toby?"

Toby rolled an extensive arpeggio on the keys.

"You take the lead—I'll sing harmony," Lily whispered.

"What? You always—" Flustered, she missed the opening note and jerked her gaze to Toby. He smiled up at her and gave her a reassuring nod.

"Go ahead—I'll sing harmony," Lily said under her breath.

Honey smiled stiffly and nodded almost imperceptibly.

> Beautiful dreamer, wake unto me,
> Starlight and dewdrop are waiting for thee.
> Sounds of the rude world heard in the day
> Lull'd by the moonlight have all passed away.

Lily joined in, singing a lovely high harmony. She had heard Honey practicing the song when she thought no one listened and had noticed that her voice had improved markedly over the past weeks. Lily had often sung this particular song with Augusta at home, and Augusta had always sung the melody. That this would be her farewell song seemed somehow fitting.

> Beautiful dreamer, queen of my song
> List' while I woo thee with soft melody
> Gone are the cares of life's busy throng
> Beautiful dreamer, awake unto me
> Beautiful dreamer, awake unto me ...

They took their bows to thunderous applause, and Honey turned to Lily with a quizzical look. Lily flashed a too-bright smile, blinking furiously to ward off sudden, inexplicable tears. Why did this place make her cry so often? She walked briskly down the stairs, making her way to the bar to get a tray to serve drinks. Passing one table, someone grabbed her skirt, and she automatically turned to smile and give the perpetrator a playful swat and an admonition, only to have her wrist caught in a tight grip.

"Melissa? Melissa Forrester? Is that you? It is! It is! I knew from the moment I saw you! Why, I can't believe my eyes! Imagine running into you way out here!"

Lily froze. She felt the color drain from her face, and her heart began pounding high in her throat. She recognized this man's thinning hair, his florid complexion, his pockmarked nose. He looked to have lost a few pounds, but he still had an extra chin and a belly that hung over his belt. The only thing bigger than his ears was his mouth. *No, no, please, no. Not Frank Dubard.* Why on God's green earth was he in Guthrie? And of all the places in Guthrie, why did he have to wander into the Canary Cage?

She gave the man a stiff smile and tried a desperate ploy of escape.

"I'm sorry ... you have me confused with someone else. I'm Lily Woods—here at the Canary Cage, they call me the 'Songbird of the East.' What are you drinking, sir? I'll fetch you another," she said in an exaggerated southern accent.

Dubard chortled, making his wattle jiggle. "Oh, Miss Forrester, I don't recall you ever being a prankster. That was more Augusta's nature. God rest her soul." He sobered quite suddenly. Narrowing his eyes, he squinted up at Lily. "I almost didn't recognize you with all that paint on your pretty face, but you can't disguise that voice of yours. Songbird of the East indeed! You'll remember that my wife and I had occasion to socialize at your home on several occasions at your father's invitation. In fact, I seem to recall you and your sister singing that particular Foster song at more than one dinner party. That's why I called out for it. The tune was one of your father's favorites, as I recall."

Lily stared at him, then finally nodded glumly.

"May I speak with you in private, Mr. Dubard? I'd like to explain what I'm doing here and why. I'm hoping I can rely on your discretion."

"Well, that's a story I'd like to hear."

That's a story you'd like to tell.

"Lily!" Sally bellowed. "Drinks!"

Lily turned toward Sally, then back to Dubard.

"I have to—help out. I'll be back."

He nodded and then gave her a smile she tried not to interpret as insolent.

"Come on, girl—move! You got molasses in your drawers?" Sally gave Lily a poke with her elbow.

"Sally, I need to talk to that man."

"Talk to him later, Lil. We're busy."

Lily tried to keep an eye on Dubard all evening. Seemingly, he did the same with her. Every time she turned to make sure he still sat at the table, drinking whiskey and playing poker, she found him watching her. He would give her a wink and raise his glass in salute.

But then he vanished, along with his entire party. They had left the deck of cards and poker chips strewn across the table amidst empty shot glasses and overflowing ashtrays.

No one had seen him leave. No one knew who he was, where he was staying, or when he was leaving town. And she had no way of finding him. She could only pray he would seek her out before leaving Guthrie. She would also pray that she could convince him to keep her secret, otherwise she would return to Norfolk amidst a scandal. She could pray. Pray? She didn't have the right to pray, did she? She had turned her back on all she had been taught and gone her own way. Nothing had turned out the way she hoped, and she had only hurt herself. And now she would be punished even more. Perhaps she deserved this as retribution for all her subterfuge.

CHAPTER THIRTY-THREE

Finally dozing only an hour or two just before dawn, Lily didn't arise until late in the morning. She dressed in a simple cotton gown and brushed her hair into a long braid. Her head ached, and she sat at the kitchen table alone, sipping a cup of tea and nibbling dry toast. She didn't try to beg off chores but quietly wiped down tables and helped mop the floor. Afterwards, she swept the boardwalk in front of the saloon, ignoring both suggestive remarks and crude invitations from men and castigating glowers from townswomen. She kept her eyes lowered and managed to refrain from searching the street for Tyler.

She rehearsed different speeches in her head, explaining first to Merle, and then to the girls her true identity and why she must leave. She considered not giving them a reason for leaving. Did she really need to tell them the truth? Perhaps—perhaps not. She couldn't decide.

By the time she finished her chores, it was late afternoon. Lily retreated to her room to dress for the evening. Sitting on the edge of the bed, she rubbed her temples, trying to will away a headache. Despite her earlier resolution, she considered trying to find Tyler before she left town. Perhaps she would write to him when she arrived home. She must devise a plan. Should she talk to Merle first? Should she pack then buy her ticket? Buy her ticket, then talk to Merle?

She had always been organized. She considered herself a problem solver, someone who could look at a situation logically from different perspectives and discern a rational, plausible conclusion. But now she couldn't think straight. How could she arrive at a solution when she could no longer identify her heart's true desire? Peace. She wanted peace. She hadn't been at peace since the day Augusta left home.

The thought of peace made her think of Dubard. She sank onto the vanity bench. Dubard. Could he possibly be discreet? She had prayed he would come by before leaving town to give her an opportunity to explain herself. With a sinking heart, she knew he would prefer spreading the juicy gossip about the proper Miss Forrester playing the saloon singer in Oklahoma. What a succulent tidbit for Norfolk's voracious tittle-tattlers. Her hope for even the small future she had longed for dissipated with each passing moment. She could only see herself as trapped. Like Honey. Sally. Trudy.

Trapped. The word echoed in her mind. Yes, trapped. And in a snare of her own making. Try as she might, she could think of no escape. There had to be an answer, a key to freedom.

Forgiveness.

Lily moved to the vanity bench and studied herself in the mirror, chewing on her bottom lip. How many times had Augusta sat on this very same stool, looking at her reflection in this very same mirror, patting on rice powder and rouge, perhaps feeling this very same heartache? Had she and her sister indeed fallen in love with the same man? Lily pushed the thought away. She refused to admit she might be in love with Tyler Buchanan. She, an innocent woman, had fallen for the wiles of an experienced predator. Something protested that thought, turning over deep in her belly.

Time to admit defeat and go home. She would have to learn to deal with the humiliation, the bitterness, the …

Unforgiveness.

Bitterness? Unforgiveness? Surely not! How could she forgive without repentance? Tyler—the offender—had destroyed Augusta and then he had preyed upon Lily's own innocence and humiliated her as well.

How could he have known of your innocence? You acted the part of a saloon girl—and played it well.

Lily shot to her feet, knocking over the vanity bench, arguing with her own thoughts.

Whether a saloon girl or a society debutante, he had no right to treat me the way he did—pulling me toward him with one hand, pushing me away with the other.

And Augusta! How could you? How could you leave me alone? Papa was barely cold in his grave and you left me! There were so many decisions to be made, so many things to be done … and I had to handle everything all alone. And all your letters … you told such tales of the places you saw—the fun you had, while I was at home alone, keeping the books, making decisions, taking care of Papa's affairs alone … always alone.

Forgive, my child.

Forgive? Forgive Augusta? Surely, she did not harbor unforgiveness against her own sister. She had always been the one who forgave offenses and slights easily, hadn't she? How many times had she cautioned Augusta against holding a grudge or harboring ill will?

Judge not and ye shall not be judged. Condemn not and ye shall not be condemned. Forgive and ye shall be forgiven.

Judging? Condemning? Refusing to forgive? How could she be guilty of those offenses?

She so wanted to deny the thought—but it rang true. Devastatingly true.

If she wanted to go home, if she wanted to start her life again in … yes, in peace, then she must forgive Augusta for her selfishness, her willfulness, for abandoning her.

And Tyler.

Lily closed her eyes. And Tyler. For whatever his part had been, for hurting Roxie, for sensing her own vulnerability and taking advantage.

A surge of anger and resistance threatened to rise, but she refused to let the emotions overwhelm her. Weary of insisting on her own way, she must listen to a voice other than her own.

Yes, I forgive—though my heart aches and I don't understand all that has happened or why, I forgive. I forgive you, my dear sister. And I forgive you, Tyler.

She sat for what seemed like ages, amazed at the ensuing peace springing from deep within, saturating her, cleansing tears coursing freely and sweetly. Crying yet again.

"Oh, my, my." She gave a little laugh. "Astounding what a little forgiveness will do for the soul!"

Now she could move on.

Lily crossed the room to the wardrobe, opened the door, and studied the contents. Yanking out her carpetbags, she opened the latches, and set them on the floor. She pulled open a drawer, then folded a few of her undergarments, and laid them on top of her Bible and the photograph of Augusta, her father, and herself she had hidden at the bottom of one of the bags. Straightening, she propped her hands on her hips and let loose a heavy sigh. Healing had begun.

Next, she layered the skirts and blouses she had brought and decided what she would wear on the train home. The dresses Rae Ann had made for her and the ones she had altered would remain behind. Perhaps she would take one of Roxie's dresses with her. No, when she left here, she would leave Lily *and* Roxie behind.

Picking up the carpetbags, she put them back in the wardrobe and closed the door securely. Turning, she knocked her bottle of gardenia scent to the floor where it rolled beneath the bureau and out of sight. With a sigh, she got to her knees and hunkered down, her cheek pressed to the floor. She stretched her arm as far as she could and touched the bottle with her fingertips. Wiggling her fingers, she managed to advance the bottle toward her until she could grab hold. Her cologne in hand, she noticed a piece of paper in the corner, covered in dust. She inched over a bit and reached out again to retrieve it. Grabbing the parchment between her index and middle fingertips, she pulled it out, got to her knees, and shook the dust off the yellowed paper.

Lily's eyes opened wide and her heart pounded double-time. She recognized Augusta's flowery script on too-familiar stationery. Sitting on the floor, she leaned back against the bed, and propped a forearm on one raised knee. *Dearest Melissa* ... dated the day Augusta died. Lily's hand dropped to the floor onto the hated rug, and all her grief coalesced and rose again to the surface.

After several minutes, her tears subsided, she smoothed open the letter, reprimanding herself. Tears, again. When she left this place, she would never cry again. The letter was shorter than Augusta's typical multiple-page missives and unsigned. Unsigned. Had she changed her mind about mailing the letter, or had something happened to stop her? Lily's heart clenched. This couldn't be a goodbye letter. If Augusta had planned to kill herself, she would have mailed the letter before she—Lily shook her head as if she could banish the thoughts by doing so.

Dearest Melissa,

Yes, my darling sister, the day you have either prayed for or dreaded is finally on its way ... I am coming home. I have much to tell you—much to confess. I do not know what you have told our friends and neighbors to explain my extended absence. We shall discuss that immediately upon my return, so I am sure not to contradict your account. However, I do, at long last, desire you know the truth—the entire truth—regardless of how painful it will be for me to tell you and how uncomfortable it will be for you to hear.

I do want you to know now that I have misled you often in my most recent letters. You see, I often wrote for the eyes of those who were reading my correspondence before posting it. I admit this was childish and self-gratifying, and I ask for your forgiveness, dear Mel. There existed such a rivalry between myself and another that, at every opportunity, I indulged my desire to provoke her jealousy by inventing tales regarding a most blameless and courteous gentleman. This letter, however, I intend to post myself, so there will be no opportunity for anyone else to read my confession.

Lily settled herself more comfortably before continuing.

While I have described to you his physical attributes most accurately, Mr. Buchanan is otherwise nothing like I have painted him to be. He is a charming and most gracious gentleman, never having propositioned or even complimented any of the women here except occasionally on a song. His reasons for even frequenting this establishment are obvious to all. He merely socializes with the chief of police, the mayor, and others to discuss politics and other issues of interest. He does not even imbibe alcoholic beverages. I did, for a while, imagine he would fall madly in love with me and whisk me away from this life to another of luxury and undying love. But he never gave me—or anyone else here at the Cage—reason to believe he cared. Mr. Buchanan is a gentleman of quality and has always treated me and the others with respect and kindness. I have felt quite guilty after writing each letter in which I stated otherwise, though the falsehoods had their intended effect ... Miss Busybody did indeed believe every word, and I had my triumph.

I have written Mr. Buchanan a letter, a full confession, if you will, and will leave it for him as I leave for the train. And I— having now confessed all to our heavenly Father and having received His abundant mercy—must declare all to you and plead for the same.

Also, my darling sister, I must tell you this before I leave—

The letter ended in mid-sentence. Lily sat, stunned, too many truths coming at her from too many directions. Augusta had been planning to come home. Why would she have killed herself? She couldn't have. What did that mean? And Tyler. *He is a charming and most gracious gentleman.* So Augusta fabricated stories in her letters about Tyler and her feelings for him to tease and torment Honey? They amused themselves and played fast and loose with Tyler's reputation, his good name, because of a juvenile rivalry?

Lily covered her face with her hands. *Mr. Buchanan seems to be a gentleman of quality and has always treated me and the others with respect and kindness.* Yes, and that was the thanks he received for his benevolence. She could not count herself as better than they. She came to town to ruin him, and she would have done so except events had not played themselves out to her advantage. Thank the good Lord she had failed.

Rummaging through her carpetbag, Lily retrieved the bundle of Augusta's letters she had brought with her from home. She untied the ribbon and reread them in order. Afterwards, she straightened her shoulders and stood.

Oh, my.

An odd relief flooded over her that her own heart had been broken instead of Tyler's. Served her right. In all of this ridiculous perfidy, Tyler appeared to be the only innocent. And she would tell him so. She would write to him and explain everything, then leave the letter at the newspaper office on her way home. Maybe if he knew … she dared not finish the thought. She dared not hope.

Taking paper and pen, she sat at the vanity and dipped the nib in the ink and wrote,

Dear Tyler,

There is so much to tell you, I scarcely know where to begin. Perhaps the first thing I should say is I believed a lie …

She heard movement behind her and a brisk chill caused her to shiver. Turning, she gasped to find she wasn't alone. Eldon LaMotte stood by the open window drawing a pistol from his coat pocket.

"You're just like Roxanne," he said, spittle flying, the gun wavering a little. He wiped drops of saliva from his chin with the back of his free hand. "Are you leaving, too?"

Lily stiffened at the mention of her sister's middle name, and her throat constricted. Dragging her horrified stare from the barrel of the weapon to the muddy brown of the man's eyes, she struggled to subdue rising hysteria.

"Like Roxanne?" she repeated, fear and dread mounting. "What do you mean?"

LaMotte waggled the gun again, motioning first at Lily and then at the unfinished letter on the desk.

"Are you writing to Buchanan? Are you pouring out your heart to him like she was doing when I came here that last time? You're just the same, you are. Ungrateful harlots, taking love and charity and grinding those gifts beneath your heel like you were crunching cockroaches." His eyes watered and he sniffed. Lily wondered if he might be a bit drunk. A sober man waving a pistol about would be frightening enough. Add the recklessness of liquor to his instability and the situation deteriorated to terrifying.

"Is that what she did to you, Sexton?" Lily tried to imbue her voice with concern, remind him of his calling, and not include herself in his thinking all in one sentence. "Did you love her? Did you offer Roxie love and charity?"

"Don't call her Roxie. Roxie is a name for strumpets." He leveled the gun at her.

Her eyes widened. Just as abruptly, he relaxed his arm, the weapon dropping to his side as he nodded.

"Roxanne, my beautiful Roxanne. I loved her, oh, yes, I did. I would have lifted her from her fallen state. I would have embraced her in her disgrace and then have taken her away where we could start a new life—a new life free from the stigma and shame of what she had become."

As he spoke, the fervor that had shown itself in the pulpit stole into his voice. Perspiration beaded on his forehead.

"Did she know you loved her, Eldon? Did you tell her?" Lily prodded.

"Of course I told her," he threw back, his emotions swinging wildly, "and she laughed. She laughed at *me!* As though *I* were the one beneath contempt. As though *I* wasn't good enough for *her!*" Sexton LaMotte's glazed eyes, filled with personal demons, stared vaguely at the wall behind Lily.

She stood slowly and took a step sideways, toward the door. Her movement alerted him, and he again jerked the gun in her direction.

"Don't even try, Lily. I know you want to run—she did. You're just like her, just as I said. You won't make a fool of me a second time." He suddenly seemed so dispassionate he frightened Lily even more.

"You killed her." Horror and relief washed over her. "She didn't kill herself. You killed her."

"An accident! It was an accident!" he yelled, waving the gun and coming toward her. "She tried to grab the gun, and it went off in the struggle." He calmed and the coldness of his glare petrified Lily. "Then I was glad she was gone. She deserved to die."

Lily inhaled sharply at his callous words.

"Things were fine until you came along. I imagined you to be different—sweet," he said. "I actually believed you somehow managed to remain pure and untouched even though you lived in this devil pit. You had an innocent glow and a wounded look in your eyes. I know you've been begging me to save you. You accepted my friendship—you encouraged me to visit you. You acted as though you were interested in me, and I fell for every bit—just like before. I visited you, shared myself, and received nothing but disrespect and condescension in return." As he spoke, his voice now low and menacing, he walked toward Lily, taking the few steps slowly, methodically.

She stepped back each time he moved forward and soon found herself against the wall. He wasn't making sense.

"You enticed me, Lily," he accused, "with those wide blue eyes and milky-white—or should I say *lily*-white—skin." His wild eyes raked across her body. Reaching out, he snatched roughly at her neckline. The soft cotton fabric tore, and Lily instinctively slapped at his hand.

Sexton LaMotte sucked in his breath, flicking his tongue across his lips.

Lily cringed and crossed her arms protectively. He laughed, the sound grotesque and humorless to her ears. The gun again waggled, inches from Lily's nose.

"Drop your arms, Lily," he whispered, his eyes narrow and dangerous. She did as he commanded, shuddering when he used the cold steel of the gun barrel to stroke her collarbone. He issued a guttural warning when Lily shrank away from him.

"She looks so innocent, doesn't she?" He reached out with a shaking hand and almost reverently caressed the curves of her face, her neck.

Lily gasped, her fists tightly clenched, her nails piercing her palms. "Please."

"*Please,*" LaMotte mimicked, his voice falsetto, his mouth twisting in derision. Then he whispered hoarsely, his breath hot and wet in Lily's ear. "*Please, oh yes, please.* That was what you said to him, wasn't it? *Please, Tyler, please.*"

"What?" Stunned, Lily's thoughts tumbled. "I don't—"

"You don't what? You don't remember? You don't know what I'm talking about?" The sexton wagged his head in mock sympathy, his lips twisting in a perversely amused smile. "You don't remember begging Buchanan to touch you again and again, over and over?"

She shook her head, though her mind flickered with a sudden memory of Tyler, his muscular arms holding her, his eyes hidden in shadow, his deep voice murmuring words of encouragement, she wanting more and more kisses.

Oh, Tyler, where are you now?

Sexton LaMotte jabbed the gun into Lily's ribs and, with his thin body, pressed her against the wall. Clenching a handful of her hair in his fist, he yanked her head back and glared.

"I saw you. I saw you at his house. You thought no one saw you go there, but I did. I was watching. I'm always watching, and I followed you. I saw you through the window."

Lily's face flushed.

"I watched him kiss you. I heard you begging for more. I saw him kiss you here—" he kissed her neck sloppily.

Nausea washed over her at the touch of his soft, fleshy lips, and she almost gagged. She twisted her head, trying to escape him. The pressure of gun metal beneath her jaw demanded she cease struggling. Grappling with him seemed only to fuel his ardor, and Lily's stomach curled in dismay.

"But you must have left. You didn't see what happened next, Eldon," she gasped.

"I didn't have to see you to know what happened. I'm no imbecile. I know what happens with women like you."

"But nothing more happened—a kiss—just a kiss, then I left. I came here …"

He yanked her head back even farther, and she yelped.

"Shut it!" he hissed in her ear. "Lies! Lies!"

Desperate, she tried a different approach.

"You don't want to do this," she said. "You're a good man. You've dedicated your life to doing good, to taking care of people. This isn't what you want." For a brief moment, she thought she had reached him, touched one small part of him that still had a tenuous hold on sanity. But the fleeting lucidity in his eyes vanished again, and he snarled at her.

"You're wrong. This *is* what I want—what I've wanted since the first time I saw you in church, sitting in the sunlight, looking like an angel. You're an angel of light sent to tempt and destroy me. I've lain awake nights burning for this. Oh, yes, Lily dear, this is what I want. And this is what you want, too. It's what all fallen angels want. Now say it." He gave her hair a vicious yank.

Lily's mind reeled. What did he want her to say?

"Please," she begged.

"Yes. That's it, say it again. Beg me just like you begged him. Just like Roxanne begged. Say the words … *Please, Eldon* … say it." He kissed her again, so hard she tasted blood on her teeth.

"Stop! Please stop!" The words tore from her throat, as the cold steel filled her with degradation. Memories of the first attack assaulted her senses. How could this possibly happen to her again? "I'm not Roxie—I didn't know—I promise I didn't know."

He snorted. "You knew. Devil-women can always see into the hearts of men—ever since the Garden of Eden. And they have to be put down. I put Roxanne down, and I'll put you down."

Her own heartbeat thundering in her ears, the truth slapped her with an ice-water chill. The sexton had shot Augusta. In his demented mind, he had merely punished her for rejecting him. He had climbed through the window, just as he had done a few minutes earlier, and he had killed her. What had Augusta written? Someone fancied himself in love with her, the last person anyone would believe. But he frightened her, and she hadn't known what to do. Augusta hadn't had time to decide what to do—this man had decided for her.

"You're right. I am like Roxanne—just like her—I'm her …"

The door burst open, the hinges splintering. Lily sank weakly to the floor as someone yanked the sexton away and easily wrested the pistol from his grasp, tossing the weapon across the room. Through a blur of shock, Lily barely registered Tyler lifting the smaller man off the floor, punching him in the stomach. Tyler's rugged face was distorted by fury. He landed another powerful swing to the minister's nose and pulled his bloodied fist back to strike him again. Merle grabbed his arm from behind.

"Enough, Tyler, let Carson handle things from here. LaMotte's had enough."

CHAPTER THIRTY-FOUR

Tyler relaxed his grip on LaMotte's shirt, and the man crumpled to the floor just as Rae Ann burst into the room.

"Merle went to get the chief." She struggled to catch her breath. "I had a tough time keeping everybody downstairs. They all want to know what's going on." Her jaw dropped when she saw Lily.

Tyler knelt beside her, draping a robe around her shoulders. He smoothed her hair, and murmured low words meant only for her hearing.

Lily raised her eyes to Tyler. "He killed Augusta," she whispered, her eyes imploring him to understand. "All this time I blamed you, and he's the one who killed her."

Tyler's brow furrowed. What was she talking about? Catching her hand, he pressed her palm to his cheek. "Who is Augusta? What are you talking about, sweetheart? You're saying LaMotte killed someone?"

She nodded. "Yes, Augusta. Roxie. My sister." Her gaze wandered to somewhere over Tyler's shoulder.

Chief Ward bustled his way into the room with Merle at his heels. "What's going on here, Buchanan?"

Tyler jerked his chin to where LaMotte lay, still somewhat dazed, on the floor. "He came after Lily with a gun. I had just come in downstairs when Sally yelled something about trouble." Turning his attention back to Lily, he grasped her elbows and lifted her to her feet. When she fell against him, he swung her into his arms. Laying her gently on the bed, he sat beside her.

At a sudden cry outside, everyone looked toward the curtain waving in the cold early-evening air. LaMotte was gone, apparently escaping the way he had entered.

Rae Ann rushed to the window. "Oh my! He fell off the porch! Surely he's dead!"

"Good riddance," Merle muttered.

"I doubt he's dead," Carson said, leaning out of the window. "It's not that far to the ground. Fall probably just knocked the wind out of him. I hope he comes around pretty quick. I'd hate to have to carry him all the way to the jail." Turning, he motioned to Lily. "See to her, Tyler. I'll come around later and get her story." The burly police chief jerked his head toward the door. "Give me a hand, will you, Merle?" At the saloon owner's answering nod, they headed downstairs.

Rae Ann turned back to the window, then gasped. "He's gone."

"What?" Tyler leapt from the bed and bounded to the window to search the yard below. "Merle and Carson just ran out the back gate." He sighed. "Don't worry, ladies. They'll find him before he hurts himself or anyone else. There isn't anywhere he can go." Tyler closed the window with a resounding thud.

Lily's pale face caused him no small amount of concern. He sat beside her again. Taking her icy hands in his, he rubbed them gently between his warm fingers. "He won't get far. Besides," he added, quirking a half-grin at her, "have you ever seen him ride a horse?"

To Tyler's relief, a smile tugged reluctantly at Lily's lips and a spark of laughter glinted in her eyes for a moment.

"Don't worry about a thing, Lily," Rae Ann said. "Tyler's right, Merle and Carson'll catch him right quick. I'll be back in a blink with some tea. It'll help settle your poor nerves." She hurried from the room closing the door quietly.

Tyler hooked Lily's chin with a gentle forefinger and turned her to face him.

"Can you tell me what happened? Sally said she was on her way downstairs and heard an angry male voice. Since she knew Merle, Toby, and Malcolm were already downstairs, she assumed there to be some sort of trouble. Why was LaMotte in here, and why was he holding a gun on you?"

Lily shuddered. "He wanted …" A look of horror brushed her face, and Tyler fought a surge of anger towards the man who had caused her fear. "He killed Augusta—Roxie—he said he loved her, but she had spurned him because of her love for you. He said we were alike—Roxie and I, and he planned to—to," she stammered to a halt and launched herself into Tyler's arms, burying her face in his neck.

He held her tightly, trying to piece together her convulsive sentences into some sort of cohesive sense.

"Roxie's real name was Augusta?"

"Augusta … Augusta Roxanne Forrester." She leaned back against the headboard.

"And she was your sister. Is that why you came here?" At Lily's nod, he frowned in confusion. "Why didn't you say so?"

"Because …" Lily faltered. "Because I wanted to get to know the people she knew, learn how she spent her last days. To see if I could find out why she had killed herself. I didn't think anyone would talk to just me."

"So, you're not—or weren't—a saloon singer before you came here?"

Lily shook her head.

Tyler's thoughts whirled. "Let me get this straight. You came to Guthrie to find out about your sister, and you couldn't do this by being yourself. So you pretended—I don't know what you pretended. Would you just please start at the beginning?"

The beginning? How could she tell him she had concocted such a ridiculous plan, hoping to exact revenge from the man she had believed to be directly or indirectly responsible for Augusta's death? Her last letter totally erased all possibility of Tyler's involvement in Augusta's unhappiness and reinforced what Lily had herself discovered about the man but had refused to admit.

Why had she continued trying to see Tyler in a poor light when he had proven her wrong at every turn? Why had she not taken him at face value, shown him her true self from the start, and let their relationship—if they were to have one—develop naturally? Why had she tried to let what she mistakenly believed Augusta had said overrule her instincts?

When she had reread the letters, the words she had almost memorized didn't sound the same in her mind. She didn't hear the same hurt, the same heartbreak, only infatuation for a handsome, virile man that was no different from any other infatuation Augusta had suffered since the age of fifteen. An infatuation that had faded into admiration and had provided only a fantasy escape from a life in which she felt trapped.

Then the overtone of rising panic became evident. Augusta, who had learned at a young age how to manipulate the opposite sex, had found herself in unfamiliar territory. There had been many overly aggressive admirers, but none so infatuated with her that desire had mutated into deadly obsession.

Lily, after sorting through the facts, the misconceptions, the emotions, what was real and what wasn't, had finally decided to confide in Tyler, and had begun writing the letter. How could she have known writing a letter to Tyler would be the final action that would push Sexton Eldon LaMotte into an abyss?

Looking into Tyler's warm eyes, filled with a mixture of confusion and concern, she wondered again how she could tell him the whole story. How could she tell him she had stayed in Guthrie under false pretenses because she had wanted to seduce him and then reject him the way she believed he had rejected Augusta? Could she tell him her actions toward him had been false, fed by anger and hatred and her desire to see him punished?

If she told him of her deceit, would he believe her when she told him she had never lied to him while he held her in his arms? Would he believe her passion had been real, even though reluctantly born? Would he believe her if she told him her feelings had changed—no, no—her feelings hadn't changed. She'd been attracted to him, enthralled by him from the first moment she had seen him from behind the veil. No, her feelings hadn't changed—they'd been there all along, only she had hidden them beneath her anger and her grief.

She had to tell him the truth. There had been too many lies between them. He deserved to know everything. A good man, kind and gentle, perhaps he would also prove to be forgiving. After all, hadn't she forgiven him when she thought him guilty of spurning Augusta? Hadn't she forgiven him for rejecting her?

"My name is Melissa Lillian Forrester. Augusta and I always used our middle names when we would playact as children. When I got the harebrained idea to accept a job here, I followed Augusta's lead. She used Roxie, so I used Lily. We grew up in Norfolk, Virginia, with our father—"

"So that part was true. What about your mother dying when she gave birth to your sister? Truth or prevarication?"

She should have anticipated his reporter's mind would automatically ferret out every detail.

"Yes, she died at Augusta's birth—I was four. My sister and I were very different, in looks—she took after our mother. I'm more like Papa—in temperament, in interests. Augusta always wanted to play, to be the center of attention, to have fun. I was more than content to watch her make the social circuit daily—and nightly—while I attended the minimum of gaieties and stayed at home, keeping the household accounts and playing hostess to Papa's literary circle meetings. That difference earned us our reputations—mine for being proper and very much the bluestocking, Augusta's for being fun loving and a bit … wild. With Papa being quite strict and Norfolk society quite censorious, I'm still somewhat amazed she managed to acquire such a label."

Lily shifted to a more comfortable position and accepted the handkerchief Tyler offered.

"Augusta chafed under all the restrictions. When Papa died two years ago …" Her voice broke, the love she felt for her father plain to see and hear. Tyler squeezed her hand and waited until she regained her composure. "After Papa was gone, she ran away, leaving me a note saying she had taken the household fund and the cash we kept in the safe, quite a substantial amount. She told me to take her monthly allowance from our inheritance as repayment, as though the money mattered. She begged me not to be concerned over her and promised to write. Still, I worried myself sick without a way to find her. I came up with various explanations for her disappearance and assured everyone she was fine, though I had no idea where she had gone or even if she still lived."

Lily searched Tyler's gray eyes for some measure of understanding or sympathy. He listened intently without interrupting her, but his handsome features refused to betray his thoughts. She released a labored sigh before continuing.

"She finally wrote to me from St. Louis. She had joined a theater troupe, of all things, and was having the time of her life. She didn't want me to tell anyone for fear what she had done would reflect badly on me. She was right, of course. I was the same person I had always been, living my life as I always had. But having a sister who was an actress would have been the end of me socially. I didn't really care … I stayed so much to myself anyway. Still, her small gesture of concern meant a good deal to me.

"I heard from her every few months. She settled here and the letters came quite regularly for a while—which was when I first learned of you."

Tyler's eyebrows jerked upward in surprise, but he said nothing to stop the flowing narrative.

"She wrote about you, pages and pages, about the attraction between you, how you led her on."

Despite his earlier stillness, Tyler shifted as if in protest, but Lily raised her hand. He need not defend himself.

"At first her typical exhilaration at having an exciting new man in her life set the tenor of the letters. I could discern the change to hurt and disappointment, then to what sounded like despair. I had no way of knowing she was only articulating her frustration at being caught in a life where the very freedom she craved proved to be a prison of another sort. All I knew—I *thought* I knew—was she loved you, and you had rejected her affections because she wasn't good enough for you.

"Then the letter came from Chief Carson saying she had killed herself, and she had been buried here. All I had was a tiny box with a cameo someone had given her, the letters I had written her, and a picture of her with someone I didn't even recognize. I couldn't believe she was dead. Sometimes, I still can't. She was always so full of life. I could only place the blame for her senseless death at the feet of the one who had scorned and humiliated her. I believed, since she had only known adoration in her life, she couldn't deal with what you'd done to her. I believed that was why she took her life. To me, you killed her, just as surely as if you pulled the trigger yourself."

The color drained from Tyler's face. He stared down at their joined hands for a moment before pulling away abruptly. Standing, he automatically shook his trousers down over his boots, absently wiping his palms on his thighs. Even in her preoccupation, Lily couldn't help but admire the leashed strength of his movements, the virility evident with every rippling muscle.

Tyler didn't speak but moved to the window, his hands clasped behind him, the clenching and unclenching of his jaw the only evidence of his agitation. The moments passed silently and Lily's guilt grew.

"Tyler, please try to understand." She reached out her hand. "I finally realized how wrong I was. Though my motives—my *reasons*—for coming to Guthrie were understandable, my reasons for staying and for blaming you were totally absurd."

"You finally realized this?"

"Yes." She willed him with all her being to understand.

He turned from the window, studying her face with eyes the color of cold steel, reporter's eyes probing deep beneath the surface, daring her to even try lying. "Exactly when did you realize you were wrong and your assumptions were just that—*assumptions,* based solely on your conception of what your sister might have meant? When, Lily—I mean, Miss *Forrester*—when did this truth finally dawn on you?"

He didn't understand. His anger almost sizzled, and Lily could no longer bear to face him. She stared nervously at her hands, picking at the coverlet he had considerately drawn over her legs. She tried to find words to lend some measure of logic to her actions.

"I realized the man I was beginning to know didn't fit what Augusta …" She stopped. Tyler didn't want justification—he wanted an answer.

"When—exactly *when*—were you convinced I had absolutely nothing to do with your sister's death?"

"I forgave you before I knew—"

"*When?*"

She could feel his eyes boring into her, certain if she met his scrutinizing glare, she would burst into flames from the intensity of his fury. When had she become convinced? Convinced, unfortunately, was the telling word. She had submersed her feelings and resisted her instincts about the man from the moment she encountered him at the graveyard when he had been so solicitous. But convinced? Totally certain? She had decided his actions toward her sister had been innocent, and he hadn't intentionally meant to hurt her. He could not be blamed if Augusta couldn't deal with the rejection. He couldn't have been aware of her emotional vulnerability. Still, only upon finding Augusta's last letter had she truly understood Tyler's total lack of involvement. At the same time, she had admitted her own true feelings for Tyler and allowed them full rein. But she had forgiven him before learning of his complete innocence. Shouldn't that count for something?

Tyler demanded the truth—he deserved the truth, though the truth would no doubt condemn her. He still waited, and she lifted penitent eyes to his and confessed.

"Today. This afternoon."

Unprepared for the spasm of pain ripping across his face, her heart constricted in answer. His expression once more stoic, only the gruffness of his voice betrayed him.

"All this time you thought me guilty of perpetrating your sister's death." Incredulity accented the statement.

Lily could only nod, a small reluctant jerk of her head. Her voice strangled somewhere in the back of her throat, unable to exonerate her. She knew what he had wrapped in the words *all this time*. Laughter, confidences, and the most incriminating of all—almost overwhelming passion.

Tyler paused just before he reached the door, one hand rubbing the back of his neck. He half-turned toward Lily.

"And you found out my innocence—how?"

Lily hesitated. Everything had crumbled into one huge debacle. What could she say to thaw his frigid stare?

"I found a letter from her ... one explaining everything ... and exonerating you—"

"*Exonerating* me? I see."

And she was terribly afraid he did.

"In this letter, she mentioned she planned to write to you as well—and Sexton LaMotte also said she was writing to you when he—when he came after her. Didn't she explain all this to you?"

"I received no such letter."

Lily frowned. "You didn't get the letter? Honey was supposed to—"

"I came by and was told Carson had been mistaken. The letter was addressed to someone else."

The finality in his flat tone would brook no further discussion.

Had Honey destroyed the letter? Lily wouldn't be surprised if she had.

"So, you believed me guilty of driving your sister to suicide and guilty of shooting my own brother, yet you let me hold you. Let me kiss you. Let me begin to think ... I can't believe I came here to ..."

He turned toward the door again. But, before taking a step, he shook his head, as though disbelieving what had transpired in the last few moments.

"What kind of woman are you?" The repugnance in his voice cut into Lily more deftly than any razor he could have wielded.

He stared at her for a suspended moment, his eyes gun-gray and condemning. His upper lip curled in derision. Before he could speak, Rae Ann burst through the door, breathlessly calling out to Tyler. She grasped his arm, her fingers white-knuckled, and pulled him into the hallway.

"Fire! Tyler, there's a fire! The newspaper building is ablaze!"

CHAPTER THIRTY-FIVE

Tyler looked as if Rae Ann had punched him in the gut. Without sparing a backward glance at Lily, he shook himself free of Rae Ann's grip and bolted downstairs.

Lily, already on her feet, yanked open the door to her wardrobe. She pulled out the first dress she found.

"How bad is the fire?" Her fingers trembled, fumbling with the buttons. Rae Ann hurried over to assist.

"It's bad. It's blazing like the fires of hell, and if they can't stop it ..." The women stared at each other in mute understanding and dread.

"You go on, Lily. I'll be right behind you. I have to find Trudy."

When Lily joined the melee on the street, the air had already thickened with billowing smoke. Two of the town's fire brigades had arrived on the scene, but the citizens formed a bucket line to do what little they could to help. Lily took a place in line between Sally and Mrs. Wanderman who owned the shoe shop three doors down from the Canary Cage. Lily scanned the line, spotting Toby and Honey a little farther down.

They worked, coatless, as the blaze lit the early evening sky.

Tyler headed the brigade, his expression grim. His only responses seemed to be yes and no as evidenced by a nod or shake of his head, his face already blackened with soot. Lily overheard someone say he had tried to push his way past a fireman to salvage whatever he could. Hit by a blast of scorching air, he had reluctantly allowed himself to be dragged back to safety on the street.

A woman screamed and gestured wildly at the roof of the building. Balancing precariously on the roof's edge, a man stood, legs akimbo, his arms spread wide, and his head thrown back to the skies. The flames reflected off his spectacles, and the crowd gasped in recognition.

Lily shrieked as she handed Sally another bucket. "Oh, my heavens ... it's Sexton LaMotte."

"What's he doing up there?"

"Is he crazy?"

"He's gonna git hisself kilt!"

The sexton laughed, a crazed howl. He pointed an accusing finger at Tyler and bellowed in a voice both commanding and demented.

"Hear the word of the Lord, Tyler Buchanan!" He threw his hands above him as if embracing the night sky and flung back his head, the flames illuminating his form in eerie, undulating waves on the street below.

"'Her lips drop as a honeycomb and her mouth is smoother than oil. Her feet go down to death and her steps take hold on hell. Remove thy way far from her and come not nigh the door of her house. With her much fair speech she caused him to yield, with the flattering of her lips she forced him. Her house is the way to hell.'

"You, Buchanan, you killed the brother of your own blood, and you have taken to your bosom the fallen angel of the brothels. You shall be punished for your wickedness!"

Stunned, Lily's gaze darted down the line to find Tyler. He had disappeared.

"Look!" Sally grabbed Lily's elbow and pointed again to the roof at two figures now silhouetted against the blazes.

"Oh, no ... Tyler!"

"What's he doing? He's as crazy as the sexton!"

"Pass the buckets, girls. This fire isn't going to put itself out," Mrs. Wanderman urged, handing a sloshing pail to Lily.

Lily handed it to Sally and reached for another, then looked to the roof again. Both men had vanished.

"What happened?" Lily cried. "Where are they?"

Marsdale, the grocer, stood on the other side of Mrs. Wanderman passing two buckets at a time. "Buchanan knows the design of the building. If anyone can get that idiot LaMotte down, he can."

The roof suddenly gave way with a tremendous crash, smothering the shrieks of horrified onlookers. The crowd stood by helplessly, the stunned silence broken only by the crackling of timbers and the roar of flames.

"Oh, dear Lord, please ..." Lily prayed.

"We need some help here!"

Lily's knees nearly gave way at the sight of Tyler carrying an unconscious Sexton LaMotte over his shoulder. He dumped the cleric on the ground, leaving him to the ministrations of Reverend Scott and others before rejoining his place in the bucket brigade. He shrugged off attempts to examine the scratches and cuts on his forearms and face. As far as Lily could see, he never even glanced in her direction.

When the fire department finally doused the fire, barely anything remained of the newspaper building except smoldering stone. Miraculously, no doubt due to the efforts of the town's citizens, the neighboring businesses suffered only slight damages.

The sexton's words echoed and magnified in Lily's head. While she had not set the fire nor intentionally scorned the affections of the disturbed rector, she felt a heavy numbness engulf her along with the weight of guilt. Didn't responsibility for the destruction of Tyler's livelihood and for the pain he so deftly disguised rest on her shoulders? Wiping her soot-grazed face with her sleeve, her eyes finally met Tyler's. He stared at her, his glare hard and blaming. He would leave no room for doubt—he plainly spurned her unspoken plea for understanding. Lily's heart shattered into thousands of trembling pieces when Tyler clearly turned his stiffened back to her and, leaning on Libby's shoulder, limped away.

Sally took Lily's arm, and together they walked wearily across the street to the Canary Cage. They entered to find Malcolm washing down the bar and pouring shots of whiskey for Merle and Toby. The kitchen door swung open, and Rae Ann carried a pot of coffee and a plate of gingerbread. Honey and Trudy sat at a table, their feet propped on chairs, nursing blisters on their fingers.

"Aren't we a sight?" Sally laughed ruefully.

They stared at each other, covered in soot and ash. White tracks carved by perspiration trailed across their blackened faces, and Lily said a prayer of thanks that no one could tell the difference between sweat and tears. She took a deep, steadying sigh. Now was as good a time as any.

"I would like to say something." Her voice sounded as loud as a thunderclap in the silent room.

"Oh, what now?" Honey said with an exaggerated sigh. "Are you going to explain why LaMotte was in your room? Why he set the *Courier* on fire? Why he thought Buchanan was your lover when we all know he wasn't? Or was he? For all your high-and-mighty Miss Purity ways, do you owe Merle some coin after all?"

"Would you shut your mouth?" Sally snapped. "If Lily has something to say, let her talk, for St. Pete's sake!"

"Now, girls," Rae Ann said, putting down the coffeepot, ready—as always—to referee. "This isn't the way to behave."

"We're saloon girls. We don't behave, remember?" Honey was in a temper.

"Can't Lily just say what she wants to say?" Trudy wound her bright hair around a finger. "I'm so tired. That fire was scary. Can I sleep with you tonight, Rae Ann?"

"Yes, dear, of course you can," Rae Ann said, rubbing Trudy's back in comforting circles.

Honey heaved a loud, exasperated sigh. "Would you just get on with whatever, Miss Lily-White?"

"Girls!" Merle stepped in. "Enough!"

"Have mercy," Malcolm grunted beneath his breath.

Lily's knees wobbled. Sitting down, she tried to neaten her braid.

"You might as well give up on that," Honey said. "We're all past hope tonight."

Sally threw Honey a warning glance, but Lily gave a nervous little laugh. She had to agree with Honey. How silly to worry about her hair, when exhaustion and soot claimed them all. There was no easy—or correct—way to say what had to be said. She might as well just jump right in.

"I have decided to leave—to go back east. As soon as I can. I think there's a train tomorrow."

Lily hadn't known what to expect, but the total silence left her speechless. She looked from one face to another—frozen, they stared at her wide-eyed. They finally spoke. All at once.

"No, Lily, you can't," Trudy whined. "We have to stay together."

"Oh, no!" Rae Ann began, obviously distressed, "Why? LaMotte's no longer a threat—"

"Tomorrow? Can't we talk about this before you make a decision?" Merle said, frowning.

"Aren't you happy here? I thought ..." Sally added, already close to tears.

Honey said nothing but began applauding—a slow, rhythmic clap.

"Stop!" Sally pounded her fist on the table, jiggling the teacups.

Honey did so but still shot Lily a smug smile and raised her coffee cup in silent salute.

"What's going on, Lil?" This from Merle, his voice stern, all business.

"Merle, first of all, I want you to know I appreciate how kind you've been to me all these months. My decision has nothing to do with—with anything here—I just want to go home."

"Yeah, well, nobody's stopping you. But what was going on with LaMotte? Why was he in your room waving a gun around?" Honey asked.

"Yes, that was a horrid shock. I was sitting at the vanity writing a letter. I didn't hear him come through the window. From what he said, he had done so before. He said he had been in love with Roxie, and she had rejected him. He felt I had spurned him too, though I didn't even know he was—enamored ..." Shaking, she clasped her hands tightly in her lap, looking from one face to the other hoping someone would help her make sense of things.

Honey broke the silence.

"Oh, come on—LaMotte was in love with Roxie and with you? Are you saying she killed herself over him? First Tyler and now LaMotte. Are you really so vain? Not every man in the world is in love with you. I can see LaMotte being infatuated, the little toad. He'd fall in love with any female who gave him half a smile, but Buchanan—"

"I'm not saying that at all, Honey," Lily took a deep breath. "I'm saying Sexton LaMotte killed Roxie. He said the shooting was an accident, a tussle over the gun. Everyone assumed she killed herself—well, she didn't. Didn't anyone wonder why she had a gun in the first place? And Sally ..."

Sally jumped. "What'd I do?"

"Sally, you said you heard a male voice shortly before the gunshot—"

"Well, yes ..."

Merle's eyebrows drew together.

"Sally, why didn't you say anything? Carson would have wanted to know."

"I did say something! I told Rae Ann, and she told the chief, right, Rae Ann?"

Rae Ann hesitated, then nodded. "Yes, of course I told him. I told him what Sally said when I gave him Roxie's belongings. At least I think I did."

Toby dragged a chair over and joined them. He swung the seat around backwards and sat down, crossing his arms over the back, resting his chin on his hands.

"So," Toby said, "Sally heard LaMotte in Roxie's room, and *he* shot her?"

"Yes!" Lily nodded. "You see, there was no reason for her to have killed herself. She had plans to come home and was not in a despairing mental state that might have led to suicide. Sexton LaMotte brought the gun to convince her to leave town with him. When she would not, he—he assaulted her and killed her, either purposefully or in the struggle." She stopped to catch her breath and felt her cheeks pinken. "He can be quite forceful when he's of a mind to be."

Toby cocked his head. "You say she had plans to go home? How do you know?"

"Reverend Scott told me. And I found a letter she'd written."

Rae Ann's brows pulled together. "A letter? Where? I cleaned her room myself. There was no letter."

"I found it beneath the bureau, back in the corner. I dropped a bottle of scent, and it rolled underneath. That's when I found the letter."

"Enough, Rae Ann. We all know you're an exceptional housekeeper," Merle said. "You say you found this letter, and Scott told you about Roxie's plans. Who was the letter to?"

Lily looked down, busying herself by wiping away some of the grime on her hands on her skirt. The dress would only be good for rags anyway.

"The letter was addressed to me."

"You?"

"But Roxie didn't even know you!"

"What are you saying?"

"What game are you playing?"

The questions and accusations came so quickly the voices seemed like one.

"I came to Guthrie because of Roxie." She continued despite the questioning murmurs, not meeting anyone's eyes. "Her name was Augusta Forrester. My real name is Melissa Forrester. The woman you knew as Roxie was my sister."

"Your sister? But you don't look anything like her," Trudy said.

"Why didn't you say so from the start?" Merle asked. "Why the pretense?"

"Because she's as much of a liar as Roxie," Honey said with an all-knowing scoff.

"Will you all be quiet and just let the girl talk!" Rae Ann said, as usual, the voice of reason.

"Thank you, Rae Ann," Lily smiled, then continued. "I had planned to. I came to Guthrie to ask questions, to …" She quickly decided to keep her suspicions about Tyler to herself, especially since she had discovered he was completely innocent. No need to expose herself as even more of a fool. "To get to know more about my sister and her life. But when I walked in here—"

"You lied," Honey said. "You said you were a singer and you wanted a job. You never said who you were."

"That's not exactly what happened," Lily said. Did Honey ever keep her tongue still?

"Close enough," Honey muttered.

"Lil?" Merle prompted, still frowning.

"Well, truth be told, when I walked in, no one seemed like they would be, shall we say, forthcoming with information about Roxie. You all looked at me as though I were a fish out of water. I hadn't planned to hide my identity. Nor had I planned to accept employment as a singer. The idea occurred to me only when Merle asked if I could sing. Then I recalled how Augusta told me she used her middle name as a sobriquet—"

"A *what*?" Sally's face scrunched in confusion.

"Don't be such an imbecile," Honey said. "She means an alias, a stage name. Lily—or what did you say your name was—Melissa?—stop showing off with such big words. We know you don't consider yourself to be of our class—"

"That's not true—"

"She's never looked down her nose at us like you do, Honey," Sally broke in. "Neither did Roxie."

"I'm not the one using fancy words," Honey spat back.

A sudden loud crash silenced everyone. Trudy squealed, Sally gasped, and they all turned as one to the bar. Malcolm shrugged.

"Dropped a glass," he said, waving a whisk broom. "You said something about Roxie not using her real name?"

Lily nodded and gave Malcolm a grateful smile. "Yes, I remembered Augusta used her middle name—Roxanne shortened to Roxie, so the thought occurred to me to do the same—Lillian shortened to Lily, like when we put on plays for our father. I apologize to you all for my subterfuge—my deception. As I said, I simply wanted to find out about my sister—how she lived, what life was like for her ... to try to understand why she had taken her life."

"So now you've had all your questions answered, and you're leaving," Toby said.

Lily shrugged and spread her hands, palms up, in an appeal for understanding. "I've already started packing. I'll talk to Chief Ward in the morning, then check the train schedule."

"Lily, that greasy man who kept watching you last night and then disappeared," Sally asked. "The man you were looking for? Who was he?"

Dubard. Lily's entire body grew numb at the reminder of the odious man. "Someone from back home. Someone who knew my father ... and me."

"He recognized you?" Honey laughed. "Well, Jim Dandy. You just might have a welcome-home party waiting for you. Ow!" She rubbed her arm and scowled at Rae Ann who had pinched her.

"You behave, Honey. Apologize to Lily for your meanness."

"Not happening," Honey said.

"Not necessary," Lily said at the same time.

Merle heaved a loud sigh and stood. "Lil, I won't lie. I'm mightily disappointed. Things have livened up since you've been around. Take tonight and sleep on your decision. Fine with me if you change your mind." Without another word, he left the room.

Lily watched him go with a sadness that surprised her. She had actually become quite fond of him. She rose with a heavy heart. Trudy's lip thrust out in a pout, her head cradled against Rae Ann's shoulder. Sally gaped at Lily, her brown eyes brimming with tears. Toby stared at Lily, his eyes narrowed thoughtfully. Only Honey smiled. She held up her hand and wiggled her fingers in an insolent wave.

"G'night, Lily—or whatever your name is."

"Honey ..." Rae Ann shook her head.

"I don't want her to go," Trudy sniffled.

"Hush, child, it'll be all right, you'll see. It'll all be just fine," Rae Ann said.

"Goodnight everyone." Lily turned toward the staircase, holding up a hand to Malcolm who gave her a solemn nod. As she climbed the steps, she comforted herself that the ordeal had come to an end.

In her room, she turned on the lamp and stopped. Several pitchers of water, a clean towel, and shavings of fragrant soap on a saucer sat atop the dresser. On the floor by the wardrobe, a small washtub awaited her. Rae Ann. What a thoughtful woman. No doubt the other girls would find the same courtesies in their rooms.

She stripped off the soiled satin dress, stepping out of her life as a saloon girl. Getting in the tub, she scrubbed herself with the sweet-smelling soap, pouring the now-tepid water over her body, rinsing off the soot and the grime. After drying herself with the soft towel, she donned her nightgown and settled herself in bed. She tried to think about tomorrow. She tried to think about the future. Everything promised to be as empty as that last look in Tyler's eyes.

CHAPTER THIRTY-SIX

Lily took a deep breath, chilled by the brisk morning air. She wrapped her shawl tightly around her and headed back toward the Canary Cage. She had been awake since dawn. Her belongings were already packed. Leaving her room before anyone else had awakened, she had walked resolutely to the train depot to wait until the doors opened. Now she had her train ticket in hand.

Walking past Gibson's Sundries, she noted the *Closed—Please Come Again* sign still hanging in the doorway. Disappointed, she shaded her eyes and peered in the window. She could see Amy emptying items from a crate. Lily tapped on the window and waved. Seemingly startled, Amy turned, frowning at the interruption, then shot Lily a sweet smile. She bustled toward the door and ushered Lily inside.

"Good morning, Lily! How lovely to see you!"

A rush of wistfulness flooded Lily at Amy's honest pleasure. Amy was most likely the only person left in Guthrie who thought of her with any degree of goodwill. How long would that last? She offered her a tremulous smile.

"What are you doing up so early?"

"Me? I'm up this early every day. There's always stock to inventory or shelve, displays to arrange and rotate—and ..." She gave a shy, little smile and blushed, looking up at Lily from beneath her lashes. "Can you believe Carson Ward himself has been coming by every day!"

Lily pulled her eyebrows together, pretending concern, but inwardly smiling at Amy's blissful discomfiture. "Chief Ward? Oh, dear! Every day? Has there been some thievery he's investigating? Has Theo Peebles been threatening you again?"

"Oh, no, Lily! Nothing like that, let me assure you! He comes by to ... to see ... because he ..." Amy blushed again, unable to meet Lily's eyes.

"He comes by to see you because he thinks you're wonderful. I'm sorry I teased you. Of course he comes by to see you! Every day? Is he courting you? Tell me everything!"

"Oh, Lily, I'm so happy!" Amy impulsively threw her thin arms around Lily, hugging her tightly, rocking her back and forth. "And it's you I have to thank! Cutting my hair and wearing my hats … just watching how you walk … gave me confidence. But most of all, you told me to smile, because you said I had a pretty smile. It wasn't easy but I tried, and he smiled back—and now he comes by every day. At first, he said it was because I was a single woman, and he wanted to make sure I was safe. Then I offered him coffee. Now he comes by a couple of times a day to buy candy or a cigar, and every evening right after closing he comes by for cake and coffee. And, oh, Lily, I know he's a bit older than I, but I think I love him!"

When she finally stopped to breathe, they held each other by the forearms, laughing. Amy beamed with the joy of first-time love. Lily's heart ached with delight for the young woman's happiness along with the sorrow of losing a friend … one who seemed like a sister … a woman who accepted friendship from a saloon girl. Would she accept a liar, a fraud, as easily?

"Amy, there's something I have to tell you."

Lily checked the watch brooch pinned to her blouse. Time to head to the depot. The train would leave for Atlanta in less than two hours. Her carpetbags stood ready by the door, while her handbag, hat box, and hat lay on the bed. Checking her reflection in the mirror, she pinned a few errant curls and studied her somber face now totally devoid of cosmetics. With no pink in her cheeks or on her lips, her pale skin seemed transparent. Dark circles emphasized her lack of sleep and the shedding of too many tears. Sighing, she comforted herself with the thought that she was unlikely to cry ever again. She'd wept so much since coming to Guthrie—surely, she'd fulfilled her allocation of teardrops for her lifetime.

Only the plea to Tyler remained. Her attempt at writing lay on the vanity … unfinished. She still hadn't decided if she would complete the letter. She hadn't decided a lot of things.

Crossing to the window, she stood with her forehead pressed to the glass, in much the same way as in her first moments there. Looking down at the backyard, she remembered her earliest thoughts of the struggling roses, when someone tapped lightly on the door.

"Come in," she called, not moving from the window.

"I brought tea." Rae Ann entered carrying a cup and saucer. "It's cold in here, Lily." Setting the teacup on the vanity, she stood by the wardrobe, rubbing her arms.

"Thank you, Rae Ann, tea sounds lovely," Lily said. "I had the heater burning earlier, but I'm leaving soon, so I let it burn down."

"I don't remember seeing that hat before."

Lily half-turned, smiling at the beribboned traveling bonnet on the bed. "Amy Gibson gave it to me this morning."

"You told Amy you're leaving?"

"Yes. Saying goodbye was more difficult than I thought it would be. Her friendship has come to mean a great deal to me."

"Don't go."

Lily sighed and drew a heart on the pane where her warm breath had fogged the glass.

"It's sweet of you, Rae Ann, but I can't stay, I—"

"Don't go."

"I have to."

Rae Ann crossed to the bed and picked up Lily's hat.

"You can't go, Lily, we're a family … and you can't break up our family. We'll just unpack your bags and put your things away. We'll tell Merle you changed your mind. Everyone will be happy—except for Honey—but she'll come around. I'll make you a nice lunch—and we'll have peach cobbler for dinner … I know how you love my peach cobbler. Things will be back to normal in no time."

"You know I'm going home—back to Norfolk. You'll still have Trudy and Sally and Honey, Toby and Merle and Malcolm—"

"I don't know if we can be a family without you."

Lily smiled. "Yes, you can."

Rae Ann helped Lily pin on her hat.

"Well, things won't be the same around here."

Together they picked up her bags and hatbox and headed downstairs. At the doorway, Lily surveyed the room for the last time, taking in the tableau. Rae Ann gave her a fierce hug. No one rose to bid her farewell.

Toby and Honey sat at the piano. Trudy and Sally huddled at a table, dabbing at their eyes with handkerchiefs. Merle sat alone at another table—papers spread out, glasses perched on the bridge of his nose.

"Thank you all …" She'd begun a little too loudly, but no one seemed to give her any notice. A lump rose thick as a goose egg in her throat, and she struggled to speak. "Goodbye …"

Finally, Sally and Trudy looked up and lifted their hands in silent farewells, and Lily braved a grateful smile. She turned toward the swinging doors and met Malcolm's gaze. He gave her that strange, lopsided grin.

"Give me your bags, Lil. I'll walk you to the station."

CHAPTER THIRTY-SEVEN

Spring came gently to Norfolk, Virginia, bringing the promise of an early summer. Dogwood bloomed in whites and pinks, the dainty blossoms ruffled by the same balmy breeze ushering clouds across a startling blue sky.

Lily squatted on her heels and leaned her head back. With her eyes closed and the sun warm on her face, she inhaled deeply, filling her lungs with fresh, cool air. She opened her eyes, sunspots dancing before her, then bowed her head to allow the brim of her sunbonnet to again shade her face.

She inspected all she had accomplished and gave a little nod, pleased with her progress. While she entrusted pruning the few trees and upkeep of the front yard to Lee Vance, a skilled gardener who maintained the grounds of many of Norfolk's gentry, Lily claimed the tiny backyard for her own. She had spent almost two long, lonely months staring out the window, waiting for spring.

The winter had been unusually cold, and the snow blanketing the flagstone patio and lifeless garden seemed to have settled on Lily's heart as well. At first, she spent the nights unable to sleep peacefully, her mind burning with Tyler's memory and her own shameful behavior. She resolved herself to the reality that she was now irrevocably doomed to spinsterhood. Truth always had a way of coming out, and Dubard had done just as she had feared. He spread the story of having seen her in Guthrie, masquerading as a saloon girl. She could no longer accept a marriage proposal from any upstanding gentleman in Tidewater. Since her return to Norfolk, she had already turned away the two suitors who had expressed an interest in courting her before her father's death.

Graciously declining their attentions by reminding them the mourning period for her sister had not ended, Lily admitted only to herself that she could not give her heart to any man. She had given it to Tyler—and he had given it back, bruised and broken.

She allowed herself to think no further than tomorrow. The prospect of a future bereft of husband and children—no, she amended solemnly, a future without Tyler—was not only incomprehensible but unbearable.

She had tried to see him, to ask his forgiveness one last time the day she left Guthrie. He had already borrowed an old printing press from his competition and had set up temporarily in a vacant shop next to Amy's store. When he saw Lily standing by the doorway and Malcolm at her shoulder carrying her baggage, his face had stiffened. With deliberate and insulting slowness, he again turned his back on her. Libby had stopped sweeping and confronted Lily with a frown.

"Haven't you caused enough harm? You came here to hurt him and you've hurt him, along with a lot of others. The Courier building is destroyed, and so is Tyler. Go away, Lily. He doesn't want you. Nobody here wants you."

So Lily had gone. She made arrangements for a proper headstone for Augusta's grave—Augusta Roxanne Forrester—Beloved Daughter and Sister—and left money in an account with Reverend Scott to pay someone to keep the gravesite tidy. She left Guthrie just as she had arrived, on the train with sorrow as her only companion.

She had received a letter from Amy before a month had gone by, but Amy had not mentioned Tyler directly. Still under construction, the Capital Courier building would, to all appearances, be grander than before.

Yanking a weed from amidst a bed of red and yellow tulips, she tried again to think of anything or anyone except Tyler—the effort, as usual, futile. She craved the sight of his smile, the gray of his eyes, the sound of his voice, his intelligence, and wit. Though she had sworn to never cry again, tears dampened her pillow every night when she relived their moments together in Guthrie.

Tears from embarrassment.

From yearning, came the arguing voice.

From shame, she insisted.

Love, she admitted.

She heard the side gate open, and she looked up with a smile expecting to see Gordy the delivery boy bringing her weekly groceries. Her smile faded, and her heart beat high in her throat. She forgot to breathe. She stared at him, uncertain if she had merely conjured up a hallucination by the strength of her longing. Lily rose slowly, her knees wobbly. She couldn't take her eyes off him for fear he'd disappear.

"Tyler?"

He swept off his hat and nodded somberly. "Hello, Lily."

Unable to form even one coherent sentence as fragmented thoughts and questions stormed her mind, she remained silent, content for the moment to soak in his presence.

She must look a muddle standing there in her apron and gardening gloves. The ribbons from her sunbonnet hung free, and tendrils of hair had escaped her chignon. She wore a simple muslin day dress in a cornflower blue that Papa had compared to her eyes. Swallowing with difficulty, she let her gaze travel over his handsome face, taking in each beloved feature from the cleft in his chin to the molten gray of his eyes and his finely carved lips.

Dressed in a charcoal gray wool suit, a white shirt, a black bolo tie with a silver clasp, his boots shone like black mirrors. He held his hat in front of him, working the brim in both hands. The motion of his hands drew her attention to her own. She tugged off her gloves, dropping them in her gardening basket.

"I tried knocking at the front door. But, as there was no answer, I thought I'd try the back entrance. I hope I'm not intruding."

Lily shook her head and smoothed her hands over her apron. The sound of his soothing voice had the opposite effect. Her blood thrummed through her veins, and her heart beat against her chest like a blacksmith's hammer on an anvil. She had thought of this moment, dreamed and prayed for the opportunity to talk to him one more time. But now that the miracle had happened and he stood only a few feet away, she realized a yawning chasm still gaped between them. All her carefully prepared words evaporated, leaving her unable to utter one civility, one explanation, one plea.

"Lily," Tyler began and then stopped, confusion clouding his eyes. "Do I call you Lily or Melissa?"

She smiled, a grim smile both understanding and self-deprecating. "I'm not sure how to answer. Sometimes someone calls out to me on the street—or Annabelle, my maid, will call me 'Miss Melissa,' as she's done for fifteen years—and I don't realize they're calling me. I don't associate myself with the Melissa everyone knew. And yet ..." She gave a pathetic little shrug and turned away. Raising her face to the sun, she closed her eyes and drew in a long, slow breath.

"And yet?"

"Yet, I'm not really Lily either. She was a fabrication. I created her out of what I perceived as necessity. I made her up as I went along. Now I'm not sure how much I invented and how much was really me."

Tyler nodded as though he understood and waited for her to continue.

"I never knew Roxie—I only knew Augusta, but the more I learned about Roxie from Sally and Rae Ann, from you and Honey, the more I realized Roxie was only Augusta without the mask, without society's constraints. As Roxie, Augusta could finally be herself."

"We're back to my question. Who are you now? Melissa or Lily?"

This time she looked at him with a steady gaze. He stared back at her, and she wondered how she could have ever thought the gray of his eyes to be as threatening as storm clouds.

"I don't know, Tyler. That there actually was a Lily came as a great surprise to me. Melissa is the lady I was raised to be. But as Lily—there was a certain freedom—"

"And now you're caught somewhere in the middle."

She nodded. "I never considered the possibility of having a life beyond this town and these people. I never realized I lived under so many rules. Or that my opinions and beliefs were supposed to be like everyone else's and expressing a contrary thought would be tantamount to social suicide.

"I learned so much as Lily. Things I couldn't learn from books. Things I never could have learned as Melissa."

"Such as?"

She plucked a leaf from a hydrangea bush. "People are people. Having a certain social status doesn't mean you're one whit better than anyone else. I discovered that a socialite can be mean-spirited and a saloon girl can be generous. And"—she paused for a moment when her voice broke—"I learned that my dear, beautiful, silly sister in her quest for freedom only traded one prison for another."

"Nothing else?"

Lily's eyes flew to meet Tyler's steady gaze. Did she hear disappointment in his voice? She couldn't be sure, but he was doing the one thing he had refused to do that last encounter in Guthrie—listen.

He had not yet told her why he had come, and her happiness at seeing him overwhelmed her so that she hadn't thought to ask. As usual, he asked question after question. But his tone seemed unlike his typical reporter's voice … and she felt undone. She had lost so much, and what remained didn't matter to her in the least. She had found love for the first and last time in her life, and she had allowed that precious commodity to be ruined through deceit. Swearing she had learned her lesson, she promised the Almighty daily—if given another chance—she would never lie to Tyler again. He waited patiently for her answer, and she recognized his presence as nothing short of a miracle.

Had she learned anything more? Another question she had yet to answer.

"How is Sexton LaMotte? Has he recovered from his injuries?"

Tyler shrugged. "I believe so. From the physical ones, at least. Barring a touch from God, he's not likely to recover from his mental illness. I dropped the arson charges."

Lily stared at him open mouthed. He spread his hands apologetically.

"He would have gone to a prison for the criminally insane. Those places are horrific. I wouldn't wish such a punishment on anyone. He's sick and should be in a place he can get help."

Lily marveled at his compassion. Tyler was a good man. She had wronged him in so many ways, and guilt once again overwhelmed her.

"I left Guthrie a month after you did."

Her hand flew to her throat, her eyes widening in dismay.

"Oh, Tyler."

"It's all right. Leaving was my decision. I'd already started over once—when I left Charleston for Guthrie—so I wasn't worried about relocating again. After the fire, I borrowed a press, rented another building, and went back to work. I even started rebuilding *The Capital Courier*. But things weren't the same. You're right about people. Class isn't necessarily a positively defining characteristic. Some decided they had been wrong about me—that the man I had been and they had known for more than ten years was a fabrication. Before long, I figured out they were more than willing to believe the howling of a lunatic."

She had destroyed him, just as she'd sworn. She had hurt him and ruined his most prized asset, his reputation. But worst of all, she had thought him responsible for her sister's death. Perhaps he felt that wound the deepest. When LaMotte bellowed his recriminations quite literally from the rooftops, she knew the townsfolk would put Tyler's good name on trial. People seemed naturally disposed to want to believe the worst. Watching everything crumble before her eyes, she would have given anything to call back every wish, every hope, every promise and prayer leading to Tyler's undoing. He, above all others, was innocent. Even she had contributed more to her sister's death by her vanity. She had thought of herself as the good daughter, the level-headed sister.

"At first, I worked day and night to rebuild what I had accomplished in Guthrie. Going at such a breakneck pace, the newspaper would have been up and running again in no time."

He set his hat on the bench and pushed his hands into his pockets.

"Before long I had to admit there was nothing in Guthrie I still wanted. Nothing. I spent over ten years building a business, a reputation I could be proud of, yet was never happy. I attained a certain degree of satisfaction, a measure of respectability, and even a few moments of genuine pleasure in the company of a few friends. But happiness? The only true happiness that ever came my way was when I allowed myself to enjoy being with you. And after you left, no matter where I looked, all I could see was you."

Lily didn't know what to think, how to feel. Could he really be saying the words she had so longed to hear?

"I decided to leave, start over yet again. In a moment of painful honesty, I admitted, no matter what I do anywhere, I won't be happy unless you're with me." He turned and pinned her with a warm, earnest stare. "Will you come with me, Lily?"

She didn't answer immediately. When she did answer, she asked the question that had kept her awake so many nights, tormenting her because she thought she would never know its answer.

"Have you forgiven me?"

"Forgiven you? Sweetheart, when I allowed myself to stop running long enough to think, forgiving was the second thing I did—the first was to admit to myself you had my heart. Given the information Roxie—*Augusta*—had given you, it wasn't much of a leap for you to think I was responsible for her unhappiness. The similarities in our stories were too great to ignore. I already blamed myself for Rogan's death. Knowing you blamed me for your sister's death was a bit much."

She started to protest, and he held up his hand.

"No, let me finish. You obviously knew the public record when you showed up New Year's Eve wearing one of Allegra's—"

"That was foolish, childish of me, Tyler. I'm so sorry. My anger, my vindictiveness—"

"That's not my point, Lily. What I'm trying to do is tell you my side of the story. Finally. Shall we?" He gestured to a garden bench under a flowering dogwood. She nodded and sat, arranging her skirts around her, being sure to cover her ankles, the proper lady once more. Tyler sat beside her, leaning forward, his elbows on his knees, his fingers laced together.

"I punished myself every day over my brother's death." He gave a sad, lopsided smile she couldn't return. "You weren't the first to accuse me of being a murderer."

"Tyler, stop."

"No, Lily, you deserve to know the truth."

"No, I don't. I know everything I need to know about you and your past. Regardless of how I've behaved, I trust you. I really do."

When her admission had settled and found its place, Tyler sat back and took Lily's hand, pressing his lips to the inside of her wrist.

"So, you *have* forgiven me?" she asked.

He chuckled and kissed her fingertips.

"Yes, my dear, I've forgiven you. And what about you? Have you forgiven me?"

Lily's emotions fluttered. Oh, how she had missed his touch. "What? Forgiven you? For what?"

"For rejecting you. For refusing to talk to you. For turning my back on you when you came to see me before you left Guthrie. For being a …"

She pressed two fingers against his lips.

"Amazing and kind and chivalrous and the most wonderful man I've ever known?"

Tyler sighed.

"There you go finishing my sentences again."

"At least I was correct this time."

"I'm glad you think so. Well, have you?"

"Have I what?"

"Forgiven me?"

She smiled and, leaning forward, kissed him gently.

"You are forgiven," she said, blushing at her aggressiveness.

"Ah, there's Lily."

"She does appear at the oddest times."

"How so?"

"When Mrs. Johansen asked what I thought of her new dress, I told her I was reminded of a frock I saw at a fine establishment in Guthrie. She took my words as a compliment until she spoke with Mrs. Dubard a few days later and found out exactly what that fine establishment was. Now she won't speak to me, though I did apologize. I don't know what gets into me at times."

"I guess the secret is out."

Lily released a long sigh. "I believe all the secrets are out."

"With truth comes freedom, don't you think?"

She nodded. "What a relief not having to keep track of every lie."

A soft breeze blew through the garden ruffling Tyler's hair and Lily's bonnet strings. He touched the tip of her nose.

"Well, the truth is, I love you, Melissa Lillian Forrester."

She sucked in a little breath and stared at him in wonder.

"You do? Truly?"

Tyler nodded somberly. "It took me a long time to admit the truth and even longer to come to the place where I could admit my feelings to you. I finally realized I had nothing more to lose. So … what do you say?"

"I can't believe you're here, saying these beautiful words to me. I feel like winter is finally over and spring has truly come. I love you, too. And I've missed you desperately."

He took her in his arms and held her so tightly she could barely breathe. She didn't care. He had come—truly, a miracle—and she would gladly give up breathing to stay there in his arms forever. Then he eased her away, his hands on her shoulders, looking seriously into her face.

"Can you give all this up?"

She looked around her—at her neat little garden, at the ivy-covered stone wall, at the house that hadn't been a home since her father died and Augusta had run away.

"There's nothing for me here—or anywhere—without you."

Tyler's smile threatened to split his face wide open.

"We can be married in Charleston. My parents will love you. I think I can tell them everything now. Then we'll head for Houston. You can be Melissa or Lily or any magnificent combination you want to be. Texas is still wide-open territory with millions of stories yet to be written. And ours is one of them."

"Let's write one with a happy ending."
"With you in my arms, it will write itself."
And then he kissed her.

ABOUT THE AUTHOR

In addition to writing inspirational romance novels, Evelyn J. Wagoner writes "Love Stories" for entertainers to present at wedding receptions, edits manuscripts, mentors fellow writers, and has led a local writers group since 2004. She is a member of ACFW and ACFW/Virginia Chapter and serves on the advisory board for Hampton Roads Writers. Having won several poetry and short story awards, she was thrilled to find *The Kulwicki Chronicles,* her tribute to Winston Cup champion Alan Kulwicki, on display in the NASCAR Hall of Fame in Charlotte, NC.

Evelyn married Rod, her favorite cowboy and best friend, in 2008 and lived happily for several years in the country with Kizzy-Me-Too, their toast-loving horse, several barn cats, and the constant threat of wisteria consuming the porch. They have relocated to Virginia Beach, Virginia, where they are thrilled to have city utilities and pizza delivery.

AUTHOR'S NOTE

THE FACTS BEHIND THE FICTION

When I chose Guthrie, Oklahoma, as the setting for *The Canary Cage,* my first step was to call Peggy Cook, the town's librarian. Excited at the prospect of helping a novelist write about Guthrie, she supplied me with two historical books from the library's archives.

I had already decided that Tyler Buchanan, my "hero," would be the newspaper publisher. I had also determined that, near the end of the book—at the turn of the century—the newspaper building would burn down. In reading through the history books, I particularly noticed a photo of a handsome man named Frank Greer. I smiled when I read that he was the publisher of the town's first newspaper (*The State Capital*) and was quite influential in Guthrie's history. In fact, he had published one of the very history books I was reading! Here was someone I could model Tyler Buchanan after in several ways. Continuing to read, a chill shimmied up my spine when I discovered his newspaper building had actually burned to the ground in 1902!

With these two books in hand, I wove authenticity into *The Canary Cage* using genuine street and business names, women's clubs' names, and actual town events, such as The Opening and the Flower Parade (also known as the Novelty Parade). The parade, now called the '89-er Day Celebration, is still held each year.

While there were several saloons and gambling houses—including one almost directly across the street from the newspaper building!—the Canary Cage saloon itself is fictitious, as is Gibson's Sundries.

The story of The Opening as related by Sally Brown is true. The Oklahoma territory was "opened" to settlers at noon on April 22, 1889, following a proclamation by President Benjamin Harrison. Expectations were that, once the territory was opened, small station points established along the railroad line would become communities. Guthrie was one such "station point."

By the end of the first day, Guthrie boasted a population of approximately 10,000 people. Sadly, the burgeoning town was ill-equipped to handle such an influx of settlers. New residents found refuge in tents (had they thought to bring them), empty boxcars, and whatever makeshift shelters they could build.

The U.S. Land Office was under construction and the line of hopeful settlers must have seemed interminable. Lawyers launched their practices on makeshift desks to file claims and battle lot disputes.

Eleven years after "The Opening," at the time *The Canary Cage* is set, Guthrie had 3,200 residences and 416 business houses. There were 8,400 feet frontage of brick and stone buildings, including several of the most magnificent structures in the Territory. The Brooks Opera House was one of these.

Today, Guthrie is still a beautiful and fascinating town. Sadly, Guthrie met its peak early and, with the move of state capital status to Oklahoma City in 1910, the town was left behind. The current population is only a little over 11,000—much the same as it was in its thriving early days. The Guthrie Historic District, which has been added to the National Register of Historic Places, boasts over 2,000 buildings covering 1,400 acres. Guthrie itself boasts National Historic Landmark status.

For more information on this unique territorial city embodying the essence of the era and the spirit of Oklahoma, please visit historicguthrieok. com or guthriechamber.com/history-of-guthrie. You may also look up Guthrie Historic Buildings on Wikipedia, which includes photos.

Thank you, Peggy. It's taken a while, but here it is.

My thanks also to Erin Brown, Collections Specialist for the Oklahoma Territorial Museum, for her knowledge and her willingness to keep The Canary Cage as historically accurate as possible while understanding there are just some things a writer is compelled to make up.

Evelyn Wagoner
Virginia Beach, VA

Archival documents used for reference include:
The Oklahoma State Capital (1889—1900 Art Edition; published Saturday, May 26, 1900; Frank H. Greer, Editor and Manager)

Guthrie: A History of the Capital City 1889—1910 (Lloyd C. Lentz III; Logan County Historical Society, Guthrie, OK)

75697181R00167

Made in the USA
Columbia, SC
24 September 2019